THE UNDEAD TWENTY THREE: THE FORT

RR HAYWOOD

CHAPTER ONE

D ay Twenty One

L illy wakes before dawn in a set of rooms near the back of the fort. The same ones she took over the night she killed the crews.

She rises silently, gathering a change of clothes, her rifle and a few bits before heading over to the middle section of the fort to one of the newly built toilet cubicles that still smells of freshly cut wood.

She thinks about yesterday and the attack on the fort as she was facing off against a dozen gypsy men who ended up fighting with her to buy time for everyone else to get off the beach and back to the fort. Howie came back with his team, ending the battle and prompting Reginald to conclude the travelling community hold natural immunity.

After that was a blur of Howie and Paula getting everyone ready to leave again with Heather and Paco tasked to go and find the immune people on a list provided by

Reginald that he had acquired from Doctor Neal Barrett, and while that chaos was unfolding, Nick and Lilly sneaked upstairs to have sex while Dave told Mr Howie his concerns over safe sex.

Mr Howie then left, taking Maddox with him and amongst all of that, Lilly and Peter - the man in charge of the gypsy men - made a deal. Lilly said they were welcome to stay in the fort, seeing as they had fought so valiantly.

Peter said they didn't like living within walls and anyway, it would be difficult to get their caravans over the water and through the gates. Lilly frowned, unsure if he was joking until he winked, at which point she noticed Kyle was wearing two pistols on his belt with the butts facing in. 'You're armed,' she said to him.

'Aye. I am,' Kyle replied, his deep blue eyes twinkling in his craggy face.

'Oh. Why are they facing in? Is it so you can draw them across your body? Yes, that does make sense...' she paused, frowned and turned to Peter. 'If you don't wish to stay in the fort do you want the outside space here in the bay?'

Peter made a show of looking about as though the idea had not occurred to him until that very second. 'Aye, that might work,' he said. 'Are ye happy with having us?'

'I am. If you assist in providing external security for the fort and work with me to check new people arriving. In return we have doctors, a fully stocked armoury and the fort of course should you ever need to take refuge.'

'That sounds fair to me,' Peter said.

'Aye, does,' Kyle agreed.

Handshakes sealed the deal and the world moved on into another hard day, gruelling, hot day.

Today will be harder too. There is so much to do. Food. Security. Shelter. The order of needs in order to survive, but to achieve each thing requires mammoth work and the weather right now is beyond comprehension. A searing, magnified heat that seems to radiate from the ground as much as the sky above.

They need to flatten the structures on the bay and open the view, but those buildings need emptying first, and the contents need to be sorted to see what can or should be brought over into the fort, and that's all at the same time as dealing with a constant flow of new people arriving.

It's been three weeks since the infection took over and decimated the world, and that defined period seems to be bringing more people than ever to the fort. Perhaps they all hunkered down for three weeks until their food ran out, and now they're seeking refuge.

Maybe Howie's constant battles have cut the numbers of infected down enough for people to risk going out, or, perhaps those infected are so occupied with Howie that survivors are simply slipping through unnoticed.

Lilly thinks of all those things while washing her hands and heads off towards the soft orange light glowing in the old police offices. Walking in to see old Alf leaning on a mop talking quietly to Kyle. She smiles at seeing him, remembering that it was Alf who cleaned the gore from the rooms and disposed of the bodies after she threw the grenades in.

'Morning,' she says quietly, her voice suitably muted for the earliness of the day. 'Any losses?'

'Two passed,' Alf replies. 'Old lady who came in a few days ago. Heart gave out...'

'And the other?'

'One of them young lads from that night. Shot in the chest. He was in a coma.'

'I see,' Lilly says with a second's worth of reflection to

examine the guilt inside while weighing up the actions taken with a decision that it was still the right thing to do. 'The bodies?'

'Ready for the sea, all wrapped in sheets and weighed down.'

'Thank you, Alf.'

'Anytime,' he says as she walks out of sight. A shared look between him and Kyle. A shrug and they go back to mopping and making drinks.

Lilly washes in the end room. A packet of wet wipes to clean her body. Her hair brushed that now seems thicker. She doesn't feel tired either, despite only getting a couple of hours sleep each night. She also doesn't feel pain like she used to, and the injuries from the beatings she took from the crews in charge of the fort are now hardly felt, despite still being visible on her body.

She has changed. Lilly knows that, and not just physically. She has become harder emotionally too. But then she will do whatever it takes to make this fort safe for her brother and the other children.

In the main office, Kyle sits at the main table. His cup of coffee steaming away. His shirt sleeves rolled up showing old faded tattoos almost buried within the thick grey hairs. One of the pistols stripped down for cleaning. His face reflective, showing the deep thoughts within his mind.

Kyle knows he must tell Lilly who he is and what he did before. He wanted to tell her yesterday, but the day got away from them. Everything was so frantic and rushed, and he could see Lilly, Lenski and the others were being pulled in a dozen different directions, so he jumped in to help out and the day went by. Days have a habit of doing that. You start off with good intentions and things just flow in a certain direction. Life is organic like that.

'Organic,' he snorts quietly, shaking his head. That's the sort of thing Henry would say. Dear Henry. That rueful smile and his impeccable manner. Kyle wonders where they are now. Where the team are from the Office of Fiscal Studies for Her Majesties Treasury Department.

Kyle did try and retire from his position within the Office of Fiscal Studies once. He'd had enough and felt the church calling him.

'Bloody godbothering twat,' Frank used say, rolling his eyes. 'He wants to go and hand out pamphlets in the High Street on Wednesday afternoons...'

They let him go. It was never like in the movies where old spies and operatives could never really retire. There was always the *call-back* proviso though. The agreement that you would go back if needed. And that happened frequently too, and in a way it was nice. It meant Kyle kept a foot in his old world.

Henry would call now and then and say *Kyle old chap, sorry to disturb you, only we've got a thing going on you see, and Frank is rather busy. You wouldn't mind doing a day for us would you?*

The *odd day* turned out to be missions of varying complexity and being posted all over the world, but Kyle didn't mind. Henry had that way about him. Henry once walked into an American roadside biker bar and came out ten minutes later with thirty new best friends who all helped him *liberate* Frank and Kyle from a couple of Russian operatives. Not that Frank and Kyle wanted liberating, seeing as the Russian operatives were both female and very attractive.

'They were going to kill you,' Henry told them later.

'Before or after the sex?' Frank asked.

'You know, I'm not awfully sure. Would you like me to ask them?' Henry asked.

'Yes. I bloody do, and if it was after then bloody put us back in,' Frank grumbled.

Being semi-retired meant Kyle still worked with the team: Henry, George, Howard, Frank and Carmen. Dave was recruited after Kyle left, and although Kyle saw Dave a few times, Dave never saw him. Kyle was always covert, in disguise or hidden, and Dave was very carefully controlled by Henry and George.

Kyle was tending a herd of goats in native dress only a few hundred feet away when Dave blew the cow up to kill the terrorist cow-herder. He saw it with his own eyes. An actual cow blowing up, and nothing on this planet seems to produce as much blood as a cow blowing up.

'How the feck did he get a bomb that size into a cow in the first place?' Kyle asked later. 'Was he shoving C_4 up the thing's arse now?'

'It's probably best not to ask,' Henry replied.

Kyle was also there when Dave's endeavours made international news. The whole team was deployed on that one. They had to make an oil refinery stop working to slow the flow of oil to slow the flow of cash to undermine a certain political group, or possibly a government. They were never really told the full details. Henry and Howard probably knew.

The problem was that the refinery was very bloody big, and very bloody secure with armed guards all over the place.

'Whatever we do, we need to do it now,' Howard said. 'We're under pressure to get it done...'

'Yes of course,' Henry drawled, as calm and as passive as ever. 'Best get Dave on it.'

Dave was called in, and after being briefed by Henry, he was driven to the drop off point with a big rucksack full of things that go bang, a pistol fitted with a sound suppressor, and some knives.

Kyle was already in the desert at that point. Observing the refinery from a distance while pretending to be a pile of rocks. He saw Dave go in from one end and a few seconds later he heard the gunshots that increased in volume and urgency as Dave moved through. A little while later he saw Dave running out and Frank pulling up in an unmarked SUV to take Dave away. Then the coded message was passed to Kyle to bug out now. Right now. Run. Get out.

Kyle ran. Covered in a sand coloured sheet with bits of twigs and desert debris stuck to it and he ran for all he was worth as the explosion came behind him. An explosion so big it was witnessed by a Russian astronaut on board the International Space Station. An explosion so big it made Kyle's ears ring for nearly a month and registered on seismic earthquake detectors hundreds of miles away. Frank said later it was one of the only times he saw Dave smile.

'Why the feck did he blow the whole thing up?' Kyle shouted later, unable to detect his own volume.

'It's probably best not to ask,' Henry said ruefully, and the world moved on, as it always does.

Then about a year or so ago, Kyle received a coded message from Henry.

S*tay in reach. Something big coming. We'll need you. Will be in contact. Henry*

K yle had no idea what it meant. He hadn't been active for a while. Not since the mission in Mogadishu that went so wrong and that big bust up with Frank. But he stayed local to the UK. Moving about as he did to help the Catholic church. Checking on priests they were unsure about and *'advising'* the odd one here and there to *feck off and find another career you dirty bastard before I break all your fingers off and shove them up ye arse.* That was for the ones seducing widowed women or pilfering funds. He did actually break fingers and shove them up arses on a few really bad ones, especially that one he caught with the images of children.

Then the world fell, and Kyle figured that might be the thing Henry was on about. He tried to get into London to their old HQ, but every time Kyle made a run for it he would spot someone in trouble and so he kept stopping, torn between his moral dedication to helping those in immediate need, and his loyalty to his team. He kept hearing about a Mr Howie and Dave and although it resonated, it never clicked or registered fully until, on the eighteenth day after the world ended, he reached a town thick with infected. Thousands of them. Maybe ten thousand or more. He could have kept going but Kyle saw there were people living in the flats in the main square and there was no way in hell he could leave them alone in their hour of need. He got inside, intending to try and get them out when Howie attacked. That alone was a staggering thing. That Howie led so few against so many.

None of Howie's team had any idea that Kyle fought with them that night. He stayed on the flanks, protecting the weak and plugging the gaps in the carnage of battle. His cut-throat razor slicing necks open in the wild chaos. He even picked a fallen pistol up at one point and emptied it into the infected. He stopped one from killing Paula by taking it down from behind. He covered Charlie's back when she ran for the horse, and then later slipped back into a covert nature as they fled for the golf hotel, intending to see who these people were and what they were about, and if they were linked to Henry, but Howie never mentioned his father and gave no indication that he knew Howard had a double life. So Kyle stayed quiet. Watching and learning, and of course feeding lots of biscuits to Blinky and making sure they all got a decent meal.

Footfall brings him back to the now, his pistols cleaned, and he looks up to see Lilly standing by the table drinking coffee and thinks this is as good as time as any.

'Do we have a moment to talk?' he asks.

Then the scream comes and everything else is forgotten as Lilly dumps the mug and starts running. Kyle goes after her, bursting to his feet to run across the room and out into the still dark fort as another scream rips through the air. Loud and shrill. Full of pain and anguish and fear.

'Coming from the back,' Lilly shouts, running hard as people in the fort come awake to cry out in alarm as that scream goes on and on. Raw and harsh. 'JOAN!'

'COMING,' Joan shouts, running from the rooms she slept in with her rifle already up and aimed. Sam and Pea behind her.

'ONE OF YOU STAY WITH THE CHILDREN,' Lilly shouts.

Kyle runs with her, trying to see through the commotion of people running in panic. A glimpse ahead. A woman on her knees outside the door to a set of disused rooms. Her whole face twisted in pure pain as she screams.

Lilly aims her rifle at the woman, not sure what to

expect   and   planning   for   the   worst. 'JOAN...COVER HER...'

'Covered,' Joan calls out, her voice clipped and terse as she takes aim at the woman while Kyle and Lilly go forward.

'Lilly, wait now,' Kyle orders. Something in his voice brings the girl to a stop and he sweeps past, his pistols already drawn, and he kicks the door open to the set of rooms and goes right to clear the doorway, pausing for a second before surging in with his pistols up and aimed and Lilly hot on his heels ready to kill the world to keep her brother and the children safe.

A second to see it. A second for the image to process and she blinks at the sight of the body hanging from the rope tied to an old light fitting.

'My husband...he's my husband,' the woman screams outside, her grief and shock so strong she doesn't see Joan aiming at her or Sam and Pea facing out with rifles up.

'It's just a suicide,' Lilly calls out, her heart beating a drum in her chest and her mind instantly replays her own words, bringing forth a rush of guilt. 'I didn't mean just a suicide,' she adds quickly.

'She won't have heard you,' Kyle says heavily, staring at the body. 'What a shame, what an awful shame...'

Lilly nods, feeling relief that it wasn't something more serious then feeling bad for feeling that relief while still wishing she hadn't said it was just a suicide. Then the smell hits and she pulls back, turning her head away.

'Aye, the bowels open sometimes when people hang,' Kyle says.

'You've seen this before?' she asks in a hoarse voice, staring up at the folds of skin all crumpled up from the ligature around the neck and the twisted facial expression. The man's eyes still open but staring lifeless and thankfully not red or bloodshot.

'Jesus,' Sam says, stepping in long enough to draw a breath. 'Oh fuck that stinks...' she rushes back out, already gagging as Pea comes in, frowns, inhales and rushes out just as quickly.

'Ah now that's a shame that is,' Alf says walking in to shake his head. 'Guess that makes three overnight then,' he adds with a sad tut before peering closer at the body. 'Here, that's my rope he's used. I was going to use that today I was...'

'Right,' Lilly says, struggling with the surreal reality for a second.

'Ah well. Done now. You hang on a jiffy, pardon the pun, and I'll get my barrow and some sheets up here. Actually, I might be able to use that rope after all,' Alf adds, stepping closer to stare up at the noose. 'He's only tied it on hasn't he.'

'I reckon he has,' Kyle says. 'He's not cut it anywhere.'

'No, I don't think he has,' Alf says. 'Good rope that.'

'I can see,' Kyle says.

'We do need more rope if we see any,' Alf says, looking at Lilly.

'Right. Yes. Of course. More rope.'

'Always need good rope,' Alf adds, tutting again. 'I'll get that barrow then...'

'Give me a hand cutting him down first,' Kyle says.

'Don't cut that rope now, just untie it from the top.'

'Take his legs then and ease the weight off,' Kyle says.

'Right you are, Kyle. Hurry up now though. He don't smell so good if you catch my meaning.'

'Aye I do. Don't let him shit on ye.'

'I'm trying not to,' Alf says as Lilly watches on, as

equally mesmerised as she is appalled. 'Have you done it yet?'

'Does it look like I've done it yet?' Kyle asks, grunting as he works at the knot on the light fitting. 'I'll have to cut it.'

'It's good rope. Don't cut it.'

'I'll get ye more rope for the love of god, he's too heavy and making the knot all tight.'

'I'll push him up a bit more,' Alf says with a grunt.

'Should I help?' Lilly asks, moving in to grab the legs of a corpse to push up with Alf while Kyle works at the top and the smell hits worse. The close proximity to it making her eyes water and her throat pinch with a pre-cursor to vomiting. 'What do you need the rope for, Alf?' she asks, trying to distract herself.

'To tie the bodies in the sheets...'

'Are ye being serious ye daft bugger?' Kyle snaps. 'Ye want the rope to use on the body it's attached to? Are ye drunk, Alf?'

'It's good rope!'

'I'm cutting the bloody rope.'

'I think I will vomit,' Lilly says.

'Cut it cleanly so it doesn't fray,' Alf says.

'I'm cutting it cleanly...'

'Did that man do a poo?' Amna asks from the doorway, staring in awe with Rajesh, Milly and Billy.

'Go on and get out,' Kyle shouts as Lilly tries to shout too but pukes instead as the body drops. A literal dead weight coming down and Kyle winces at not giving warning as Lilly tumbles with a shit and now vomit covered body landing on top of her while Sam and Pea drag the entranced kids out.

'That knife is sharp,' Kyle says, staring at his blade.

'Went right through that rope it did...are you alright there, Lilly?'

'I'm fine!' Lilly calls, scrabbling out from under the body already stiff with rigor mortis and her own clothes now soaked in shit, piss and puke. 'Fine. I am fine...great,' she looks at the body then at Alf already checking the rope and Kyle still marvelling at his blade. 'I think I shall go outside,' she announces, sucking clean air in as she steps through the door and spots the four kids still trying to peer in at the body 'You four are in trouble...' she says sternly, pointing a wet finger at them.

'They run fast,' Lenski says. 'Subi she yell and I yell and they run...they are like goats. They run like goats...'

'Goats,' Lilly mutters, finding a hose to use to rinse the goo from her hands and clothes. 'You four come here, right now,' she adds, turning to glare at them. 'I mean it. Over here now. Amna, that means you too. You do not run if you are told to stop. Do you understand? All four of you are on punishment and will stay in the reading tent until I say otherwise. Have you had breakfast? Go and have breakfast and wash your hands and faces. Yes? Got it? Say yes Lilly.'

'Yes, Lilly,' four small voices grumble as Subi leads the kids away past Norman, a middle aged man with a hawkish nose standing nearby who woke suddenly to the yells of Lilly and Kyle running past and everyone surging up. Mothers and fathers grabbing their children. Men and women rushing in all directions in pure panic and Norman scrabbled to his feet, his heart jack-hammering in his chest. He heard the woman screaming and saw the people with guns all aiming for that one point and instead of running away with everyone else he found himself going towards the point of danger but without knowing why.

Now he looks to the woman screaming as Sam and Pea

try to offer comfort, but she seems locked in a cycle of pure anguish. Her eyes not focussing, and he watches the veins push from her neck and her face flushing deep red. Her voice starts to crack too as the scream changes from that of pain to an unpleasant tone that is hard to hear. Like nails on a chalkboard. A noise that pushes into his head and makes him tense inside.

'Shush, it's okay, you're okay...' Pea at her side giving soothing words to no effect.

'Love, you've got to stop screaming,' Sam says, her tone firmer than Pea's but the screeches go on. The woman on her knees. Her children dead. Her husband now dead. Everything she ever had in life is now gone in the most awful ways and so her mind fractures, breaking apart.

Kyle looms in the door, a frown on his face at the woman. Lilly winces and Norman spots Joan stiffening and reads the sympathy is lessening by the second. He turns to see children crying and fear spreading through the fort from the awful noises.

'Jesus, love, stop screaming,' Sam says, her voice now harder.

'Hey come on, shush now,' Pea says.

But it goes on. Repeating over and over. The sound becoming less human and more animalistic.

'Enough of this,' Lenski snaps. 'Is more people here...'

The woman pays her no heed but keeps going. Not hearing anything. Not seeing anything. She starts clawing at her own face, digging her nails into her cheeks.

'Hey, no...stop that,' Pea says, trying to take hold of her hands but the woman tenses and screeches harder, driving her nails into her own flesh, drawing blood that pours down her face. 'HEY NOW...'

Lilly moves in, Pea, Sam and Lenski too with Kyle. All

of them trying to grab the woman's hands but she fights hard, thrashing and kicking, lashing out with a hand that knocks Pea flying before getting a foot into Sam's gut.

'She's got the strength of the devil in her,' Kyle grunts, trying to hold a wrist as the woman bucks and heaves, pulling him down on top while all the time screeching that awful noise and in the midst of that loss of her mind she spots the pistol on Lilly's belt and makes a lunge for it, not knowing why, not knowing reason or coherent thought. Seeing only the gun.

'LILLY!' Kyle shouts as Lilly tries twisting away. A flimsy safety strap holding the pistol within the holster the only thing preventing the woman from yanking it free and she tugs hard, surging into Lilly to drive her back, still screaming and fighting wild. Kicking and lashing out with her other hand, smashing her knuckles into Kyle's mouth, splitting his upper lip.

Everything a blur. An explosion of escalation and Norman snatches a glimpse of Joan moving next to the desperate fight, her rifle aim locked on the woman's head as she tracks and readies to end it should the woman get the gun free. Lilly hitting at the woman's arm, Kyle bleeding and grappling. Lenski taking kicks to the arms and shoulders as they roll over in the dirt.

'YOU...GET IN AND HELP,' Joan snaps, using her left hand to point quickly at Norman. A blink, a balk and he darts forward, hesitant and fearful then a second later he's amongst the scrap. Feeling the heat of the bodies about him and Kyle's head butting against his own. A snag. A ping and the safety cord snaps, freeing the gun from the holster.

'SHE'S GOT IT,' Kyle roars. Norman senses the urgency and grips harder, throwing himself in to use his body weight to crush her arm as the woman starts plucking the trigger. The safety on but in this melee, it could so easily get knocked off. 'HOLD HER HAND DOWN,' Kyle shouts. Norman tries harder as Lenski lands on his back, adding her own weight. A dull crack. A bone breaking but the woman still pays no heed, screaming and tugging at the trigger.

'HOLD HER,' a fresh voice. Female and strong. A rush at the side and Norman feels someone leaning over his head. 'Keep her down...I'll get a sedative in her...okay, going in now...it takes a few seconds...hold her...'

'SHIT!' someone screams out at the fresh surge of energy as the woman thrashes so hard she starts lifting Norman, Lenski and Kyle all trying to pin her body down as Lilly fights to keep the gun aimed away from people. Sam lands in the fray. Pea too. Joan still holding aim should the situation worsen.

'GIVE HER MORE,' Lilly yells.

'I AM,' Ann shouts in reply, readying the syringe as Norman struggles to draw air from the press of bodies on top of him. 'GOING IN...'

Then it comes with a sound they all hear and the dull click of a pistol safety switch turning off.

'JOAN!' Lilly cries out as the woman squeezes the trigger on the pistol, sending a round bouncing off the ground. The danger of death now immediate. The danger of a round ricocheting into a child and Joan moves forward to get clean aim.

'No! She's going...' Ann says urgently. 'Hold on...don't shoot her...'

They all feel it. The sudden lessening of strength and energy. They hold on for dear life, waiting for the motions to grow still. Lilly's hands gripping the wrist holding the gun until she sees the knuckles turning from white to pink in the woman's hand and she moves fast, wrenching the gun free to roll clear, clicking the safety back on. 'Got it,' she gasps.

'Jesus,' Sam says, rolling off as the others starts to disentangle and Norman goes last. A strong hand on his arm pulling him off as Kyle rolls him clear before sagging at his side. All of them gasping for air as Ann moves the woman into the recovery position.

'I think her arm might be broken,' Norman says between hard breaths, feeling like his insides have been re-arranged.

Ann nods but doesn't reply. Her own face flushed. Her medical bag open at the side. Two empty used syringes lying on the ground. Kyle's mouth bleeding. Pea rubbing her face. Sam grimacing at the pain in her belly. Lenski's shoulders and arms kicked and sore. Everyone stunned at the speed it all happened and the sky only now showing the first rays of daylight.

'I got the rope off that fella...' Alf says from the doorway to the rooms as Norman hears the groans coming from everyone around him.

CHAPTER TWO

D ay Twenty One

'I think here will do,' Kyle says.

Lilly cuts the engine on the small boat, bringing forth a silence broken only by the waves gently slapping the hull. She moves to the feet of the first body bound in sheets and after a nod from Kyle they heave the body over.

'Into thy hands dear lord. We commend the soul of thy servant departed, now called unto eternal rest and we commit this body to the deep...'

Two more bodies go over the side and she watches as they slide down into the deep waters where they'll sink to rest on the seabed.

'Beautiful morning,' Kyle remarks quietly after completing his prayer.

'It is,' she says. Admiring the view of the sunrise bathing the land once more in light, banishing the shadows of darkness and they both stare to the gypsy camp that has grown overnight.

Lilly stood on the high fort walls last night watching them for a long time. Hearing the metallic clangs and voices calling out. Watching the lights glow as the camp got bigger.

'Perhaps now is the right time for us to talk openly,' Lilly says.

Kyle nods, figuring this is why Lilly said they should take the bodies out together.

'I was considering if it should be you and Joan in charge. You are older, experienced and people look to you as a figure of authority. I can help of course, Sam, Pea and Lenski the same. What do you think?'

'Oh, I try not to think too much. Gets me in trouble... but aye, there's some logic in what you say,' he trails off, watching her closely for a second. 'Leading is a funny thing. Some can be taught, trained as it were. Others just have that ability. Mr Howie for instance. People will always follow him. I can see it in Blowers too. Henry had that ability. He was in charge in my old team. He once talked a whole bar full of bikers into helping him rescue me and Frank. Of course, we neither wanted nor needed rescuing, but that's a different story. George could lead and plan when needed, but me and Frank? We were never leaders. We were doers. Carmen's the same. She's a cracking section head so she is. Aye, we all are really. We can lead for the task or objective, but it's not our natural way. There was another member of our team too. He did comms, intel, a lot of the background work. He gave instructions and briefed us, but he was never a leader...'

He falls silent, thinking about Howard and Howie. Thinking about Dave and all of them and that Henry will have the team bedded down somewhere waiting for the first month to pass as per protocol, but then something isn't right. If Howard, or any of them knew Howie was the one fighting back, they'd be here now. He guesses one of two things, either they didn't make it through the first day of absolute hell, or they're in complete isolation.

'But I'm not going to lead, Lilly. Nor will Joan. That is your path,' Kyle says into the silence.

'I am only sixteen...'

'Aye. Tell me, do you want me to lead? Be honest now...'

She pauses, caught out by the question.

'Let me ask you this instead, what needs doing today. Answer quickly,' he urges, his voice a bit harder.

'We need to clear those buildings,' she says, pointing to the bay.

'Why?'

'The infected can hide behind them...'

'And?'

'And because they block the view. I can't see beyond them. I want the whole bay flattened but that means we have to empty the houses first and get the contents into the fort...'

'Why?' he cuts in.

'Kyle. I appreciate the...'

'Why?'

'So I can put the wall in...'

'Why do you want to put a wall in?'

'To enclose the bay so we have control over the flow of anyone coming towards us. Kyle, look, I don't know you, but you are clearly trained and...'

'Pah! Training is overrated. Frank and I always said wits and guile will get you through most scrapes. Don't fret now, Lilly. I can see you disliking the fact I'm are not doing as you wish which is one of the reasons why you need to lead here. Do you know what Henry did when someone wouldn't do what he wanted?'

'I don't know who Henry is,' she replies before cocking her head over and breaking into a smile at his comical expression. 'What would Henry do?'

'Nothing at all! He'd smile his polite smile and be as passive as you like.'

'How does that work?' she asks.

'It doesn't. But he'd also then call me and Frank to go and make them do what he wanted. He's a canny man is Henry. You'd like him a lot...and I'm not going to lead, but, I will be your right hand man and give you what guidance I can. Something tells me our paths are already chosen for us...'

Silence again. Both of them thinking while also simply enjoying the beautiful view and the serenity of the moment before another gruelling day starts.

'There is a connection between you and Mr Howie. I've worked that out.'

'Have you now?'

'I have. Mr Howie says *aye* all the time. I didn't know anyone else that said that until I met you. You say it too, and now because you say it lots of other people here are saying it. Which makes me think Mr Howie was either in contact with you before this, or someone connects you both...I'm guessing the latter.'

Kyle has been to many places and seen many things in his long life, but right then he feels genuine surprise and remembers what Reginald said. *Lilly is a most incredible young woman. She is ruthless, capable and highly intelligent. You'd do well not to underestimate her.*

'It was Howie's father,' he says quietly. 'We worked together.'

'Howie's father was called Howard,' Lilly says, looking at him. 'You said you worked for Henry. You, George, Frank and then later Carmen joined you. You said before that someone else handled comms and intelligence, but you didn't say who at the time. I'm guessing that was Howard. Howie's father.'

'Jesus,' he says, glancing at her. 'I'm never playing poker with you. Are you sure you're not related to Henry?'

'I don't know. You haven't said who Henry is.'

'Ach, good point. Do you want to know?'

'Do I need to know?'

'You might need to know.'

'Then tell me when that happens. My brain is some-what occupied right now.'

'Right you are, we'll do that,' he says.

'Three questions,' Lilly asks. 'Does Howie know his father did these things, because he's never mentioned it. And my second question is did you know Dave before this?'

'Right. No, Howie does not appear to know what his father did, and yes, I knew Dave, or rather, I knew who Dave was and I saw him working, but Dave never saw me. I was freelance by then and mostly covert. What was the third question?'

'Did you know this was going to happen?'

'No,' he says honestly. 'Henry sent me a message six months ago saying something was coming, but that was it...'

'I see,' she says, thinking for a second. 'Good luck,' she adds, starting the engine on the boat again.

'Good luck with what?' he asks.

'Good luck explaining to Mr Howie why you didn't tell him all this before...'

'I needed to be sure who he was, Lilly. I've been out for a while now. When I met Howie, I didn't know if he was something bad or good and until I see the old team I'm still not sure what it is we're dealing with…'

'Like I said, tell me when I need to know,' she says, shouting over the thrum of the outboard engine. 'Anyway, Mr Howie isn't here. But we are and that's all that matters… I'm glad you're with us, Kyle. I mean that.'

She aims the boat towards the shore of the bay as they both look ahead to the camp that has formed overnight. Dozens of caravans grouped together amongst cars, vans, trucks and lorries. More coming down the road and no doubt more will come during the day. In fairness, Peter did say there would be a few.

'Good positioning,' Lilly remarks. 'They're at the converging point of the two roads…'

'Aye,' Kyle says, seeing what she means. The camp now sitting at the meeting point of the shore road and the road running in from the north and that nothing can approach the fort without going past the camp.

They come to a stop in the shallows of the bay and clamber out to wade through the waters. Lilly bringing her rifle to the front. Loaded, made ready, safety on. Kyle's pistols on his belt. Loaded, made ready, safeties on.

They reach the road and pause to take stock of the new camp. People still setting up from positioning their caravans overnight. Men in groups smoking as they chat with rifles and all manner of weapons held on slings or within reach. Swords, bats and weird looking old medieval weaponry that Lilly saw in history text books. Guns too. Lots of guns.

The scents of fires and wood smoke mingled with coffee and tobacco drift over. Music too and it makes Lilly frown lightly. She hasn't heard music since this all started. Just an old track, something from the sixties maybe and the volume is low but it's still music.

'You alright there?' a man calls out, his expression hard and his voice signals more to stop and look with a long second of silence as others turn to look.

'Miss Lilly! Are you alright? Father, it's good to see you,' a man strides towards them. A huge smile on his face. Tall and lean with dark and hair and startling green eyes, and Lilly recognises him as the guy with the Stengun in the fight yesterday.

'Elvis,' Kyle beams, moving in to shake his hand. 'Can't forget that name can we,' he adds in a way that makes Lilly think it's for her benefit. 'Willie, you rascal,' he adds, grinning at a ginger-haired shorter and stockier man walking over. Another one that Lilly recognises.

'Father, Lilly,' Willie says. 'Come in, come in...PETER! MISS LILLY IS HERE NOW SHE IS...' he shouts out as the mood instantly shifts from weariness to something else as the men and women drift over with big smiles on tired looking faces.

'We just brewed up, coffee is it?' a woman asks at Lilly's side, pushing a steaming mug into her hand. 'It's got milk in it...from a goat mind, not a cow...'

'You have goats?' Lilly asks.

'Course. Where do you think the milk comes from?'

'I said there'd be a few of us,' Peter calls out with a grin, striding towards them.

'A few ye say,' Kyle says with a comic look about. 'More than a few there is. You'll have the council serving notices you will...'

A few laughs. A joke well served and the mood softens a bit more as Lilly sips the coffee and looks about, hoping like hell inviting them all here was the right thing to do.

'We'll have more coming,' Peter says, shaking hands with Kyle before moving to Lilly. 'This is Miss Lilly,' he calls out, proudly presenting her. 'She's in charge of the fort now…'

'The wee girl with the grenades?' someone asks.

'Aye, that's the one,' Peter says. 'Fights like a demon she does. Hard as nails too, don't let them blue eyes fool you.'

'It is very nice to meet you all,' Lilly calls out, looking around. 'And thank you for coming here.'

'You won't say that when the rest arrive,' a voice shouts from inside a caravan. Female and loud with a strong accent.

'Mary,' Peter calls, a warning edge to his voice.

'Mary my arse,' the voice says, a woman appearing in the doorway of a big caravan. Early twenties with flame red hair down her back and she drops out to stride on past them, holding eye-contact with Lilly as she goes. 'What you looking at, Blondie?'

'Pack it in,' Peter chides.

'Mary, go on now,' Willie says, making Lilly realise they must be brother and sister.

'You go on now,' Mary fires back, flicking a middle finger up at him. 'And you can feck off gawping, Elvis…'

'Daughter?' Kyle asks as the young woman walks off.

'Niece,' Peter replies with a sour look. 'Strong willed too…anyway, a few people that turned up during the night for the fort. I think they were startled to see us here, but we've put them at ease, given them some tea and a place down the way to rest. I've got a few lads keeping an eye to make sure they're safe now and we've said the fort opens back up in the morning. I'm hoping that was about right? And we've got some lads posted on the roads in…you said I had the security of the outside and I take that seriously. We all do…' he adds as the other men gathered about them murmur in agreement.

'How many more are likely to come?' Lilly asks.

'Hard to say,' Peter replies. 'Is there a limit now?'

Lilly spots the joke in his manner and smiles. That's he likes him is obvious. The way he speaks is so lilting and nice. An energy so similar to Kyle too. 'There's no limit,' she says. 'But if you're happy to come over I can show you the fort and explain what I have in mind.'

CHAPTER THREE

'Fucking joke. I mean...what the fuck was all that about? Sleeping all night on a hard floor then got some screaming bint waking everyone up...' A meaty looking tattooed guy says as Norman heads back, his limbs still trembling from the adrenalin of grappling with a woman trying to fire a gun.

'Norman, are you okay?' Patricia asks, seeing him walking back into their patch of ground in the bizarre little street of invisible houses.

'What happened?' Keith asks, his face as stricken with fright and worry as everyone else. 'Someone was screaming and everyone ran...we didn't see you...'

'Silly twat ran the wrong way,' the tattooed guy sneers. Balding and with days of growth on his jaw flecked with grey. A faded and torn England football shirt and ripped shorts showing tribal inkwork on his legs 'We're all going that way and that idiot's going the other direction. Fucking numpty.'

'What on earth did you do that for?' Keith asks.

'Did you see what happened?' another man asks from

inside his own section of ground as a few other people nearby stop to listen.

'A man hung himself,' Norman explains. His head spinning from it all. His mind still feeling not like his own at all. His voice quiet. 'His er, his wife found him. That was her screaming...'

'Oh god, how awful,' Patricia says, covering her mouth in horror as the tattooed guy snorts a blast of air while shaking his head.

'Gave her a good kicking though by the looks of it...' he says loudly.

'I'm sorry, what?' Norman asks.

'We saw 'em all jumping on her. Gave her a right going over. That's what happens if you get upset in this place is it?'

'She tried to grab a gun,' Norman says.

'A gun! Which fucking numpty let her near a gun? Jesus. Who's running this place? Fucking kids?'

Norman thinks to reply, expecting his mind to kick in with answers to counter but he comes up empty and dry and shakes his head instead. Feeling dull and lifeless again. He could tell them what happened and describe it all but what's the point? Why bother?

He sits down and rubs his face as images of Robert rush through his mind bringing forth a surge of raw emotions, and his face changes, showing the angst and pressure.

He breathes deeply as he looks about the rushed and hastily thrown up refugee camp.

He came in late yesterday evening with Patricia and Keith. Neighbours from his high-end expensive street in Surrey. They'd heard about the fort and a man called Mr Howie fighting back. They said the fort had security. It had soldiers and order. They were heading south and asked if

Norman wanted to go with them. Norman said no at first but then Patricia said Robert was gone now. He was dead, and it was time to leave.

Norman didn't so much as agree as not refuse and so he tagged along, riding in the back of their Mercedes SUV in grey suit trousers and a white office shirt.

They arrived at the fort to see mounds of bodies on fire and chaos everywhere, but people too. People that seemed to be trying. A doctor on the beach. A boat over to the fort. A Polish woman called Lenski asked them to give their food over, so it could be given out fairly. She told them to share what they had but to ask if they needed anything.

She then led them to the far side next to huge gazebo and open-sided tents rigged up for the children to play in. She said she called it tent-town and showed them to a patch of ground and said they would get them a tent as soon as they had some.

That was it and the Polish woman rushed off. She had a pistol on her hip but other than that there were remarkably few armed people. Norman couldn't tell if that was a good thing or not. He was too tired to think. Too exhausted. Too drained and so he curled up on the hard ground then woke this morning to the screams.

'This fucking heat,' the tattooed man mutters. 'Where's the fucking tents? Seriously. I've had enough of this. Walked all fucking day to get here yesterday...it's a joke this is, leaving us without food...'

'I think we eat in a minute,' the man in the next patch of ground says. 'The kids eat first apparently...'

The tattooed guy sneers. 'Joke though yeah? Fuckin' joke. Where's the tents? They say to you about the tents?'

'I dunno. It's chaos though. Nobody seems to know anything...'

'Fuck's sake. What's your name then?'

'Mathew.'

'What about you?' the angry guy asks, looking over to Norman.

'Norman,' Norman says.

'Tommy,' the tattooed guy says, lifting his chin in greeting. 'They say what else happens? Where do we shit and piss?'

'I don't know,' Matthew replies, holding his hands up.

'I think they're building some toilet cubicles,' someone down the line says, a voice hidden within the shadows and gloomy light.

Tommy tuts again, blasting another snort of air through his nose. 'Bit fucking late doing them now with all these people here...'

'BREAKFAST,' a voice yells as a metal ladle is whacked against a metal pot. '

'About time,' Tommy says, walking out of his square of ground like he's walking from his house. 'You two coming or what?'

Norman holds back, pointing at Patricia and Keith as though to show he's with people.

'You go on, Norman,' Patricia urges. 'We'll probably just sleep to be honest...'

A weird feeling inside Norman. That he's imposing on his group somehow. Daft for sure but the feeling is there nonetheless, but then he doesn't want to go with Tommy either.

'Fuck's sake. Come on,' Tommy snaps. 'Greedy wankers will eat it all...'

'You on your own, Tommy?' Mathew asks.

Tommy shrugs as he walks on. 'My wife got bit didn't she, stupid cow. The things had her. I had to hide in my garage. What about you? Wives get bit did they?' Tommy asks.

Mathew nods, his face showing pain. Norman stays silent and stares ahead to the queue already forming at the big serving tables with a view like a news report from a third world country.

Sullen, bedraggled people in filthy clothes. Some emaciated from not eating enough. The signs of deep stress, anxiety and worry showing in their faces. The way their heads are bowed. The way people who know each other cling together. Everyone scared and fearful and nobody quite knowing what to do or how to be.

'I bet they eat alright,' Tommy grumbles, his voice still too loud and aggressive for the quietness about them. He nods towards the offices and the people Norman saw trying to help with the screaming woman. 'Bet they sleep in proper beds eh? Creaming the best shit for themselves. I was told everyone has to give up what they got when they come in. I said *what for?* They said to share out. I was like *fuck that, I'm not giving my stuff up...*'

'I think they're doing the best they can,' a woman further in the queue turns to say.

'Who asked you?' Tommy fires back, puffing his chest out. 'Jesus. Can't even say anything without someone having a go. That what it's like here is it?'

Norman lowers his head and folds his arms wishing he'd waited and not come with Tommy in case anyone thinks he's with him.

'Hi, can you wash your hands please,' a man says, motioning them over to a hose held over a huge bucket. 'Hands under the flow and use the soap...then anti-bac up...'

'I know how to wash my hands mate,' Tommy says.

'We're just doing the best we can,' the man says, looking fit to drop.

'Don't jump down my throat. Bleeding hell. Only made a remark...'

Norman waits his turn, nodding a thank you to the man.

'Is that it? Sausages and beans? Fuck me. Go on then, load me up, love,' Tommy's voice ahead, flecked with hard humour and Norman glances down to see Tommy's plate already steaming from a pile of food and a nervous looking woman holding the ladle she used to serve him with from a big pot. 'That's not enough...I get medical issues if I don't eat enough. Blood sugar and all sorts going on. Docs said I has to maintain my weight...'

The woman serving him glances nervously at his plate. 'There's so many people,' she says quietly.

'Eh? What? Jesus, I'm only asking for a few more beans...'

The woman complies. Too tired, too scared and too drained to argue or oppose Tommy's aggressive voice and she dollops another spoonful of baked beans on his plate then keeps her gaze down when she serves Matthew.

Another table set further aside with a small generator chugging away to give power to a big water heater for tea and coffee. Bottles of water stacked on the ground and rows of disposable cups on the table top.

'Tea or coffee?' a man asks as Tommy ventures close.

'You got any pop?' Tommy asks.

'Pop?' the man asks.

'Yeah. Coke, lemonade, fizzy stuff...'

'I don't know. We've got...'

'Fuck's sake. I saw piles of it on that fucking beach. Fucking joke...'

'Everything okay?' Sam asks, walking towards the food tables as Tommy overplays a double-take at the rifle strapped to her back and the pistol on her belt.

'No need for that. Fuck me. I was only asking...' Tommy says, pulling away.

'I have no idea what just happened,' Sam says to the other people standing nearby.

Norman moves off from the table, not wanting to go with Tommy and Mathew but unable to summon the energy needed to make any other decision, and so he simply follows as they lower down onto the hardground.

'Tastes like shit,' Tommy says. 'Still, best not say anything. Probably take you outside and execute you or sumfin.'

Norman finishes with a sudden desire to be alone and away from people. A need for isolation and he gathers his things, the empty plate, cup and bottle of water and starts to rise.

'Where you going?' Tommy asks, snapping his head up. 'Getting another brew yeah? I'll have tea...Matt? What you having?'

'Er, tea, cheers,' Matthew says.

Norman walks off, not saying anything at all. He finds the returns table and simply stands for a moment, watching people work. Seeing they are like him. Broken, terrified and exhausted but at least they're doing something to help.

He walks away and stops a few metres from the inner gate and an old man in his sixties sitting on a chair eating from a plate with a rifle propped against the wall next to him.

'You alright?' Donald, the old soldier asks, glancing up.

'I'm just looking around,' Norman replies.

The man nods and chews another mouthful. 'You can

go out if you want...I got to tell people they ain't prisoners or anything...' he takes another mouthful, speaking as he eats. 'Gates are locked at night though. Makes sense really.'

'Sure,' Norman says quietly.

'They use ex-army blokes for the guards, I'm saying that in case you served. There's only me really...'

'I didn't. Sorry,' Norman says, looking over as a small group come through the gate. A young blond woman with an assault rifle strapped to her back leading others inside.

'And this is the fort,' Lilly says.

'Ach, will you look at that now,' Peter says, walking through with Willie and Elvis. 'A double gate system. That's a good design that is...and look at this in here. Bigger than it looks and you've got a cooking area all set up. Breakfast time I'm guessing.'

'It is yes. I'll show you the infirmary,' Lilly says, motioning for them to follow her across the fort and in through the medical section doors. 'Doctors Heathcliff and Andrew Stone,' Lilly says, pointing at the two male doctors talking at the bedside of a teenager covered in bandages from the night Lilly took the fort back. 'Doctor Lisa Franklin is here somewhere too, and Ann is normally about...but your people are welcome to come over if they need medical help.'

'Ach, you got a father and son doctor team there now,' Peter says with a bright smile. 'Like a family business is it?'

'We're married,' Andrew says.

'Aye that's grand so it is, and good luck to your wives I say too,' Peter replies, his lilting voice so friendly and warm.

'To each other,' Andrew says pointedly, pointing at his gruff looking bearded husband.

'Right,' Peter says without missing a beat. 'Right you are...to each other you say? Right...'

'Did you hear that, Elvis?'

'I did, Willie. Got the gay doctors so they have. That's modern that is.'

'Modern as you like, Elvis. Are they good dancers, Peter? That Brendan was gay and he was a good dancer. You'll have to come over for a dance one night fellas eh?'

'I'm sorry, what?' Andrew says, thinking first to take offence then realising they're speaking without any hint of malice.

'Ah, we've moved in so we have,' Willie replies. 'Across the way there.'

'New neighbours,' Elvis beams. 'Gay doctors. Will you fancy that now. Was that Brendan gay was he, Peter?'

'Aye,' Peter says. 'Terry's lad. I think he was.'

'Do you know Brendan?' Elvis asks, smiling at Andrew and Heathcliff.

'Terry's lad,' Willie adds. 'He's a good dancer.'

'Big lump he is,' Elvis says.

'Huge dick. I saw it once,' Willi says. 'I said to Elvis, I said I wouldn't want that up my...'

'Okay, shall we move on,' Lilly says quickly, ushering them out into the blazing sun to continue the brief tour. 'The walls have got dozens of rooms in them. Some haven't been used in years so we're clearing them out and putting them to use. The clean ones are used as sleeping sections by the children...then over towards the back we have the armoury and...'

'Lilly, come and eat,' Sam calls from the office door.

'And that is our main office area,' Lilly adds, guiding them over and into the chaos of the office and four children sitting at the main table eating from bowls. 'What are you doing in here?'

'Don't even ask,' Sam says with a dry laugh. 'Agatha

caught them pilfering sausages from the big pot.'

'Sausages?' Kyle asks. 'Have we got sausages?'

'No! The little hotdog things in tins. Agatha put them in with the beans,' Sam says, holding her bowl out to show them all her beans and mini-sausages. 'But apparently our four little sods thought they could help themselves and got caught under the serving table covered in bean juice... they're running poor Subi ragged. Anyway, Peter, nice to see you again. Willie isn't it? You had that old gun...'

'They both had old guns,' Joan cuts in. 'Stenguns belong in museums. Lilly, okay if I take these two up for some new hardware?'

'Please do,' Lilly says.

'Lilly, I want to talk to you,' Dr Lisa Franklin says, rushing in through the door, making them all step back. 'Who are they?' she asks, glaring at Willie and Elvis. 'And who are you?' she asks Peter. 'Why is there a new camp on the beach and aren't you the cook?' she snaps at Kyle.

'That's a lot of questions in one go,' Kyle says.

'Lisa, we've got a lot going on this morning. Was there something you needed?' Lilly asks.

'Eat, Lilly,' Pea says, pushing a bowl of sausages and beans into her hands.

'No, just...well yes,' Lisa says. 'Why are you sending new people for medicals.'

'Lilly, we need to know what we're doing with the toilet block,' a large man asks, walking in to stop and blink at the already busy offices. 'The pipes are a mess but Steve's a plumber, he reckons we can get something rigged up...for the flushing I mean...'

'Okay,' Lilly says. 'Peter, this is John...he's sort of taken charge of our construction side of things.'

'Move your backsides,' Agatha calls, pushing into

the room. 'Lilly, I know you're busy love but I've lost Kyle and I need more help and we need to know where you want the food stacked now. The first rooms are rammed and the shelving isn't ready for the next lot...'

'You can't put food on the floor in a place like this,' Peter says, rubbing his jaw. 'Be damp and you'll have rats and vermin all over the place.'

'That's what I said,' John cuts in. 'It has to be kept off the floor...'

'Lilly?' Lisa calls, staring at her pointedly. 'Why are you sending new arrivals to the medical centre when Ann has already checked them?'

'Just a minute please, Lisa. John, the toilet block. Privacy is the first thing, we can use buckets of water to flush for now, then after that we need washing areas...'

'Lilly, we need more shade for the kids,' someone else calls, rushing into the room. 'Have we got any more tents?'

'We're running low on tents,' Sam calls from the back of the room. 'Use the gazebos for the kids...'

'And smother them in sunblock,' Pea adds.

'Where's the sunblock kept? Is that in the food store?' the man asks.

'Do ye eat sunblock ye daft twat?' Kyle cuts in. 'It's in the general store rooms up yonder. Now for the love of god will ye start thinking for yourselves and stop bothering Lilly every few seconds with daft questions...'

'Er, it's called responsibility?' Lisa points out.

'Hi, sorry guys,' Colin says, pushing into the room. Permanently red-faced but polite and willing to help where he can. 'Blimey, busy in here. Er, so the tent situation? What's happening on that front?'

'If anyone sees any rope will they grab it for me,' Alf

says, pushing his way towards the big table at the back of the room laden with boxes of teabags, jars of coffee, packets of sugar and pans of water heating to make drinks.

'Wow,' Ann says, walking into the hubbub of noise.

'Coffee, Ann?' Agatha calls.

'Love one please! What's going on? We having a meeting or something?'

'That is exactly what we are doing…' Lilly says. 'Everyone grab a seat please…'

CHAPTER FOUR

D ay Twenty One
The Meeting

'A re we ready?' Lilly calls, bringing a spreading
quietness through the room. A few people at the
main table. John the builder. Doctors Ann and
Lisa sitting opposite each other. Peter and Kyle. Joan, Sam,
Pea and a few others.

'Finally,' Lisa mutters. 'First question. Why are you
sending people to the infirmary when Ann has already
checked them?'

'We've been through this, Lisa,' Ann says with more
than a touch of frustration.

Lilly sits down, a notepad and pen laid in front of her.
'Ann does not have time to complete thorough medical
checks on the beach. She can check for signs of the infection
and immediate risks to health and that's it. However, if you
wish to come over and assist then I am sure we can

complete more thorough checks on the beach and reduce the burden on your services in the infirmary.'

'Okay, first of all.' Lisa replies, holding a hand up in emphasis. 'Do not patronise me. It isn't safe over there. We were attacked yesterday and neither I, nor Andrew or Heathcliff will risk our lives and the medical security of this fort by going over there.'

'In which case we will maintain our current system. In time we may find others with medical training, nurses perhaps, who can assist Ann...' Lilly says,

'Er no, that isn't acceptable,' Lisa says. 'We are far too busy for every shell-shocked, stressed, blubbering new arrival coming in to tell us they once had a bunion removed...'

'Everyone is busy,' John cuts in.

'Excuse me?' Lisa glares at him with open irritation. 'I don't think you can compare sawing wood to saving lines and quite frankly, we don't have time or capacity to deal with every single tiny medical issue! Do you realise how many people have been injured by Lilly throwing grenades about...'

'Whoa,' Sam says. 'Do I need to bloody remind you what Lilly did?'

'Killing a bunch of kids is a bit different to running a growing society with complex needs.'

'Thank you,' Lilly says before the situation can escalate. 'We'll do what we can but Lisa, the current process will remain for now unless you can suggest a viable alternative.'

'Yes! Don't bloody send them to the infirmary unless they actually need something.'

'I think Lilly has made it clear we are to remain doing as we are,' Ann says. 'Or, one of you can come and give me a hand on the beach.'

'We can talk more on this later,' Lilly says. 'The priorities right now are our immediate security and ensuring we have enough supplies to stay alive. Everyone, this man is Peter. He and his men assisted yesterday when we were attacked...they have set up camp outside and will provide our external security.'

'Great. Just what we need,' Lisa mutters.

'What does that mean?' Sam asks, looking at Lisa.

'It's obvious what it means,' Lisa replies to a sudden quiet spreading through them all.

'Um, so...elephant in the room,' Colin says, lifting a hand. Lilly looks at him, thinking he looks like a can of Coke Cola. 'And er, yeah so, shall I just say it?'

'Say what?' Sam asks.

'You know,' Colin says with a wince. 'Don't want to offend anyone but...'

'But what?' Sam asks, rubbing her face. 'Spit it out.'

'He means the big pikey camp that just set up outside your fort,' Peter says as Willie and Elvis snorts laughs while standing just outside the door.

'Right. Yes, wasn't going to use that word per-se,' Colin says carefully.

'Gypsies? Is that the right word?' Sam asks.

'We were told to use travellers in my old job,' Pea says.

'Travellers, that's the one,' Colin says, pointing at Pea. 'Everyone happy with travellers?'

'Well, Peter said pikeys,' John says. 'Or is that like a black person saying nigger...'

'John!' Sam sputters, spraying tea over the table. 'You can't say the n word.'

'I didn't!' John says quickly. 'I meant...like...I didn't call anyone a nigger...'

'Stop saying it,' Sam says.

'Confusing me all this PC talk,' Agatha says with a huff.

'While we're on the subject of verbal abuse,' Lisa says, leaning in to glare at Peter. 'Your men gave homophobic abuse to Andrew and Heathcliff,' Lisa continues, pointing at Peter.

'Who did?' Peter asks, trying to think how Willie and Elvis can get in trouble so quickly.

'When they came in. Saying all queers are dancers...'

'That wasn't said at all,' Lilly says.

'Ah, the lads were talking about Brendan being gay and dancing and wanted to know if your gay fellas liked dancing too...'

'That's homophobic!' Lisa shouts.

'Jesus, will ye can it with the shouting,' Kyle cuts in. 'We're barely surviving at the end of the world here. Fecking worried about someone asking if they like dancing... Peter, are you happy with the word gypsy.'

'Aye,' Peter says with an amiable shrug.

'Great and tell ye lads not to ask gay men if they like dancing. Lilly?'

'Thank you, Kyle. As I was saying Peter has also agreed to take on the work we have going on to flatten the land which in turn means we can give workers back to you, John.'

'Oh bless you,' John says with obvious relief. 'That'll help loads...and honestly, I didn't mean anything when I said nigger,' he adds, looking about the table.

'John, it's fine. Stop worrying,' Sam says, waving a hand at him.

'Just don't want anyone thinking I'm racist.'

'John! Nobody thinks your bloody racist,' Kyle snaps.

'Moving on,' Lilly says again. 'There are a few things I want done quickly...everyone listen in please...' she takes the pen and draws a circle on the notepad. 'This is the fort...this is the sea...this is the bay, can everyone see that?'

'Aye,' Kyle says.

'Aye,' Peter says.

'This is where the gypsy camp is...' Lilly pauses, thinking it sounds wrong to say gypsy camp before shaking her head and carrying on. 'I want a wall from here to here...' she adds, drawing a curved but unbroken line from one side of the bay to the other. 'That will enclose the entire bay...' she looks up to a sea of faces staring at the notepad and a stunned silence as everyone takes in the huge area she just referenced in her sketch.

'That's a big wall you're needing,' Peter says, rubbing his chin.

'That's a very big wall,' John says.

'Aye, it is,' Kyle replies. 'Of course, in a perfect world you'll be wanting a concrete sectional wall...'

'I've seen the ones you mean,' Peter says.

'Aye, they're used on military bases all over the world. It's said a good wall is an army's best friend.'

'I'm sure it is but where are we going to get a twelve feet high concrete sectional wall from?' Peter asks.

'Most army bases have them. I'll do you a list I will.'

'You'll do me a list now?'

'Aye. I just said that. I'll do you a list.'

'And a cook who isn't a priest that isn't a soldier knows where all the army bases are that have concrete sectional walls, is that right, Father?'

Kyle thinks for a second as everyone in the room looks from Peter to him. 'Aye,' he says finally.

'Aye,' Peter says, rolling his eyes. 'Now if we can't find your concrete sectional wall for any reason, would shipping containers do the job for you?'

'Shipping containers you say,' Kyle replies. 'Aye. Would. Stacked right they're good walls they are. Of course they'll be needing razor wire and other such deterrents.'

'Aye, naturally,' Peter says.

'Aye,' Kyle says.

'Aye,' Lilly says before being able to stop the words coming from her mouth. 'I am so sorry. I wasn't mocking you...'

'It's okay, I already said nig...'

'John! Stop saying it,' Sam says.

'I just said I said it. I didn't mean it like...'

'Drink your tea, John,' Kyle says.

'Indeed,' Lilly says. 'Now, there are two main roads in. The seaward road that runs adjacent to the shore, and the other that goes through where the housing estate was...'

'Is that what it was,' Peter muses. 'What happened to it?'

'Dave blew it up,' Lilly says, remembering what Nick told her.

'I bet he bloody did,' Kyle mutters, earning a look from Lilly before she continues.

'We need to make sure we control access, so my plan is to construct a wall and control those two roads with barriers and vehicle check-points for the initial safety check on entry...then new arrivals can be escorted down to a secondary checkpoint for registration and so forth.'

'Aye. That would work,' Kyle says.

'Okay, that's one thing,' Lilly says. 'Moving on and we need to address food. Agatha, how are we looking on that front?'

The big woman sucks air in, shaking her head as she speaks. 'Plenty right now, but we've a lot of mouths to feed we have. At this rate, allowing for new people coming in, I'd say we've got about a week's worth of eating well. More if we ration...'

'Only a week?' John asks as the ripple of concern goes around the room.

'Lot of bellies to fill,' Agatha says. 'That said though, Peter my love, are we feeding your lot too? That'll cut it down if we do...'

'We've enough for now,' Peter says. 'Maybe about the same I'd say. A week or so.'

'We need foraging parties,' Lilly says, bringing the attention back to her. 'But the priority is emptying the buildings in the bay and flattening that area ready for the wall...'

'We're going to run out of people,' John says. 'Between that and buildings inside the fort...'

'We've new people turning up every day,' Kyle says. 'Get them rested, fed and put them to work. It's that simple.'

'Kyle's right,' Lenski says. 'You eat, you work.'

'And look for rope while you're out,' Alf adds, lifting his tea mug while leaning against the wall at the back of the room. 'And some new mop heads, and a few buckets wouldn't go amiss either. Maybe a new wheelbarrow. Can't beat a good wheelbarrow. You can use the barrow to put the other things in and bring them back. Barrows are good like that. But mainly the rope.'

'Rope. Got it,' Lilly says into the sudden quiet of the offices. 'Those are the priorities for now. We get the wall up and we gather as much as we can...after that is living accommodation. What options do we have to house people inside the fort? John?'

'Crikey, yeah we've been thinking on this. Comes down

to materials. Wood is the easiest so it'll be wooden structures...'

'We'll need a big one for people to eat in,' Agatha says. 'And for cooking. We can't cook in the rain outside.'

'Sorry to place burden on you, John, but that needs to be done as soon as possible too,' Lilly says after a few seconds.

'This weather worries me if I'm honest,' Pea cuts in. 'What if this thing has changed the weather and winter comes early? That sounds stupid but this summer is way beyond anything I've ever known...'

'Aye, I guess we can't rule that out,' Kyle says heavily, wondering if Henry knows more of exactly what *this* is.

'All we can do is try,' John says.

'It's not a question of trying,' Lilly says. 'Failure means people die...'

Hard words that bring forth another heavy silence. 'Sure,' John says. 'We'll do what we can.'

'Agatha, are you happy to take charge of the food issues?'

She nods deeply, 'yes love, I'll do what I can.'

'Thank you, Colin the Co...ahem, sorry. I meant Colin, would you take charge of the other rooms please. Bedding, clothes and hygiene supplies. Organise the rooms for them.'

'Wow, yeah sure, happy to jump in,' he says quickly.

'Great thank you, please report to Lenski on matters relating to the fort if I am not here. Lenski? Are you happy to oversee them?'

'I do this. Yes.'

'Sorry, just so I have this right,' Colin the Cola says. 'I like things clear in my mind. Lilly, you're in charge and Lenski is like your deputy? That about right?'

'I no do this,' Lenski starts to say. 'I just help...'

'If the shoe fits, Lenski,' Kyle says, patting her back.

'What shoe? I have shoes.'

'It's a saying,' Pea explains.

'Lenski, Sam, Pea, Joan and Kyle can all make decisions regarding the fort and the things we need.'

'Got it,' Colin says. 'So like they're all deputies. That right? And we're like section heads? I just like to be clear on things.'

'Does it matter?' Sam asks.

'He just said he likes things to be clear,' Pea explains. 'That's fine, Colin. Think of it like that.'

'Great. So. Just to be clear. I'm a section head of the clothing, bedding and hygiene department. That right?'

'Yes,' Pea says.

'Great. Got it. Thank you. Do we get t-shirts or anything? You know, like a uniform or...'

'No,' Pea says.

'Great. Got it. Just thought it might help that's all. So people can see who the section heads are if they need help.'

'Is that a bad idea?' Sam asks. 'Might help put people at ease. Colin, you carry on if you want...'

'Great. Anyone else want a t-shirt? I'll get a list going... sizes? Colours? Preferences?'

'I think we're done,' Lilly says. 'You can sort the other things out between you. We need progress and quickly. Thank you everyone...'

CHAPTER FIVE

D ay Twenty One

'T inned beans and hot dog sausages. Fucking joke
that is. Either that or fruit. Some fucking choices
that is. Bet they've got bleeding crossonts to eat or
those pain o'chocolate buns...and what we supposed to do
all day? Sit in the sun?' Tommy grumbles in his patch of
ground. Sat on his backside with his legs stretched out. His
belly full and a large Styrofoam cup filled with strong tea at
his side. The sun now rising higher into the sky with the
promise of another scorching day.

'This tea tastes like gnats pee as well,' Tommy adds after
sipping from his cup. 'They need to get a fucking grip in
here...where you going?' he asks when Norman rises to
his feet.

'I need to stretch my legs,' Norman says.

'Make sure you go the right way this time you numpty...'

Norman walks off. Simply unable to sit in the heat

listening to Tommy. Too many images of Robert in his mind. The pain inside so very terrible it makes him feel strangely numb, like there is a void where his heart and soul once existed. He needs something to do. Something menial and hard so he'll be exhausted and sleep without night-mares. It felt good for those few seconds this morning when he helped with the woman in shock. Not the action of it all. That was frightening, and never in his life did he think he would ever need to try and wrestle a gun from someone.

No, it was the doing that helped. The having something else to focus on. That's what he needs now.

He lifts his head to look about, trying to discern who he should ask and walks to the door where all the fort workers seem to go in and out, hearing the sound of chairs scraping and people chatting as the meeting ends.

'Excuse me! I have work to do?' A female voice snaps and Norman watches the angry female doctor he saw yesterday storm out and walk off across the fort.

'Give me five minutes,' Lilly calls while walking out. 'Oh hi,' she says, coming to a stop on seeing Norman. 'You helped us this morning...I didn't have a chance to say thank you...'

Norman nods, offering a tight quick smile. 'Is this where we volunteer to work?'

'Yes, it is. Thank you so much. Go in and see Lenski... she's right in there.'

'Lenski?' Norman asks, stepping into the offices to see people standing and chatting.

'I'm just saying it'll help if we have t-shirts,' a red-faced man tells Sam nearby.

'Sure,' Sam replies. 'Sorry, who are you after?' she asks Norman.

'Er, Lenski?'

'Down there,' Sam replies, pointing down the room to the tall Polish woman talking to Agatha the cook.

'Lenski? I'd like to volunteer...to help I mean,' Norman says, coughing to clear his throat. His voice sounding so weak and feeble. His voice was always so strong. So resonant and powerful but then everything feels weak and feeble now.

'Name?' Lenski asks, waving as Agatha walks off.

'Norman.'

'Last name?'

'Calloway. Norman Calloway...'

'Wait please...' Lenski says, flicking through a stack of sheets on a table. 'Calloway with C yes?'

'Yes, it is. I can pick litter up or...clean the dishes maybe. Open tins. Carry wood or...'

'Were you builder? Soldier?'

'Er, no...no, I wasn't...'

'I have now,' she says, pulling a sheet from the pile. 'Calloway. Yes. Norman Calloway. It say you were a lawyer.'

'Er yes.'

'You have education yes? Wait please...Ann?'

'Over here,' Ann replies, pushing through the people chatting. 'What's up?'

'I have man to help you. Is lawyer. Is smart.'

'A lawyer eh?' Ann asks, stepping in close with that doctor's way of invading his personal space without the slightest bit of worry. She reaches out to feel his neck, nodding at him as she does. 'I'm happy with menial work or just labouring,' he adds while she pulls a small torch from a pocket to shine in his eyes.

'Look that way...have you eaten this morning?'

'Sausages and beans but...'

'Drank much?'

'Tea...'

'Passed water?'

'What?'

'Had a piss? Have you had a piss?'

'Yes.'

'Any pain? Did it hurt?'

'No but...'

'Close your eyes, hold your arms out...checking you for balance now. Just going to push gently so resist me...that's good. From this side. That's good...'

'Sorry, what's this for?'

'Checking to make sure you're fit to work with me. Expect a long day. Hot too. Not much shade either. Probably looking at twelve, maybe fourteen hours before we come back to the fort. That okay?'

'Right. Er...doing what?'

'Working with me on the other side. Could do with a thinking man giving me a hand.'

'I just wanted to pick litter.'

'Oh I recognise you now. You helped this morning with that woman. Of course you did. You're with me. Wait here and we'll go when Lilly gets back...actually, that pan has just heated. Make yourself a cup of tea and I'll have one too. No sugar in mine...' she rushes off, making Norman turn as Lenski walks in from his other side.

'Radio,' Lenski says, pushing one into his hands. 'Channel two, you are the beach, yes?'

'What?'

'If I call for the beach you answer if Ann does not hear me. Yes?'

'Right.'

'Take this clipboard. Names, details of the people.

What skills they have. You write this down when the new people come. Yes?'

'Right.'

'Yes, write. Write on sheet. If builder, if doctor you say urgently. We need people with skills. Yes?'

'Right.'

'Thank you so much for this morning,' Pea says, walking by while quickly rubbing his shoulder. 'Really means a lot.'

'Right,' Norman says.

'Okay,' Ann says, appearing at his side with a huge red paramedic bag that she dumps at his feet. 'Did you make a brew? No? I'll do it. Look after that bag...'

'Okay, everybody ready?' Lilly calls, prompting an exodus of people starting to move.

'Grab that for me,' Ann says, passing Norman the big red medical bag while she hoists another one from the side onto her shoulder.

Lilly leads the way with Kyle and Peter as they head out and down to the gates and through to the beach and the workers all chatting and smoking on the shore with the boat engines idling, ready to load.

Into the vessels with Lilly's and Ann's boats moving side by side through the still water as Norman takes it all in. Looking at the sea, at the sky, at the people about him that appear so tired and exhausted but still functioning and still trying to help.

'What's your name?'

Norman blinks then spots Kyle staring at him from a few feet away in the other boat. 'What's your name?' Kyle asks again.

'Norman.'

'Norman is it? Thanks for your help this morning. Appreciate that.'

Norman nods. Not knowing what else to say. 'We've got new arrivals already waiting,' Ann says to him, pointing ahead to a fleet of vehicles waiting on the shore road flanked by armed men and women. The refugees drinking water and sitting in the shade. Men, women and children. 'Going to be a very long day...'

'What do I do?' he asks but she just smiles at him. A middle-aged woman with laughter lines in the corners of her eyes and a great and awful sadness within them.

'Whatever it takes,' she says with raw honesty. 'We do whatever it takes.'

If there is order, Norman cannot see it. From the minute he steps from the boat to the beach there is only chaos and noise with many people doing many different things at the same time.

He wades through the shallows onto the beach. His wet office shoes sinking into the soft sand. Grey suit trousers and his white office shirt now grubby and worn. The sun already glaring down. The heat already so high it makes him squint from the sunlight bouncing off the water, shielding his eyes as he looks this way and that while carrying one of the big red medical bags.

'We're over here,' Ann calls, bringing his attention to her at the edge of the sand. 'Give me a hand with these...' she starts grabbing large sun umbrellas. Norman tries to help but every action feels feeble and weak. Like he's not in his own body. 'They are a bit tricky,' Ann says kindly, having already put four up. 'How do you like it?'

'Like what?' he asks.

'Our office,' she says, staring at the shaded section formed by the umbrellas. 'Grand isn't it. Right, grab a clipboard, we'll get stuck in...'

Clipboard in hand and he trudges after Ann striding

confidently from the soft sand onto a road surface that only three weeks ago would have been swept daily to keep the sand off. Now it's barely visible.

'Hullo!' Ann calls out to two armed men. 'Are you with the camp?'

'We are,' one of them replies. Blond haired and smiling. 'I'm Patrick, that's Tyson...'

'Alright,' Tyson says, tanned and lean with short dark hair. A wooden stocked rifle held on a strap across his front.

'Great stuff,' Ann says. 'I'm Ann. This is Norman. Right, what have we got here?' she says, coming to a stop to address the silent and worried looking people that arrived during the night. 'Listen in please. We'll get you over to the fort as soon as we can, so please get yourselves ready to be checked. Norman, we'll start at the far end and work backwards...'

Into the fray they go. Norman rushing after Ann towards a car at the front. A family sitting beside it. Two young children. A mum and a dad. All of them looking fearful.

'Hi! Doctor Ann Carlton,' Ann says, walking towards them. 'We just need a few details. Come on, up you get... where are you from?'

'Gloucester,' the man says, clearing his throat to speak.

'Not too far then,' Ann says. 'Are any of you in pain? I mean serious pain from injury or illness? No? All good? Children drinking plenty? Have any of you been bit, scratched, cut or had any bodily fluids go on you from the infected? No? Right, very briefly. This is the fort. We're getting set up as we go, okay?'

'Is Mr Howie here?' the man blurts, glancing at his wife. 'We heard about him. They said he's immune and he's got soldiers and it's safe here...'

'See that group over there,' Ann says, pointing down the road to Lilly talking with Kyle, Sam, Pea and Joan. 'They're all part of Mr Howie's team. He's not here right now but he does come back. We're doing everything we can to make you safe while Mr Howie is out there keeping them away from us...'

Norman spots the looks of relief in the faces of the two adults. That there is hope and someone doing something.

'Norman, we need names, dates of birth, who they are here with, allergies and what skills they have, weapons, engineering, cooking, crafting...anything that can help us. Lenski also does the same in the fort to make sure nothing is missed.'

Into the fray a bit further and Norman starts his job proper. A pen in one hand. A clipboard in the other and he feels strangely nervous, like it's the first day on a new job and he's being scrutinised. Then a few seconds later and his mind floods with images of Robert and those nerves go because nothing really matters now.

'Okay, great,' Ann says, finishing the first family. 'Norman, can you radio Lenski and tell her the first lot are on their way.'

'Er...' Norman juggles the pen and clipboard, everything awkward and weird. The radio in his hands and he presses the button, not knowing if it's working. 'Is that it?' he asks, hearing his own voice blast out from several radios held by people nearby.

'I'll do it,' Ann says, rubbing his arm as she plucks her radio from her belt. *Lenski, it's Ann. First family coming to you very shortly.*

Yes. I hear this, Ann, Lenski's voice transmits back.

Into the fray a bit more and he rushes after Ann striding on towards the next set of people. The same things repeated. This is the fort. Mr Howie is not here but Lilly and her team work with Mr Howie. Names, details, allergies and skills.

'Sally love! Next lot are ready to go over...*Lenski, It's Ann. Another group on their way.*'

Norman rushes after Ann as the morning plays out. The same things repeated. This is the fort. Any pain? Names, details. What are your skills? More caravans arriving. People shouting out. Voices constantly on the radio with people in the fort and on the beach talking to each other. Boats going back and forth. Vans and pick-ups whizzing up and down the shore road carrying the contents of the houses being flattened. A frantic pace that only gets worse as more people turn up. Terrified, confused, bedraggled and desperate.

'*Er, Lenski? Hi, it's Norman. I'm on the beach and Ann asked me to tell you the er...I mean we have some more people coming over...when Sally...*'

'*I hear this,*' Lenski cuts him off and on they go, working down the line to the next vehicle. A tall man with a turban and a dark beard turning to look at Ann and Norman. Two more men in turbans. Women, children and older people. All of them the same as everyone else. Silent and fearful looking.

'Hi, Doctor Ann Carlton. Welcome to the fort. I just need to check you over and we'll go through everything with you. That okay?'

'Sure,' the tall man in the turban says. His accent distinctly Birmingham.

The same as before and Ann gets working, moving from person to person. Asking about cuts, bites, scratches and bodily fluids.

'Just need to take some details please,' Norman says.

'Names, dates of birth, who you are here with then skills and that sort of thing.'

'Sure mate, whatever you need. I'm Pardip...the other two ugly ones are my brothers unfortunately, Jaspal and Simar, we're all Singh though mate. Surnames like. I don't think anyone is allergic to anything. Best ask the wife though...Sunnie? Is anyone allergic to anything, love?'

'You're allergic to cleaning,' she fires back in a strong brummie voice. 'No love, nobody has allergies. Jaspal gets windy if he eats too much bread...'

'Okay,' Norman says, writing it all down. 'I need to ask for skills too, builders or soldiers or...'

'I'm a builder, well, a construction manager to be precise like,' Pardip says casually.

'What?' Ann snaps, spinning around. 'Say that again?'

'I'm a builder,' Pardip says with a shrug.

'Not a good one,' Jaspal mutters.

'Builder!' Ann says, rushing over. 'I could kiss you! I will kiss you! A builder...' she grabs the tall man, planting kisses on his cheeks in a way that makes his family all smile in puzzlement.

'Jaspal's an electrician,' Pardip adds. 'And Simar is a joiner...'

Ann shouts in delight as she rushes to hug Jaspal then on to Simar. 'WE'VE GOT BUILDERS!' she shouts, making the workers on the beach turn to call out and wave as she grabs her radio. *'John! It's Ann. I've got a strapping family here. Builder, electrician and a joiner...'*

A brief pause. A burst of static. *'Really?'* John's voice booms from the radio. *'They fit to work?'*

'Sure, I guess so,' Pardip says, clearly thrown off but smiling all the same. 'Sunnie's a cook too if that helps, and Anika's a nurse.'

'FUCK ME,' Ann shouts, lifting her arms into the air, making them all jump. 'You're the family from heaven...are you a qualified nurse?'

'Yeah course,' Anika says, her own voice as strong with the brummie accent as the others.

'You beautiful woman,' Ann says, hugging her too. 'Right. We'll get you over to the fort and sorted out, then as soon as you are ready please get back over here to work with me and Norman. Is that okay? Best family ever...gold stars for everyone.'

'That's a nice welcome that is,' Pardip says as his family nod and murmur in agreement. 'We were worried like. You know. Being Indian and all that...and from Birmingham...'

'You could be aliens and I would still kiss you,' Ann says.

'Hi, Ann? I just heard on the radio,' Lilly says rushing towards them with Kyle. 'Builders?'

'Oh no, not just builders,' Ann says, grabbing Sunnie's hand. 'This lady is a cook, and this lady is a nurse, Jaspal is an electrician and Simar is a joiner...'

'Oh now, will ye look at that,' Kyle says, striding in to clasp hands.

'Brilliant,' Lilly says, joining in with the greetings, and it hits harder, right then on a sand covered road at the edge of a beach between a fort and a gypsy camp as Norman realises just how desperate times are now. And that this family, simply because of the skills they have, are instantly elevated up in terms of just how bloody essential they are.

Lenski walks through the outer gate onto the beach outside the fort. Tall, blonde and born with an instinct for survival coupled with a desire to work and be useful, to be productive and make things run properly. Things should be done properly.

She nods at Donald straightening his posture as though coming to attention from slouching. A man in his sixties with a big paunchy belly, a rifle strapped to his shoulder and a pipe stuck in his mouth, but at least he's working.

The first family reach the shore. The mum, dad and two children from Gloucester.

'My name is Lenski. I no smile so much. I not angry though. Is just me and way I am. Yes? Come...' she leads them into the fort, pausing to let them gawp at the size of it and the spectacle of people working. 'I take names please,' she asks as they walk, her mind thinking of Maddox as she jots the names down. Lenski likes Maddox but holds no real deep feelings for him. Maddox was kind and gave her security when she needed it. In return, she gave herself. Not like a hooker. Lenski isn't a whore. It wasn't like that, and besides, Maddox is handsome and strong. A good man too. He's just young and needs guidance.

'You have the two children yes?' she asks, feeling a pang of awful sadness that the mum and dad have tried to make them look clean before bringing them into the fort.

'Lenski, It's Ann. Another group on their way.'

'Is busy,' Lenski mutters, thinking to ask this family to wait while she collects the next one up as she spots a large woman trying to slink out of the offices. 'What you do?' she snaps in her hard voice.

'Eh?' the woman startles, looking trapped for a second. 'I didn't do anything.' A big round belly and a set of chins that wobble when she speaks. Dark greasy hair pulled back. Filthy clothes and stained teeth that show as she smiles nervously. Lenski has seen her about for the last few days, skulking at the back and staying quiet.

'What your name?' she asks bluntly. 'What you do in office?'

'Pamela. Nothing! Honestly, I was just...like um, seeing if you wanted a cuppa or something?' she trails off, trying to smile as she edges away.

'You want to work? Yes? This is good. Go down to the gate. Wait for new people. Bring them here. Wait with them. Take names, write down. Ages, dates of birth, skills, you see like on the other sheets. Is so busy. I cannot be in all the places...'

'But, so right...I mean, I've got this bad knee and...' Pamela trails off, offering another smile of dirty teeth. 'But sure. Like, totally glad to help...' she limps away, too startled and too scared of Lenski to do otherwise.

She saw the office was empty when she walked by and only wanted to see the rooms Lilly killed all the kids in. The last thing Pamela wanted was to do any actual work.

'How do,' Donald the guard says, puffing on his pipe.

'Lenski told me,' Pamela blurts watching as the scared people clamber from the boat. All adults. All sullen and scared. Pamela sets off through the gates and gets several steps before realising she is alone and goes back to see them on the shore with their bags.

'I think you need to tell them to follow you,' Donald says.

'Er...right...so...follow me then...' she offers a smile and watches as they struggle to carry their bags and traipse in after her and she doesn't pause to give them a few seconds to gawp at the fort.

'Jesus,' one of the men mutters at the size and sight of it.

'Yeah right,' Pamela says. 'Wasn't always like this. Maddox and his lot like totally fucked it over and kicked off and Lani got killed but then Lilly threw some grenades in and blew the little shits all over the place, now it's better...'

'What the fuck?' the man mutters, sharing horrified looks with his group as they reach the offices and stop with Pamela standing in the doorway, remembering that Lenski told her to take their names. She grabs a clipboard from a table and finds a pen.

'Er, I need to take your names, and like dates of birth and...er...something about peanuts or bee-stings. So...'

'Sorry what?' the man asks.

'What?' Pamela asks.

'What did you want?' the man asks, clearly confused.

'You might as well do it,' Pamela says, thrusting the clip-board and pen at him.

'Do what?'

'Write your names down and ages and if you're allergic to bees and stuff.'

'Bees?' someone else asks. 'Are there bees here?'

'Why would we have bees?' Pamela asks.

'You just said...' the man starts to say.

'And peanuts,' Pamela adds, nodding at them. 'I don't know. Lenski just told me to do it. I don't even know why...I was just like walking past and she was like all angry and *go and get the new people and make them write their names down...*'

'Right,' the man says. 'Sure. Er...yeah I can do that...'

Pamela waits as they write on the clipboard, stealing glances at their stuff and the clothes the women are wearing and assessing if the men are hot or not. She turns to look inside the offices, spotting the tea and coffee stuff at the back and a packet of open biscuits. Anyone in the fort can get a brew whenever they want from the central section. The hot water thing is always on, but they don't have biscuits, and Pamela really likes biscuits.

'I say you do this...'

Pamela snaps her head over as Lenski takes the clipboard from the group while glaring at Pamela. 'I say you write down. Not them. They not put dates of birth or allergies or who they are with...'

'Oh, oh right,' Pamela says quickly. 'Your accent sorry, didn't hear you. I thought you said tell them to write it down.'

'I do this now. Go to gates. Bring next ones here...you write down names. Not them. Yes?'

'Okay!' Pamela says, seeing everyone staring at her. 'Like I'm totally happy to help and do my bit, like...you know...all working to get the fort going after Lilly killed the little fuckers...'

'Go!'

'I'm going!' Pamela blurts, rushing off back towards the gates, adding her limp then forgetting it when she goes through.

'How do,' the guard says.

'Fuck,' Pamela says, spotting the next boat coming in. 'That's all we need...'

'You meeting them again?' the boat driver calls.

Pamela nods, looking at the dark-skinned people and their dark beards and turbans and the women in clothes that look halfway between normal and Indian. 'My. Name. Is. Pamela,' she says slowly when they disembark, clustered together with bags and rucksacks. 'I. Am. Going. To. Show. You. The. Fort...yes?' she asks, nodding at them.

'Are you alright, babs?' Pardip asks her, wondering why she is speaking so slowly. 'Anika, she alright?'

'You banged your head, love?' Anika asks.

'What! Oh...haha! Right...yeah, sorry...thought you were like foreign or something,' Pamela says. 'I mean like foreign foreign and not just like...er...'

'Did you want us to follow you, love?' Pardip asks when Pamela walks off.

'Yeah you need to follow her,' the guard says.

Pardip leads his group in through the gates, pausing as he runs a professional eye over the space and constructions while Jaspal instinctively looks to the wirings running about the place feeding from solar panels set against the walls. 'Lot of wood work going on, Sim,' Pardip adds. 'You'll be busy.'

'If they want it all falling down you mean,' Jaspal quips, earning a dig in the arm from his brother.

'They seemed nice on the beach though,' Sunnie says.

'Fiver on someone thinking we're Muslim within an hour,' Simar says.

'Sorry!' Pamela calls, walking back towards them having rushed off towards the offices. 'You need to follow me...'

Up to the offices and Pamela grabs a clipboard and pen then turns back to the group coming to a stop outside and feels a rush of panic that their names will be really complex and hard to spell.

'Er, so...I have to take your names and...'

'We did that on the beach,' Sunnie says.

'Sorry what? Your accent is really strong,' Pamela says, leaning towards her.

'I don't have an accent, love,' Sunnie says.

'Sorry, can you just speak slower. I'm doing my best

here...I need to take your names. Er...just spell them for me, oh hang on, are you called Muhammed or something?'

'Boom!' Simar says. 'Less than a minute...'

'That doesn't count,' Jaspal says.

'We don't have a mosque,' Pamela adds, rushing the words out.

'Cock it,' Jaspal mutters as Simar laughs.

'Hello there!' John's voice booms out as he rushes towards the group with Lenski. 'You're the golden family, right?'

'I wouldn't say that mate,' Pardip laughs, moving out to grasp John's hand.

'I heard we have a cook here,' Agatha calls, appearing from the other side while pointing at them all in turn until Sunnie lifts a hand and gets a hug in greeting. 'Bless you, we're desperate we are,' Agatha says.

Pamela watches on. Confused as to why John and Agatha are being so nice and figures it's because the new people are Muslims or something and they're just trying to show they're not racist. Then she worries she appeared racist and then worries it will stop her being able to hang about in the offices and eat biscuits. 'I love Indian food...' she blurts, earning a confused look from Anika.

'You have drink. I do this now,' Lenski says to Pamela.

'In here?' Pamela asks, motioning the office.

'Yes. Sure. Get drink. Stay in shade. Is hot. Sit down, see sheets, learn what we do and help. We need help...'

Pamela slips into the offices proper, relishing being inside the place where Lilly threw the grenades, glancing at the walls and the chunks of masonry missing from the blast. To the back and she sets water to heat while staring at the biscuits. It's not that Pamela eats a lot. It's a thyroid thing. A gland problem. She practically doesn't eat. Still, at least she told the new family she likes Indian food so they won't think she's racist.

She makes tea with three sugars and four mini-pots of long-life milk and the second Lenski walks off she stuffs two in her mouth to chew quickly while more go into her filthy pockets for later.

CHAPTER SIX

It's taking too long. Everything is taking too long, and Lilly looks down the shore road to the beach and clenches her jaw, feeling nothing but frustration and inadequacy inside.

There are too many structures to pull down and not enough people working. New caravans are arriving every few minutes, bringing new people that can work and help, but they need to find a position to pitch on and then get set up and sorted, and that takes time. Everything takes time. Too much time.

She stands on the shore road staring this way and that. Plant machines flattening the structures already pulled down, but there are so many more to go and every one of the standing buildings is a place the infected can hide in.

She needs more drivers for the vans and more people to help unpack the houses and she needs them to be faster in dumping the contents on the beach, but then the people on the beach can't cope with the amount of stuff they've got coming in. More refugees too, which is good as that means more workers, but they need to rest and recover, and so the pressure grows. Pressure unrelenting. A crackle on the radio and she cocks her head over, listening to the transmission.

'*Lilly. It Lenski. Simar, he is the carpenter. He say the houses there are made of wood but he needs the wood, oh shit, I have no idea what he says. Wait please...*' another crackle of static. A few voices heard talking before a deep male brummie accent comes through. '*Alright, it's Simar. John said you're pulling them houses down. They're timber framed they are. Can you get the wood to the fort? We can use that...*'

Lilly looks up the road to the houses and structures. At the moment they are simply flattening them, so picking the wood out means a whole new effort. Another priority. Another task that needs doing as soon as possible, but it has to be done. If they fail then people will die. If the weather changes and they don't have sufficient shelter then people will be exposed, and Agatha cannot cook food out in the open for very long.

'*Sure,*' Lilly says. '*We'll get the wood to you...*' she breaks the transmission and turns with a sinking sensation in her gut at the shore road now completely blocked. The vans and pick-ups jammed in with the caravans and the new arrivals. People on foot walking down with bags. Kyle and Joan in amongst them all trying to get people to pull over to make room to ease the backlog as Lilly tracks the line of vehicles all the way down to the beach and grabs her radio.

'*Lilly to the beach...what's going on?*' she pauses, waiting for a reply and tries again when none comes. '*Lilly to the beach...can anyone hear me?*'

'I DON'T THINK THEY CAN HEAR YOU,' Kyle yells.

'WHAT'S GOING ON?' she yells back. He shrugs,

holding his hands out as she nods grimly, motioning back that she'll go down and see.

On the beach, Norman stands back to mop the sweat from his brow. His once white office shirt now glued to his back. His grey suit trousers clinging to his legs, rubbing and chafing.

Why did he dress like this? He looks down at himself, barely remembering leaving his house. He was in such a state of shock. He just got dressed and must have reverted to putting his normal work clothes on. Someone shouting on the radio. He thinks it might be Lilly, but he misses it.

A glance about. The end of the narrow shore road now clogged with the ditched and abandoned cars used by the new arrivals. Too many of them stretching down alongside the beach. He spots piles of crap on the edge of the sand too. The van drivers ditching their loads at the closest point possible to get back up the road, and those piles are now preventing cars from moving over to create space. Caravans too, blocking the road as they try and punch through to the camp.

Vehicles sounding horns. Van drivers waiting to ditch more loads so they can get back for more. Workers on the beach drowning under the sheer weight of goods they have to deal with and Sally shouting at everyone, the stress and heat getting too much. Caravan drivers tooting horns to get through, so they can pitch in the camp and help out. Diesel fumes in the air. Men with guns. Women with guns. Everyone seems to have a gun. Norman doesn't have a gun.

'What's going on?' Lilly shouts out, striding towards him. Her face as red and sweating as everyone else but etched with determination and annoyance as she looks to the blocked beach and the blocked road and the sheer bedlam in every direction.

'The cars,' Norman says.

'Pardon?' she walks up to him, her arms at her side. Her rifle strapped to her back. Startling blue eyes and her hair pulled back in a tight ponytail.

'The cars,' he says again. 'We need to move these cars...'

Lilly follows his gaze and spots the abandoned cars left at the end of the road and turns as she looks back down, following the line of them as she brings her radio to her mouth.

'Peter, it's Lilly. We need somewhere to put the cars being left here...we can't move at the moment.'

'Get them into that burnt out land behind my camp...I've got a few lads flattening it out to make room...and we're having the fuel out to run the generators too...'

'Brilliant. Thank you, Peter...can anyone near the beach that can drive come and grab a car please...WE NEED THESE CARS MOVING...'

More minutes wasted finding people to drive, then more time goes by as they rush over and ask what's happening and did someone say they need drivers?

'You're looking busy there, Blondie...' the red-haired woman from the camp calls as she saunters into view. 'You wanting these cars moved are you?'

'Yes please,' Lilly calls over.

'Right. So I can drive a car but I can't carry a gun, is that right?'

'Pardon?' Lilly asks as she realises Mary is staring past her to Tyson and Patrick.

'Jesus, Mary. You're like a broken record,' Tyson yells.

'And you're a broken record sexist prick,' she yells back, getting into the car and slamming the door closed. 'AND YOU PATRICK,' she yells from the window.

'I can drive one,' Norman says, seeing people rushing in

to grab cars and wishing to keep busy and stay busy to try and stop the pain in his heart from swallowing him whole.

'I'll come with you,' Lilly says without hesitation. 'I want to see it anyway. Ready?'

They take an old Ford Focus and Norman adjusts the seat as Lilly takes the passenger side, pushing her rifle between her legs as she gets in. 'Just follow them,' she says.

'You can't drive then?' he asks.

'Not safely,' she replies. 'And not with so many people about...just follow everyone else I guess.'

Norman starts the engine and sets off. Driving from the road to bounce over the grass and heading north towards a wide access point leading to a place that looks like hell. Everything blackened and broken. Piles of bricks, masonry and chunks of houses scattered all over the ground and he slows as a huge digger goes thundering by driven by a spotty bare-chested teenage boy with a huge grin scooping a big pile of masonry away. More plant machinery doing the same, flattening the ground to make it usable and Norman follows the other cars to the far side.

'What was this?' he asks.

'Housing estate,' Lilly replies. 'Dave blew it up when the fort was attacked.'

Norman doesn't reply. What do you say to that anyway? It stinks something awful, and the searing heat of the day seems so much worse for the broken surroundings.

A row of cars already parked with the kids sliding them in with handbrake turns, laughing and joking as they make a game of it. More kids with tubes, syphoning the fuel from the vehicles into big pots that get poured into bigger drums. An access road leading in with more men with guns standing sentry.

He parks up at the end of the row and gets out into a

wall of heat and noise and fumes. Something happening in every direction and he spots the red haired woman getting out of a car and walking off back towards the camp.

'You want a Snickers, Miss Lilly?' a boy shouts, ten, maybe eleven years old. A wide grin showing some of his teeth missing. His hands and arms smeared with grime, but he looks absurdly healthy and is clearly having a great time. 'We've got a box of them...'

'Thank you, very kind,' she shouts back, slowing in step as the kid ducks into the side of a small van and comes out to throw a Snickers over. 'Nice and cold,' she calls, holding one of them up.

'Aye, got a fridge we have,' Bobby grins, giving her a thumbs up before launching one at Norman who wasn't expecting it and reacts too slow, fumbling and knocking it across the ground. 'What was that?' the kid asks with disdain, waving a hand as he goes on about his business.

The day grows hotter too with every passing hour. A searing sun glaring down without mercy or care and in the fort, Tommy watches Pamela closely. Taking in her bulk and the way she waddles as she works. Sweat pouring down her face and her clothes look filthy, but what gets his interest most is the way she goes into all the store rooms while showing new people about.

'And so, like this is your little patch,' Pamela says, bringing the next group over.

'Is that it?' a woman in the group asks, looking at her large brood and then at the small patch.

'I dunno,' Pamela mumbles, losing all interest as she walks off and spots Tommy grinning at her. She slows to look behind, thinking he must be smiling at someone else because people never smile at Pamela. She puts it down to everyone being a judgemental twat rather than the fact she hasn't washed in days of staggering heat. Pamela doesn't like washing. She does, however, quite like the dark unused rooms within the fort. She doesn't even mind the bugs or spiders and happily shoos the rats away when they scuttle too close. She even woke up with one sat on her big belly a few nights ago and just farted then went back to sleep.

That's how she stayed safe when everything went so wrong in the fort, by crawling into dark places and hiding. She did think to maybe tell someone there were a few hiding places when it got really bad, but then she didn't want to ruin it for herself, so she kept quiet.

She aimed for the room at the back last night but stopped when she saw someone else go inside it. She snuck over and peered in to see a crying man fasten a rope to the ceiling then drop from a box to gargle and kick as he died. Pamela felt funny watching him and thought maybe she should shout for help, but she didn't. She went in when he fell quiet and checked his pockets for food, but he didn't have any so she went off and crawled under a big length of tarpaulin in another room. Now she blinks at the meaty tattooed guy smiling at her and slows her pace.

'Alright love,' Tommy says, friendly and nice. 'You look hot.'

'Like so hot,' Pamela says, nodding and wobbling her chins.

'They working you hard are they?'

'Yeah,' she says, scratching at her arse. 'Lenski's like *do this, do that, don't stop...*'

'That's a fucking joke that is,' Tommy says with a heavy sigh. 'Been watching you go up and down all bleeding morning. Come and have a sit down. You want a drink of water?' he asks, clearing space within his patch. 'Go on, five minutes won't hurt will it...'

Across the water, Norman helps unload the contents from the vehicles bringing goods back from the houses. His slippery office shoes sinking in the hot sand. His white shirt soaked with sweat, the tails pulled out, the sleeves rolled up. There is only work. Only the sanctity of it that gives blessed relief from the utter horror deep within.

More people arrive. He takes their names and details and shows them down to the boats then goes back to carrying things. More caravans arrive. He helps wave them into the camp, showing them the route to take. The chaos doesn't end, and if anything, it just gets worse as the day gets hotter.

Mid-afternoon and he wades into the sea to steady the prow of the boat, offering a hand to Anika jumping out. Taking her to Ann's shady umbrella office.

'Anika is here, Ann...' he says.

'Oh bless you,' Ann says, close to tears, overwhelmed by everything as she hugs the young Indian woman.

'We'll be okay, love,' Anika says kindly, an experienced nurse clearly used to dealing with overwrought doctors. 'Let's have a cuppa and you can talk me through it...'

Norman walks away to work and keep working. More vans and pick-ups waiting to off-load. The drivers under pressure to empty their vehicles and get back so Peter's men can flatten the structures. Everyone under pressure. Everyone hot and stressed and rushing about without any real order or structure.

'We can't fucking cope!' Sally shouts on the beach as she finally snaps and launches a bottle of water across the sand. 'Just dumping shit then fucking off for more...what we supposed to do with it?'

'Take a break,' Pea calls out, rushing onto the sand from the road. 'Sally! Go on now, go and sit down...'

'IT'S TOO MUCH,' Sally shouts. 'It's too much...I can't...it's just...' Norman watches her break. Seeing the very second the emotional surge takes over as she simply crumples to sob.

'ANN!' Pea yells out, rushing to Sally as Ann and Anika run out from the umbrellas to give aid. Everyone stopping working to watch.

'What we doing with all this?' the driver Sally shouted asks. Stricken to the core with worry etched on his face that he made Sally so upset. 'Lilly said...she said it's got to be cleared and we can't stop. Peter's lads are waiting to knock it all down...' he looks for someone to tell him what to do as his imploring eyes fall on Norman. 'What we doing mate?'

'Er,' Norman hesitates, glancing about at the absolute chaos and the beach strewn with so many piles of things.

'*Lilly to the beach, what's the hold up? I need those vans back here...*'

Norman edges closer, thinking to tell Pea or Ann that Lilly is calling.

'*Lilly to the beach...can you hear me?*'

'Norman, can you tell her we need a few minutes,' Ann calls.

'Sure...er...' he fumbles with his radio, finding the button to press. '*It's Norman, er...Ann is busy and Sally is...*'

'*Norman, it's Lilly. Where's Pea and Sam?*'

'*Pea is with Sally and Ann. Sally is er, she's not very well. Sam is helping Joan on the road. We've got caravans turning up and vans, it's pretty mad down here...*'

'*I need those vans back...*'

Norman can hear the tightness of her voice. The pressure growing upon them all. Pressure unrelenting. He looks to the vans stacking up waiting to dump their loads and the few workers on the beach struggling to cope with what they have already. There are simply not enough people. Then he spots more new arrivals coming towards them. Some in vehicles. Some on foot. Sally now broken and weeping hard. Ann and Anika trying to get her into shade.

There are too many piles of stuff here and too many smaller tasks underway. They need to focus on as few things as possible. '*Lilly, it's Norman. It's too manic here...*'

'*It's bloody manic everywhere,*' Kyle cuts in. '*Just do what you can...we need those vans back out...*'

'*We can't,*' Norman says. '*There's nowhere to put it all... Sally is hurt and...there's piles of stuff everywhere...the vans can't get in because they're dumping it too close to the road...*'

'*That's not our fault,*' someone shouts on the radio. '*We're told to get it unloaded and get back...don't fucking blame us...*'

'*No, I don't mean that,*' Norman says quickly. '*I just mean if we re-organise the beach we can make it faster...*'

'*Norman, it's Lilly. Can you do that please...*'

'*Me? Right...er...I...not on my own. Jesus, no chance...*'

'*This is Lilly. Anyone not busy go to Norman on the beach...Norman, we'll be with you in two minutes...*'

A surge of worry rises in Norman that he should have kept his mouth shut. What is he doing here? Why is he on this beach? Why is everyone staring at him? He blinks at people heading over from the road. Sam and Joan. Drivers and people from the vans.

A shout in the camp from Tyson. 'WE NEED A HAND ON THE BEACH...'

Norman turns his head, watching as a few more men

head out from the camp towards him. A pick-up weaving through the vehicles backed up on the road. Lilly and Kyle in the back. Peter and more of his men jumping out.

'Where do you want us?' Lilly asks, and he blinks again, his mind empty and blank. Without a clue of what to do. A woman in front of him. She looks austere and stern. A bottle of water in her hand.

'Drink,' Joan says, pushing the bottle at him.

He gulps quickly, wetting his mouth and throat.

'Better?' she asks.

He nods.

'Get on with it then. Can't stand dithering...'

'Er...we don't need so many piles here. It's too chaotic... clear it all back into one big mound over there. Food stacked in one place. Wood for building in another then everything else. That's it. Three clear sections...we do that, and we can turn those vans around in half the time...' he trails off as everyone looks at the beach strewn with debris and crap. A silence of a second.

'You heard him,' Joan snaps, clapping her hands. 'Three sections...come on! Chop chop!'

Everyone works. Lilly, Peter, Kyle, Joan. Everyone. Men from the camp grabbing stuff from the many mounds, hefting it over to the far side to stack and dump then rush back for more. Joan harrying them on. Lilly, Kyle and Peter urging them to keep working. Faces pouring with sweat. Clothes sodden and Norman in amongst it all, but work is good, work stops the pain inside.

'We need to call it a day,' Kyle says as another van drives off towards the beach. His sleeves rolled up showing his arms knotted with muscle, covered in old tattoos. The top few buttons undone. His pistols still worn but he looks beat. They all do. Peter the same. A long day yesterday then he was up most of the night organising the camp and now another day of solid work.

Pea yawns, her feet burning in her boots. Her skin feeling raw from so much sweat and motion in the heat. Sam sags against the side of a van, her head bowed. Joan remains upright, not showing any signs of fatigue despite her age but she feels it inside. My god she feels it inside and it's only pure grit and courage that prevent her from showing it.

Lilly stares about. Norman's re-organising of the beach made it all work a lot better and progress has been made, albeit not enough and too slow. Lilly would work through the night, but she spots the expressions of the people around her, exhausted to the bone and so weary they look like could drop right now and so she nods, knowing she pushed as much as she dares for today. 'Enough for now, we'll pick it up tomorrow...'

Gasps of relief. Peter nods, signalling his men to shut down and head back. Engines cutting off. Men dropping from driving plant machinery and they simply head down the road as one group. Not speaking for no words can be given right now. They are too hot, too tired and too drained.

'I know you're all done for,' Peter says as they walk down to the now much larger camp. 'But will you show your faces in the camp, just so they can all say hello and know who you are.'

They've nothing left to give but they nod and murmur agreement all the same. 'Of course,' Lilly says. 'Ann? Anika? We're calling in at the camp…join us? Norman? You too please if you will.'

That a sixteen-year-old girl can require the presence of a doctor, a nurse and a lawyer without raising question is neither noticed or mentioned. It is just the way of things now and Norman heads over, joining Ann and Anika as they tag onto the filthy and very drained ad-hoc delegation going into the camp.

'Quick brew?' Peter asks them quietly.

'Ach, we'd love that, Peter,' Kyle says, sensing this is his part to play now, a wink at Sam, a nod almost hidden.

'We'd love a cuppa,' she says with a big smile, getting the silent message loud and clear. 'This looks great in here…'

'Lovely,' Pea says. The three of them taking the lead while Lilly remains quieter, somewhat aloof and reserved but watching everything.

'Have you learnt to catch yet?' a young voice asks, prompting Norman to look down at the smiling kid with the missing teeth from earlier who threw the Snickers at him. 'Do you want some food? My ma's just made a rabbit stew so she has. I'll get you a bowl…'

'Er,' Norman says, thinking to politely decline as the lad runs off.

'Made a friend?' Ann asks him. 'And you really need to change your clothes, Norman. You look dreadful. See Colin when we get back.'

'You could do with some sunblock too, love,' Anika says. 'You're gonna peel something awful if you keep burning. I've got some aloe-vera gel in my bags if you need it…'

'Right,' Norman says, feeling a tug on his arm.

'Stew,' the lad says, beaming a huge grin at him while

holding a bowl out with a spoon already in it. 'My ma made it.'

'Yes, you did say,' Norman says, feeling somewhat touched by such a simple act of kindness and he looks at the child. 'Thank you...' he says sincerely.

The lad shrugs. 'You look like shit mister, thought it would help...'

Ann snorts a laugh. Pea and Sam the same as the lad walks off leaving Norman holding the bowl. 'Is it nice?' Sam asks. 'It looks nice...try it...'

Norman tries it. Tentative at first but then the taste hits. The seasoning and rich flavours and he nods eagerly, eating more. 'Delicious...'

'Bobby?' a woman calls, walking into view from behind a caravan. 'My lad give you the stew did he?' she asks, glaring at Norman.

'Er yes, he did,' Norman says. 'Sorry. Did you want it back?'

'No! I don't want it back. Got the manners of an ape has Bobby. Come on, got plenty more round here. Peter, I'm taking 'em for a stew now.'

'Right you are, Kathy,' Peter calls. Motioning them to follow her into a clearing with a big central fire underneath a big metal pot. Mix and match bowls filled with stew and handed round with spoons so clean they can see their reflections gleaming in them.

'We shouldn't take your food,' Lilly says.

'Ach, get off now, we've plenty to go round,' Kathy says.

The food is delicious. Heartening and rich, filling their stomachs quickly. Tyson and Patrick stroll over. Others they saw during the day. Weapons on belts or in reach. Candles and lights shining as the light fades. Muted conversations, men laughing. Life rolling on and people living.

'Is there many more to arrive, Peter?' Kyle asks.

'A few maybe. We're different families...different groups. Some are tucked up here and there nice and safe and don't feel the need to come here. We'll see...maybe when we get the wall up we'll get more. They'll see it's safer.'

'Soon as possible,' Lilly says. 'The wall I mean...'

'YOU DUMB PRICK...' a female voice shouts from somewhere close making Lilly tense from the aggression in the voice.

'Jesus,' Peter groans as Kathy closes her eyes and sighs while shaking her head.

'Mary! Will ye just calm down...' a male voice yells. The sounds coming closer through the twisting lanes of the camp.

Lilly watches on, reading the reactions of everyone else in the camp, all of them tutting and shaking heads, rolling eyes and muttering but not showing signs of fear or worry as the shouting flame-haired woman Lilly saw before comes steaming into view.

'Mary,' Peter groans. 'It's been a long day...'

'Mary!' Willie yells, running behind her.

'Mary, will ye calm down,' Elvis shouts, rushing with Willie.

'I'll not calm down,' Mary yells. 'I can shoot better than these wankers, Peter, and I can bloody hit harder too...'

'Mary,' Peter says, a jaded, weary tone to his voice.

'Cooking? I'm not bloody cooking...I can carry a gun and be a guard you sexist fucking pricks...'

'You're a mentalist,' Willie shouts. 'We ain't giving you a gun...'

'I've got my own gun. Do ye want to see it? I'll go and

get it shall I and we'll see who can shoot better and it won't be you you fecking ginger prick...'

'We've got the same hair colour you daft bitch!' Willie shouts back. 'We're related.'

'No, you ugly shit. I'm a redhead, you're a ginger prick, there's a bloody difference...'

'Mary, ye too angry to be a guard...' Elvis says to a few more murmurs of agreement.

'Right, back with you now and calm down,' Willie says, moving towards his sister.

'Don't bloody touch me, Willie,' Mary warns, backing away.

'I will bloody touch you, Mary.'

'You'll not be bloody touching me, Willie...'

'Pack it in,' Peter shouts.

'Mary, have some stew love,' Kathy calls.

'Fight him, Mary,' Bobby yells.

'Bobby! Shut up,' Kathy shouts.

'I mean it, Willie,' Mary says, coming to a stop. 'Elvis, you'd best not be helping him now. I'm warning you both fair and square. You can all hear this. I'm being provoked I am...'

Willie stops, rolls his eyes, huffs and shakes his head. Elvis the same. Lilly watches. Norman too. All of them holding bowls of soup and thinking the argument is now over, only it isn't and Willie, with a mischievous glint in his eye, reaches out to poke his sister in the arm.

A pause. A heartbeat. Peter groans and Mary punches Willie in the face, knocking him off his feet.

'Oh shit,' Sam whispers.

'GO ON MARY!' Bobby yells.

'Shut up, Bobby,' Kathy shouts as Elvis moves to restrain Mary and gets punched in the face too. One hit and he goes down with a thud, both the men groaning on the floor as the camp explodes in uproar with a couple more men running in to try and grab Mary but she darts back, weaving and slamming fists out, sending them flying until enough of them go in together, grappling the yelling girl out and past Lilly and her group.

'I'm leaving this bloody camp,' Mary yells as she goes. 'It's shit anyway... wankers...'

'She's out tonight,' Peter yells as Lilly and her group turn on the spot to watch them all go by.

'That bloody girl,' Kathy says. 'Will you be wanting some more stew now?' she asks, smiling at her guests.

'Is she okay?' Sam asks.

'Oh, this is normal for Mary,' Kathy says as Willie and Elvis come back, rubbing their jaws but with a bizarre air of normalcy and resignation.

'Right. Well. We should be going,' Lilly says. 'Thank you for the food and hospitality. Peter, are you happy to come for the meeting in the morning?'

'Aye, I'll be over,' he says, helping take the bowls from them. 'Don't mind Mary none. She's just got a temper on her...'

They exit the camp and head over the road towards the beach, seeing everyone else has gone back.

'What a day,' Sam remarks as they trudge over the sand. 'Wish I could punch like that though.'

'Blondie!' A voice behind making them all stop and turn to see Mary striding across the sand. Her face still furious. 'You're in charge of the fort are you not?'

'I am,' Lilly says.

'Good. I'm moving in I am,' Mary says, sweeping past them. 'Stuff Peter and them sexist wankers. Your fort takes refugees and I'm a refugee I am. Is this our boat is it?' she asks, wading in to grab the front of it.

'Forgive me. I do not want to intrude on your issues, but will this cause upset to Peter?' Lilly asks, holding still.

'Peter doesn't bloody own me. I can go where I want...I said to him. I said I want to be a guard not bloody cooking and making fires and peeling spuds. He said maybe. That's all he ever says. *Maybe Mary. I'll think about it Mary.* I said to him, I said *why can't I be a guard? Blondie has female guards and she's only a wee girl, and I can bloody shoot straighter and hit harder than most of them pricks I can...* how do you drive this? Is this the on switch? Ah I got it now I have...right. Are you getting in or what?'

'I guess we're getting in,' Sam says, wading out to climb in as the others do the same.

'Your shoe's knackered there,' Mary says, pointing at Norman's shoe. 'And why are you wearing office clothes? Are we all in? Right...I've never driven a boat before. What do you do? Twist this? Ah right, there we go...STUFF YOU PETER,' she yells, sticking a finger up at the camp. 'I'M MOVING TO THE FORT WITH BLONDIE...'

Across the water to the shore on the other side and out with Mary striding to the gates, glaring at old Donald smoking a pipe in a deckchair. 'You telling me he can be a guard and I can't?' she asks, walking off then rushing back. 'I wasn't being angry at you old fella,' she tells Donald. 'But you are a bit fat like...'

Outer gate locked. Inner gate locked. 'Good,' Mary says, watching them chain up for the night. 'Keep them pikeys out... seriously now? Did you hear that? Saying I'm too angry to be a guard? What a crock of shit. Oh wow, is this your fort now is it? It's a grand fort it is. Bigger than it looks. Where are we going?'

'Just to the offices,' Lilly says.

'You've got offices have you? Where? Through here?' she asks, going in first.

'Who are you?' Lenski asks, standing at a table.

'Mary, who are you?' Mary fires back, walking over with her hand held out. 'This your offices is it?'

'Evening,' Kyle calls, coming in next to see Lenski shaking hands with Mary. 'That's Mary. She's kipping down here for the night.'

'More than the bloody night,' Mary says. 'They said I can't be a guard,' she tells Lenski. 'I said I can shoot better and hit harder any day of the week. Wanted me to do cooking. Cooking? Me? Stuff that...'

'How's my smiling girl anyway?' Kyle asks with a heavy groan as he drops into a chair and brings his feet up to rest on the table.

'I no smile,' Lenski says, watching them all traipse in. 'Who say this? Why you here? Go back. This my fort now...'

'Day of days or what,' Sam says, heading straight for the table to sit down.

'Get them off,' Joan says, hooking Kyle's feet from the table as she goes by.

Ann walks in with Norman and Anika, dropping her medical bag and stretching her back out. 'Is this starting to feel like home for anyone else?' she asks.

'I had that,' Pea says. 'Soon as we walked in...'

'Where do the bags go?' Norman asks, trying to pick Ann's medical bag up with the others already on his back.

'I'll grab that I will,' Mary says, scooping the heavy thing off the floor with ease.

'Out the back,' Pea says. 'I'll show you...' she leads them through to a complex of small rooms at the rear of the larger office. 'We're using that one for storage, the bags can go in there. That one down at the end is where we're washing and changing, so if the door is closed don't go in, or knock first.'

'Nice,' Mary says, looking about. 'This where you all sleep is it?'

'Er no, we're up the wall a bit more.'

'Right,' Mary replies, dumping the bag in the storage room with Norman. 'What's your name anyway?'

'Norman,' Norman says.

'Mary,' Mary says, offering her hand. 'Your Pea aren't you, love?'

'Paula, but everyone calls me Pea. Cuppa?'

'Aye, cuppa will be grand,' Mary says, following her back into the office as Norman aims for the main door out.

'I should head off,' he says, lifting a hand.

'Norman! Have a cuppa with us,' Kyle calls, dragging a chair out.

'I need to wash, thank you,' he says stiffly, that feeling inside again that he's imposing.

'Norman, thank you for today,' Ann calls. 'Same tomorrow? Go and see Colin, get some shorts...'

He offers a wave slips out with a nod to Pamela going in who balks at the sight of the room now so full and quickly wipes her mouth to hide trace of the chocolate bar she just ate.

She stays quiet at the side, watching as a young woman with long red-hair moves from person to person, shaking hands and giving them her name. Her voice so strong and lilting with an accent that sounds mostly Irish but something else too.

'These are from our side,' Lilly says, joining Lenski at another table and placing a stack of sheets down, weighing them in place with a big stone with the word 'BEACH' written on it.

'Mine here,' Lenski says, tapping her stack held down by a stone with the word 'FORT' written on it.

'Busy day?' Lilly asks.

'Busy, yes. Busy day. Many people they come. We still need tents, shelves, we need wood, we need tools, we need this and that. Is okay. People they eat, they breathe, they alive. They not suffer...'

'Amen,' Kyle says to a few murmurs. 'We need more Lenski's in this world.'

'We do,' Pea says.

'I say this all the time,' Lenski says seriously. 'More me, less you, is good...' she adds a quick smile to get a few chuckles. 'Pamela, she help...' she adds, motioning towards Pamela.

'I didn't see you there, love,' Mary says, striding over with her hand held out. 'I'm Mary...'

'Hi!' Pamela says, taking the handshake nervously while seeing everyone staring at her. 'I'm Pamela, or Pammie, or Pam, or Pam Spam or Pamelo or like Spammie or...'

'That's a lot of bloody names you've got there,' Mary says, blinking at her. 'Can I just call you Pam?'

'Pam's fine,' Pamela says quickly.

'What do you do?' Mary asks her.

'Nothing,' Pamela blurts. 'Lenski told me...'

'What now?' Mary asks.

'She take names,' Lenski cuts in. 'Greet new people then she take them to doctors and to Agatha and Colin...'

'That's great,' Pea says.

'Cheers, Pammie,' Sam says.

'Aye, grand work that is,' Kyle adds.

'Oh it's like...like totally fine and...yeah,' Pamela says,

nodding hard enough to set her chins off. 'Just doing my bit and...so like, everybody is saying how great you guys are. And like so grateful and, they're like...wow, you guys are doing so much for them...'

'That's really nice to hear actually,' Pea says.

'It is,' Sam mumbles.

'It's not a popularity contest,' Joan says, as blunt as ever. 'How long have you been here, Pamela? I've seen you about...'

'Oh like...' Pamela thinks fast, not wanting to admit she hid in back of the filthy rooms during the bad times when the crews were in charge. 'Er, yeah, like...I had to...you know...keep my head down because of...the boy and...he wanted to sex me, like fuck me and I was like...really scared and...'

'What?' Sam asks as the focus sharpens. 'What happened?'

'One of the boys tried it on with you?' Pea asks. 'The crews you mean?'

'Like yeah,' Pamela says, smiling nervously. 'Kept touching my...like my boobs and then he...like er...put his penis in me...'

'He raped you?!' Pea asks.

'Jesus,' Sam says. 'I had no idea. That's awful...'

'A boy raped you?' Mary asks, blinking at Pamela.

'They had assault rifles, Mary,' Pea explains quickly. 'Long story but basically we couldn't do a thing. Lilly sorted it but...Jesus, I didn't know they did that. Which one was it, Pamela?'

'Er, the um....' Pamela thinks fast while glancing repeatedly at Lilly. 'The spotty one...'

'Zayden!' Pea asks, stunned to the core. 'The one that went for Lilly?'

'Yeah like...I mean...I didn't know he was going for Lilly too, otherwise I'd like have totally tried to stop him and...'

'Zayden raped you?' Pea asks.

'Pea,' Sam says, frowning at her. 'You can't ask that. Pamela, that's awful...'

'Come and see me if you need to,' Ann says. 'We'll discuss it privately...unless you want to go over to the infirmary now?'

'Oh I'm fine,' Pamela says, a little too quickly. 'Like, I'm not fine. Like it hurts inside...'

'He hurt your insides?' Mary asks, standing straighter. 'Where is he? I'll cut his bloody dick off and stuff it up his arse...'

'He's dead,' Lilly says, her voice cold and hard.

'He wants to be dead,' Mary snaps. 'What did he do to your insides now there, Pam?'

'No, my insides, like my soul and my heart...cos of what he did to Lilly and...like...if you ever want to talk about it...' she says to Lilly.

'I do not,' Lilly says.

'Cos like, you know, we've got that in common and...so... like sharing that pain could be...like...'

'I have no pain,' Lilly says without trace of emotion. 'But I am hungry, and I want to wash and then see my brother. Excuse me.'

'Ach, Blondie sounds like a right tough one she does,' Mary says as Lilly walks out into the back rooms.

'You have no idea,' Pea murmurs.

Lilly heads into the end room. A couple of candles already burning in jars bathing the room in soft orange light. She strips her top off, wincing at feeling so grimy and starts to clean herself using wipes. Tension inside her mind that has been growing all afternoon, but she doesn't know why.

A disquiet inside. A gnawing worry like a sense of dread building up but without reason. Something to do with Howie's team but she doesn't know what.

She wipes her body, cleaning the sweat and grime away without knowing the team are captured within an army base, crying from tear gas as they are systematically tortured, and she brushes her teeth, her face set and hard, sensing trouble while knowing there is nothing she can do. No phones. No radios. No contact. She doesn't know where they are even. Only that feeling inside.

Norman washes too in one of the rough and ready wooden shower cubicles knocked up by Simar. A simple design of two fixed sides and one hinged door propped against a few of the tap and hose connections running around the inner wall.

He dries using the towel he got from Colin the cola and dresses in the shorts, t-shirt and slip on trainers he also got from Colin the cola, that was after spending ten minutes listening to Colin discuss being a section head, and how that was a big thing, and that Norman was now the beach section head. Norman said he wasn't the head of anything, but Colin carried on and said they should have a section head meeting and elect a section head of the section heads. Norman didn't say much after that.

He thinks of Robert as he dresses. Robert would be so good here in the fort. Pain inside. A surge of emotion that threatens to bubble up but he swallows it down and heads out.

'Hi, Norman...'

He startles at hearing his name and looks to see the

family from Gloucester staring at him within their allocated ground section.

'Hi,' he replies, coming to a stop with the light of the day fading fast. 'Er, you okay?'

The man nods, the woman offers a smile. 'Fine, thank you.'

Norman nods back. 'See you,' he sets off again, realising how many more people there are now, then realising that he already knew that because he processed them all.

'Hello, Norman...' another greeting and he slows down, nodding back at the woman. A woman from Wales. Gwen Jones.

'Hi, all well?'

'I guess,' Gwen says quietly. 'What time do we eat?'

'Very soon,' Norman says.

'Thanks, Norman.'

'Sure. See you...' he sets off again, navigating the invisible streets towards his own patch, nodding in greeting as he passes the people he registered and processed.

'There's the numpty,' Tommy calls as he reaches his own section. 'What happened to you all day? Go in the wrong direction again?'

'Sorry, Norman...hi, I saw you walking by,' a man asks, stopping at the edge of the section.

'Ken, hello. Are you okay?' Norman asks.

'Er...Janet and I were just wondering about the food side of things?'

'Keep bloody wondering, mate,' Tommy snorts. 'You'll be lucky to get a few beans...just don't ask for more or they shoot you...'

'They don't shoot anyone,' Norman says. 'It'll just be a few minutes I should imagine. The kids eat first then...'

'Norman? Sorry...We can't remember what the Polish woman said about the evening meal?'

A woman behind him. Joanne Broadmoor. She worked in a launderette. Actually, he should let Colin know. She'd be good in his section.

'Joanne, yes don't worry...her name is Lenski and it'll just be a short while I should imagine,' he replies.

'Fuck me. Norman's putting himself about,' Tommy mutters.

'Hi, sorry...did I just hear someone mention the food times?' someone else asks.

On his feet and Norman clears his throat. 'HI! EVERY-ONE...HI YES. THE EVENING MEAL WILL BE VERY SOON. KIDS EAT FIRST...THEN THEY CALL ADULTS OVER. OKAY?'

'Look at old big bollocks making announcements now,' Tommy remarks. 'Eh Matty? Old Norman's got himself shoved up someone's arse...but then he likes shoving things up arses apparently...'

'What did you say?' Norman asks, his heart missing a beat as he looks to Tommy while the people that gathered about him asking questions drift off.

'Just a joke. Jesus, mate. Only having a laugh you bleeding snowflake. Fuck me, remember that, Matty. Snowflake ain't got a sense of humour...' Tommy says in that hard tone, aggressive and surly, like he's constantly on the verge of erupting in violence. He stares hard too. Unblinking and goading and Norman wilts back, thinking this world is not the old world.

'Ah don't look so hurt,' Tommy laughs, sensing the weakness in the other man. 'Mind you, queers are sensitive aren't they...'

'Ignore him, Norman,' Patricia says as Norman sits

down. His wits gone. A brutal day already and he just can't summon the mental fortitude to say anything and risk escalating the situation. So he does nothing and says nothing.

'Oh, there goes another one,' Tommy says, watching a man in a turban walk by. 'Hope they checked them properly...'

'Oh Jesus,' Patricia groans. 'He's been going on about that all day.'

'Well,' Tommy grumbles, his voice carrying too clearly. 'I heard them's the ones that caused it. Jihad or whatever... fucking holy war...'

'They're Sikh's,' Norman says.

'Don't even bother,' Patricia says. 'Keith and I tried explaining it.'

'Have you been here all day?' Norman asks.

'Keith's been resting,' she says. 'He doesn't feel well...'

'I don't feel well,' Keith says.

'Oh here we go, someone thinks they can boss everyone about now yeah?' Tommy calls.

'I just asked what you'd been doing today,' Norman says.

'And I just replied with mind your own fucking business,' Tommy snaps in a voice filled with instant aggression again.

'OKAY...KIDS FOR FOOD PLEASE...' Agatha bellows out. 'ADULTS CAN HEAD OVER TOO BUT WAIT FOR THE KIDS TO EAT FIRST...'

'Bout fucking time,' Tommy says, on his feet in a second. 'You ready, Matty?'

'Seriously though, Norman,' Keith says as everyone about them starts stirring. 'Are they checking foreigners properly? I mean, we really don't know where this started from...'

CHAPTER SEVEN

D ay Twenty Two

B linky is dead.
Lilly does not how or what caused it, but only
that she feels it inside. She can't even explain what
that feeling is, or where it comes from, she only knows that
Blinky is dead.

Lilly does not cry because crying will not help. She
doesn't know where they are or what happened and so she
feels an intense frustration that she cannot do anything
to help.

What she does know however, is that if she can feel
Blinky is dead, then it also means the others are not dead,
and specifically, Nick is not dead, and so, while the sadness
and worry is there, she is also able to process it and seek
logic and reasoning within those emotions.

Nor does she plan to tell anyone else because to impart
such news will dampen the fragile energy they have right

now, and so she makes coffee in the office as dawn breaks on the twenty second day since the world changed forever and keeps her counsel private.

A noise in the back rooms. A creak. The sound of footfall. Her hand drops to the pistol on her belt, easing the safety strap off as the noise comes closer with a hearty yawn that makes her put the safety strap back on and she goes back to making drinks as Mary stops in the doorway, stretching noisily. Her gorgeous red hair poking up all over the place, sleep lines on her cheeks, her eyes somewhat puffy but the glint is there and the smile forms easily.

'Morning, Blondie. Slept like the dead back there I did. Some wee fella called Colin gave me some bedding. Nice man but he doesn't half talk and he looks like a can of cola, don't you think so? Like his face is all red and his hair is all light and you know what? I thought I talked a lot but dear god, he doesn't stop. Must have told me he was a section head at least twenty times he did...'

'Coffee?' Lilly asks when she stops to draw air.

'Aye, Kyle? You wanting a coffee now?' Mary calls over her shoulder.

'Aye, I will,' a gruff sleepy voice calls.

'You both slept here?' Lilly asks.

'Aye,' Mary says, watching Lilly with her hands on her hips. 'Plenty of rooms back there. Kyle took one and I took another, but he said you all sleep up the way. I said why not sleep down here? He said he didn't know and would suggest it.'

'And now you've beaten me to it,' Kyle calls.

'I have,' Mary says, winking at Lilly. 'We need a toilet though. I don't like pissing in a bucket and it's a fair trek to the toilets. I had a shower mind in one of those cubicles last night though. Cold but nice. Should have one for ladies.

Men always piss when they shower the dirty bastards. Sorry, Blondie. Am I talking too much?'

'It's fine,' Lilly says.

'You don't smile so much eh?'

Lilly glances at her, unsmiling and impassive, a glance and no more before she pours the hot water into the mugs.

'Right, that wasn't awkward at all then. Good chat there, Blondie. Anyway, so you'll let me be a guard right? Joanie said you got a full armoury here...'

'Coffee,' Lilly says, handing a mug over. 'No offence but I don't know you and I'm not giving a gun to anyone I don't know...'

'All of Peter's lads are armed,' Mary cuts in.

'What Peter does is down to him. I run my side and until I know someone they are not carrying a firearm.'

A rush of annoyance flits across Mary's face. A frustration showing clear. 'You got that old bloke on the gate but not me?'

'Donald? He's an ex-soldier and we tested him...he's lovely.'

'Test me then. Joanie can do it, Pea and Sammie said she's like a markswoman...'

Lilly blinks at the familiarity, unsure how to take it. 'She is, but it's more than being able to shoot straight. It's having a gun in the first place...we had too many people with guns here...'

'Ach yeah, they told me about that,' Mary says with a nod and an almost comical expression. 'But if I'd have been here it wouldn't have happened...that's a fact. Try me out. Let me be a guard for you...;

'Lilly!' Sam at the door, her voice low but urgent. Lilly turns to run out as Kyle sprints from the back, cursing under his breath while doing his shirt up.

History repeats itself and Lilly runs fast, seeing ahead to Pea and Alf outside the same room as yesterday morning. Joan rushing over with her rifle and a sense of dread builds in Lilly's gut. A foreboding as it were.

Lilly rushes into the room with Joan on her heels, sweeping in with her rifle up as Kyle draws his pistols, all of them coming to a stop at the sight of an old man and woman lying on a blanket on the ground with their bodies entwined.

'Are they dead like?' Mary asks as Joan lowers down, pushing her fingers into the necks. Both of them cold and stiff.

'No pulse,' she says quietly. 'Both dead...'

'Another one,' Lilly says to herself.

'Another one?' Mary asks.

'A man hung himself in here night before last,' Sam says quietly as Alf walks in, joining the group in staring down.

'Found 'em when I checked the room,' he says. 'Didn't want any more rope being wasted...'

'Alf,' Sam groans.

'Good rope's hard to find. At least they done it with pills this time. Couple of pots over there...sleeping pills and painkillers by the looks of it...'

'Well now,' Mary says sadly. 'You've got yourself a suicide room.'

'We don't have a suicide room,' Lilly says.

'Sure,' Mary says.

'It's not a suicide room,' Lilly says.

'Anyone know who they are?' Pea asks.

'I saw them yesterday, on the beach,' Joan says.

'Mr and Mrs Kepple,' a voice behind says, making them all turn to see Norman in the doorway who was wide awake thinking about Robert as they all sprinted past. 'They arrived in the afternoon. They were looking for their children and grandchildren...'

'Ach now, have you seen this?' Kyle asks, picking a sheet of paper up from the side. 'They left a note now...*we're really sorry to cause any fuss. We both wanted to say thank you for trying so hard to help people, but if our families are gone then we'd sooner be with them now.'*

'Jesus, that's awful sad that is,' Mary says.

'Is,' Sam says as Joan pushes up to her feet with a heavy sigh and a silence that stretches on for a few seconds.

'Right. Well,' Mary says. 'Are we saying a prayer then, only I've got a coffee going cold.'

'Prayer?' Pea asks, still trying to wake up properly and now blinking at the concept of saying a prayer.

'Aye, there's two dead people there,' Mary says. 'Someone should say a prayer. Father, are you doing it?'

'I'll say a prayer when we take them out I will.'

'Why not just say it now? I'd do it but I don't know the words. Go on now, Father. Say a few words,' Mary says, closing her eyes, bowing her head and clasping her hands to the front.

'Fine, I'll say a prayer,' Kyle says, bowing his head, closing his eyes and clasping his hands to the front. Sam and Pea share a look. Alf clears his throat, doing the same. Joan too. Norman just stares at the floor while Lilly stares ahead.

'God our Father,' Kyle says. 'Your power brings us to birth. Your providence guides our lives, and by your command we return to dust...'

'Amen,' Mary says.

'I haven't finished,' Kyle says.

'Sorry. I thought you'd finished,' Mary says.

'I say amen, then you say amen after me.'

'Yeah I thought the priest always said amen first,' Sam says.

'They do,' Mary says. 'I just jumped the gun a bit.'

'Can I carry on now?' Kyle asks.

'Aye, but don't drag it on. Blondie and me have coffee going cold.'

A tut from Kyle. A blast of air from Sam as Pea clears her throat.

'What happen?' Lenski asks, walking in.

'Morning, Lenski. We're praying,' Mary says. 'And the amen comes at the end from the Father...'

'What?' Lenski asks.

'Am I saying this prayer or not?' Kyle asks.

'Ach, you are,' Mary says.

'Oh, they are dead?' Lenski asks, seeing the bodies on the floor.

'No, we like to pray over sleeping people...'

'Our Father,' Kyle continues. 'Will ye take these souls in heaven and forgive them their sins...these are hard times they are, and not everyone will see it through to the end...'

Lilly stiffens, lifting her head to stare into the darkness of the room.

'And so many will come to you early, many souls who have suffered but by your divine right they will suffer no more. We ask you guide us to work hard and do the right thing to help those that come our way...and we ask that you help Howie and his team wherever they are. Amen.'

'Amen,' they chorus the words.

'Can you ask God for more rope next time you talk to him.'

'Alf, I'm not asking God for more rope.'

'There's rope on the beach,' Norman says.

'What kind of rope?' Alf asks.

Norman shrugs. 'I don't know. It looked long and thin...'

'That's a good rope description there,' Mary says.

'Can you get it over to me?' Alf asks.

'Er, sure,' Norman says.

'Appreciate that. Right. Let me work then. You lot go off...' Alf says as they shuffle out with Lilly striding ahead. Her mind thinking of Blinky as the fort starts to wake proper. The first rays of light pricking the sky, bringing forth hues of purple and orange that seem to streak from horizon to horizon.

A new day. A new dawn and Agatha leads the first charge. Stopping by the door to her stores with her arms hanging at her sides as Sunnie kisses her husband and rushes out of her patch of ground, nodding at Agatha. The two women marching first into battle as they go forth into the fray to get food into the bellies of the people.

Their troops soon join them. Fetching and carrying tins of fruit from the stores to the central cooking area. But fruit alone is not enough. Some of these people will burn thousands of calories today, so they need fuel. They need carbs and fats. Pasta for energy. Beans and canned fish for protein.

Gas burners started to heat water. Generators chugging to life to get power into the big electric water urn used for teas and coffees.

People queuing for the toilet blocks. More heading for the new shower cubicles. The back gate open for men to rush out and piss in the sea.

John leads the second charge. Weaving his way through tent-town, rousing his men and women. Telling them to get fed and watered because today is going to be hell.

'You up lads?' he says, pausing at the edge of the Singh family patch.

'Two of us are,' Jaspal replies, kicking Simar's sleeping form.

'Come over to the offices for the meeting,' John says, heading off.

'Will do mate,' Pardip says, standing tall enough to see his wife already working in the cooking section. 'You on the beach again babs?' he asks his sister.

'I am,' Anika replies. 'Crazy over there like. Worse than A and E on New Years Eve. Right, I'd better go and find Ann. Laters.'

'Crazy everywhere,' Jaspal says, booting his brother a bit harder. 'Sim, wake up.'

'Sim, if you don't wake up I'll grab your ear,' their mother says, walking back from the toilet block. 'Anika, make sure you drink lots.'

'I'm a nurse, mum!' Anika calls back as she rushes off.

'Simar!' his mother snaps.

'I'm up, I'm up,' Simar grumbles, sitting up to rub his eyes.

Pardip blasts air from his nose. Nodding at his mum who went straight to work with everyone else yesterday. Allocating herself to the kids area and the many orphans that need care while looking after their own young ones at the same time. A deep sigh and he looks about, spotting Tommy and a few other surly looking faces staring over. 'Morning,' Pardip calls.

Tommy lifts his head an inch and no more before looking away with distaste. 'Fucking joke,' he grumbles. 'Think they own the place already...'

Patricia sits up. Her dyed blond hair plastered to her face. Her husband yawning as he wakes next to her. 'Where's Norman?' she asks sleepily, looking to his empty bedding.

'Gone off to bum someone probably,' Tommy quips.

Lenski leads the third charge. Wide awake from the double suicide and she showers in one of the new cubicles before rushing back into their sleeping rooms.

'Up, come on, up,' she claps her hands, bringing the sleeping children from their slumber. 'You sleepy,' she bends to tickle Rajesh's sides, making him giggle. 'I no like children...I no like any children...' she switches aim to tickle Amna, making her giggle then attacks Billy and Milly as Subi sits up to yawn. Lenski so straight-faced and serious being engulfed by four sleepy bodies rushing into her. 'Get off me, I hate children...no kissing! I no like cuddles...go away.' She disentangles herself, winking at Subi. 'You make them brush teeth, wash and change, yes?'

Subi nods, smiling at Lenski who crosses the room to bend and kiss the girl's head. 'Come down to office when ready...stinky children! I hate children...yuck...'

She rushes out and heads down, greeting Colin already opening his rooms. The proud section-head of bedding, clothes and hygiene products ready for the day.

'Alright, Lenski love,' Agatha calls, rushing out of the food storage rooms.

'Morning, yes, hello,' Lenski replies, moving on to stride into the offices and the smell of coffee hanging in the air. 'Doctor, you see suicides?' Lenski asks.

'Terrible,' Ann says. 'I went up and checked with Anika.'

'Peaceful though,' Anika says. 'That Alf is amazing. Wraps them all up he does. Ooh, he said to mention he needs more rope...what?' she asks at the groan sounding in the room.

'Morning, morning,' John says, walking in.

'John, you want a coffee now?' Kyle calls from the

back table.

'Hi guys,' Colin says, walking in behind John. 'Morning prayers is it? I've got a few things I want to raise with the other section heads.'

'Are you a section head, Colin?' Kyle calls.

'I am yes,' Colin beams.

'Ach, I didn't know. Pea said she wants to hear all about it she does,' Kyle adds.

'Of course,' Colin says as Pea eases back into a corner while glaring daggers at a grinning Kyle. 'Pea! Hi, yeah so, section head of bedding, clothing and hygiene products.'

'I know, Colin. I was at the meeting yesterday,' she replies.

Pardip heads towards the office door. Norman just ahead of him, slowing as he looks inside to the already busy room.

'Alright, mate,' Pardip says, as Norman turns to look. 'Ah it's you, the guy from the beach. Didn't recognise you there mate,' Pardip adds. 'This where the meeting is?'

'I'm not sure,' Norman says, reaching the door to peer in.

'Go on inside,' Joan says from behind them. 'Dithering about blocking the door. How are you today? You look better in those shorts anyway. Caught the sun too. Watch you don't burn.'

'Ah, Norman,' Ann says as he's bustled in by Joan. 'You look better...'

'Par,' John calls, seeing the tall guy walking in. 'Come in mate, brew?'

'Love one ta. Anika should be about somewhere too.'

'I'm here you idiot,' she says from behind him. 'Bloody hell, and they're trusting you to build things?'

'If I need a plaster I'll let you know,' Pardip replies,

pushing past her with a friendly shove.

'Jesus,' Lisa says, arriving at the door to glare inside. 'This shit again. Right, we getting on with it or what? I've got work to do and sick people to try and stop dying. I'm sure that's not important though.'

'Bloody hell,' Mary says, walking in from the back to see Lilly and Lenski in conversation. 'What's this then?'

'Meeting,' Lilly replies.

'A meeting is it now,' Mary says, looking impressed. 'Right. What about?'

'So we stay organised,' Lilly says, walking off into the room.

'Is so we *try* and stay organised,' Lenski explains. 'We are not organised. There is organised, and we are at the other end. Yes?'

'Gotcha,' Mary says. 'Bit like how we do things then. Is that the office man there is it?' she asks, spotting Norman now in shorts, t-shirt and trainers. 'Is that you is it?' she calls, walking over. 'Bedlam here or what?'

'Who are you?' Lisa asks her with a scowl. 'Who the hell are all these people? Is anyone gripping this?'

'Morning, am I on time?' Peter asks, knocking on the door. Mary, what the hell are you doing here?'

'Moved in I have,' she says as Norman and a few others tense, expecting the row to start again. 'Anyway, morning uncle Pete, you alright?' she asks instead, moving in to kiss his cheek.

'Aye, you'll not be starting nothing over here though, Mary. These people have enough going on and I promised Lilly we'd abide her rules. Come back over and we'll talk later.'

'The meeting is starting,' Joan calls. 'We've a busy day so we need to get going...'

Lilly takes the head of the table again. Stern and unsmiling. Blinky is dead, but she still will not share that news. Instead, it makes the energy inside burn harder. The risk of death is there if they fail. Winter will come. The food will run out. So many things to do. So little time to do them in.

'Morning, thank you for coming,' she says as the room settles with nearly every seat in the office now filled. Norman and Mary standing at the back as though showing they are not included by leaving some distance. Agatha rushes in, wiping her hands on a cloth as she heads for the table.

'We need to be quick,' Agatha says.

'We will be,' Lilly says.

'Are we doing this every day?' Lisa demands.

'For now,' Lilly replies. 'The priority is still clearing the bay to open the view. That has to be finished today. Norman's got us moving faster so there is no reason we cannot match that pace and get it completed today. John, how's it going here?'

'Er yeah, yeah we've got three more lads now. Pardip, Jas and Sim. Sim knocked up the shower cubicles yesterday and said he'd do another couple of toilet cubicles this morning.'

'We need structures,' Lilly presses. 'Buildings for people to live in...somewhere for Agatha to cook and serve the meals.

John nods, seeing the determination within Lilly. 'Par's going to project manage it all...'

'What does that mean?' Sam asks.

'Par?' John asks.

'Er yeah sure, hello everyone. I'm Pardip. I wear a turban...it's not a hat,' he says to a few chuckles. 'And we're not Muslims either. So, if we project manage we can plan it all in advance, so we do it the best way...John said you need housing right? We need wood for that and materials. I can plan ahead, work out where the structures go, what material we need and how much and then when we start it's not so manic and crazy like. Honestly, doing that prevents so many snags later. We've got to think about drainage, weather proofing, space per person, distances between the buildings, fire safety...'

'Health and safety?' Lisa asks. 'Are you joking?'

'No, I'm not,' Pardip says seriously. 'We're building from wood. Wood burns. You put them close together and if one goes up they all do. Great fire of London went up because of that. Buildings constructed too close together and made from flammable material. We can build close but then we need to fire-proof them. Plus, we're on flat ground so the water will pool, which means we need to stilt up. And, if we get it right we can build two story structures to get the most from the space...'

'He's right,' John says. 'We plan it now then it goes so much quicker when we start.'

'Okay,' Lilly says. 'Please make a start. We cannot delay. If the weather changes we are exposed. Peter, the wall?'

'As soon as the buildings are flattened I'll free some men up to go out. Kyle's given me a list he has. We'll get it started soon as we can.'

'We need food,' Agatha says, cutting in. 'Got more people turning up every day now...I said we had a week's worth yesterday but that's down to four or five days already...'

'Bloody hell,' John says as a few others murmur in alarm.

Agatha shrugs, showing apology in her features. 'People

need to eat...'

'I'm going to cut in here,' Lisa says. 'You're pushing people too hard. We had too many patients coming in yesterday with heat stroke and exhaustion. People passing out all over the place...this fort is hitting nearly forty degrees C in the day...it's not safe. And we had people coming in from the beach, that woman, Sally? She had to be sedated... she's still in there now on a drip she was so dehydrated.'

'The work continues,' Lilly says. 'We have more people arriving. They can work and let others rest for an hour.'

'An hour? Are you bloody joking?' Lisa snaps. 'Do you have any idea how dangerous heat-stroke and exposure are?'

'Yes,' Lilly says, staring at her.

'Who the hell do you think you are? People will bloody die.'

'They'll die if we don't.'

'Are you being serious? Can you hear yourself? You're sixteen. You're a child. You have no right to make people work like that and while we're all here, why the hell has Ann got the nurse?'

'The nurse? I've got a name, love.'

'Doctor. Not love,' Lisa snaps.

'We need Anika on the beach to work with Ann to free Norman up to process the vans to get them turned around so we can flatten the view and build the wall,' Lilly says.

'That's good project managing that is,' Pardip says with a dip of his head at Lilly.

'We've got an infirmary full of sick people,' Lisa continues.

'You've also got Hannah and Amy over there,' Ann says. 'Train them up. They can do a lot more than count bandages...'

'Thank you,' Lilly says as Lisa goes to fire back, seeing

the doctor simmering with anger.

'Er, so hi guys,' Colin says, raising his hand. 'Couple of things if I can change the direction quickly?' he asks, unfolding a notepad.

'Please do,' Sam murmurs, casting a look at Lisa.

'Excuse me, I find that look threatening,' Lisa says, calling her out.

'You find me looking at you threatening?' Sam asks. 'Fuck me, you're a sensitive soul aren't you...'

'I beg your bloody pardon?'

'Colin,' Lilly says as Mary cocks her head over while looking at Lisa.

'Right yes,' Colin says. 'Sorry, I know you've all got important things going on but er, any news on the tent front?'

Groans and heads shaking. 'Nothing,' Pea says.

'I can take a run at a few outdoor stores later if we get time,' Kyle says. 'Best we can do for now, Colin.'

'Er, well, I have another suggestion,' Colin says. 'I was chatting to Pardip and a few other section heads yesterday...'

'Are you a section head, Colin?' Kyle asks.

'I am, yes!' Colin says. 'Bedding, clothing and...'

'We know,' Sam groans.

'Spit it out, Colin. We've a lot to do,' Joan says.

'Right yes, sorry, lots going on, er so...we've got quite a lot of tarpaulin.'

'Great,' Kyle says as everyone stares at Colin.

'And poles,' Colin adds, 'and I don't mean Polish people before anyone...'

'Oh my god, we're not doing the racist thing again,' Sam says. 'Colin, what's your point?'

'We can make tents and shelters. I saw it on the telly.

Poles, sticks, tarpaulin. We just stretch it over and make shade...we can use sheets to blot the sun out, anything really...' he trails off into the silence. 'Sorry, just a silly idea...er, moving on...'

'Anyone else feeling an urge to kiss Colin right now?' Sam asks as a few hands lift up.

'The simplest solutions are often the best,' Kyle murmurs. 'Colin lad, that's a grand idea that is.'

'Very good,' Lilly says. 'Can you organise it today?'

'Wow, yes, sure,' Colin says, almost lifting off his chair with pride. 'The other thing is the t-shirts? I know you all think it's a stupid idea but...people in the fort don't know who to ask for help other than Lenski and she's getting run ragged...'

'Is true,' Lenski says. 'I am hardest working person in fort, yes?' she adds to a few smiles.

'Notice board,' Norman says from the back, the words spilling out before he can think. 'Put a notice board up with meal times and information. Lenski can show that to people when they come in...I had a lot of people asking me questions last night.'

'Colin, can you organise that?' Kyle asks.

'I'm on it!' Colin says, scribbling in his pad. 'How big should it be?'

'Big as you like,' Kyle says, winking at him. 'Big as you can make it.'

'Right,' Colin says, nodding eagerly. 'I'll get it done.'

A nod from Kyle to Norman. 'You got any more ideas in that head there, Norman?'

'Not right now,' Norman says, dropping his gaze.

'Aye, well just say when you do.'

'Indeed,' Lilly says. 'That's enough for now. To work please...'

CHAPTER EIGHT

D ay Twenty Two

I f yesterday was bad, today is worse and it feels like Norman blinks and they're striding out through the fort with Lilly leading the way to the gates.

Norman blinks again and he's in one of the lead boats heading across the water. Mary next to him looking about at their fleet of open-topped vessels all chugging in one direction. Everyone sucking air in. Fidgeting nervously with a sensation akin to going into battle. He looks up the bay and notices how more of the houses have been pulled down, but from this position he can also see how easy it would be for dozens of people or infected to get closer to the fort using the structures as cover.

The boats land and out they go. Once more unto the breach and what a difference a day makes. Yesterday, Norman was in office clothes and felt nervous and slow, but today his clothing is suited to the tasks. He has knowledge of what to do too, and with that comes direction and purpose.

'Mary?' Peter calls as they head over the sand. 'Are you heading back into the camp?'

'I don't know, Uncle Peter. Am I being a guard?' Mary asks, vaulting from the boat.

'Ach, Mary. We've been through this.'

'Aye, we have been through this. Stuff your camp. I'm working with my mate Norman now I am.'

'Are you?' Norman asks her, slightly alarmed at the turn of events.

'Fine,' Peter says, waving a big arm as he stomps off.

'FINE!' Mary yells. 'BLONDIE LETS HER GIRLS BE GUARDS...'

'It's nothing to do with you having tits, Mary,' Elvis yells from the road. 'It's cos your bloody mental...'

'Piss off, Elvis. I'm working with Norman. He's the section head of the beach and he said you can get off his sand you wanker...'

'I never said that,' Norman calls quickly.

'Blondie, if I work hard will you let me be a guard for your fort?'

'Don't let her, Miss Lilly!' a voice from the road shouts.

'SHUT UP, TYSON YOU TWAT...Blondie, I'll work hard I will. I'll show you...' she adds with a grin. 'Right boss,' she says to Norman. 'What's the crack then? What we doing?'

'Hang on a second,' Norman says, dumping his bag with Ann and Anika setting the umbrellas up and he runs off over the sand with Mary frowning behind him, thinking he's going to tell Lilly he doesn't want her help.

'Just you bloody hold on now,' Mary shouts, reaching to

grab Norman's arm. 'If you don't want me working with you bloody tell me not Blondie...'

'What?' Norman asks, blinking in confusion as he looks from an angry Mary to an impatient Lilly. 'Sorry, I saw it from the sea when we were coming over...'

'Saw what?' Lilly asks.

'The view. I saw it. How important it is to open that view up, so we can see what's coming.'

'Okay,' Lilly says, nodding at him to continue.

'I was just thinking I can work here with Ann and Anika, and you take everyone else to strip the houses and dump the contents by the side of the road then the vans can take it from there...it'll be much quicker.'

'Right,' Mary says, staring at him. 'So, this isn't about me working with you then?'

'What?' Norman asks, looking from Lilly to her. 'No!'

'Great,' she beams. Slapping him on the back. 'Good idea. Like it. What do you reckon, Blondie? Nice bit of project managing there or what?'

Lilly stares at Norman for a second. Her blue eyes studying his features. The same slim build as her father. The same hooked nose. But her father failed. He was weak, and this world has no place for weakness. 'Good idea. Thank you...please tell everyone working here to meet us at the end of the shore road...'

'Will do!' Mary says, giving a thumbs up before striding off. 'LISTEN UP. GET TO THE END WITH MISS LILLY. NORMSKI'S CHANGED THE PLAN HE HAS...'

'I did mean to use a radio,' Lilly says.

'I don't think Mary needs a radio,' Kyle says.

They sit in the sun at the back of the fort on the edge of tent-town. A group of a dozen or so all clustered around one loud, tattooed figure. Some listening. Some dozing. Some thinking about everything they have lost and all of them unable to summon the energy or wherewithal to work and help.

'So you were literally just walking past then?' Tommy asks.

Pamela nods. Her chins wobbling as she does so. 'Honestly. Lenski was like *you work. Go to gate. Get people. Take names. Don't rest. Don't drink. Don't eat...*and her accent is so strong and then she's yelling at me when I got it wrong because she didn't explain it...'

'Fucking joke,' Tommy mutters, shaking his head. 'And she's got a gun too...'

'I was so scared,' Pamela says. 'Then all that lot turned up,' she adds, nodding towards Pardip, Jaspal and Simar working with John and the others to build another set of toilet cubicles.

'Bet they weren't so angry at them,' Tommy says, urging Pamela on.

'God no,' Pamela snorts. 'All over them they were. Like, couldn't be nicer...*do you want a drink? Do you want food? Pamela can carry your bags. Pamela can get what you need...*'

'No way,' Tommy asks as a few others tut and shake their heads.

'I know people need to work,' Pamela continues. 'But I was like totally beaten and raped by those kids...like that one that went for Lilly? He totally got obsessed with me too. And I was trying to keep him away from Lilly and was going to kill him then Lilly did it and me and Lilly we've been talking about what it did to us...'

Pamela slept under the tarpaulin again last night, that was after she stuffed more chocolate bars in her mouth and smoked a lot of cigarettes, all of them pilfered from the stores. She'd never worked so hard as yesterday. The fact that Pamela has never really worked in her life did not factor in her thought processes.

She did try and sleep in the back room again, but was beaten to it by a selfish old couple sneaking in there. She hoped they'd piss off, but they didn't.

'Seen that, Tommy?' Karl asks, a middle-aged man with a London accent.

'What?' Tommy asks, following the direction of Karl's nod. 'What the fuck are they doing?' he asks at seeing Colin and a few of his red-faced sweaty workers driving sticks into the ground nearby.

Patricia and Keith look over. Mathew the same. Everyone in that section paying attention.

'Jesus,' Tommy mutters, watching Colin and a few of his workers try and fix a length of tarpaulin over some poles. 'We're all fucked. Seriously...what are they even doing? Is that meant to be a fucking tent? Like something that wanker Bear Grylls would make on the telly. This is what it's come to eh? Living under fucking shelters like savages. Mind you, I bet them fucking darkies don't mind it. Eh now! Best watch what I say. Patricia will have the PC brigade shooting me for racialism...'

'Idiot,' Patricia tuts at him.

'Oh god, he's seen us, quick hide...' Tommy quips as Colin turns and grins at the group, waving a hand as he rushes towards them all red-faced.

'Hi guys! Wow, there's a few of you over here...'

'What's that supposed to bloody mean?' Tommy asks.

'We're just minding our own business and you're coming over having a go.'

'Oh gosh no, no I wasn't doing that. I just saw there was a few of you,' Colin says, trailing off into an awkward silence with a few of Tommy's group just staring flatly while others look away. 'Right. Well, er...just to let you know we'll be getting some shelters up today...which is nice...'

'Where's the fucking tents we was promised?' Tommy asks, his tone hard and demanding.

'Ah no, afraid not. We're just having the hardest time in finding any, just got to make do with what we have eh? Bit of the old British stiff upper lip...'

'Fucking joke. We get our stuff taken away and told we'll get a tent then just left to sit in the blazing sun all bloody day...'

'Gosh I am sorry for that,' Colin says with genuine worry. 'But you guys are more than welcome to help...we've got so much that needs doing and Lenski is running about like crazy and...'

'You taking the fucking piss?' Tommy asks.

'Oh I really wouldn't do that. I could pop some sticks over, some sheets? Maybe put your own up or...'

'Jesus fucking Christ! My wife's dead...I saw her being killed with my own eyes right in front of me I did. I can't fucking sleep. Literally not a wink. Pat's the same. Keith's in bits. Poor Karl don't stop sobbing and Matty ain't said hardly a word...I got a slipped disc from fighting the things and you're over here yelling at us to work...fucking joke that is. That's what this place is yeah?'

'Oh gosh, I'm so sorry,' Colin says quickly, panicking at the level of aggression and the looks coming from the group.

'Er, I mean...I hope you feel better soon...' he rushes off, startled and shocked.

'That got rid of him,' Tommy snorts, looking round at the others. 'Fucking joke though right? Saving it all for themselves. Sleeping in rooms on beds...yeah I know their game. Tommy ain't stupid. I can see what they're doing. Making people into slaves so they can cream the best for themselves...wankers...'

P ressure grows. Pressure unrelenting. They have to empty the houses so they can be flattened, and at the end of the bay Lilly drives them on with a sustained energy, rushing in and out of the houses. Dragging furniture through doors. Sweeping the contents of kitchen cupboards into bags. Kyle, Joan, Sam, Pea and everyone else working with her, trying desperately to keep up with her relentless pace.

Martin Jones rushes down the stairs with his arms laden and his vision misted from sweat. A pressure inside to work fast and he doesn't see his shoelace come undone that snags under his foot and he goes down hard, flying head first into the bannister and he tumbles down with a crack of bone in his arm. A yell. A scream and he writhes in pain as Kyle rushes in to find him.

'What's happened?' Lilly asks, running in with the others. Her face coated in sweat.

'Fell down the stairs,' Martin gasps.

'Wrist is broken for sure,' Kyle says, feeling the bone in a way that makes Martin suck air.

'Get him down to Ann,' Lilly orders.

Twenty minutes later and Jane Parker collapses in a heap. Dehydrated and red-faced.

'Down to Ann,' Lilly orders. 'Everyone else, back to work.'

Arms lacerated. Fingers trapped. The air thick with curses. Heads hurting from thirst. They can't drink enough to replace the fluids lost.

'Come on!' Lilly claps her hands, rushing back in to the next house. Six houses emptied. Six to go. 'We have to get this done....'

Brian Collins twists his ankle. Yelling out as he goes down. 'I can work,' he grunts, using a wooden curtain pole to hold his weight up. 'I'll drive the automatic van...'

Seven houses done. Five to go. Emily breaks a finger as she carries a sofa out that gets trapped between the edge and the doorframe. A burst of temper as she screams and stamps her feet, her face flushing red. 'Get down to Ann,' Lilly says.

'I'm fine,' Emily growls. A timid librarian before this. 'Strap it up and get me back in.'

'That's my girl,' Kyle booms. 'We need that energy. Come on! We can clear this...'

***

Chaos on the beach too. The boat drivers and everyone else now up the road working with Lilly.

Norman, Mary, Ann and Anika start off working together to process the new arrivals but then the builders in the fort soon start calling out for more wood, and the new arrivals need ferrying over. Mary jumps in, driving boats back and forth, carrying heavy wood, sweating and cursing the same as everyone else, and when the road fills with cars they call grinning Bobby down to help drive them away into the blackened old estate and a landscape changing all around them minute by minute. Back to the road. Back to work. Back to sweating. More new people. More cars. Load the wood. Ferry the boats. Drive the cars into the old estate.

Then it gets busier as the hurt workers soon start making their way to see Ann and Anika. People with cuts, bashes, bruises and broken bones.

'We need shelter,' Anika says, surrounded by people near-on passing out from heat-stroke and dehydration. 'There's no shade here...'

'Right you are,' Mary says. 'Norman, give me a hand now will you,' she heads off into the camp with Norman close behind, ducking under washing hanging out to dry, smelling fires and spotting women and girls everywhere, preparing food and scrubbing clothes. Norman recognises a few of the faces from his previous visit and nods in greeting as Mary gets jibes shouted at her. Mostly good natured and without malice, although Norman does spot a few desultory glances.

'There she is,' a woman calls out, grinning at Mary. 'Heard you left us, Mary.'

'Cooking's not good enough for you is it, Mary?' another asks with a smile.

'Cooking bores me stupid,' Mary tells Norman.

'It's very traditional here then,' Norman remarks as they walk through.

'Aye, is,' she replies. 'Not so bad now maybe. Some girls get to college, a few go and have careers too, but most want to be married by eighteen and popping babies out. Don't get me wrong now, I'm not judging them but there's more to life than wearing a frilly dress and growing things in my womb.'

'Right. Yes of course,' he says.

'Uncle Jack,' she says, coming to a stop to knock on an open caravan door. 'Will ye let me have that big old tent thing.'

'No!' a shout from inside. A harsh voice, old and deep.

'Ach, you grumpy old shit,' she yells back, marching inside. 'Give me the bloody tent...'

Norman listens to the shouts and yells as more people join in, all of them seeming to go from calm and passive to all out screaming in a split second. Bangs sound out and even what sounds like a punch until Mary comes out dragging a big white roll. 'Grab the end of that will you,' she says with a grin to Norman.

'Did you want a hand?' Uncle Jack asks, appearing in the door, old, stooped and grey.

'Nah, you go and rest Uncle Jack.'

Norman grabs the end and sets off back to the beach, wondering what just happened and shooting glances back to the caravan. 'He was okay with you taking it then?' he asks.

'Ach, course he was. My Uncle Jack is lovely,' she says. 'In a manner of ways...' she adds as they cross the shore road towards the beach.

———

At the other end of the shore road, Lilly counts the structures. Eight houses emptied. Four to go. Heavy plant machines roaring as they work, and the air fills with bangs and crashes as brick and timber structures are taken down and the good building timber dragged free. Nearly every man capable of work from Peter's camp sweating and cursing while Lilly's teams rush in and out of doors to stack the contents at the side of the road, and that road stays busy with the diggers and scoopers and new cars coming in every few minutes filled with terrified refugees. Some arrive on foot. Tanned, weathered and shell-shocked only to be told to keep going down to see Norman.

A scream from inside a house. They all run in to see Jillian spraying blood from a deep laceration in her hand caused by the glass on a broken mirror. A dressing applied, and she goes out into the automatic van driven by a cursing Brian. Down to Ann and Anika. Localised painkiller injected. Stitches given. Half hour later she's back with Martin. His arm now in a sling. Jane Parker now hydrated with water and Lucozade and back in the fray they go.

'They're fecking mad,' Peter mutters, wiping the sweat from his head with the back of a hand.

'FUCK!' Sam shouts, a chair landing on her foot.

'WANKER,' Pea yells, banging her elbow hard enough to jar her teeth.

'Keep it going, fast as you can now,' Kyle shouts, clapping his hands. Shirt sleeves rolled up. Buttons undone. Face gleaming with sweat.

'Almost there,' Lilly calls, sweeping the contents from a food cupboard into a big bag. A grunt from a huge splinter driving into her arm. She uses her teeth to pull it free, spits it out, binds her arm in a tea towel and carries on.

Ten houses emptied. Two to go and she speeds up. Pushing harder. Moving faster. In and out. Stacking goods. Bedding dumped. Food scooped into bags. Another collapse from the heat. 'Get her down to Ann,' Lilly snarls. Furious at the delays.

On it goes. It will never end. This work will last forever

and every minute seems to take an hour to pass, and each hour feels a day as that agony goes on.

But then, after several gruelling hours the last wooden dining room chair is thrown onto the last mound outside the last house and those still on their feet stand with their arms at their sides and chests heaving while the sweat drips from noses and chins, running in rivers down faces in the awful, crushing heat. A battle waged and won. Victory claimed.

'Good,' Lilly says, hand on her hips. Her rifle slung on her back. 'GOOD,' she booms, her face flushed, her eyes blazing. Blinky is dead. She doesn't know where Nick is. Howie left her here to do this on her own. Fuck him. Her father failed to protect her and Billy too. Fuck him. Fuck all of them. She will make it happen. She will absolutely see it through and that energy flows out, touching everyone around her, making them work when any sane person would say no, it's too much. Something raw and pure and strong. 'From that fort,' she calls, pointing down the bay. 'We will be able to see past this point to where the wall will go. That will save lives if we are attacked. We did this. You did this. Well done...'

A few words spoken but enough to lift chins and spirits. They might not be out with Howie fighting, but not every battle is fought with a gun or an axe.

'Okay, van drivers, get the loads sorted...everyone else back to the beach.'

'Is it alright for you, doc?' Mary asks on the beach, standing back with her hands on her hips while blowing up her face to rid the strands of red hair falling over one eye. A big marquee tent now in place where the sun umbrellas were. Old and torn in places. The sides covered in stains and grime, but ready to function as a very rudimentary field hospital HQ filled with furniture taken from the huge mound on the beach.

'It's perfect,' Ann calls, tending a drowsy woman taken out by heat and dehydration. A panicked glance up to more people coming in from Lilly's work-team. Broken bones. Twisted ankles. Cuts needing stitches. Men from Peter's work teams the same. Kids from the old estate and all of them suffering the effects of heat-stroke on top of whatever else has hurt them.

'We'll be okay,' Anika says. An emergency room nurse used to frantic pressure. An unflappable manner, her voice so calm and soothing.

Norman takes over on the road, processing the new arrivals. Asking the questions. Filling the forms out and only sending people to Ann and Anika if they look like they're about to die.

He glances down the beach as he draws air, spotting Ken and Janet from the fort heading up towards him. 'Norman? Hi...sorry...Lenski said to ask you about a vehicle?'

'A vehicle?' Norman asks.

'Yeah, er...we're going to see if we can find our daughter...she's down near Bournemouth.'

'Sure, yes of course. See that road? Go up that to the old estate. Bobby's in there...he's only ten but...whatever, see Bobby. He'll find you a car, and probably give you a Snickers too, but they're nice and cold.'

'Right,' Ken says, nodding slowly at Norman. 'Snickers. Sure.'

'He's got a fridge. Good luck,' Norman says, turning away to work on. 'Oh and ask him if he knows where we can find a spare generator from.'

'Will do,' Ken says. 'Right. Generator. Yep. We'll er, we'll ask Bobby.'

'Aye,' Norman says, waving them on as he stops at the next vehicle on the road. A white mini-van. Sleek and modern looking. A woman behind the driver's wheel. Middle-aged and worried looking. 'Hi, I'm Norman. Welcome to the fort...just need to go through some things with you. Can I ask you to step out and open the back for me please...'

'They said on the way in to ask you,' the woman says, dropping out.

'Sorry, they said to ask what?' Norman asks, following her around to the back of the van.

'About the cats,' the woman says.

'What cats?' Norman asks as she opens the back door. 'Oh, those cats,' he says, seeing the crates stacked up in the back of the van. Each of them filled with a cat. 'Right. You have cats.'

'I said I had cats,' the woman says. 'Up the road. I said I had cats. They said to come down and tell you I had cats.'

'Right,' Norman says. 'How many cats are there?'

'Ten cats.'

'Right. And er...they're all yours are they?'

'Yes. I don't steal other people's cats.'

'No, of course not.'

'They're all my cats. From my house.'

'Right.'

'I like cats.'

'I can see...'

'I'm not leaving them. I'm not. I won't go in without my cats...'

'Right,' Norman says again, wiping the sweat from

his face.

'I've got food. Cat food I mean. And some human food. But mainly cat food...and the good stuff. Not the cheap stuff. My cats don't like the cheap stuff...'

'How's it going there?' Mary asks, sauntering around to stand next to Norman staring into the back of the white mini-van as the road starts filling with Lilly's teams all returning. 'Ah, that's a lot of cats.'

'Ten cats,' Norman says.

'Ten cats you say?' Mary asks.

'Yes,' the woman says. 'Ten cats.'

'Right,' Mary says. 'Are they all yours?'

'She doesn't steal other people's cats,' Norman replies.

'I don't steal other people's cats,' the woman says. 'And I have food.'

'She has cat food,' Norman says.

'Cat food you say,' Mary says.

'Not the cheap stuff,' Norman says.

'They don't like the cheap stuff,' the woman says.

'Right,' Mary says. 'Well, I guess if our food runs out we can always eat the cats...'

'She's joking,' Norman says quickly at the reaction of alarm on the woman.

'I'm joking,' Mary says. 'But seriously, I'd eat a cat if I was starving I would...'

'What's that in there you're looking at?' Kyle asks, walking over with Lilly as everyone else heads for the new HQ marquee on the beach and some blessed shade.

'Cats,' Norman says. 'How is it at your end?'

'Done,' Kyle says. 'Peter's team are on the last one now.'

'Cats,' Lilly says, staring into the back of the van.

'Ten cats to be precise,' Mary tells her.

'Ten cats?' Lilly asks.

'They're all hers,' Mary says. 'She doesn't steal other people's cats.'

'I don't steal other people's cats,' the woman says.

'New marquee is it?' Kyle asks, nodding past the minivan to the new marquee.

'Mary sorted it,' Norman says.

'Cracking good stuff there, Mary,' Kyle says.

'Cheers, Father.'

'Kyle, not Father.'

'Right you are,' Mary says. 'We've got furniture in it too. Beds and chairs and the like. That was Norman's idea. And we're on the scrounge for a generator too.'

'I've asked Bobby,' Norman says.

'Bobby?' Lilly asks.

'The Snickers kid. His mum gave us the stew last night.'

'Oh of course,' Lilly says. 'That was nice stew.'

'Aye, it was a nice stew,' Kyle says.

'Kathy makes a nice stew she does,' Mary says.

'What was in it?' Lilly asks.

'Cat I think,' Mary says.

'She's joking,' Norman says to the panic-stricken cat owner.

'I'm joking,' Mary says. 'But seriously, I would eat a cat if I was starving. Not a dog though. I like dogs.'

'Do you like dogs?' Kyle asks her.

'Aye, do you like dogs?' Mary asks in reply.

'Aye, I like dogs,' Kyle says.

'What about these cats?' Norman asks.

'*WATCH   IT...THE   FECKING   IDIOT WON'T STOP...*'

A shouted radio transmission as shots ring out. Rifles firing from the end of the shore road. A burst of them and at that second, so the noise of a diesel engine screaming out in third gear punches through the other noises. Snapping every head over to a big red panel van accelerating towards them with guards firing shots into the engine block as the van swerves left and right, careering madly.

Mary and Lilly spin round and burst away to run down past the line of vehicles holding the new arrivals waiting to be processed as Lilly reaches back to pull her rifle forward. Angry yells and shouts of alarm on the radio almost lost in the noise of gunfire. Kyle running on the other side of the row of vehicles. Norman a few steps behind and everyone else pouring from the marquee tent on the beach. Shouts of alarm. Men shouting in the radio and another flurry of shots.

Everything happening so fast. No time to think. No time for thought. The van coming in hard with no signs of stopping. The distance closing. The van will smash into the cars or worse, it will veer onto the beach and into the people there or hit the big tent. The engine screaming out. The speed still gaining but with the sunlight bouncing off the windscreen they can't see anything inside.

'THE WHEELS,' Kyle yells out, drawing his pistols while knowing the distance and the motion of the vehicle is too much for his small calibre rounds. He starts firing, aiming for the tyres. 'SHOOT THE WHEELS,' he shouts again. If they kill the driver the van could still slam into them all.

Lilly brings her rifle up and tries tracking the van, plucking shots off but worrying about missing and hitting the guards chasing the van down the road.

Everyone else is too far back on the beach. Joan trying to run but the soft sand impedes her speed, the same for all of them. Sam and Pea, Tyson and Patrick. Other guards with guns too far back and with other people between them and the van.

Kyle brings his pistols side by side, sighting both on the driver's tyre and he fires fast, sending shots in that miss and ping off. Then a burst of air and the tyre blows out, sending fragments of hot rubber spinning off as the van drops down onto the rim. The steering hit and the van slews at an angle as Kyle turns on the spot, firing both pistols at the other wheel as Lilly fires her rifle. Both missing with several shots until it blows out with a pop and once again sending chunks of rubber flying off across the road. The van drops with a bang. The steel wheel rims digging into the road. Sparks flying. The van careering and swerving. The engine still screaming out as the van gets close enough for them to see a single person in the front. A man waving his arms in panic as the van slews out of control before coming to a juddering stop.

'DON'T SHOOT,' the man screams as he drops from the van, tripping and slipping as he runs around the front. Blood on his clothes. Blood on his arms and hands. 'DON'T SHOOT! MY DAUGHTER...' he aims for the big sliding door, every motion filled with panic. Everything happening so fast. 'SHE'S INFECTED...'

'NO!' Lilly and Kyle both shout the word as the door starts going back.

'IT'S FINE,' the man yells back. 'MY FAMILY HAVE HER...'

'Oh fuck,' Mary gasps, seeing a look of hope etched on the man's face that will stay with her forever. A second poised in time. Held for eternity. Then the door rolls back, and the first adult infected woman flies out. Her eyes red. Her hands clawed. Her lips pulled back and her mouth already open for the bite as she slams into the driver. Taking him down with a spray of blood arcing in the air from her teeth tearing a chunk of flesh from his neck.

A wild scream sounds out. People shouting in alarm and panic as those running towards the road suddenly stop and try to go back the other way, blocking the path of Sam, Pea, Joan and Tyson and Patrick. An explosion of chaos and noise as more infected pour out of the van behind the first woman. A teenage girl. Red eyed and wild. More behind her. All of them infected. All of them pumped and ready to bite and take more hosts as they sight the people on the beach.

'GET DOWN GET DOWN,' Sam shouts out.

'MOVE,' Joan yelling but even she cannot get a clear shot through.

Kyle opens up, his pistols already nearly empty from pouring so many shots at the wheels. The guards on the road still too far back and unable to shoot down for fear of hitting their own.

'Fuck it,' Tyson curses, seeing it all happen but he can't get through and he can't fire either. A glance to the road, to Lilly and Kyle trying to fire at the infected already running fast. 'PATRICK,' he yells out, pulling his rifle overhead.

Patrick turns, seeing Tyson throw the rifle, knowing instantly what must be done and he darts forward, catching the weapon. 'MARY,' he yells her name.

She turns on the road, seeing the rifle go from Tyson to Patrick then Patrick turning and the weapon sailing over the heads of everyone else. She runs in to catch the wooden framed ten magazine bolt-action Lee Enfield 303 rifle, yanking the metal lever back as she spins to face the van with the rifle butt braced in her shoulder.

'DOWN BLONDIE!'

Lilly ducks left, firing as she goes. Kyle shouting out as

his pistols click empty. Mary sights, tracking the teenage girl in the lead of the small horde, streaking out ahead of them all. A sharp crack and the rifle bucks with a round sent whizzing a few inches past Lilly's head to slam into the teenage girl, sending her spinning off to the side and Mary yanks the bolt back, aiming again. Her face a mask of calm focus. Another shot and she takes the next one in the lead down as Lilly switches from single shot to auto and burst fires to hit targets. Seeing them closing the distance towards the beach. She hits several, not kill shots but enough to buy time.

'RE-LOADING,' Kyle shouts. Joan and everyone else still trying to get through. Mary shooting fast with every round taking one down.

'EMPTY,' Lilly's rifle clicks, she slings it back and draws her pistol, bringing it up in a double handed grip as she strides in towards the incoming attackers. Firing single shots. Sighting each target.

'STAY STRAIGHT BLONDIE,' Mary yells out and Lilly feels the displacement of air beside her head as Mary shoots them down. The last two coming. A big male. An old woman. Mary takes the old woman out as Lilly fires her pistol into the male, the rounds hitting his chest and doing nothing at all. Mary yanks the bolt, aiming again as Lilly fires but the big man comes in hard and fast. Kyle gets one pistol re-loaded, Mary sights, Lilly aims and all three fire, pouring rounds into the solid dense body until Mary's larger calibre bullet takes the back of his head off and he finally drops to slide along the road, a spray of hot blood splatting across Lilly's face who doesn't flinch once as she tracks the body until it stops at her feet.

A few seconds from start to finish and it's done. Over.

Bodies lying dead and the man that drove in now shot and killed.

'CEASEFIRE,' Kyle yells, his guns held out in front. Ears ringing. Chests heaving. Joan finally gets to the road. Sam, Pea and the others the same. Every gun aiming in. A hiss from an infected woman rolling over and pushing up to her feet.

'BACK,' Kyle shouts. Firing once into her chest. 'BACK YE HEATHEN...BACK TO THE DARKNESS...' he fires again, slamming her into the van. 'THIS IS NO PLACE FOR YOUR KIND...'

The last shot comes from behind. A sharp crack of an assault rifle and the woman's head blows out, killing her instantly.

Norman blinks, his head spinning at the speed it all just happened. He looks to the dead bodies on the road. Blood everywhere. A metallic tang in the air mixed with diesel fumes. A glance behind him, looking to see who fired the last shot, expecting it to be Pea or Sam, maybe Joan or one of the lads from the camp. A glance and no more and he faces forward only to double-take at what his eyes saw that his brain took time to process.

Men with guns behind him. He spins to face them, his heart lurching again. A man with a police issue assault rifle braced in his shoulder. Another man standing next to him with a rifle. Another slightly behind them with a shotgun. Not men from the fort or the camp. Dark skinned men with beards dressed in loose fitting trousers and robe style tops. Their style, appearance and dress giving instant recognition as Muslims. All of them gathered about an executive style mini-bus with blacked out privacy windows that was waiting in the line to be processed.

A blink of an eye. A beat of a heart and he sees the

figures in burkas at the side of the mini-bus. People covered from head to toe in black robes with only a mesh screen to see out from.

Patrick sees them next from the motion in his peripheral vision. A glance over. His own heart racing. 'SHIT!' he yells out, seeing the Muslim men with guns and the black-robed figures hidden within the burkas. Everything on instinct. Everything happening so fast and he turns to aim his assault rifle, yelling loudly. 'BEHIND US...'

Lilly spins on the spot, seeing the new threat, seeing men with guns behind them but her eyes fix on the figures in black robes. Their eyes hidden and she moves quickly, striding across the road while ejecting her pistol magazine and slamming a new one in.

Mary turns as Lilly brushes past, her rifle still in her shoulder as she too sights the new threat and goes forward, keeping pace at Lilly's side. The two women aiming hard. Kyle moving behind them. His pistols up and raised. Joan striding in, her own gun up and ready. Sam and Pea swivelling on the spot.

A chain reaction of events. Everyone turning to aim at the men from the mini-bus and they, in turn, aim back, yelling at each other in a language no one else can understand. The figures in burkas causing as much fear as the men with guns. Their faces covered. Their eyes hidden.

'GUNS DOWN,' Patrick yells.

'PUT THEM FUCKING GUNS DOWN,' Tyson's voice.

'CAN'T SEE THEIR EYES,' Mary shouts. 'THEM IN THE ROBES...CAN'T SEE THEIR EYES...'

Norman's heart whumps in his chest. His mind processing the fractional changes as the situation plays out.

'EYES,' someone else shouts.

'INFECTED...THEY'RE   INFECTED...'   another voice.

The tension ramps. The men at the mini-bus bristling with fear and worry, shouting at each other in a rapid-fire language. Female voices heard crying out from those within the burkas as they shield children with their bodies.

Lilly moves in. Unwavering in her intent. Ruthless, brutal and ready to kill. 'I WILL SHOOT YOU ALL. SHOW ME YOUR EYES...'

'DO WHAT SHE SAYS,' Mary shouts, keeping pace at Lilly's side. Kyle next to them. The air thick with fear-loaded aggression coursing through all of them. Everyone shouting. Pushing it to the brink. Pea's heart racing in her chest. Sam's face etched with something between deep angst and determination to hold the line and do what must be done.

'EVERYONE CLEAR BACK NOW,' Joan shouts, ordering the others away onto the beach.

'I SWEAR IT,' Lilly shouts, her own face spattered with glistening blood. 'EYES...SHOW ME YOUR EYES OR I SWEAR I WILL KILL YOU ALL...'

'Mummy!' A voice screaming out. A child. A boy. Ten or eleven years old at most. Slight build. A mop of dark hair on his head as he clings to a figure in a burka. His tear-streaked face etched with tears. He tries reaching for her head covering as she panics and grabs at his hands. Everyone shouting. Men and women calling to Allah. Men and women praying to whatever gods they hold dear. Children screaming in fear and right then, at that second, the click of a safety switch being taken off by a trembling hand brings them all to the point of death where many will die and the road will run red with blood spilled as both sides prepare to kill and be killed.

Norman can see it will happen as though it is foretold and will not be stopped and in that second, so his mind finally runs clear. The adrenalin ridding the fug within his mind. Giving him his voice. 'DO NOT SHOOT,' he bellows out. The voice of a man used to gaining attention from juries in courts across the country. 'DO NOT SHOOT...DO NOT SHOOT...'

'Mummy,' the boy cries, still tugging at her head robe. 'Show them...please!' She grabs his hands, caught up in panic. Her mind not processing it all fast enough and the boy turns, screaming out. 'Don't kill my mummy...don't kill my mummy...'

'DO NOT SHOOT...' Norman yells. Fingers pressing on triggers. This will happen. It has to happen. The fear is too great. The pressure too high. He has to stop it. He has to find the words to give in this single second. 'THEY'RE JUST PEOPLE...'

'I WILL SEE THEIR FACES,' Lilly shouts back. 'OR THEY WILL BE SHOT...'

'Do not shoot them,' Norman says. 'You, please...lower your guns,' he pleads to the men by the mini-bus, waving his arm to make them understand.

'SHOW ME YOUR FACES...' Lilly shouts.

'Mummy, show them...please...' the boy cries out. The moment poised on a knife-edge. Snatches of words in a foreign language as the men shout to each other. Confusion and fear in their faces.

'Don't shoot,' Ann says, rushing into the road. 'Just wait...all of you...just wait...'

'They were helping us,' Norman adds, the words rushing out. 'That man,' he points to the closest, the one holding the assault rifle. 'He shot the infected woman...not us...they weren't aiming at us...'

'EYES,' Lilly shouts. Heedless to anything else.

'It shows in the eyes,' Ann calls out, turning to the men and women at the mini-bus. 'The infection...it shows in the eyes...'

'Eyes,' Norman shouts, pointing at his own face. 'We have to see your eyes...'

'Lilly, in the tent,' Ann says. 'We can take the women to the tent...they're Muslims. They can't be seen by men.'

'No. Not an option. Here. Now. One step in any direction and I will shoot...'

Kyle holds still, wishing he were a leader like Henry with words to give and a mind fast enough to think ahead. He swallows, sucking air into his lungs, forcing a calm tone. 'We respect your faith and your beliefs...this isn't about that...this is survival...we have to see your eyes...'

One of the men speaks out. His language rushed and filled with worry. A rustle among the figures in the robes. The men stiffening. Everyone else bristling as that tension surges back up, the air thick and charged. Sweat pouring down faces and the knuckles of the hands holding the guns grow white.

'Mummy,' the boy turns back, reaching up to her head. 'Please...' pleading in his tone. Sudden motion from his mother. A movement that makes everyone yell out as she looks through the mesh to her son, to his face so sweet and innocent, to his pleading voice and she lowers her head, stooping so his hands can grip the hem of the material. She drops lower then slowly pulls back and rises. Her face feeling the coolness of being free from the confines of the burka. The sun too bright and so she squeezes her eyes closed, bringing a hand up to shield her vision as the silence stretches on. Tense, hard and with every finger ready to give death.

She blinks and lowers the hand showing black hair wet

to her scalp with sweat. An open dignified face etched with fear as she looks at Lilly. 'I am not infected,' she says, her voice accented but clear. She turns her head to the women about her. 'Show your eyes...'

Rustling fills the air. Material being drawn overhead to show faces glistening with sweat. Women old and young and as their ages come to be seen, so everyone can see the older women were shielding the younger. 'We are not infected,' the woman says, her arms about her son, holding him close. 'Ameer, tell your uncles to lower their weapons. There has been enough death today...' she looks to her son then up and out to Norman, to Mary, to all of them in turn and finally to Lilly. 'I am sorry to cause you fear...we heard this is a safe place. We will leave...'

Lilly exhales slowly, lowering her pistol as she looks behind to the corpses and the red van. She holsters the weapon and takes a fresh magazine from a side pocket in her cargo trousers and swaps it over in her rifle. Loaded. Made ready. Safety on.

'Welcome to the fort. My name is Lilly. We have food, medicine and we'll give you what protection we can. Your guns will be placed in our armoury. You can take them out if you leave. Your faces must remain uncovered when you are in the fort...Norman and Ann will deal with you from here.' She turns away, plucking the radio from her belt as she goes. '*Lenski, it's Lilly. Everything is fine here. A minor incident that is now dealt with...*' she listens to the reply then pauses to look back at everyone on the beach and road. 'Back to work please...'

Mary blinks at the people in robes and the men with them. At the sudden lessening of the tension in the air. Everyone's limbs trembling from the come down. She spots

Lilly walking away and goes after her, finding her own legs feeling somewhat funny.

'Blondie,' she calls, her voice now a bit quieter. Lilly turns to look at her, staring into Mary's green eyes as the gypsy girl comes to a stop, caught out by the icy cold gaze. 'Er, you got some blood on you,' she says, motioning her own face.

Lilly doesn't reply but pulls a packet of anti-bac wet-wipes from a pocket, gets one free and starts rubbing at her cheeks, smearing blood further up her face.

'Ach no, you're missing it...' Mary says, 'here, let me...' she takes the wipe, noticing how her own hands tremble while Lilly's remain completely still. 'Bit exciting eh,' she says, reaching out to start wiping Lilly's face. Her skin golden and tanned.

'I guess so,' Lilly says. 'You want to ask me if you can be a guard now?'

'Right, yes, that's exactly what I was going to ask,' Mary says, blinking at Lilly as she pulls another wipe free to clean her face more. 'Close your eyes now, got some on your eyebrow...you don't want the anti-bac chemicals in your eyes now do you...'

'Thank you,' Lilly says politely, closing her eyes. 'And thank you for what you did just then.'

'No bother,' Mary says. 'Okay, all done...give me your hands now. I'll give them a wipe too.'

'I can do my own hands,' Lilly says.

'Aye, and this blood is dirty so maybe we can both do it and reduce the risk,' Mary says, taking Lilly's hand as Lilly watches her. Seeing there is an intelligence and seriousness hidden behind the young woman's humour. 'Uncle Pete said you're immune like us, but that doesn't mean everyone else is...'

'Of course not,' Lilly says.

'I don't want to just be cooking in the camp and making babies, Lilly. I can shoot and I can fight...'

'It's fine. I'm happy for you to be a guard, however, I do not want to annoy Peter.'

'Uncle Pete will be fine with it. I promise,' Mary says.

'Can you fire a pistol?'

'Aye. Can. Right, you're all done,' she says, letting go of Lilly's hands.

'Thank you. Speak to Joan, but people on my team wake first, eat last and work hard,' she says, staring into Mary's eyes again. Holding her entranced and silent. 'We do whatever it takes to get the work done. That's the deal. If you work in my team then we all jump in.'

Mary nods, swallowing as she listens. 'Right. Will do. I piss about a bit, like crack jokes and stuff. Is that okay?'

'It's fine,' Lilly says, offering a rare smile as a digger rolls past that starts scooping up human forms to take away and burn. The sounds of squishes and bones snapping sounding clear in the air, sending some people moving away as others carry on as though nothing is happening.

'Ach, that's great,' Mary says. 'You've a lovely smile you have, Blondie...'

'Mary! I'll be having my rifle back,' Tyson says, walking over as Lilly nods politely and goes on about her business.

'I don't know what rifle you mean there, Tyson.'

'My bloody rifle in your bloody hands, Mary. It was my Grandfather's rifle.'

'You dumb shit, he was my Grandfather too...now what we doing with them cats?'

CHAPTER NINE

D ay Twenty Two

L enski kneels on the shore outside the gates, shielding her eyes as she stares across the water to the bay and the figures all holding still on the road. Donald standing nearby. Her own weapon heavy in her arms.

She ran as soon as she heard the first shot. Sprinting from the offices to the armoury to grab a rifle, loading it quickly and taking spare magazines before sprinting back across the fort. Everyone calling out in alarm at the popping sounds of gunfire coming so clearly across the water.

Now she waits. Wondering why the people on the beach aren't fleeing for the boats, wondering what's happening.

'Lenski, it's Lilly. Everything is fine here. A minor incident that is now dealt with...'

'Ask her what happened,' Donald says.

'*Lilly, is Lenski. That is understood...*' she says simply. Detecting the hard edge in Lilly's voice and figuring it doesn't really matter what just happened because things are happening every half an hour and if you worry about what just happened you'll lose focus on what is happening now. At least that's how Lenski sees it.

She heads back in and comes to a dead stop at the sight greeting her. A crowd of people waiting grim-faced and silent.

John and Pardip in front of everyone else. John holding a big metal pipe. Pardip clutching a sledgehammer. Others behind them. Simar, Jaspal and Steve the plumber. More workers from John's section holding heavy things to hit with and sharp things to stab with and Lenski blinks at the sight of Agatha clutching a huge rolling pin. Sunnie standing next to her with a heavy metal ladle. Colin between them holding a tent pole looking terrified to the core but she can see they are prepared to fight and hold the line.

'They alright over there, babs?' Pardip asks, his voice breaking the silence.

Lenski nods, caught out by the sight of them all. 'Yes, Lilly say is minor incident...'

'Right...er...back to work then I suppose...' Pardip says.

'We'd have given 'em what for,' Agatha says, patting the rolling pin against her leg while striding off with Sunnie. 'Rotters think they can get in here now...'

To the armoury and Lenski unloads her rifle, stacks it away and heads back to the office, deep in thought of many things and walks in to grab her clipboard. Adding *train fort defence force* (*speak to Lilly*) to the ever-growing list of things-to-do.

'Lenski,' Jaspal leans in through the door, bracing his weight on the doorframe. 'Sorry, I know you're busy...Par and John reckon they've found the place to put Agatha's cooking section up...they want to run it past you.'

'Yes. I come,' she says, trying to think of a hundred different things at once. 'Where is Pamela?' she calls.

'I don't know who that is,' Jaspal says as he pushes off to go back.

'Is fat woman,' Lenski shouts after him. 'Has big chins... big belly and...' she trails off, spotting another larger built lady in the new arrivals glaring at her. 'Pamela is fatter than you. Wait please. I come back...'

Out of the office into the wall of heat rising higher within the walls of the fort. No breeze, no air and the sun glaring down.

'Lenski!'

'What?' she turns as she walks, looking to Agatha throwing a bottle of water over.

'Drink love, you look hot...'

She catches the bottle, unscrewing the top to glug the warm water while glancing over to the rows of rough looking shelters already put up. Everyone now back to work. Everyone back to sweating and she reaches the hub of building work near the new toilet blocks. Timber stacked ready for cutting. Sheets of ply wood of varying thickness. Tool boxes and bags. Boxes of nails and screws. Hand tools everywhere. People with pencils behind ears and cigarettes hanging from lips.

John spots her coming, waving for her attention. 'Lenski...was there a building here before?'

'Yes. A place for visitors.'

'Visitors centre,' Pardip says, clicking his fingers. 'Makes sense now.'

'What happened to it?' Simar asks.

'Same as everywhere,' Lenski says. 'Things break.

Things burn. Things fall down...old world is broken. We are the new world yes?'

'One way of looking at it,' John mutters. 'Anyway, we've got foundations here...'

'To build on,' Pardip says. 'We've got drainage, water pipes....'

'And we spoke to Agatha,' John continues, making Lenski look from one to the other as they speak.

'She said it's the right size for her,' Pardip says. 'We can put a cooking section and a covered area for people to eat in...bench seats, big tables...like a refectory.'

'I know this. Canteen yes,' Lenski says.

'What do you think?' John asks.

'Yes. Do this. Build this here. Is good. But we only have five toilets and four showers. Is many people now. Build one more of each then do this next. Is okay? Agatha needs more shelves too for food rooms...' she says, spotting a group of people standing by the edge of tent-town watching Colin and a couple of his workers fashion another shelter. She frowns, squints and nods to herself. 'Pamela...' she mutters, finally seeing where the woman has been hiding.

Pamela stands back while watching people try to get a shelter rigged up over their section, her arms at her sides. Her face, arms and neck red from the sun. A dozen people about her, all of whom were lying in the sun when Colin politely asked if they wouldn't mind just moving over a little bit so they could quickly pop a shelter up.

'Um, so...if you get your end in first there, Joanne...yes that's it. Try and drive it in,' Colin says, holding a pole at one corner. The three other corners held by volunteers working all day to help get shelters up. A big expanse of tarpaulin already tied onto the poles making it unwieldy and hard to control, all of them sweating, all of them struggling in the intense heat and all of that made so much worse by the running commentary coming their way.

'How fucking hard is it?' Tommy calls. 'Fucking incompetent...why'd do you make it so bloody big?'

'Just the size it came in,' Colin replies, his face a deep shade of crimson from both the heat and the pressure of being watched by so many people.

'Who's using it then?' Tommy asks, seeing it stretch over several patches of ground.

'Well, as many as can get under it I would think...'

'Oh right. We're fucking sharing then are we. The fucking golden bollock family get their own shelter but we have to share...'

'Sorry, who?' Colin asks as Joanna struggles to get her pole in the ground, her eyes constantly darting to the angry Tommy and his group.

'Them!' Tommy yells angrily, pointing at the Singh family section covered by a sheet.

'We're just using what we have,' Colin says nervously. 'Come on now, we're only trying...'

'Fucking joke. They get the best patch... a shelter all of their own...letting 'em work in the kitchens to get more food. Eh? Bigger portions is it? Creaming it off the top yeah?'

'Other people have their own shelters too,' Joanne says.

'Who asked you?' Tommy demands, making her flinch. 'Sticking your oar in. Fuck me. Can't say a fucking word in this place...'

'Sorry, I didn't mean anything,' Joanne says.

'Perhaps you could help,' one of the workers on another corner says.

'I watched my fucking wife die,' Tommy shouts, bridling instantly, chest puffing up, eyes glaring. 'Right in front of my own eyes...I got slipped discs and...'

'Pamela!' Lenski snaps, cutting Tommy off as she steams towards them. 'Why are you here? What this? Why you all watch? Why not working?'

'Oh here we fucking go,' Tommy sneers. 'Comes over with a gun threatening everyone...'

'I no threaten. You work. Pamela, go to office. Is new people...'

'But my knee and...I think I got heatstroke and...' Pamela blurts.

'Go!' Lenski snaps, glaring as Pamela rushes off.

'Alright alright, Jesus love,' Tommy says, holding his hands up in mock surrender. 'We're all sick we are. Got slipped discs in my back, Pat here can't think straight. Keithy is a mess. Karl's got problems with his...'

Lenski tuts, scowling at them all. 'You here for days now. Not new. You rested. You work now. Put shelters up. Colin. Leave this...they do it.'

'Fuck me! Trying to explain and you get threatened! Get told to work or get a kicking. This what this place is yeah? I watched my FUCKING WIFE DIE,' he screams the words out, flushing with instant rage designed to make her wilt and run away but Lenski just tuts at him, shaking her head with disdain.

'Colin, take this shelter. Put in other place. Over there... yes? Working people need shade. These people no work. They no have shelter...'

'What did you fucking say?' Tommy demands.

'Colin, go,' she says, waving the frightened man and his workers away before looking back to Tommy and the dozen or so people about him. 'You lazy. You no work. You lie in sun. Drink tea. Everyone else sweat and get sick from working in this heat. You want shelter. Make it. Put it up. Work...'

'You can't do that,' Keith says. 'We've got human rights...'

'Now just hang on a moment,' Patricia snaps.

'I no wait moment. You want shelter. You ask for material and you make it. You want to eat. You work for it...'

This isn't right. Tommy is used to scaring people. His tattoos. His angry voice and the projection of violence but Lenski shows no fear and just withers him on the spot with a single look.

'You lazy,' she says simply, giving them all a disgusted look. 'All of you. I speak to the cooks. You get basic food only. Water only...' she strides off after Pamela, leaving a stunned Tommy behind in her wake.

'Sorry about that,' Pamela says, pausing to let her catch up. 'I was like trying to make friends with them so I could encourage them to work but they were all, *fuck this, fuck that* and I'm like *hey come on guys, everyone has to do their bit and Lenski's working so hard and those guys are like doing everything they can and Lilly is so amazing and we...*'

'You smell,' Lenski snaps, catching a waft of body odour, stale urine, shit and filth coming from Pamela. 'Use showers. They work now,' she adds, heedless to the look of shock mingled with horror on Pamela's grime streaked face. 'Take new people around then please go and wash. Get new clothes. Disease is spread by not washing.'

'But but...the kids were trying to sex me and...like I was too scared to go into a shower cubicle in case they came back and...'

Lenski walks off. A hundred other things to do and a hundred other things to think about.

Tommy watches them go. Seething with righteous anger. Furious at the way Lenski spoke to him in front of everyone. He glances to Colin rushing away with their shelter and balls his hands at his side into fists. 'Fucking joke,' he mutters.

'Half rations?' Karl asks quietly, looking at the others. 'Can she do that?'

'Course she can't fucking do that,' Tommy snaps. 'Keithy said it. We've got human rights...fucking cheeky cunt. Did you hear her? Couldn't say a word. Had that gun she did. Fucking coming over here threatening us all with a gun...'

'Er, she didn't really like do anything with the gun,' Mathew suggests, lifting a hand as he speaks.

'But she bloody had it,' Tommy shouts, glaring so hard it makes Mathew look away. 'And you can bet she'd have pulled it out and started firing the bloody thing. The Polish are like that. Mark my words. That's what this is. Fucking immigrants telling the English what to do in their own fort. Got the fucking darkie family eating the best food and getting the best shelter and the fucking Polish making everyone else eat their scraps...fucking joke. I got slipped discs. S'not our fault we can't fuckin work...' he trails off. Thinking of all his old tricks he would use when the government started insisting he got a job. A nod. An idea. 'Wait here,' he says, marching off with his thick arms swinging by his sides.

Five minutes later he steps inside the infirmary. The air cooler. The atmosphere quieter. Muted even.

He moves from the door into the main section, eyeing the people in beds. An old woman drugged and unconscious. Kids in bandages and dressings with life-altering injuries caused by grenades and bullets the night Lilly took the fort back.

He spots others too. Workers from John's section with

work-related injuries. Cuts, sprains and many with heat-stroke sitting quietly. Some with drips attached.

'Help you?' Andrew asks, spotting Tommy loitering. 'We're really busy...so unless it's something serious...'

'Yeah I need a note.'

'A what now?' Andrew asks.

'Got slipped discs haven't I. Putting me on half rations cos I got a back injury and...'

'Sorry,' Andrew says, lifting a hand to cut him off. 'Not now. Come back another time...'

'What's going on?' Lisa asks, walking down the central aisle.

'He wants a note or something,' Andrew says, already turning away.

'What for?' Lisa asks, looking from Andrew to Tommy, seeing the tattooed arms and legs, the unshaven face, the roughness about him. 'What for?' she asks again.

'Slipped discs and she said we can't eat or have shelter just cos we can't carry heavy wood about and...'

'Listen, you need to take that up with someone else,' Lisa says, turning away the same as Andrew.

'Fucking figures,' Tommy mutters. 'In it with them are you? Getting the best food yeah?'

She looks back at him, ready to tell him to piss off. She's knows his type from her time as a GP. People that don't want to work. Angry, cynical, bitter, entitled and vicious at anything that doesn't mirror their own exact identity, except she pauses, thinking for a second. 'Come down to the office,' she says, motioning Tommy to follow her.

'Lisa?' Andrew asks, watching her walk off with Tommy.

'Be five minutes,' Lisa says, leading Tommy into a private room. 'Tell me again what happened...'

'We's all hurt ain't we. Me, Keithy, Pat, that's Keithy's wife. Er, Matty, Karl, few others...like we've got hurt. I got slipped discs and I watched my wife die and tried to fight the things having her then hid in my garage and like, I saved loads of people on the way here then we get in and we're trying to get better so's we can help but that fucking Polish woman comes screaming over with her gun saying we's got to work and we don't get any shelter and like, we can just eat scraps...didn't fucking listen to a word we said. We're trying to explain and she just fucks off...'

'Sure,' Lisa says, listening intently. 'Slipped discs you say? Which ones?'

'I dunno, like I was ready for tests when it all happened, but they reckoned that's what it was. Fucking joke. We're like slaves. Can't say a word, and I ain't racist or anything, some of my mates are black but they're giving everything to them Pakis...'

'They're Indian, but I understand,' Lisa says, turning away to rummage through boxes, opening drawers. 'So basically, Lilly is denying you your basic human rights. Shelter, food, time to recover...'

'Yeah,' Tommy says, nodding eagerly at hearing what he wants to hear.

'That's the way it's going in here I'm afraid,' Lisa says. 'It's how dictators start. But...ah here we are,' she finds a notepad of white pre-formatted sheets. 'NHS sick-notes,' she says, pulling a pen out. 'What's your name?'

'Tommy. Tommy Barnstable.'

'Better just check you over...turn around...pain in your back?'

'Yeah, like...'

'Down here I would say,' Lisa says, prodding a random point in his back.

'Ouch! Fuck me, yeah that's sore as anything...'

'Sure,' she says, writing on the pad. 'Severe back trauma, possible damage to the sciatic nerve, rest needed for recovery,' she explains as she writes. 'There you go,' she peels it off, handing the note to Tommy. 'Find someone to present that to and I hope you feel better soon, Mr Barnstable. If you get any more concerns you come straight back to me...'

'Yeah cheers,' he heads out feeling pleased as Punch and stops at coming face to face with Pamela on her way in with a group of new arrivals behind her.

'Oh my god,' Pamela whispers. 'She's so fucking rude. That Lenski. I said to her, I said *they're all sick and just resting and you should, you know, totally go easy on them* and she's like *they no work they no eat. I am in charge. This is my fort...* then she's all like *you stink like a pig, Pamela. You dirty fat cunt. Go and wash you dirty fat cunt...*'

'She said that?' Tommy asks, thinking actually Pamela could do with a good wash.

'Yeah,' Pamela says, nodding eagerly. 'I said I was raped by all of those kids and I'm scared to go in a cubicle on my own, but she said I was a liar and told me to fuck off and get back to work and said I couldn't eat or drink until she says. What's that?' she asks, seeing the note paper in Tommy's hand.

'Sick note,' Tommy says, winking at her. 'That lady doctor did it. She said to tell anyone else that can't work to go see her...here, do me a favour if you go into them food rooms. Get us a choccy bar to eat yeah? Fucking starving. There's my girl...'

He heads off, thinking to take his sick-note to the office to that Polish bitch. She's fit though. Tommy would do her. He'd bend her over a table and have a right old go on it. Mind you, he'd need some Viagra. His dick doesn't stay up like it did a few years back. That Lisa will probably give him some.

He spots Lenski coming back in through the gates. Admiring her body but then remembering he heard she only fucks black guys. Then he spots the people with her and comes to a stop. Men with beards. Dark skinned men. Baggy trousers, linen robes and those hats they wear. Muslims. Women in black robes with head-scarves wrapped about their heads. Full on fucking Muslims coming in like they own the place with Lenski stopping to explain how they can take what they want and do fuck all, and Tommy rushes off, the forgotten sick-note still clutched in his hand.

CHAPTER TEN

D ay Twenty Two

The days draws to a close and the fort grows busier as the bay workers return. All of them burnt from the sun and so exhausted they should be cowed and sullen with heads drooped.

Except they're not.

They trudge back in smiling and joking from a bond between them all. That they set forth this morning in the boats and not only attacked the day head on, they saw it through even when they were bleeding and hurt.

'Here they are,' Agatha calls out from the cooking section, her eyes constantly flicking to the gate to see who is coming and going. 'What happened to your arm, Martin? Bless you all. You limping, Brian? Blimey. Been through the wars eh? Over there working so hard. Food won't be long now. Come and sit down, have a cuppa. Colin's rigged some shade up he has...'

Lilly and her team come in after them. Securing the gates before they head up to the office to see Lenski as the four children sprint across the fort to see them.

'It's changing,' Agatha remarks.

'Changing?' Sunnie asks.

'The fort, it's changing...people are getting some confidence back they are...'

Sunnie stops working, drying her hands on a cloth draped over her shoulder. 'Was it that bad?'

'Bloody awful it was. I told you, them bloody kids had everyone too scared to do anything. Lilly's turned it around she has, and now we've got John and your Pardip, and Colin's doing his work...makes a difference. I'm telling you... everyone working so hard and getting it done.'

Tommy works hard too. Sweating freely with his top off and his swollen gut wobbling and hanging over the edge of his shorts. 'Get your end up, Matty...good lad...now, Karl, you get over to Matty and drive it in...Pat, what you doing, love?'

'It's really awkward,' Patricia says, struggling to hold the pole.

'Keithy, get over and help Pat...Gwen love, lift your end up. Bleeding hell, Gwen. Up a bit more. That's it. Right, now hold it nice and tight....'

They made the shelter themselves after Tommy got back from the infirmary and told them about the muzzies invading, and how everything was going to shit, and they needed to stick together and get their own base sorted out pronto.

'I'm tellin' ya. We need to protect our patch before those fuckers take over...right, where we getting the material from? Might have to ask that wanker, Colin...'

'I know where there's some of that waterproof stuff,'

Pamela said, hunkering down out of sight from Lenski while handing out stolen chocolate bars taken from the food rooms.

'Where?' Tommy asked.

'One of the rooms in the walls,' she said and took them over. A big group skulking across to a far corner in the back wall.

'Pat, Keithy, you speak posh so you keep an eye out,' Tommy said, slipping inside the filthy rooms with Pamela. A length of rolled up tarpaulin. Big too. They carried it back to their section then went back to root through the rooms, finding poles, sticks and string.

A hard afternoon then commenced with much sweating, cursing, squabbling and bickering while also trying to hide their activities from everyone else, while in truth everyone else was either too stressed, too exhausted or too busy to give a shit.

'Whack 'em in properly,' Tommy urges. 'We don't want the wind ripping it all out...that's it. Cor, look at that...' he says, standing back. His hands on his hips as the others join him to look at the fruit of their labours. Something between a small crappy circus tent and a yurt with a slit cut into the material on one side to make a doorway. More string used to pin the flaps back. A communal home covering all of their patches with room to spare. Easily the biggest shelter in the fort. 'That's fucking brill that is,' Tommy says with genuine feeling.

Pat and Keith nod and smile. Both sweating freely. Wealthy suburbanites from a big detached executive house in Surrey now feeling proud over their new shared home.

'Right,' Tommy says, clapping his hands together. 'Hang on there a sec...' he rushes in, grabbing his bag and mooching through the contents before dragging a large beach towel out that he ties onto one of the poles by the ad-hoc door. 'Ready?' he asks, looking at the others. A grin and he lets it unfold, showing them the creased, faded and stained white material emblazoned with a big red cross upon it.

'What's that?' Keith asks.

'What's that? That's the Saint George's Cross,' Tommy says. 'Fuck me, Keithy. It's the flag of England...'

'That's racist though isn't it,' Matty says. 'Don't all the far right groups use that?'

'Fuck off,' Tommy snaps, bridling instantly. 'Fucking fake news shit...this is our flag for us...it's what we fought for in the war...telling them Germans to fuck off and them wankers over in Pakistanighan or wherever the fuck, and them muzzies blowing our troops up. This is our land. This here, what we just made. For us. Ain't no fucker can just walk in neither. We've got our human rights we have. We got the right to...the right to...' he pauses, frowning.

'Right to privacy?' Keith suggests.

'Right to privacy,' Tommy says eagerly.

'Right to life too,' Keith adds.

'And that,' Tommy says.

'Freedom of expression...'

'Yes!' Tommy says, clapping his hands together. 'Some decent British fucking laws eh?'

'Er, so...I think those laws came from Europe, didn't they?' Mathew asks, lifting a hand.

'European court of human rights,' Keith says, nodding at him.

'Fuck them!' Tommy shouts. 'They're English laws now.'

'English or British?' Keith asks.

'Yeah, you keep saying both, Tommy,' Karl says.

'Alright, bleeding getting hung up on the details. Point is...the point is...right, look over there. That proves my point right there...' he says as they turn to watch the new Muslim family all kneeling on mats facing in one direction while giving the sunset prayer. 'See that?'

'What?' Mathew asks.

'The fucking muzzies doing that weird shit,' Tommy snaps. His temper starting to show from his group asking too many questions. 'You wanna go and suck 'em off, Matty? Wanna go pray on a rug with them?'

'Eh? No, I was just...no course not.'

'Wankers,' Tommy says.

'Yeah, yeah wankers,' Mathew says, not quite as angrily as Tommy.

'English only in here,' Tommy says.

'I'm Welsh,' Gwen says, lifting her hand.

'Yeah, that's English,' Tommy says.

'British,' Karl says.

'You taking the fucking piss? English, British, same thing. Our country...for us. No fucking queers and homos and fucking terrorists...and I heard they started this. I told you that. I heard that from a good source. Lad in the army. He said it came from Pakistanighan and it's part of that Jihadi holy war stuff...'

He trails off, watching the Muslim family pray. Everyone does. The sight draws the eye and the surrounding area grows still and quiet enough to hear the murmurings. The way they're all lined up under their shelter. The way they all face the same way. The way they all rise and lower at the same time. Something mesmerising about it. Peaceful and calming.

Norman watches them too. Stopping on his way back to his patch of ground, marvelling at the changed landscape about him. Shelters everywhere with a tiny step closer to homes and privacy. Now he stops to watch the new family praying, thinking back to the beach and how close it came to them all being killed. He thinks of Lilly and her absolute determination to keep the fort safe and how she simply flicked the aggression off the second the threat was negated and in so doing, she proved she had no fear of their religion.

It does look peaceful though. An act of shared worship in a world that now only really knows pain and suffering.

A sigh and he walks on, blanching at the sight of the big shelter looking so different to everyone else's. 'That's a big tent,' he remarks, noticing how quickly Patricia and Keith appear awkward and glance away.

'Your crap's there,' Tommy says, pointing at Norman's single rucksack.

'Right,' Norman says, frowning at them all.

Tommy shrugs, everyone else looks away, watching the family in prayer or finding something else to stare at.

'Sorry, what's happening?' Norman asks.

'I just said your stuff's there,' Tommy says.

'I heard you,' he says, noticing the hanging towel England flag and Tommy standing proud with his top off and the tattoos on proud display. He turns to look at the new family praying under their shelter so clearly in view.

'You going then?' Tommy asks, his voice hardening, the atmosphere tensing instantly.

'Going?' Norman asks. 'Going where?

'Somewhere else,' Tommy says.

Norman nods. His presence no longer desired or wished for. He has outstayed his welcome and he sighs long and heavy, noticing the way Keith and Patricia continue to avoid his eye contact. 'Sure,' he says quietly, walking over to grab his bag. 'No problem.'

'Good,' Tommy snaps.

'One question though,' Norman says, pulling his bag onto a shoulder as he looks at Tommy. 'Is this because I am gay?'

'Nah, it's cos you're a cunt,' Tommy replies after a heavy pause. Winking at him as he speaks. 'What do I care if you like sucking cock. No skin off my nose is it...'

Norman smiles. 'Sure,' he turns to walk off, nodding at Patricia and Keith as he goes. 'Nice to see you again...'

'Fucking wanker,' Tommy mutters, the words reaching Norman. His heart beating a drum and an absurd sense of shame creeping up his spine. He wasn't going to stay there anyway but it does sting that Patricia and Keith were like that and he heads to the closest shower cubicle as the dong of a metal ladle being whacked against a pot rings out.

'FOOD,' Agatha yells. 'KIDS FIRST BUT YOU CAN ALL START COMING OVER...'

Tommy grins with a sense of victory, watching Norman walk off. 'You all got your sicknotes? Right. We queue up all good and proper, no swearing, no fucking about and if that Polish bitch says anything then we've got our slips.'

Lenski doesn't say anything.

She forgot about the interaction with Tommy five minutes after it happened and never had any intention of reducing their food. She only said it to try and make them work, and so Tommy's group get their food without hinderance and rush back to eat within the walls of their new home. Grinning and laughing with another sense of victory.

The fort eats and starts to unwind from another gruelling day. Bellies filled and mouths yawning. The shower cubicles in near constant use. Solar light shining, creating little pools of light.

Groups of people sitting near the cooking area, drinking

tea and talking about what happened on the beach today. The van full of infected. A father trying to save his daughter but killed his family and himself in the process. Awful and shocking, but unifying because so many saw it. So many saw Lilly and Mary and Kyle shooting and the blood on Lilly's face. They saw the Muslims too and how quickly Lilly relaxed and accepted them the second she saw they were just people. '*She seriously didn't give a shit about them being Muslims,*' Emily says, her hand wrapped in a dressing. '*And that Mary! Oh my god...and Kyle was firing his guns and I'm telling you, I thought we were all dead. We all did. The infected were right there but they didn't even touch us. Didn't even get close...*'

The back shore. Lanterns on a big folding table taken out. Pistols and rifles stripped with Joan and Kyle showing how they work. John, Pardip, Jaspal, Simar and a few others John said would be suitable. The first of Lenski's fort defence force. Mugs of tea on the side and the air filled with the clunks and clicks of moving parts. Dry firing exercises. Norman with them, a pistol in his hands.

'I would like you trained and armed please, Norman,' Lilly said as they were eating.

Norman figured he could refuse but refusing Lilly didn't feel right. 'Sure,' he said instead. 'Er, is there anywhere I can sleep? I think I've been evicted...'

'Room at the back of the offices if you don't mind sharing with me,' Kyle said.

'He bloody snores something awful though, Norman,' Mary said, butting in. 'Makes the whole fort vibrate he does.'

'It's not that bad,' Kyle said.

'It bloody is,' Mary scoffed. 'I almost quit and went back to me Uncle Peter last night. I was like *Uncle Pete, can I come back, the Father makes a terrible racket he does...I'll peel the spuds and make some gypsy babies with a nice gypsy boy I will...'*

'I make new rooms,' Lenski said, hearing their conversation. 'You stay with Kyle tonight yes? Mary, she sleep in back too. I get something sorted tomorrow.'

'Okay, er...' Norman hesitated, looking at Kyle. 'I'm gay. Does that make a difference? Only I know some men don't like sharing rooms if...'

Kyle just looked at him. 'I know I'm a handsome man, charming too, rakish, rugged, did I say charming?'

'You said charming,' Norman said with a smile.

'Aye, very charming, and I've shared many rooms with many people and I have yet to be seduced or molested in my sleep by anyone...so if you can keep your hands of my toned body then I think we'll be okay.'

'Idiot,' Joan muttered.

'I am charming,' Kyle said.

'You're something,' Joan replied, giving him a look.

'Are you gay, Norman?' Pea asked casually.

'I am,' Norman replied.

And the world moved on. That was it. Nobody cared that much. What was, and what they were before is not now, and now is busy. Too busy to stop and dwell and think.

'You've got it,' Kyle says, watching Norman load the magazine into the pistol and make it ready. 'We'll do some shooting tomorrow...'

A chorus of giggles from the far end of the small beach as Mary reaches into the water to grab at Milly's feet, making the girl squeal with laughter.

'Ach, I thought it was a fish I did,' Mary says, tutting to herself at seeing Milly's foot in her hand. All of them sitting with their trouser legs rolled up and their bare feet dangling in the water. 'Ah, there's another fishy,' Mary cries out, leaning over Lilly to grab at Billy's foot in the water. 'Ah bum, it's another foot...all wet and stinky it is too...'

'Get Lilly's foot,' Rajesh laughs.

'I'm not touching those huge things,' Mary says. 'Bigger than my hand they are...'

'My feet aren't big,' Lilly says.

'But, little Raj, I'll get your feet I will,' she says, leaning the other way to get his.

'My feet really aren't big,' Lilly says, still staring at her feet.

Pea yawns, yelping with the effort and setting a chain reaction off as Subi does the same then Sam and the others, all of them yawning loudly.

'Sucking the air from the world you lot are,' Mary remarks, making them laugh. 'Fish!' she lunges over Lilly again, grabbing at Billy's foot again then at Amna's, making them kick and spray water. Lilly laughing as she turns her head and ducks down behind Mary's back, her world filling with a vision of flame red air. 'Don't you be hiding behind me, Blondie,' she says, grabbing at Lilly's foot. 'Are you ticklish? Billy, is your sister ticklish is she? Get her feet...'

'Don't you dare,' Lilly cries out as four children pile on top of her with little hands tickling at her ribs and sides while others go for her feet. 'No! Billy...get off me...' she rolls and laughs, making Pea and Subi chuckle as they watch. Sam grinning as the people working at the table glance over to a sight none of them have really seen. To Lilly laughing properly. Not just smiling at a joke or giggling from exhaustion but full on belly laughing and even Joan grins at the sight, watching as the kids and Mary subject their brave fort leader to a merciless attack.

'Subi! Save me,' Lilly calls, the words almost lost within the mound of laughing bodies.

'Go on,' Pea whispers, urging Subi to go in and have some fun. 'Save Lilly...'

Subi grins, shy and wanting to play but unsure and hesitant. Old enough to think she should be serious but young enough to still feel the lure and she doesn't see as Lenski hands her assault rifle to Joan and runs over to heft Subi up with a laugh, making her squeal out as she dumps her into the big bundle.

'I think we'll call that a night,' Joan tells her trainees all smiling at the play underway.

Lilly doesn't hear them leave. She only hears the laughs coming from her own body and those coming from the children. Her ribs being tickled, and she does the same back, grabbing Amna then Rajesh. Milly then Billy. Mary in amongst them all, tickling anyone she can reach. Tears falling from eyes that soak cheeks. Faces flushed and hot. The temperature still so high. The giggles come to them all. The deep giggles that take hold within their bellies and keep surging up and out in waves. Subi diving in. Lenski plonking down at the side to watch before being engulfed by Milly and Raj.

Sam and Pea ease away to lean back against the fort wall, chuckling at the games underway. Taking genuine pleasure at watching them play.

'She's like a breath of fresh air,' Sam whispers, nodding at Mary.

'Lenski's changing too,' Pea whispers back. 'She even winked at someone earlier.'

Sam smiles, turning back to watch them all laugh and play. The world is over. Society has fallen. Law and order are gone, and the threat of death is now real and very immediate. They took life today. When that van came down the road, and then when they saw the women in burkas, that was so tense, so raw and awful, which just makes this now more meaningful and special, but all things must end, all things must cease and eventually the children, worn out by heat and playing all day in fresh air, eventually tire and grow sleepy, snuggling in while giggling and snorting.

'Bed time,' Lilly says, trying to sit up with two children draped across her.

'We'll do it,' Sam says with a nod at Pea. 'Stay out here a bit...'

'I'll come in,' Lilly says.

'Stay,' Sam says, a firmness to her voice as she hefts Billy up first before scooping to lift Amna. 'It's fine. We can do it. Relax for five minutes, have a paddle...'

'Yeah, Lilly, have a paddle,' Mary says.

'Yeah, Lilly, have a paddle,' Lenski says, a Polish girl trying to mimic an Irish gypsy accent which just sets them off again.

Sam and Pea head off. Four sleeping children within their arms and a very sleepy Subi at Pea's side.

'That was the worst accent ever,' Mary says.

'Aye,' Lilly says, making Lenski giggle again which just sets them off.

'Aye,' Lenski says.

'Am I being racially abused now?' Mary asks.

'Aye,' they both say at the same time with another fit of giggles taking hold.

'I get ya,' Mary says, 'two blondies picking on the redhead.'

'Is ginger,' Lenski says.

'I'm not bloody ginger, my brother is a ginger. I'm a redhead...' Mary says, her accent making them both laugh again. 'Will ye quit laughing at me now. Anyways, I'm hot as anything. Do you mind if I have a swim?'

'A swim?' Lilly asks.

'Aye, it's when you get in water and don't drown.'

'I know what swimming is,' she laughs, looking up as Mary gets to her feet and starts tugging her trousers down.

'Are ye coming then?' Mary asks, looking at Lilly. 'Come on, Blondie. Cool off a bit.'

Lilly thinks to say no. Her mind already forming the intent to say the word and explain she should go inside and check on Billy. She should make sure things are okay. She should work, and if not work then she should rest and get ready for work, and besides, she doesn't have a swimming costume. That makes her think of her old bedroom and her old clothes. She remembers the drawer her swimming costumes were kept in. A white chest with brass handles. She remembers her room next and how the light fell through the net curtains. She thinks of her mother and everything they had. She thinks of the long days before her father finally decided to set out and leave and she thinks of how quickly and easily he died. She thinks that he isn't here now, and that she, at the age of sixteen, has had to kill so many people to protect her brother.

She thinks of Howie and Paula and that they should have left someone behind. Any one of that team would have stopped the crews taking over. But they all left and so she had to do it.

She thinks of today and how hard it has been. Gruelling. Brutal even. She thinks of the Muslim family and the van full of infected. She thinks of all of those things but that after that happened, the mood changed a little. She couldn't explain it, but everyone seemed a bit different after that. Chattier, talking more, helping each other. It's hard to define or explain, but maybe just a shift in energy.

She thinks of tomorrow and how it will be even harder than today, and the day after that will be harder still because this is the new world and the old world is gone. This is life now. This is living now. So why shouldn't she swim in her underwear at night to cool off? Where's Nick? Where is he? Where's Howie now? They're off fighting. They're off doing hard work, but that doesn't mean the work here is any less hard, and they left her on her own. All of them went. The same as her father.

'You know what,' she says firmly. 'I will have a swim. Lenski?' she asks, turning to see Lenski already stripped off. Her body so tall and lean, statuesque really. Her ribs showing and her flat stomach sweeping in. Long shapely legs. Her breasts small and covered by a white bra and Lilly cannot help but steal glances at the shape of other women's bodies. She looks to Mary. Seeing she is shorter and wider, her frame more solid but not fat. Bigger boobs, bigger hips, muscled thighs and a soft belly that is every bit as attractive as Lenski's defined shape and she blinks as Lenski strides past and dives into the water, going deep and long before surfacing with a gasp.

'Is so nice,' she says, somewhat breathless while sweeping her blond hair over her head.

'I'm in,' Mary goes next, plunging in with a splash as Lilly unfastens her pistol belt and trousers, tugging them down and off before taking her top off as Mary surfaces. Gasping the same as Lenski did. Splashing as she turns with a grin and wild red hair plastered down her face. A look from her to Lilly. The moonlight shining down as Lilly walks to the edge of the beach in her bra and knickers. Moonlight coming down. Darkness about them. The air sultry and heavy and she looks from Lenski dunking back under to Mary and the gypsy woman's broad, beautiful face staring back at her with a slow smile forming. A moment in time. A feeling inside. Lilly smiles back at her. Mary widens her eyes and motions with her head, inviting Lilly in. She goes for it. Diving out with a splash and feeling the contraction in her chest from the lower temperature of the water. The instant coolness of it. The heat of her body seemingly robbed within a second and she kicks out, seeing nothing but darkness in every direction before she surfaces to see Mary still smiling at her.

'Nice?' Mary asks softly.

'Aye,' Lilly says. 'Very nice.' Both of them treading water. Mere feet between them and in that moment, Lilly does not think about Mr Howie or Paula. Not the infection or Reginald's ideas or what it all means. She doesn't even think about Nick.

They are not here.

They left.

Agatha was right. The fort is changing, and with it, the people too.

CHAPTER ELEVEN

D ay Twenty Three

L illy wakes before dawn. Darkness outside but a feel about the world that it's almost ready to wake up. She stretches, languid and slow. Her muscles flooding her body with chemicals that help bring her mind to the fore and she lifts her head, blinking as she looks about the room.

On her feet. Her heart racing as she grabs her rifle and runs hard. Her mind spinning. Her brain frantic. Light coming from the office. Noise within. 'The kids are...' she stops at the doorway, her chest heaving. 'Gone,' she says the last word, shaking her head at seeing Amna, Rajesh, Milly and Billy at the table and Mary at the back by the drinks table in shorts and a vest. Her red hair piled on her head.

'They dive bombed me,' Mary says.

'What are you doing?' Lilly demands, striding in to

glare at the kids suddenly freezing as they look at her. 'Why did you sneak out? Answer me!'

'Lilly,' Mary says from the back. 'They're fine...'

'It's not fine. I've told you not to sneak out. You wake me if you need anything...look at me. All of you...'

'Sorry, Lilly,' Billy says quietly.

'Sorry,' the others join in. Quiet, soft and all filled with that special kind of remorse reserved for small children.

'It's dangerous.'

'Aye, it is, but there's plenty of people about,' Mary says. 'And the gates are locked...plus they came and woke me so....' She trails off, not wanting to undermine Lilly but trying to gently suggest Lilly doesn't need to be so angry. She offers a smile. Her green eyes twinkling in the soft light.

'Even so,' Lilly says, wincing inside at her harsh tone.

'No, it's a fair point it is,' Mary says. 'You kids, don't do that again. Okay? If you want to dive bomb me in the morning, you'll have to wake someone up, or better yet, move down to these rooms so we're all in one place. Lilly, you wanting a coffee now?'

'I will. Yes please,' she says, moving to kiss her brother's head. 'I panicked...I couldn't see any of you.' She moves from one to the other, leaning down to give kisses and hugs. 'What are you doing anyway?'

'Drawing,' Rajesh says. 'I drew a doggy...it's Mr Howie's doggy.'

'That's very good,' Lilly says, looking at the big black splodge that kind of resembles a thing with four legs and a tail. 'Is that Mary?' she asks Billy, seeing a stick figure with a big red splodge of hair.

'And you,' Billy says, pointing at a stick figure with yellow hair. 'And Lenski, and Pea and Sam and Joanie...'

'Amna, what are those?' Lilly asks.

'Cats,' Amna says, scribbling away. 'All running and running...'

'Nice,' Mary says, bringing a mug of coffee over for Lilly. 'Who's that then?' she asks Milly, staring down at her drawings.

'That's Cassie and that's Gregory and that's the boy,' Milly says.

'Ah is it now?' Mary says. 'You seen this, Lilly? Good little artist here.'

'Let me see,' Lilly says as Mary holds the picture up. Crude figures but the lines are clear, the sizes too all appearing in scale. Two adults and a child all hand in hand. All three of them smiling and drawn in lighter shades but with darker figures behind them. Scale given to show they are further back and all of them with red eyes. Lilly smiles sadly as Mary bends down to hug Milly.

'Did you know them?' Mary asks gently, thinking the figures to be family taken by the infected.

'No,' Milly says. 'They live far far far far away,' Milly says, turning to grin at Mary.

'Ah I see,' Mary says. 'And what's the boy called?'

'Cassie calls him the boy and Gregory calls him the boy and they play frisbee. Can we play frisbee later?'

'We'll have to find a frisbee first, but I'll keep my eyes peeled I will. Kids eh?' she says, standing up to look at Lilly. 'You've got a bit of bed hair going on there, Blondie.'

'I woke up with a start,' Lilly says. 'And I don't have a hair band.'

'Ach, how do you modern girls cope?' Mary asks, grabbing a pencil from the table as she walks over to stand behind Lilly. 'Just pull it all back,' she says, taking Lilly's hair in her hands as the four children watch on with interest. 'Nice and tight, then twist it over...and stick the pencil in there...'

Lilly frowns, reaching back to feel the pencil poking through the rough bun. 'I've never been able to do that.'

'Gypsy magic,' Mary says, winking at the children before leaning to whisper in Lilly's ear. 'Go and put a bra on before people wake up...'

'Pardon?' Lilly asks, glancing down at her chest showing a bit too clearly through the thin material of her top. 'Right.'

'This fort's hot enough without them bouncing about,' Mary says with a laugh, heading back to the drinks table. 'Can your kids drink tea? I think it's decaf? It might be decaf. Ah hell, it's probably not decaf...it'll be fine. I'll make it weak.'

'I shall go and dress,' Lilly says, holding her hands over her chest. 'Tea's fine, but not coffee.'

'Blondie,' Mary tuts. 'I wouldn't give a kid coffee,' she says, rolling her eyes as Lilly goes out. 'Who wants coffee?'

'Me!' Milly calls as Lilly ducks back in to glare over.

'Ah, I'm joking. Go on with you. They can go and jump on Kyle in a wee bit.'

Lilly smiles, walking towards her own sleeping rooms while thinking they really need a set of rooms where they can all be together, preferably with a lockable door. 'Morning, Alf,' she says, spotting him walking towards her pushing his wheelbarrow.

'Miss Lilly,' he says, ignoring her hands clasped over her boobs.

'Any losses?'

'Just the one. Old fella from the infirmary. Blood poisoning, I think. He's wrapped up and ready to go...'

'Yes, of course,' she says. 'Er, don't suppose you've

checked the suicide...I mean the room at the back, have you?'

'Not yet, want me to look?'

'No, it's fine. I can do it,' she says as he nods and walks off then tuts at herself still holding her boobs. She carries on walking, looking at the first hints of light in the sky, thinking of yesterday, thinking of the work they need to do today, thinking of Lenski, of Mary and smiling at the jokes last night. It was nice swimming with them both. They sat in the offices and drank tea while drying off after. Lenski is changing, she's more natural now and less stern. Mind you, everyone is like that.

A few minutes later and she groans softly in the doorway. Staring in at the figure slumped against the wall. Then she frowns at hearing strange noises and her hand moves instinctively to her hip, ready to draw her pistol that isn't there. She thinks to back out then realises what the noises are. Cats purring. The ten cats are in here. She spots the crates, the shape of them becoming clear as her eyes adjust to the gloom. A heavy sigh and she heads in, moving to the corpse. A dead woman with a big cat purring on her lap. Whoever the person is came in and opened one of the crates before dying.

Something moves against her leg. Soft, warm and also purring, and Lilly corrects her thought processes; whoever this person came in and opened all of the crates before dying. Awesome. That means they now have a fort full of cats.

She bends down, wincing as she presses her fingers to the neck of the corpse that twitches and snorts, making Lilly panic and punch it in the face while jumping back, thinking it's only the infected that makes noises when they should be dead.

'Ow!' the corpse cries out, keeling over. 'What the fuck?'

'Oh shit,' Lilly says, her heart booming, her fist still clenched.

'Why'd you bloody punch me?'

'Oh my god, I'm so sorry…I thought you were dead.'

'Dead? I'm not bloody dead. I'm asleep…'

'I know. Oh god…are you okay?'

'No! You just bloody hit me. Jesus, right in the cheek too. That really hurts…'

'I am so sorry. Honestly, I don't know what to say. I mean, you made a noise so I punched you…'

'What!?'

'Okay, sorry, let me start again. I was going to get my bra and thought you were dead…'

'Who punches dead bodies?'

'No! You made a noise…' Lilly says, wincing at the woman. 'Are you okay?' she asks again, moving closer.

'I'm fine,' the woman says, wilting back as she gets to her feet while rubbing her cheek. 'I wanted to check my cats…'

'Oh. Right. They're your cats. Yes, that makes sense now…er, why did you let them out?'

'What? My cats are out?'

'Yes. I just said that.'

'I'm sorry, you just punched me in the face while I was sleeping…who let my cats out?'

'Oh, I thought you let your cats out?'

'Why would I let my cats out?'

'Right,' Lilly says, remembering Amna's drawing of the cats running. 'Gotcha. That's a mystery. Blimey. Never solve that one. Er…I need to put a bra on. Sorry for punching you…um…bye then! Oh the infirmary is down the other end if er…if the cheek is sore or anything…' she heads out, tutting, wincing and cursing at the kids sneaking past her to let the cats go before dive-bombing Mary and making her punch sleeping women.

'What about my cats?' the woman calls from behind.

'I'm sure you'll catch them all!' Lilly says before scarpering with her hands back over her boobs.

CHAPTER TWELVE

D ay Twenty Three
The Meeting

'Safety announcement,' Mary calls out to a packed table in the main office as the morning meeting gets underway. 'Don't anyone fall asleep or Lilly will punch you in the face,' she adds to a few laughs. The story already well-told from the cat-lady walking about displaying her black eye.

'Our little dictator strikes again,' Lisa says, sucking the humour from the room. 'Oh come on now, don't all look so offended. Or is it a case of not being able to speak out for fear of the consequences? Like say, starving people and denying them shelter from the sun?'

'What the hell are you on about?' Sam asks.

'Perhaps we should ask Lenski,' Lisa says.

'You mean what I say to the lazy people,' Lenski says as everyone looks at her. 'They shout at Colin and make him feel bad. Sit in sun all day. No work. Drink tea and go blah

blah. I said to make their own shelter and work. One man, he has tattoos...'

'That'll be Tommy,' Norman says.

'Him. This man. He shout and angry and swear. I get angry too. I say half food unless work. I no mean this,' she adds, waving a dismissive hand. 'I say it to make them work. They eat full food. I no care.'

'Oh I see,' Lisa says. 'Sorry. I didn't fully understand. Only it sounded to me that while Lilly was threatening to shoot Muslims unless they removed their burkas, Lenski was denying food and shelter to sick people...which, of course, is before our little dictator punched someone in the face for sleeping...' she lifts her hands, splaying her fingers as everyone starts talking at the same time. 'And how many people were hurt yesterday on the beach? Broken arms, broken fingers...severe heat-stroke. But hey, they work or don't eat. Right?'

'Fuck off!' Sam shouts. 'It's nothing like that...'

'We couldn't see their eyes,' Pea says.

'Sure. So you threaten them at gunpoint. Best way to resolve everything.'

'You're such a fucking bitch,' Sam yells.

'Lisa, it wasn't like that now,' Kyle says calmly.

'Wow, sure. Nobody can speak out against our little...'

'Call her a dictator again and see what bloody happens,' Mary yells, striding across the room as Norman moves to block her path.

'That's enough. Thank you,' Lilly calls out, standing at the head of the table.

'I no deny food. I only say this to make them work,' Lenski says, her tone harder and defensive.

'The sick and injured have to work?' Lisa asks. 'Are you going to come into the infirmary and make them work too?'

'Lisa, what's got into you?' Ann asks.

'Nothing has got into me. I'm just not getting sucked into the Lilly cult...'

'Ye fucking twat!'

'Mary!' Lilly says. 'Enough. Thank you. Lisa, your views are valid, but do not goad for the sake of a reaction. It is beneath you...'

'Who the hell are you talking to?' Lisa snaps, losing her cool instantly. 'Patronising little schoolgirl. Excuse me. I have work to do. May I go please, Miss Lilly?' she smiles, wide and icy before storming out.

'Well, that escalated quickly,' John says into the silence.

'Fuck her, we can have a nice meeting now,' Sam says, glaring at the door as though to send daggers after Lisa.

'Heat and pressure do things to people,' Ann says. 'This weather...it's enough to drive anyone crazy.'

'You're not lying there, Ann,' Kyle says as Peter and Mary share looks with both knowing someone saying things like Lisa would be dealt with very quickly in the camp.

'You think hot on the beach?' Lenski asks. 'Colin, what was temperature in the fort yesterday?'

'Forty two Celsius,' Colin replies with a wince to a few sharp intakes of breath. 'There's no breeze you see.'

'There's no breeze over there either,' Pea says. 'I felt like I piddled myself yesterday I was that wet...what?' she asks when everyone looks at her. 'It did feel like that...'

'No, you're right. It is like that,' Sam says. 'Still, you are getting on a bit, Pea dear. Bit of piss leaking out yeah?'

'Oh fuck off,' Pea says to a few chuckles.

'I think a storm will come, yes?' Lenski says as the others murmur in agreement. 'This worry me. If rain now we no cook for everyone...no have enough tents. People get wet and cold...'

Lilly nods, leaning in to rest her elbows on the table. 'My apologies but we'll need to work harder today. Lenski's right. We need structures up, somewhere to cook and tents...and we need to start on the wall too...'

'I'll jump in here,' Peter says. 'I took a few lads up to an army base overnight. The Father said it used to be an army prison and had sectional wall we could take...' he trails off, thinking back to a few hours before and standing in the army base in the hours of darkness with his rifle gripped and ready.

'What the bloody hell happened here?' Patrick asked quietly, looking about with distaste.

'No idea,' Peter said, staring down at a mangled corpse reading the name on the front tunic of the camouflage clothing. 'Major Donaldson...'

'He's a very dead Major Donaldson now,' Patrick said. 'Looks like he's been hung, run over, stabbed and shot a few times...oh and someone chopped his head off...it's over there I think.'

'We didn't stay long,' Peter adds after explaining what they found in the meeting. 'But we did check the walls. They're buried too deep to dig out, so I'm thinking unless we find a place with new ones then we might as well go for the shipping containers...'

'Aye, you know, I didn't think about that,' Kyle says wistfully. 'My error, apologies. Of course they'll be sunk in... Henry would know where to find new ones but I don't...'

'Who's Henry?' John asks.

'Someone I used to work with. Lilly? I'd say go for the containers then. We'll get a good wall up with them.'

'Okay, we'll do that,' Lilly says.

'Tell you what might be the best idea,' Pardip says. 'Southampton docks. They get the lorries loaded the previous night ready for the morning. Dozens of them all waiting to go out. You just need to drive them back here, oh and get a mobile crane to lift them off and pop them into place...'

'That's a good idea,' John says. 'Get a few drivers and do a fast run up the coast...'

'Put me down for that, Uncle Peter,' Mary says.

'Can you drive a lorry?' Kyle asks her.

'Ach, I can drive anything,' she replies.

'I'll have a go,' Pardip says. 'It'll be messy, but I can get them moving...'

'Yeah same,' John says. 'We might have a few truck drivers in the fort.'

'No,' Lilly says before Lenski can reply. 'I'm not risking you two outside...you're both too essential.'

'We can do it,' Peter says, interjecting after a glance from Lilly. 'Leave it with us...'

'That doesn't feel fair,' John says.

'John mate,' Peter says. 'I get bit it's just a mark...you get a tiny scratch and you die...plus you'll kill others. It's just how it is now...'

Questions hang in the air. Questions with no answers. Too many things to think about.

'We'd better get on,' Lilly says. 'Lenski, are you okay over here? I feel bad leaving you alone...'

'I not alone, I have Colin and Aggie and John and...well, John he does not count. He a bit slow yes?'

'Oi,' John says, pointing at her with a grin.

'Is fine. I sort the fort. You not far. I call if I need help. Is good. We cope, don't we, Colin?'

'We certainly do,' Colin says. 'Us section heads all sticking together eh? Bit of the old stiff upper lip.'

'Are you a section head?' Sam asks. 'Pea was asking who

they all were...'

'Oh right, yes. Happy to explain that, Pea...'

'She's taking the piss,' Pea says, whacking Sam as they all start getting up.

'But before you all dash off, do have a look at my new notice board...'

'Have we got a new notice board?' Sam asks. 'Pea was asking where it is...'

'Sam!' Pea says.

'Ooh let me show you,' Colin says.

'I have idea I forget to say,' Lenski says to Lilly, moving over to the side. 'Colin and Agatha have big rooms for food, clothes, yes? They have teams work with them. Lots of people they help. The people working with them should stay in those rooms. They work, they use the space. We do this and maybe make fifteen tents to use because we move workers out of tents into rooms...some peoples they have big tent with only two people. That was okay some days ago, but now is not okay. I organise this. Yes? I make better.'

'That's a brilliant idea,' Lilly says. 'Are you honestly okay on your own over here?'

'Yes. I fine. I not alone. Is good. Make wall. Make us safe...we do this together, yes?'

'Okay, but just say if you need me. I'll be here in a shot.'

'I know this. I come to you if need me. We team, yes?'

'We are,' Lilly says, smiling warmly.

'I think things are different now,' Lenski says, lowering her voice and laying an affectionate hand on Lilly's arm with a simple act that defies Lilly's invisible wall that projects a clear disinclination towards physical contact. She simply isn't the huggable type and does not wish that to happen. Standoffish, aloof even. Distant and often cold, so for Lenski to reach out and touch her without thinking about, and without any hint of awkwardness is a thing indeed and speaks of their journey. 'We win this. I think we will...we no make mistakes other people they make. Maddox and...' she trails off, not wanting to say it.

'And Howie,' Lilly says, finishing the sentence.

'I not know. They have bad things happen, many bad things, but we win this. We make this fort good. We no make same mistakes. We smarter than men,' she adds with a smile. 'They fight and shout. We are smart. We think. Go build a wall. I see you later, yes? Drink lots. We swim later? I like our swim. I like Mary too, she makes me laugh...'

Lilly smiles at her, amazed at the flow of words and the passion in Lenski's expression. The way she smiles and frowns, the way she jokes now.

'I feel exactly the same,' Lilly says.

'Ladies,' Joan says, moving over to them. 'I'd suggest we get some firing practise in for Lenski's fort defence fort... okay if I get it organised? Oh, and if you and Kyle are doing the sea burial can you take a boat out the back for them to shoot at?'

Further up the fort, in a big shelter that looks halfway between a crappy circus tent and a yurt, another meeting gets underway.

'Everyone here are they?' Tommy asks.

Pamela told Tommy that Lilly holds a meeting every morning. She also said her and Lilly are *like totally so close now, because, you know, that Zayden was fingering and fucking both of us and we're like, so traumatised and sharing our grief, but that's private and I can't talk about it.*

Tommy ignored the stuff about kids fingering and

fucking Pamela and Lilly. Tommy is many things, but he doesn't find Lilly attractive. She's too young. He likes them a bit older. Like Lenski. Mind you, that Pea's a bit of alright too. Tommy wouldn't mind a go on her. Nice dark hair and slim. Sam too. She looks fiery which Tommy translates to being a right little goer in the sack. He also quite likes Anika. Yeah, she'd get it. That other one. Mary, she's hot too.

When he tuned back in, Pamela had stopped talking and was stuffing her mouth with another chocolate bar. Tommy was quite glad she stopped talking, but also wished she would go and wash.

'You using them showers or what?' he asked.

She shrugged. 'Scared to go on my own, in case someone fingers me again.'

She slept in the new big tent too. Kipping down near Tommy who made a point of spraying lots of deodorant. Pamela missed that point and went to sleep.

'Fuck me, it's ripe as shit in here,' Tommy said, waking up in the morning. 'Christ, who's been farting all night?'

'Pamela,' lots of people said at the same time.

'I got IBS,' Pamela said, sitting up with dried, scabbed chocolate smeared across her cheek from when she woke in the night and tried to eat another one but fell asleep halfway through.

'Right, so...what we're gonna do is this,' Tommy finally says. 'Pammie, you stick working for them...'

'Eh? But I've got a bad knee and IBS and I was finger-fucked and...'

'Nah, you stick working for them see. You be nice and enthusiastic cos you're our mole. You give us the intel and get to see who's coming into the fort, and any good ones you send our way. No muzzies though, or darkies, or queers...I don't mind lesbians cos there's no dicks involved and it's not so fucking gross. And get into the food rooms and get what you can. Smokes, booze, choccy bars...that sort of thing... then we'll get inside here sorted out. Hang up some partitions so we get privacy, make some rooms...you with me?'

Pamela frowns, pursing her lips and looking up at Tommy while thinking the whole plan seems to involve her working and stealing while everyone else hangs out here.

'Good girl, knew I could rely on you,' Tommy says, giving her a wink. 'Right, first things first. Pammie, you go and wash. You stink like a tramp's arse.'

'But...'

'Come on. Stop fucking about. We've got loads to do. Tell you what, we'll go with you and make sure no teenagers shove their fingers in your fanny...'

The fort comes to activity and as Joan rounds up the newly formed Fort Defence Force, so Lilly heads to the gate with Kyle and Mary so Tommy leads his gaggle with a protesting Pamela ushered, cajoled, harangued and physically pushed into a shower cubicle.

'It's cold!' she bleats under the hose.

'It's heavy,' Lilly grunts to Kyle as they lift the corpse wrapped in a sheet and weighed down with rocks into the first boat.

'It's hot,' Joan says, blasting a sigh as she steps out onto the back shore.

Pamela washes. The water running black for a long time. The pungent aroma of her discarded clothes reaching the others waiting outside the cubicle.

Two boats set off. Lilly and Kyle taking theirs out wide and away from the fort. Mary driving another boat behind theirs.

'Here will do,' Kyle says. Lilly cuts the engine and shuffles forward to grab the end of the corpse. 'You want to pray with me?' She shakes her head. Her blue eyes staring at his craggy face. He smiles and nods before bowing his head to clasp his hands together, giving Lilly a chance to study his features. 'Amen,' he whispers after muttering the prayer near silently.

'I'm glad you were there yesterday,' she says, earning a look from him. 'On the beach...and in general too. Just having you nearby gives me huge comfort.'

He listens, staring at her. Sensing she is trying to say something.

'It's important to give thanks,' she says at length.

'You don't have to thank me, Lilly,' he pauses again, thinking he can detect the thing on her mind. 'For what it's worth I'm not going anywhere. I'm at your side as long as you need me...I'll not leave.'

A sudden rush inside. A surge of emotion that she swallows down in a way that hardens her features. 'Thank you, that means a lot,' she says, her voice a little too clipped and brusque.

'ARE YOU COMING TO PICK ME UP OR WHAT?' Mary yells from her boat, breaking the tension instantly.

'Aye, go on now,' Kyle says as Lilly starts the engine and sets off. 'It's a beautiful day to build a wall too.'

'Actually,' she says. 'I might go with Mary and Peter's men for the container trucks...I'm immune, or infected... either way the risk isn't there for me.'

Kyle smiles at her, seeing the iron will inside the girl and that although she is posing it as a suggestion she is really saying she *is* going to do this. Mind you, she's a born survivor, that is without doubt. 'Aye, good idea. We'll keep it running here...'

CHAPTER THIRTEEN

D ay Twenty Three

'A re you sure now?'

'Yes. I am sure.'

Peter frowns, rubbing his jaw while trying to think of reasons to stop Lilly coming with them. 'You can't drive a truck, Lilly.'

'Are you telling me that every single one of these men can drive lorries?' Lilly asks him, taking in the tough faces of the thirty or so gypsy men gathered about them.

'And don't even think about lying, Uncle Peter,' Mary says. 'I know for a fact Eggy can't ride a bicycle let alone a bloody big truck...and Callum there never even passed his car test. You're doubling some of them up. One guard and one driver so that's what we're doing. I'm the driver and Blondie is my guard...'

'But...'

'And she's immune so she's not at risk...and I already

tried to talk her out of it. I said to her *Blondie, what the hell is wrong with you? You've a perfectly nice fort to stay in with lots of busy shit to do.* You know what she said? She said *fuck that, Mary. I'm not staying back while those sexist pricks go and have all the fun driving big trucks with no cops about telling them they shouldn't be driving without a licence...'*

'I never said that,' Lilly says as everyone looks at her. 'However, I am going. So...' she smiles at Peter, expectant and ready to move. 'Shall we then?'

'Peter,' Willie says. 'Do you want to put Miss Lilly with you or me and Elvis? Or stick her in with Patrick and Tyson...'

'No,' Mary calls out, waggling a finger at her brother. 'Don't start on this ye ginger twat. Lilly and me are doubling up. I can shoot better than you and I can...'

'Ah for fuck's sake,' Willie says, turning away as the group disbands with much grumbling and muttering.

'I can bloody hit harder too,' Mary calls out. 'Wankers...' she adds with a grumble as they set off into the blackened waste-land of the old estate and over towards the now plentiful abundance of vehicles to choose from. A few vans fuelled up and made ready by Bobby and his gang of grease and oil smeared kids. 'Quick now,' Mary whispers, grabbing Lilly's elbow as she runs for the last vehicle. 'Ye don't want to be in a van with a bunch of men farting and belching...'

'You bloody stay with us now, Mary,' Peter orders through the radio. *'Don't go tear arsing off and being bloody stupid...'* he adds as Mary tear-arses past him with a wave. *'Mary! I bloody mean it. Slow down and wait...fuck's sake. Load up and get moving...'*

Mary laughs as she eases the speed off and winds her

window down to let the breeze flow through. 'It's nice to be out and moving, eh Blondie?'

'It is,' Lilly says, watching the world about her through eyes that are now so different from when she first arrived at the fort. A pistol on her hip. A knife in her belt. Grenades in her pockets and a small rucksack holding spare magazines. Simple cargo trousers. Sturdy boots and a black top. Her blond hair pulled back in a ponytail. Her skin now golden from the sun.

'I'm amazed you wanted to come,' Mary says.

Lilly was quite surprised she wanted to come too, and never thought she would willingly choose to be away from her brother. But the fort is safer now. The camp is there for a start so that gives protection from the outside. Joan and Kyle are there. Sam, Pea and Lenski. Plus, there's new people too. John and Pardip. Both big men and it's solidly re-assuring to have them about the place. Jaspal and Simar too. More guys. More people. A community growing. On top of all that, it just didn't feel right asking Peter's men to go out and take all the risks. Why should they? A blur in front of her nose brings her from the deep thoughts as Mary leans over to wave her hand.

'Mary to Blondie...are you receiving me?'

'Miles away,' Lilly says, smiling at Mary's hand being too close. 'You can move it now...'

'Move what?' Mary asks, her hand still dancing about in front of Lilly's head.

'Idiot,' Lilly laughs, reaching up to push it away.

'You're a strange one you are, Blondie,' Mary says, finally pulling her hand back.

'Me?' Lilly asks, volleying the joke back.

'Aye, you're all in charge of everything.'

Lilly nods, looking out at the world going by then

leaning forward to see Peter's van now close behind. She looks at Mary again, watching her drive and the way she grips the wheel. A simple vest top leaving her arms bare. A few freckles here and there and the fine hairs seen in the sunshine. She watches Mary's hair moving in the breeze. So gorgeous and thick and so deep and red too.

'Is it hard to manage?' she asks.

'What's that?' Mary asks. 'My hair? Nah, I don't do anything with it mind. Just pull it back...but I admire that about you. Not your hair. Although your hair is nice, I mean I like that about all of you in the fort all mucking in together. You'd never get women in charge like that in a camp. Don't get me wrong. I love my Uncle Pete, and I love my brother, although he is a ginger prick. They're good people really, but they're in the last century in someways. You know what I mean?'

'I think so,' Lilly says.

'But you though. You were like, *stuff that, I'm not waiting for a man to save me. I'll bloody do it myself*...and Sam and Pea are right there with you. Lenski too. And Joanie. You know, I was only going to come over for one night...I thought I'll get out from the camp, cool down a bit then go back, and I figured you were a right stuck up bitch too, but it kinda draws you in, does that make sense? Like all the goings on and new people turning up and stuff happening and this and that...am I talking too much again?'

'Yes.'

'Am I really?' Mary asks, shooting a glance to Lilly's deadpan face. 'Ah piss off, Blondie...' she adds when Lilly smiles. 'Go point them blue eyes somewhere else...so tell me about your lad? Nick is it? What's he like?'

'Nick? Yeah he's er...' she falters, expecting the rush to come that isn't the same as it was when she thought about him before. A deep fondness. A warmth even, but not the surge of emotion that was there before. 'He's nice,' she says. 'Nice guy...'

'I've heard he's handsome as anything.'

'He is. And sweet too,' she trails off, thinking about what he did to save her brother, thinking about missing him, about needing him, about the absolute desire she had for him that isn't quite the same now.

'Right. Good chat,' Mary says, rolling her eyes. 'He your first?'

'My first what?'

'First whatever. Boyfriend? Lover? Roll in the hay? That made you laugh...'

'Yes, he was my first. How about you?'

'Me? Ah you know. Dated here and there. A few gypsy boys courted me. That's different too. Dating in our world I mean. It can be very old-fashioned. Especially when the girl you fancy has a champion prize fighting brother called Willie, whose best mate is also a prize fighter called Elvis and whose Uncle Pete is perhaps one of the most famous fighters in our world, then imagine the girl you fancy has mad red hair and a tempter to boot and can outfight her prize fighting brother. Eh? Will ye think on that now. You think you had it bad? Come and be a gypsy girl...'

Lilly laughs hard, wiping the tears from her eyes at the way Mary says it all. The accent rising and falling. The facial expressions too.

'Ah but now I'm in your fort. Aye. So any hot men coming in. Yep, they'll do the same as the others and run the other bloody way!'

They hit the motorway and the view opens up. The world outside of the fort. Fields bursting with life. Rabbits running everywhere with their white tails seen racing into the undergrowth or sitting in the sun, content to munch. Foxes glimpsed in the treeline. Birds soaring overhead. Butterflies and insects and flowers blooming. The sky so heart-achingly blue and every colour seems so vibrant and so much more alive than it ever did before.

Lilly takes it all in. Seeing the new world moving on. A world without people. Without fumes or smog. She opens her window and leans out to breathe deep, catching scent of flowers and all sorts of things she would never have smelled before. They pass buildings and structures. Seeing houses with smashed in doors or broken windows. Others look intact. A car abandoned in the road ahead and bodies further down the road. Half-eaten by birds and whatever else creatures took a fancy. The bones showing through the skin.

They keep a wide route around the big towns and go a few miles north to get by Portsmouth as they head towards Southampton. The two of them chatting but only about the now, about life now and not the past. Not what they were. Not who they were. It's not relevant. It doesn't matter.

At the bay, the day grows hot again. Searing and crushing. Sweat pouring. Sam, Pea, Joan and Kyle doubling up as guards to slow the incoming cars down.

Pamela on the shore outside the fort smiling at the next incoming boat full of refugees. 'Hi, I'm Pammie,' she says, offering a wave and waiting as they disembark and grab their bags. 'Follow me,' she sets off and pauses inside to let them gawp at the fort and the work underway. 'I need to take your names and details again then I'll get you round the fort...'

Into the infirmary. Down the main aisle to the glowering form of Doctor Lisa Franklin

'I know right,' Pamela says, tutting and rolling her eyes. 'What a joke. Lenski's like totally making me bring them over. I said to her *look, Len, there's no point doing a double medical check.* But she's all like *you go. Do not argue.'*

'Well, we're in a dictatorship,' Lisa says, smiling coldly at the new arrivals. 'Hmmm? How do you like that? Prepared for a little tyrant ordering you about? And I hope for god's sake none of you are Muslims. You get shot for that here apparently. Anyway, you all look fine so go away...'

Pamela leads them out back into the sunshine, traipsing through the staggering heat. '...and yeah so like, I totally got fingered and Lilly was the same and we're like working through our grief together, but I can't talk about that as it's private...anyway, so this is the food section. HELLO, SUNNIE. I. HAVE. NEW. PEOPLE. HERE...'

'Why do you keep doing that?' Sunnie asks as Pamela slips past her and through to the back, pretending to be looking about in interest. A quick look about and she scurries to the end room, the one filled with the goodies, snacks, booze, packets of cigarettes and rolling tobacco. Pockets filled, and things shoved into her knickers and bra before she strolls back out, fanning her face to show she's super hot and only seeking shade.

'So, this is your patch,' Pamela tells them a few minutes later, pointing at a newly vacated patch of ground under a stretch of tarpaulin.

'Did they really start all this?' one of them asks, glaring over at the Muslim family.

'Um, dunno...probably, so like, don't go touching them or anything...bye then!'

She walks off into Tommy's tent and another hive of activity underway with more sticks and poles being fashioned to make rooms inside.

'Watchya get?' Tommy asks, leading to his private section and he watches eagerly as she pulls the front of her top down to show her fat breasts spilling from her bra and the many things bulging out of the material. 'Bloody hell,' he mutters at the sight of so many stolen goodies.

A thrill inside from him watching and she starts pulling the things out slowly, as though being erotic and tugging her bra down a bit more as she does. 'Yeah come on,' he urges without interest in her boobs. 'Ain't got all day...just flop 'em out if it's quicker...I'll give you a hand...'

He does too. Flopping her fat breasts out to grab the food and packets of smokes and she blinks, slightly stunned when he tweaks her nipples and winks. 'Good girl...you got anything else?'

'In my knickers,' she whispers with hearts shining in her eyes that a real human man touched her boobs.

'Get it out then,' he says quickly. 'You want me to do it? You dirty girl...' he tuts and winks again, hoisting her skirts up to delve into the huge knickers, hiding the grimace at feeling a mass of wiry pubic hair. 'Hiding it in the forest eh?'

'Pardon?'

'Yeah never mind...' he says, pulling a small bottle of vodka out. 'You beauty...get me more of this...booze, smokes...chocolate yeah? Good girl...off you go...'

She waddles out with a big grin and scurries off towards the gate thinking she might have actually found somewhere she can fit in. She never did in her old life. She just used to spend her time online trolling for attention, but she doesn't have to do that anymore. Now she can have a boyfriend and he'll like totally have a huge shop and be important and maybe even be a leader when Lenski and all them stuck up bitches fuck off.

Maleek stands at the edge of his section and offers a smile to the filthy look sent his way from Pamela as she rushes on by. His smile fades slowly and the worry shows in his soft brown eyes as he looks about at the barely concealed hostility coming from the people nearby and thinks maybe they made a mistake by coming here. He glances back to his family, to his brothers and finds himself caught out once more at seeing his wife's face revealed to the world. He doesn't mind that his wife must now show her face. He feels the wrongness of it in accordance with the will of Allah. Allah is everything and what Allah wills so be it, but Maleek also takes great pleasure in being able to see his wife and daughter smile.

Maleek didn't realise, when he left Afghanistan, that so many Muslim countries around the world allowed their women to show their faces. Some even show their hair and many wear make-up and drive cars, some even work, like doctors and engineers, and although he could never have admitted so in Afghanistan, he secretly wished his daughter could be educated and feel the deep satisfaction that comes from mastering a skill.

That's why he was so eager to come here, to this country after Ameer, his son, gained a prestigious scholarship and managed to get a few of their family out of the abject violence and suffering in their country.

They arrived in England with hope in their hearts, thinking it would be better, that it would be the start of a new life. His daughter would be educated. His nieces too.

His wife, Damsa, could show her face, but they were immediately housed in a predominantly Muslim area on the outskirts of London and so the same pressures came back. The same adherence to strict laws that they suffered in their home country. The same threat of violence or worse if they didn't abide and adhere to what was expected, and so Damsa and the other women remained covered and life stayed as it was before.

They stayed hidden and quiet when the world fell with skills learnt from living in warzones. Maleek and his brothers snuck out to find food now and then. That's when they found the weapons. Stumbling into what looked like the scene of an awful attack with many bodies lying about the road. The guns were right there, dropped and left. They washed them off and took them back and it was having those guns that gave them the confidence to finally set out for the fort in the south. They'd heard it had order and security and hoped they would be admitted.

But now. Now it can be different, but he feels fear in his heart. Everyone is looking at them with hatred and hostility and he doesn't know why. The blond girl, she made the women show they are not infected. Why then does everyone glare the way they are?

Maleek bites his bottom lip, deep in thought. They look different. He knows that, but they have Sikh's here, and they aren't getting the same level of angry looks. Black people too. They're not being glared at.

'Maleek,' Damsa calls from behind. Her voice so soft and warm and he turns to look at her, caught out at seeing her face in public like this. She smiles sadly, seeing the worry in her husband's eyes. 'Either come and sit down or go and try...'

'You're scaring people,' his brother Bashir says. 'Standing there like that...'

Maleek nods, swallowing his fear. He must be brave. He must show courage, for his son, for his family.

'I'll try,' he says.

'Good,' Damsa says, smiling at him standing there. 'Go on then.'

'I am.'

'You're not moving.'

'I'm praying.'

'Praying silently?' she asks, humour in her eyes.

Maleek shrugs and smiles back at her. 'I'll go then...' he sets off, nervous, scared and feeling every head snapping over to watch the Muslim man step from his patch of ground. He walks steadily, trying to show his hands, worrying they'll think he has a bomb or a weapon or something. That thought makes him lift his hands a bit more.

'What's he doing?' Damsa asks, rolling her eyes. 'He looks mad...'

'What's he fucking doing?' Tommy asks, his hard voice rolling out as Maleek passes by the big circus tent, nodding and smiling at people while showing them his empty hands. 'Jihadi time is it? You try it in here mate and see what fucking happens...yeah, grinning at me like some wanker...'

Maleek nods and grins. His heart racing. Dread inside at moving even just a short distance from his family and he heads for the middle ground, for the work going on that all stops with people ceasing what they are doing to watch him go by.

This is not nice. Not nice at all. Everyone hates him. Everyone hates his family. He should go back. They should leave the fort. But no, he must try, and he heads for the big stack of wood, stopping beside Simar standing with his hands on his hips, tutting and huffing.

'Half of this is no good,' Simar says, not paying attention to whoever is next to him.

'Half of that wood is no good for construction.' Maleek says in his own fast and flowing language.

'It's taking me too long to sort it,' Simar mutters, scratching at his beard. Not hearing and still not looking.

Maleek stares at the pile of stacked wood then turns to stare at the beginnings of the frame being constructed and nearly every person in sight watching him. *'A frame of this size needs strong wood,'* he says, finally making Simar turn to look at him. The younger Sikh man hardly showing reaction to the Muslim standing next to him.

'Sorry mate, what did you say like?' Simar asks.

'Most of this wood is not building timber...' Maleek says, earnest and sincere as he points at the pile.

Simar shrugs, not understanding a word.

Maleek purses his lips, frowns, scratches his beard and tugs a length of wood out and turns to show Simar. *'This is not building wood,'* he says and casts it aside to select another piece. *'This is splintered,'* he says, running a finger over the crack and casting it with the other piece. *'This is too short...this is brittle, it snaps too easy...this had termites or insects. Ah but this, this is good wood. Strong! Good.'*

'That's a nice bit that is,' Simar says, watching Maleek pull out a nice length of timber. 'Good wood that.'

'This is good wood,' Maleek says.

Simar goes closer, tapping the timber. 'GOOD WOOD,' he points to the rotten stuff. 'BAD WOOD.'

'Good wood,' Maleek says in a heavy accent, putting the good timber down before choosing another piece. 'Good wood,' he adds it to the first one then pulls out a rotten strip and shows it to Simar.

'Bad wood,' Simar says.

'Bad wood,' Maleek says, casting it over with the other crap stuff. 'Good wood, bad wood,' he adds, pointing at the two piles then at the big stack then at himself. 'Good wood. Bad wood...'

'Yes!' Simar says, grinning widely. 'Good wood...bad wood...Ah mate, that's brill that is. You sort the wood. Good wood and bad wood...ah that's great. I'm Simar...Simar, mate...me...SIMAR...'

'Maleek,' Maleek says, smiling as Simar takes his hand to shake.

'Maleek?' Simar asks, shaking his hand. 'Great stuff. Bang on that is...'

'*I have no idea what you are saying,*' Maleek tells him.

'Yeah sorry, no idea what you're saying now,' Simar says.

'What's going on?' John asks, walking over. 'Why's everyone stopped working? Come on...back to it,' he shouts, ending the show as the other workers shrug and carry on working.

'Alright, John,' Simar says. 'Maleek here is going to sort the good wood and the bad wood...'

'Good wood,' Maleek says, grinning at John.

'Great. Get on with it then. I want this frame done for when Lilly gets back tonight.'

'Eh? The whole thing?' Simar asks.

'Yep! The whole thing.'

'Bashir! Come and help,' Maleek calls, waving his brother over.

'Go,' Damsa urges in their patch of ground as Bashir rushes out.

'There goes another one,' Tommy calls as Bashir grins

and nods as he rushes by. 'Don't let 'em near any explosive for fuck's sake...'

'I'm telling you, Blondie,' Mary says as they hit the outskirts of Southampton. 'You let a bitch like that doctor Lisa carry on and she'll fester and make it worse...we don't put up with that shit in the camp. It's not healthy...'

'What should I do? Order her not to say anything and thereby prove her point with a totalitarian response?'

'Bloody hell. That's a big word. Can you spell that?'

'Yes,' she smiles, laughing at Mary. 'I can spell it.'

'You just tell her quietly to stop gobbing off or you'll punch her in the face...which she'll believe as you're already running about the place punching people in the face.'

'I thought that woman was dead.'

'Which is even worse...and anyway, I saw the cat woman's black eye. I'm not speaking out of turn but that wasn't a good punch. She was sitting down, you were above her, she should have been knocked out. I'll show you later...'

'Great. I shall look forward to it...' Lilly says primly, offering a quick smile with a second's worth of eye-contact held again.

'Mary, we're only a few minutes out. Pull over and let me go first,' Peter says.

'Go first? Why the bloody hell should he go first?'

'Slow down and let him go first,' Lilly says, waving her over while pulling the radio away from Mary. *'Peter, It's Lilly. We're moving over now...'*

'What the hell?' Mary asks.

'Pick your fights,' Lilly tells her. 'Peter's a good man and you arguing over every single thing won't help...'

Mary glares. Lilly lifts her eyebrows. An immovable object meeting an unstoppable force. Humour in Lilly's eyes that projects out and makes Mary grin. 'Fine,' she says, slowing down to let Peter go by. 'Happy now, Blondie?'

'Thank you,' Lilly says, turning away to look at the world about them. Mary stares at her for a second. At her golden skin and blonde hair pulled back. There's an ageless quality about Lilly. An energy inside of her that defies anyone to define her by age alone. Pretty too and Mary swallows, clearing her throat as she looks away and blasts air through her cheeks. 'Hot isn't it...'

'It is,' Lilly says, glancing across to see a flush in Mary's cheeks. 'Do you want some water?'

They take the motorway into the city from the west and the surrounding view soon gives away from rural to urban and then on to inner city with tower blocks, shops, stores and houses lining the route. Smoke billowing within the city. Fires underway. Debris everywhere. Cars and vehicles crashed and dumped. Bodies too. Lots of them. Like a carpet in some places. The storms and flood waters having scooped them to dump in troughs and dips.

Lilly hardens her mood, bringing her assault rifle up to check through, popping the magazine out then slotting it back in before yanking the bolt back, making it ready.

'We'll take the slip road ahead then over the roundabout on the third exit...it's signposted to the docks but just in case they've been taken down...' Peter's voice coming in. His tone hard now. This isn't play. This is work.

'Understood,' Lilly transmits back as Mary glides the van off the motorway and along the slip road to a large roundabout. A barricade of sorts across the first exit road.

Lorries and van jammed in end on end with coils of razor wire spooled through it all. A big gap torn in the middle. Bodies seen inside as they pass. They pass another exit road leading into the city. Corpses everywhere. Everything seemingly dark and sinister.

They take the third exit, driving fast down a straight road towards the docks. A smell of burning in the air. Unpleasant and strong.

'That's from the refinery,' Mary says. 'The smell I mean...we're right by the River Test. The refinery is just down a bit and on the other side. Or it was I should say...'

'Is that Fawley?' Lilly asks.

'Aye.'

'Howie blew it up,' she says. 'Nick told me...'

'Your Mr Howie did that? No way...we heard it from like thirty miles away. Felt the ground tremble we did...oh now, will you look at that,' she looks right as the road starts to climb up a bridge over wide sections of railway tracks. A view opening up of the docks spread out and the tens of thousands of containers stacked in all directions. A vast car park to the right side filled with brand-new cars shipped in that will simply remain where they are until they turn to rust.

'There,' Mary says, pointing off towards the east. Lilly turns her head, trying to see what she's looking at. 'The truck park...see it?' Mary asks.

Lilly blinks then spots it. The same containers as stacked up everywhere else, but these ones already loaded on the backs of trucks. Loads of them too. Easily enough for her wall, and if not then it's a very good start, all they have to do is get them back to the fort.

Then she spots the blood. Wet, red and glistening on the metal railings at the side of the road. She leans forward, looking across Mary to see the same thing on the other side. Blood smears along the railings. Fresh too. A different smell in the air now mixing with the oil and smoke. The stench of unwashed bodies and faeces. The same stench she scented in the battle.

'Trouble ahead... Peter's voice in the radio. Mary's face focussing hard as the small fleet of vehicles starts to slow.

'Seen that?' Mary asks, pointing to the other side of the road as they pass an infected woman crawling along, her legs mangled and crushed, her face wild with frenzied hunger.

'Go out wide,' Lilly urges.

'This isn't good,' Peter says from ahead. *'We might be needing to rethink...'*

'I can't see,' Lilly says, leaning over as Mary starts steering out, opening the view beyond Peter's van to a crowd of infected charging ahead down the road. Running fast. Lots of them too. Stretching the width of the wide road in dense lines all going forward. The snarls and screeches heard through the open windows of the van.

'Stop here,' Peter orders. *'We'll turn around and find somewhere else...'*

'Is there anywhere else?' Lilly asks Mary. Her eyes scanning the infected, trying to see what they're chasing.

'Up the coast maybe. Not close though...' Mary says.

'What are they chasing? *Peter, it's Lilly...can you see what they're chasing?'*

'Not from here,' Peter replies, his lips pursed. He felt the same rush as Lilly at seeing the lorry park filled and ready. But there's too many infected. The risk is too high. *'We'll turn around...'*

'You seeing that, Peter?' Willie asks, shooting his arm out ahead. 'The fence...see it?'

'The fence,' Mary says quickly in the next van back from Peter. 'Down the road...people running...they're inside that fence...'

Lilly lifts up, trying to see then spots the figures ahead of the horde, instantly recognising them as people from the scared way they run into a compound and start dragging the gates closed. Big and high with sharp metal tops and coiled with razor wire. More people seen beyond them running from a building.

'Peter,' Willie says, glancing from the infected to Peter with a deeply worried look.

'Too many,' Peter says, shaking his head. 'There's too many...'

'Jesus,' Mary says. 'Will the gates hold them back?'

'Not a chance,' Lilly says. 'They'll body pile and go over in seconds...'

'Are you joking now? Do they do that?' Mary asks, snapping her head over as Lilly drops out of the van and starts running. 'BLONDIE! YOU DAFT BITCH...'

'We can't just leave them, Peter,' Willie says, his face consumed with angst. 'They'll be over that fence in seconds...what the bloody hell? Is that Miss Lilly?'

'Where?' Peter asks, turning to see Lilly running past his van. 'LILLY! GET BACK...Ah shit, she's fecking mad. Out with you...' he shouts, spilling from his van to charge after her. 'LILLY!'

Lilly runs hard, seeing the infected will hit the fence any second. Seeing the people still trying to get the gates closed. Seeing they will die within minutes. 'HEY...HEY!' she shouts out, trying to make the infected see her but the noise is too high, the distance too far so she points her rifle to the sky and plucks the trigger, the sharp crack sounding over all else.

'BLONDIE!' Mary yells, running after her with her Lee Enfield rifle in her hands. Peter and the rest all spilling from their vans.

Lilly fires again. Screaming out as the last few stragglers in the horde turn to look. A glance back. Eyes red. Mouths open. A message spreading and more turn.

'SEE ME,' Lilly roars, coming to a stop to bring her rifle up. 'See me...' she says the words again and starts firing, sending shots into legs and bodies, blowing them back and making them spin and drop.

'Ye bloody crazy,' Mary yells, reaching her side to aim and fire. Her rifle booming louder. The shots bigger and taking the infected off their feet.

The rest of the horde turn with a wild screech and start charging back towards Mary and Lilly. A solid wall of things that were once people moving fast with pure violence etched on their faces.

'Do you know what Howie will do to me if you get hurt,' Peter yells, reaching Lilly's side as he lifts his rifle.

'Howie isn't here,' Lilly shouts, changing magazine as the line forms. Nearly thirty men firing all manner of guns and the air fills with noise and heat. With booms and cracks. Lilly slings her rifle and pulls a grenade from her pocket. Her face hard. The woman that took the fort back. The same woman that rolled the grenades into the room. She pulls the pin and lobs it overhead, sending it high and long so it drops deep and rolls before exploding with a deep satisfying bang sending a spray of blood and gore flying up.

Still the horde run. Still they charge and still the line fires. Changing magazines quickly. Pouring bullets into bodies but the horde close the distance fast. Heedless to pain. Heedless to anything.

'Come on,' Lilly fires into them. Mary the same. Her ten

shot magazine running out faster. The gap closing. The darkness coming but Lilly has been here before. She's seen this. She's tasted it. Peter too. Willie, Elvis, Patrick and Tyson. They were all there on the shore road that day. Mary wasn't there. Mary hasn't seen this, and she glances to Lilly, seeing the change in her. Fear inside her gut. Fear at what's coming and then it's too late to run, too late to re-load and as Lilly slings her weapons and draws her knife, so Peter and the others that did it before do the same and down they go, lowering into stance, readying for the impact. Mary does it too. Scared. Terrified and with adrenalin flooding inside her. 'SEE ME...' Lilly screams the words, the veins in her neck and head pushing out and she can't wait. She can't hold back. 'INTO THEM...'

They charge. The two lines coming together. A whump as they hit. A deep impact of bodies into bodies and the blades go in. Deep and stabbing. Peter headbutting one down before stamping on the face. Willie punching out hard and fast, his knife puckering flesh with each blow. Elvis beside him. Mary with bunched fists, smashing them down and away. Lilly leaping high into a big male, wrapping her legs about his waist as she stabs into his eye and steps off when he falls, going in again to open a stomach. Blood everywhere. Gore and heat. Mary stabbing and stabbing. Men grunting. Shouts and cries. Pistols drawn to fire close range. The glory of battle upon them and they get bit and scratched with blood and fluids going into wounds and mouths, but they do not turn and so they fight on. Fast. Brutal. Vicious and all of them fighting to stay with Lilly. For her energy. For her will power to do this now.

Then the gaps start to show. The horde not so thick now. 'INTO THEM...' Lilly shouts out, urging them on as the ground becomes thick with bodies and then it's done with Lilly kicking into the legs of the last one, taking it down before grabbing the hair and sticking her knife into the throat and pushing the body away. Her chest heaving. Her face so alive. Blood on her arms and down her front. Thick spatters across her face and she turns to grin at the men and right there, Mary understands why her Uncle Peter said they should go and live outside a fort run by a posh woman called Lilly.

'Ye crazy bloody girl!' Peter says, rushing in to hug Lilly. They all do. Closing in with shouts and yells, patting each other on the back and clustering about Lilly. The energy still flowing.

'What did I tell you,' Willie shouts out at the others, his head held high as he stands proudly next to Lilly. 'Eh? What did we say? We said the wee girl fights. We said that... now you've bloody seen it...'

Lilly grins. Her chest still rising and falling. Sweat pouring down. Men all around her and she looks over to Mary staring at her. Blue eyes meeting green. A smile between them.

'And Mary!' Willie shouts at his sister. 'Damn you're a pain in the arse but you can bloody fight...'

'Finally, ye ginger prick...' Mary fires back. 'I can shoot better and I can bloody punch harder...don't you all groan at me now ye sexist twats...'

CHAPTER FOURTEEN

Day Twenty Three

'Hi! I'm Pammie...follow me ...Yeah and like, so those kids were awful. They had machine guns and then me and Lilly killed them all... This is the infirmary and Lisa who is like our top doctor...'

'Hi, welcome to North Korea,' Lisa says. 'Be ready to be worked to death, or starved if you don't, or left to burn in the sun. But hey, go Lilly! Seriously, don't say a word against her or Lenski...now fuck off, you all look fine.'

Out of the infirmary and across to the food rooms. 'THIS. IS. A. NEW. GROUP...'

'I speak English,' Sunnie says. 'I. SPEAK. ENGLISH...'

'This is your patch,' Pamela says, coming to a stop. 'And apparently the Muslims like totally started the whole zombie thing so don't touch them. Bye!'

'What did you get for me?' Tommy asks, plucking

bottles and packets out of her underwear while Pamela tries leaning forward to kiss him. 'Get a toothbrush, your breath stinks, go on now. Off you go. Good girl...'

'Hi, I'm Pammie...so yeah, total orgies and like everyone was fucking until we killed them all with grenades...'

'I'm Doctor Lisa Franklin. Welcome to Lilly's concentration camp. Work or die but don't speak out. You look fine. Fuck off.'

'Don't,' Sunnie says firmly, pointing at Pamela. 'I speak English...'

'NEW. PEOPLE,' Pamela shouts slowly.

'Unbelievable,' Sunnie mutters, sorting out the food while Pamela fills her underwear.

'Oh you look so wretched,' Colin says a few minutes later. 'Let's get you all settled eh? Anyway, this is my notice board...I'm just putting a list of the section heads on it...'

'This is your section...you might get a tent later. Lenski is sorting them out I think, but then you're not Muslims and they started the infection and killed everyone, but they get the nice tents. Bye!'

'Good girl!' Tommy says, plucking a bottle of gin from her knickers while weaving side to side to avoid her puckered mouth. 'Go on now, get back at it...and do me a favour, bring the next lot to me before you take 'em to the food rooms. Good girl...we'll have a cuddle later eh?'

'Hi, I'm Pammic. We kill children with grenades but not the Muslims because they started it...this is Lisa.'

'Welcome to hell. Lilly will make you work until you are dead. Go away.'

'And this is Tommy...' Pamela says, showing them to the big tent and grinning Tommy waiting for them.

'Watcha,' he says, beaming a smile. 'I'm Tommy. It's a

fucking joke here...don't mind my language. I'm a bit rough and ready and they don't like that about me. Right thorn in the side. Speaking out. Standing up for our rights. Can't even make a joke...now, before they take all of your stuff away, anyone got anything they want to trade?'

'They take our stuff away?' a man asks, the head of the ten-strong new group of now very alarmed people.

'Bloody right they do. And you'll probably get a kicking if you say anything. Woman the other day, she saw her husband hang himself and she got a kicking for crying. Saw it with my own eyes...creaming the best for themselves ain't they...now, what you got? Any smokes? Booze? I got loads of choccy bars...Tommy's shop is open for business!'

A short while later and Pamela presents the new group to Sunnie and once more slips inside as though to seek shade.

'Hi, are you all okay?' Sunnie asks, noticing the group seem very sullen. Mind you, everyone coming into the fort is in shock in one way or another. 'Bless, you look so tired. I won't keep you long...what we ask is for everyone to give their food over and then we cook it all centrally and make sure we've got enough to feed everyone. Is that alright?' she asks, full of genuine empathy.

'Do we have to give our food over?' the man in charge of the group asks, glancing at his wife and back to the others.

'Why wouldn't you, love?' Sunnie asks. 'My family did and everyone else is...'

'But do we have to?' his wife asks, sharing glances with her friends.

'We've so many people to feed, if we store and cook it all together then we make sure everyone gets fed...'

'And what if we don't?' the woman asks.

'Don't what?' Sunnie asks.

'Don't give our food over. What then? They said you starve people and make them work until they're dead...'

'Eh? You what now?'

'I'm not having that. I'm really not. I've got kids here... we'll keep our food thank you. You're not starving my kids...'

'But...'

'No. We heard this was a safe place,' the woman says. 'Someone said the Muslims started this and you've got loads of them everywhere...'

'We've got one family love,' Sunnie replies.

'Enough of them though,' someone else says. 'All over there in their turbans...'

'They're Sikh my love, not Muslims...I'm Sikh...they're my family.'

'No. Sorry. We're not giving our food up. We just want some space please and we'll take care of ourselves...' the woman says, moving her group away while casting looks at Sunnie.

'What on earth was that about?' Sunnie asks as Pamela walks from the back rooms.

'Sorry what?' Pamela asks her.

'Them. Saying we work people to death and not giving their food over...is someone saying the Muslims started this?'

'Yeah sorry,' Pamela says, offering a confused half-smile, 'your accent is so strong.' She walks off, leading the group away into an atmosphere thickening by the minute as Sunnie shakes her head, not quite grasping what just happened as she looks past Pamela to Tommy standing outside his big tent with a nasty smirk on his face.

'Ain't so fucking cocky now is she,' he mutters.

'Who ain't?' Karl asks.

'That fucking bitch,' he says, nodding towards Sunnie. 'Thinking they can take over in here...wankers...'

'Hi, are you Tommy?' a man asks, quiet and withdrawn, his head lowered, his whole manner nervous and scared. Thin from not eating and he glances back to a young woman sitting under a shelter a few rows over.

'Depends on who's asking,' Tommy demands as the young man wilts back from his aggressive manner.

'Sorry, I'm Josh... someone said you might have some ciggies...we er...I mean...' he falters, pointing back to the woman. 'We ain't had a smoke for a couple of days...'

'Ah gotcha,' Tommy says, easing his aggression back. 'Best come in then...' he slips inside, motioning for the young man to follow him through to Tommy's section and a mound of goods that looks like an illegal tuck-shop in a prison or a boarding school. Packets of cigarettes and rolling tobacco. Cans of deodorant, chocolate bars, snack food, perfumes, cans of beer and bottles of booze. 'What you after then?' Tommy asks him.

'Just a pack of ciggies but...' Josh pauses, swallowing nervously. 'I don't have any money...'

'Money,' Tommy laughs. 'Money don't mean anything now does it. Fucking money he says. Do me a favour...what else you got?'

'Er...we've got phones and...'

'What am I going to do with phones?'

Josh falters again, his eyes glancing constantly to the cigarettes. Desperation in his eyes. His whole life ripped apart, his girlfriend crying constantly. A gnawing inside to at least have a smoke. To have something to do with his hands.

'Can't just give stuff away can I,' Tommy says. 'I worked hard to get all that...'

Josh nods again, witless, scared and not knowing what to say.

'You must have something,' Tommy says, seeing exactly what he wants. He sighs heavily, shaking his head. 'Tell you what I'll do, give me that chain round your neck and I'll slip you a couple of packs eh?'

'My chain,' Josh says, fingering his thin gold necklace. 'My mother got it for my twenty-first birthday...'

'Alright alright, fuck me...only suggesting. Jesus mate. Fine. You ain't got anything then you ain't got anything... come back when you do...'

Josh swallows, wretched and broken. He needs to smoke. Cigarettes will fix this. They'll help. 'Okay,' he whispers, finding the clasp as Tommy picks two packets of cigarettes up. 'Mum paid like two hundred quid for it...'

'Things ain't valued the same now mate,' Tommy says, clocking the wretched look on the guy's face. 'Bleeding hell, okay, fine. I'll stick another pack in for you. Just don't tell everyone Tommy is a softy now, they'll all be wanting special treatment...'

'It's worth more than three packs,' Josh says.

'Not to me it ain't,' Tommy says, hardening his manner to glare at the lad. 'You wasting my fucking time or what? Karl? Matty? You lads there?'

'Yeah what's up?' Karl asks, walking in with his big gut bulging out but looking large and frightening in the small space.

'You alright?' Mathew asks, looking from Tommy to the lad now looking even more terrified.

'S'fine,' Josh says, swapping the chain for the three packets.

'Lovely!' Tommy beams. 'Nice doing business with you,

come back when you need something. We can always work something out eh?'

'Did you want something?' Karl asks when the young man slips out.

'Nah, you did fine,' Tommy says, chucking them both a chocolate bar. 'Just make sure you come when I call…helps make sure nobody takes the piss. Know what I mean?'

'Hey, is Tommy in there?' he hears someone else ask outside. Another woman shown in. Another trade made and more after that.

Plans and schemes form in Tommy's mind. A buzz inside. A rush of energy. He likes hearing people ask for him. *Is Tommy there? Where's Tommy? We need Tommy.*

He likes it a lot, and as his pile of goods grows so his sense of popularity does too. He starts to imagine himself building an empire from scratch and having minions running around after him while he sits like a spider in a web, luring the meek and scared to give him what they have, because it should be him running this fort.

Maybe he should open a pub or something next? That would be a good step. He's got loads of cans now, and a few bottles too. Few bottles of wine, some spirits. He pictures himself holding court over everyone, cracking jokes and making them all laugh and being popular. Yes. That's what it is. That's the thing he wants now. He wants people to need and respect him. He never had that before. He was jobless and lazy, people looked down on him.

Even when he went on the anti-immigration rallies and anti-austerity marches and anti-anything parades he was put at the back out of the way.

Now look who is in charge. Eh? That's right. Tommy's here. This is a new world with new rules.

What he needs to do is build support and get enough

people on side and eventually make them upset the balance of power. Then he can sweep in and calm it all down and grab power while he's there.

Yeah. That'll work. Get some big drama going on. Stir it all up and save the day.

CHAPTER FIFTEEN

D ay Twenty three

'W e're from a fort up the coast,' Lilly says,
standing between Peter and Mary at the head
of her group of thirty or so armed and very
tough looking men. 'We're here for containers to build
a wall...

A sea of bodies behind them stretching up the road.
The gates to the compound now open and she looks at the
terrified people. Bedraggled and thin. Cheek bones showing. Hair lank and greasy. Twenty three days of barely
surviving in a commercial port truck diner. 'We have
doctors, food and security,' she adds as they all look to each
other. 'We can take you in if you're ready to go now, but you
must go now...'

'Actually,' Mary says, cutting in. 'Can any of you drive
lorries now?'

The man in front of his group stands silent and

stunned. Looking past the armed group to the bodies. The sight of it all. The way they did it. So fast. So violent. He blinks at Mary and nods. 'Most of us can,' he says weakly.

'Great. Get ready then, we're going now...' Lilly says.

'What, right now?' the man asks, caught out by the speed of events.

'Aye,' Peter calls. 'We're going now. I'll not keep us at risk in the open longer than needed...and that gunfire could be drawing them from all over the city. NOW. GO... Willie, Elvis...get in there and get 'em moving...and find a mobile crane.'

A few minutes of chaos. Into the truck park. Into the offices for the port workers to find the keys to the trucks and they pour out, running across the super-hot tarmac in the super-hot air to climb into the cabins of super-hot trucks. The air filling with noise and black smoke from heavy diesel engines firing up after more than three weeks of being idle. The people from the diner feeling terrified and rushed, urged on, shouted at to get moving. Truck drivers with shaky hands and wild eyes taking their families into their cabins while sensing this is a safer option than staying here.

'We ready?' Lilly shouts, noise everywhere. Engines rumbling. The air thick and choking. A thumbs up from Peter. From Willie and Elvis. More from the other lads and she turns to see Mary waving from a truck.

'COME ON, BLONDIE...'

She runs over, clambering up the passenger side and into the cabin. A great sense of urgency. To get going now because this is not a safe place at all.

Peter takes the lead, his truck jolting and bouncing, air brakes sounding, thick smoke spewing. Carnage again. Everyone pulling out at the same time with trucks clipping each other, shunting walls, smacking into the edges of the truck park office building. Shouts and yells but it doesn't have to be pretty. It just has to be done.

Onto the exit road, bouncing over the roundabout then bouncing over the bodies. Skulls popping. Ribcages bursting. Bones snapping and the speed builds, shaky, jolty, messy but functional.

'YES!' Mary calls out, grinding gears while jolting and bucking the truck. The wheel looking so huge in her hands. 'We bloody did it...' she shouts, grinning at Lilly.

'We did,' Lilly says, the thrum of adrenalin still spiking inside. A fleet of trucks behind them.

'You're a bloody legend, Blondie,' Mary shouts, leaning over to rub Lilly's shoulder in the excitement. 'Eh? Right up there we were. Two ladies. Fighting and shooting and talking to survivors and getting the trucks all going. Damn! Now I see why Peter bloody loves you so much. I can understand it now I can. Willie too, and Elvis and Tyson and Patrick. All of 'em going on about Miss Lilly this and Miss Lilly that. Haha! If I were a bloke I'd have the total hots for you too.'

Lilly smiles, somewhat sheepish, somewhat flushed, somewhat still feeling the rush of the fight and she laughs when Mary grabs her hand and lifts it up, whooping and calling out in victory.

W illie reaches the shore road first. Driving the mobile crane pilfered from the docks with Peter's truck behind him and the rest stretched out in a long convoy all slowing down with much jolting and shuddering but still hearing the cheers coming over the radio.

The trucks come to a stop. Crunches and bangs sounding out before the doors open and they start dropping out into the heat and chaos of the bay.

'How many did you get?' Kyle asks.

'No idea,' Lilly calls back. 'Probably close to forty I'd say...everything okay here?'

'Fine,' Norman replies. 'Lots of new arrivals. Have you looked inside the containers?'

'We just grabbed them and got back,' Peter replies.

'Could be stuff inside we can use...' Norman says.

'Okay,' Lilly says. 'Norman, can you get up and manage the contents from the containers...I think you probably know more than anyone right now what we need in the fort. Sam, Pea, can you two take over on the beach processing new arrivals and getting the wood over...everyone else just jump in where you can...' she pauses, drawing air. 'Peter, you make a start on the wall and I'm going back out...hold on. Let me speak...' she pulls a map-book from her pocket, flicking through the pages. 'I found this in the truck...there's an advert for a retail park a few miles from here. It's got outdoor stores...which will have tents...'

'You want to do a run on it?' Peter asks. 'I'll get some lads with you...'

'I need you all here managing this...I'll go with Mary.'

'Lilly,' Sam starts to say, as everyone speaks out in alarm at the idea.

'No, listen...two of us in a van. In and out. Quiet and fast...'

'Don't all look at me like that,' Mary says. 'This is the first she's mentioned it...'

'Ach, you might be right,' Kyle says. 'A light rapid unit going in fast and quiet is probably the best way...will you let me come with you?'

'We don't know what your immunity is,' she says. 'And I'd rather the fort had you here in case something does happen.'

'If you're thinking like that then why risk it?' he asks.

'Because we're not going to just survive and scrape by. We're going to live and there's no rewards without risk... and this risk is negated by what I have learnt from this experience of going out with Peter. I can move fast. So can Mary. I've weighed it all up and it's the right thing to do.'

'Ach, you are bloody related to Henry. I bet on it. I don't know how...and if not then you bloody should be. Right. Okay, good luck to you and the slightest noise then get the hell out...'

'Mary, swap with me,' Joan says, offering her assault rifle over.

'I've got a weapon,' Mary says, lifting her Lee Enfield.

'That is a bolt-action rifle with a ten-round magazine. This is an automatic assault rifle with a thirty-round magazine, and I want both of you back in one piece...besides,' she says, offering a quick smile. 'I haven't fired a Lee Enfield in years.'

'Ah, I'll have to ask Tyson, Joanie. It was his you see, or our grandfather's anyway and he gave it to Tyson. I was gonna give it back after I'd pissed him off for a bit...'

'It's fine,' Tyson calls over. 'Mary, take an assault rifle and don't fuck about with Miss Lilly...are ye sure we can't come? I think you might need some men to fight for you...'

'YOU SEXIST PRICK!' she shouts, her face flooding with instant anger as several men snigger.

'He's winding you up,' Peter says. 'Don't bloody bite all the time.'

Fast and frantic. Everyone rushing to work. Orders

being shouted. Engines starting. The mobile crane firing back up. Fumes and heat, sweat and work.

'Bobby, we need a big fast van,' Mary calls, jogging into the blackened former estate.

'Got a Mercedes or a Transit,' Bobby shouts back.

'Transit,' Mary shouts. 'Can't beat a transit,' she tells Lilly.

'I shall keep that in mind.'

'Mind you, Mercedes vans are good too. Ach, damn. Now you've got me thinking. Bobby? Which one would you use?'

'Transit, Mary. There's no choice really.'

'Aye, he's right. You're right, Bobby. Transit it is.'

A shiny new, only partially dented and scuffed Ford Transit is promptly delivered from Bobby's growing fleet of vehicles and once more they load up into the cabin and head back out on the estate road.

'I just realised I didn't ask if you minded doing this,' Lilly says.

'Are you bloody joking? I hate your company,' Mary says. 'But why us? Why not send Willie and Elvis? Or Tyson and Patrick?'

'For the reasons I said,' Lilly says.

'Is that right?' Mary asks, giving her a sideways glance. 'Not for my amazing company then?'

'God no,' Lilly replies, rolling her eyes. A smile between them, an unspoken energy flowing. A silence of a few seconds. Cheeks flushing a little as both look out the windows to the world going by.

'It's hot isn't it,' Mary remarks, blasting air through her cheeks.

'It is,' Lilly says, looking away with a smile still touching her lips.

'I s too hot,' Lenski mutters, wiping a hand across her forehead with the realisation she just spoke to herself in English rather than Polish. Then she realises she is doing it all the time now, and is even thinking in English sometimes too, but in an organic way. Like when she thinks of a conversation with Lilly or Pea. She'll remember it in English, and the other thoughts and notions that stem from that interaction will then also be in English.

She stares down at the three sheets in front of her on the table in the main office while clicking the lid of the pen on and off, a habit now formed. A blur of motion from the side. Something surging into view that lands on the table with a soft thud and immediately squats down on the sheets of paper to purr and demand attention. Lenski smiles, fussing the cat as another one strolls in through the main door and heads towards the back with the absolute surety that the whole of this fort is just for him.

A few minutes later and she slides a few of the sheets out from under the protesting cat and steps out into a gut punch of heat and heads to the food rooms and just that small motion makes her sweat and breathe harder. The heat is beyond anything she has ever experienced. She reaches the food rooms, stepping gratefully into the shade to see Agatha and Sunnie in muted conversation.

'I have list,' Lenski says, handing one of the sheets over. 'Is list of names for the people to live in these room, yes? Tell them to empty tents so I use them again...' she pauses, detecting the atmosphere between the two women. 'What wrong?'

'It's probably nothing,' Sunnie says, taking the sheet.

'Few new people getting funny with us,' Agatha says.

'Saying they been told they'll get hurt if they don't give us their food, and some are refusing to hand anything over...'

'Where this come from?' Lenski asks.

'No idea,' Sunnie says.

'And I'm sure we've had a bit of stock going missing,' Agatha adds. 'From the back rooms. Just a few gaps appearing on the shelves...maybe I'm wrong. It's too hot to bloody think...'

'Okay. I look into this,' Lenski says. 'You tell me if hear other things.' She walks on, aiming for Colin's rooms. 'Colin?'

'Colin reporting for duty,' Colin says, red-faced as ever as he rushes over to offer a mock salute. 'Ready to receive orders...'

Lenski smiles. She likes Colin. His gentle humour. His eagerness to please. 'I have list...people to sleep in your rooms.'

'Roger that. Wilco. Understood loud and clear,' he says, taking the sheet. 'Blooming good idea too, Lenski.'

'Is all okay?'

'Yeah, I think so,' he says with an affable nod. 'Hotter than anything and we're literally all sweating into puddle...'

Lenski nods, not really understanding about sweaty puddles. 'Is all good then? You hear anything bad?'

'Er, well there have been a few comments here and there now you mention it. A few new groups didn't want to share their stuff. I said they don't have to and it's not like a prison camp or anything. Then this one chap said he heard the woman that found her dead husband got a kicking. I said that never happened. Then Joanna, she works in my team, she heard some rumours from one of the new groups saying Muslims started the infection...'

'Who say these things?'

'No idea. It's all third hand silly rumours, but it's hot I guess and everyone is finding their place so there's always tittle tattle...anyway, have you seen my notice board?'

She listens to him for a minute then moves on, heading over to the central section and the bedlam of work underway.

'John, I have list...Pardip, for you too...'

'What's that, love?' Pardip asks.

'Your family, they take our old rooms. I move us into back of offices and John, you are with Kyle and Norman by the front gates...you have Muslim men working here now?' she asks, looking at Maleek, Bashir and another one sorting through the wood. 'They have trades? They builders?'

'No idea,' Pardip says. 'They don't speak English and we don't speak...er...whatever they speak. Where are they from?'

'Afghanistan,' Lenski says. 'They say to me when they come in. I never ask for skills though. I make mistake...I ask now...wait please...'

She rushes off, cursing herself for being too caught out at the sights of the robes and how different they look and not asking if they had skills.

She feels it then. A transition of mood. An instinct inside as it were, and it makes her slow and take in the immediate world about her. At the new groups of people hiding from the sun under sheets and shelters. Sullen faced, moody and quiet. But then everyone is like that when they come into the fort. The world is over, millions have died, and everyone has suffered and lost. But no, this feels a different sort of sullen.

She looks to the big ugly tent Tommy put up yesterday. She saw him doing it with his big fat belly hanging over his shorts, and in truth she simply didn't give a shit or have time to worry about what he was doing. Now she spots a young woman come out with the same sullen, cowed and distrustful look on her face as everyone else. Tommy comes out behind her, ogling the woman's backside as she opens a packet of cigarettes.

The sight makes Lenski glance about, seeing more people sucking on cigarettes and small clouds of smoke rising from under the shelters. A few cans of soda seen opened on the ground. A heavy looking woman eating a Mars bar. Another eating a packet of crisps. All of them quiet.

Another glance to Tommy, seeing him smirk as she passes. An arrogance in his manner. A cunning too. Something unkind and unpleasant.

'Is too hot for this,' Lenski mutters, ignoring him as she reaches the Muslim family patch. 'Damsa, I sorry. I make mistake. I not ask what skills you have when you come here...is my fault. Is so busy and hot...' Lenski says as Damsa rises to her feet and walks over. 'I say truth too and say you are first Muslim people in these clothes I speak to...'

Damsa offers a smile, grateful for the honesty while glancing beyond Lenski to the harsh glares and looks coming from everyone else. 'Maleek is working now,' she says, motioning the building site. 'Bashir and Tajj are with him...his brothers.'

'Yes. I see this...' Lenski says thoughtfully. 'Where you learn English?'

'My father was a translator for the American army in Kabul...Ameer, he is better...' she says, smiling at the serious expression on her son.

'Is good English,' Lenski says. 'I ask now, you have skills? Any of you?'

'My father's a carpenter,' Ameer says, blanching slightly

at Lenski face palming herself while sagging on the spot at the same time as muttering several very rude words in Polish.

'Are you okay?' Damsa asks.

'I not okay. I am idiot,' Lenski says. 'We are desperate for builders yes? Maleek is a carpenter. I not ask this...' she rolls her eyes, tutting at herself. 'I borrow Ameer please? He translate for his father...I bring him back, is safe yes?'

Damsa nods, looking again at the harsh glares coming from everyone else as Lenski sets off with Ameer.

'Lenski Benski!' a shout, a yell, Milly, Amna, Billy and Rajesh running fast through the tents and patches of ground, slamming into her legs. Subi not far behind them.

'I work now. Busy. Come, we go see John...this is Ameer. Ameer, these are other smelly children. All smell. All bad...'

'It's like seeing one of them adverts...' Tommy calls out with that smirk, adding a wink when Lenski looks at him. 'United colours of Benetton eh? All them different coloured faces. Nah, it's nice to see. Kids eh? Gotta love 'em...'

Lenski stares. Tommy smiles, and she walks on, leading the children over to the building site. 'John, Pardip. I say sorry. I make mistake. Maleek, he is carpenter...'

'I know he is!' Simar shouts from somewhere.

'How do you know?' Pardip shouts out, looking for his brother.

'Cos carpenters are all like Jedi warriors,' a grinning Simar says, popping up from the framework holding a mallet as an also grinning Maleek pops up next to him holding a set square. 'We're all connected on a deeper level than you lot...and that's not a religious thing either. We're as one...' he adds, waving the mallet between his own head and Maleek's. 'Anyway, I got this now, Lenski. Cheers for that.

Ameer, is that your name? Alright, I'm Simar. Tell your dad cheers for helping cos my stupid brothers and big John don't know the difference between a nail and a screw...and also, do your uncles know good wood from bad wood? And if they do, can they go over to the beach and only send us the good stuff...'

Lenski listens for a minute before staring back to Tommy at the epi-centre of the rot spreading through that area. A marked difference to everywhere else in the fort and Tommy's little section. Everywhere else is industrious, busy and buoyed on with a sense of hope, whereas that area is dark and sullen with Tommy right in the middle.

She looks around and spots Pamela leading a new group in from the gates and sighs heavily, feeling the sweat roll down over her forehead as the pen lids clicks in her hand and above her the blue sky stretches on, deep and endless.

CHAPTER SIXTEEN

D ay Twenty three

U nder that same deep blue sky lies a quiet road nestled between gorgeous meadows filled with wild flowers. A serene tranquillity brought on by the lack of cars on the nearby road or jet aircraft thundering overhead, and the air fills with birdsong and the buzz of insects. The calls of creatures and the sometimes faint rustle of leaves and branches moving against one another.

Another noise comes to be heard. A deep booming sound. Rhythmic, persistent, and growing closer with every passing second and those creatures grow still as the Ford Transit thunders along the road. The windows down. The music blaring. A woman with red hair driving and singing. A woman with blond hair in the passenger seat laughing.

Crazy by *Gnarls Barkley* thumping from the stereo. The addictive beat so deep, the voice so light and perfect. A CD found in the stereo by Mary poking buttons on the music system.

'*Ha ha ha bless your soul…you really think you're in control? I think you're crazy…*' Mary sings to Lilly, unashamed and filled with fun.

Lilly taps her foot, grinning along. Feeling the flow of new energy as her mind undertakes the change that Agatha detected sweeping through the fort.

The world is over, and anyone left alive now has suffered and lost. Everybody hurts, but they are alive and today is a beautiful day. They have life. They can see the sky and feel the warmth of the sun. Aye. That's what it is. A resistance to the feeling that they must be meek and cowed. A new voice. A new energy. This is life now, and without risk there is no reward, and so Lilly sings too. Giving voice to a song and Mary takes her turn to laugh. The two of them barrelling through the countryside bobbing heads, tapping feet and banging on the dashboard to make more noise, and when the song ends, so they play it again and keep going.

A short while later they coast into the edge of the car park and switch the engine off to sit quietly, staring ahead and to the sides, listening intently, scenting the air through the windows.

'Looks okay,' Mary says quietly. 'Can't see any movement…'

Lilly stares ahead to the retail park. A squared off horse-shoe shape of big fronted stores all bearing bright logos and huge windows filled with incredible offers. A few cars left in the car park. A body seen further down the road, but it looks old. The skin rotten and falling away. Bones showing.

'We going for it?' Mary asks.

Lilly nods. 'Go slow…but be ready to get us out if anything happens.'

'Right. Did you really need to say that?' Mary whispers, earning a smile in response.

The van creeps forward. The wheels crunching tiny chunks of grit and gravel as they cross the parking bays and move in towards the huge outdoor store in the middle of the row.

The van turns as they get closer, going wide to sweep the view and position the van facing out before Mary reverses it in. Bringing the back doors as close to the store front as possible. Then they stop and wait once more.

Mary turns the engine off and starts to get out, but stops from Lilly's hand resting on her arm, holding her still. 'Give it another minute,' Lilly whispers.

Ears strain as they listen to the ticks and gentle clunks coming from the engine. Birdsong close by. No other noises. No traffic. No hum of a city. No planes or anything. No wind even.

Mary realises Lilly's hand is still on her arm. She can feel it. She looks down at Lilly's slender fingers, tracking her eyes up along her wrist to her arm and up over her shoulder to Lilly facing ahead and she watches a bead of sweat roll slowly down her cheek as she sits perfectly poised. Perfectly still. Perfectly perfect. She swallows, turning away sharply. Blinking to herself and drawing air.

'I think it's okay,' she says, sliding out from under Lilly's hand to step out of the van into that searing, crushing heat. She gasps a little and half wishes they hadn't used the air-con in the van as it makes it feel so much worse now. A glance over to Lilly getting out with her rifle already up and raised. No sounds anywhere and it's almost eerie because of that silence. Thoughts in her mind. Weird thoughts that she has never felt before. Weird feelings too. She shakes her head, dismissing them from her mind. It's the heat and a result of the massive life-changes underway. That's all it is. Mary has only ever really known life within the camp, or within the circles of that life. Now there are new influences and new things so for sure, she's just a bit too excited about it all. That's all it is. She looks over to Lilly again and lifts her eyebrows at seeing Lilly already staring at her. A smile shared and they go back to taking in the world about them.

The windows to the stores all intact. Most of them clothes shops. Fashion outlets. A few jewellers, cosmetics. Things to make you look good, smell nice and glint under the nightclub lights. All now meaningless and rendered obsolete.

'There'll be some stuff in there we could use,' Mary whispers, nodding at a health food shop. 'The rest is a bit shit like...'

They head for the outdoors store and try the doors. All locked. The windows intact. 'Safety glass,' Mary says quietly. 'No point shooting it...we'll have to use the van... you want to keep watch and I'll ram the arse in...'

'Sounds interesting,' Lilly says with a smile, walking off as Mary blinks and thinks that sounded a bit flirty. Was it flirty? Lilly doesn't flirt. She's not the flirting type. What the hell is she thinking? They're both girls who like boys. Mary likes boys. Lilly is sleeping with Nick, who apparently is like a model or something. But still, it did sound a bit flirty.

Lilly moves off as Mary gets back into the van, turning to face out while holding her rifle ready and wondering if she just flirted a bit. Did she? It just came out. It wasn't flirting. It's just a lightening of the mood. It's hot too. Really hot. Mary's arm felt hot when she rested her hand on it. She frowns and shakes her head. She likes Nick. Nick is handsome and strong and they made love and it was amazing. But Nick also fucked off with Howie and left her. She blinks again, frowning harder. Howie is fighting back and that's important. Yeah but he couldn't just leave one behind to help?

Still. It doesn't matter. She's with Nick. Nick is amazing, and a man, and Lilly fancies him. Definitely.

She blasts air and turns to see Mary giving a thumbs up with a smile and grins back with all thoughts of Nick vanishing in a heartbeat and she watches as Mary starts the engine, eases forward, selects reverse then slams the van back into the window.

A hard bang. A smash and the van goes through the glass, tearing a hole through with an almighty noise. A crunch of the gears and she comes out, bringing the van clear before silencing the engine and popping out.

'How was that for a bit of arse ramming?' she asks, making Lilly snort a laugh. They head through the gap, pausing to let their eyes adjust.

'Bloody hell,' Mary says quietly. 'Doesn't it feel weird being in a shop now...like all clean and neat...'

'Apart from the huge hole in the window you mean,' Lilly says, turning to look back.

'Aye,' Mary says, turning at her side to stare at the same thing. 'Apart from that. Right, tents is it?' she asks, looking at Lilly.

'Aye,' Lilly says, rolling her eyes at using that phrase again.

'Tents are back there,' Mary says, pointing as she walks off. 'We should get boots too. And thick socks...and waterproof clothes...oh and sleeping bags and have you seen these headscarves?' she stops at the counter, fingering a display on a rotating stand. 'I like these, Blondie. Nice and stretchy. Keep the sweat out of our eyes. What do you think?'

'Try the red,' Lilly says, taking one from the display to hold near Mary's head. 'Matches your hair.'

'Yeah?' Mary asks, staring into her blue eyes.

'Definitely,' Lilly says, staring into her green eyes as that energy spikes a bit more. A bit higher. Rushing through them a bit faster. Making their hearts beat that bit harder as they both blush and laugh to hide the weird feelings. 'They're nice,' Lilly says, nodding at the display. Serious, studious and frowning as she tries to ignore her heart beating too hard and the blood rushing past her ears. Another silence. A little bit awkward. A little bit heavy.

'It's hot,' Mary says.

'It is.'

'Should we get the tents then?'

'Yes. Yes I think we should...'

'Good. Because this isn't awkward at all right now,' Mary says, winking at Lilly and making her snort as they turn away with Mary instantly regretting saying it and Lilly wanting to ask what she means. She doesn't ask. That would be weird, and so they get to work. Rushing back and forth side by side.

In and out with armfuls of tents and sleeping bags and boxes of boots. Anything that might be usable. Camping gas cylinders and stoves. Batteries. Waterproof clothing. Knives. Multi-tools. Fishing rods, reels and the sweat pours as the work. The heat sucking the air from their lungs.

'Oops, sorry, Blondie,' Mary says, stepping back into Lilly with an armful of clothes.

'My fault,' Lilly says, placing her hands on Mary's hips to guide round and past her. The touch fleeting but they both feel it and smile as they work. Joking and throwing socks at each other. Pausing when outside to listen, standing side by side, close enough to almost feel the heat coming from the other. Gentle brushes against one another become jokey nudges with Mary moving close behind Lilly to push her on, making them laugh as they go. The energy between them so natural and organic.

They work fast too. That relentless nature within Lilly not easing one jot, but Mary keeps pace and if anything, seems to relish it.

'I bloody love this!' she says, striding back in with Lilly. Both sweating and breathing hard. 'Ach, I mean like this beats camp work any day of the week. Not that I love being here with you. Not that...I mean that's cool too. Don't get me wrong now. Great...' she smiles, pulling a face that indicates she doesn't know what she's saying that makes Lilly burst out laughing. 'Are we having a swim later? We should have a swim...with Lenski! Not just...I mean...right well. We'd better keep going then. Busy or what. Do you need a drink? You look hot. Like, your face is red I mean and...wow, I'm soaked through I am...' she says, only too aware of the gabbling words falling from her mouth as she pulls her sodden top away from her body.

'Change it,' Lilly says, fanning her face as she walks to the counter to her water bottle. 'There's enough here...'

'Hey now, that's why you're in charge of everything. Being all smart like that,' Mary says, slipping her rifle off before grabbing the hem of her vest and pulling it up overhead to show her body glistening with sweat. 'Chuck us a pack of them wet-wipes on the counter there will you, Blondie...'

Lilly grabs a pack, glugging water as she turns to throw it over with a sudden nervousness stealing over her at the sight of Mary stripped down to her bra. The flare of her hips. The softness of her belly. The swell of her breasts. So very feminine in every way.

Mary feels her watching but doesn't know how to react. The energy shifting again. Charging and becoming tense, but not unpleasant, not unpleasant at all. She feigns not to notice and wipes her body, detecting in her peripheral vision when Lilly pulls her top off and steals a quick glance.

'Fuck,' she says without thinking, seeing the old faded bruises on Lilly's body. 'Is that what they did to you?'

'It's fine,' Lilly says, looking down at the darker patches on her ribs and stomach.

'I didn't see them last night,' Mary says. She moves closer and stretches her hand out to touch Lilly's ribs, but stops with a micro-second of hesitation before the contact comes. Her fingertips gently touching the bruise and so soft is that touch it brings goose-bumps over Lilly's flesh and a shiver running down her spine. 'Do they hurt?' Mary asks, her voice catching a little in her throat.

'It's fine,' Lilly says, studying Mary's features. 'I don't feel pain like I used to...'

'Why not?'

'It's possible I'm infected,' Lilly says, expecting Mary to pull her hand back sharply, but she stays still, listening and waiting for more. 'Reginald thinks we have a mutated strain of the virus...'

'Right,' Mary says quietly, knowing there should be a hundred questions forming as a result of that statement but right now not one of them comes to the fore of her mind.

'Freak, right?' Lilly says, offering a tight smile.

'God yes,' Mary says, wide-eyed and nodding emphatically in a way that makes Lilly laugh again. 'Do you feel any different?'

'I do, yes,' Lilly replies with raw honesty. 'I feel very different...but not from that.'

Another silence with eye contact held until the nerves

give out and they both smile, suddenly sheepish and shy. Turning away to wipe and dress and talk about how hot it is.

———

'Will you look at that now,' Mary says, easing the speed down as they drive along the shore road towards the bay and Lilly leans forward, hardly believing what she is seeing.

'That,' Mary says proudly. 'Is your bloody wall that is...'

It's only the start but already it makes such a visible difference. A solid line of shipping containers stretching from the sea across the land with a gap for the shore road to pass through.

They slow down as they approach to watch the crane hoist another container from a lorry trailer and drop it down for Norman and a few others to rush in and get the doors open, peering inside before waving their arms.

'*Nothing good,*' Norman's voice on the radio. '*Get it stacked in...*'

'*Right you are, Norman...mind out now...*' a male voice from whoever is driving the crane and the container goes back up into the air and swings out, only to be dropped down at the end of the row where a digger is poised and ready to shunt it into position. Men guiding it in. Men shouting out. Radio messages flying thick and fast and both Lilly and Mary hear as the digger slams into the container's end, ramming it flush alongside the next one along.

'Drop me off here,' Lilly says, looking at Mary. 'Can you take this van down to the beach and let Pea know it's full of tents...'

'Leave it with me, Blondie.'

She drops out into the heat, smiling at seeing Mary grinning inside and the van drives off, leaving Lilly to stare up at the eight and a half feet high container wall.

The infected will get over it with ease. They'll body-pile or just jump and grip the top ledge and climb over. But then the infected are not the only danger now. Other people are too, and this sends a signal.

Besides, they can easily stack another layer on the top and make it five metres high then cover it with razor wire.

'Lilly!' Kyle shouts when she walks in. 'Did you get to the retail park?'

'Aye,' she calls back over the noise, tutting at herself for saying it yet again. 'I mean yes we did. Tents, sleeping bags, camping stoves...loads of things. But this is incredible...'

'Mayhem too,' he yells back. Diesel engines roaring by them. Men shouting. The whir of the crane and the clang of metal on metal.

'Lilly, you okay?' Norman calls, coming over.

'Fine. Anything inside of them?'

'Fridges,' Kyle and Norman both say together as Peter walks over. Sweat pouring down his face. Sweat pouring down all of their faces.

'This heat,' Peter shouts, pointing skywards.

'Storm coming,' Kyle yells back.

'Got to be,' Norman says.

'Lilly, we've shoved a container in the sea,' Peter explains, pointing to the shore. 'It was shallow enough to just walk around the end...'

'Okay,' Lilly says, spotting the top of the container poking out the water. 'How many have we got?'

'Forty three,' Norman says. 'Each at twelve metres long...so just over five hundred metres which is about half the distance you wanted enclosed...'

'I've got some lads going back to the docks to bring more, we can't do as many as this morning...' Peter says.

'That's great. We can do another run tomorrow,' Lilly

says, looking past him to the trucks still holding containers parked all over the place. 'These trucks waiting...we can get them into position now...I mean where the wall will run. That way the crane only has to move along...and that hedge needs to come down. I'll get one of Bobby's team up here to rip it out...'

Mary finally reaches the beach after navigating the chocked road and bounces out while singing to Gnarls Barkley playing on the stereo again. People everywhere all packed into the tiny area and she rushes over to the marquee tent taken from her Uncle Jack and into the shade to see Pea, Sam and Joan having a quick brew made from a kettle connected to a small chugging generator. Ann and Anika tending to chairs filled with more people suffering the effects of heat-stroke or wrapping bandages on injuries.

'There she is,' Sam calls out. 'Must have heard the kettle boil...'

'Good timing or what,' Mary says, waving her hand as Sam moves to make another drink. 'I'll do it...we've got a van full of shiny new gear for the fort we have. Tents, sleeping bags...'

'Brilliant,' Pea says. 'Did it go okay?'

'Fine, all easy,' Mary says.

'Where's Lilly?' Joan asks.

'Up the road marvelling at her new wall, no doubt with a few dozen blokes hanging off her every word...'

'I bet they bloody are,' Sam says. 'I don't know how she does it...no, that's not true, I do know how she does it...'

'She gets on with it and gets the job done,' Joan says. 'No mess, no fuss. Lenski's the same and that's exactly what we need right now too...'

'She's an astonishing woman,' Sam says before sipping

at her tea. 'Or girl...' she frowns, thinking for a second. 'What do you call her?' she asks Joan.

'She's a girl to me, but then I'm old. Even you two are a lot younger than me.'

'We're not girls,' Pea says. 'We're definitely not girls...'

'We're ladies,' Sam says.

'Yeah we're definitely not ladies either,' Pea adds, earning a few smiles. 'But you're right. I keep forgetting how old Lilly is...I didn't know my arse from my elbow at sixteen.'

'You still don't,' Sam says, pointing at Pea's arse. 'Nice elbow though.'

'Idiot,' Pea tuts, rolling her eyes. 'How old are you, Mary?'

'I'm twenty one,' Mary says, stirring the coffee while listening closely.

'Twenty one!' Sam says. 'Oh my god, you're still a girl too then.'

'No,' Pea chides. 'Twenty one is a woman.'

'It's not,' Sam scoffs.

'Lilly can't buy a drink in a pub,' Pea says. 'But Mary can.'

'Er, it's the end of the world and like, there's no pubs,' Sam says.

'Good point,' Pea says.

'I think that coffee is now very stirred,' Sam says as Mary slowly realises they're all staring at her.

'What now?' she asks with a blush creeping into her cheeks. A feeling of shame from the thoughts in her head.

'But then everything is different now,' Pea continues. 'I mean, look at Lilly and Nick. He's like Mary's age...and that's okay.'

'Yeah but it's Nick,' Sam says. 'Any mother would be happy to see their daughter with him.'

'Most mothers wouldn't mind a go too,' Pea mutters.

'Paula Gabriel!' Sam laughs.

'You're quiet, Mary,' Joan says. 'Everything okay?'

'Aye,' Mary replies, offering a smile with too many confusing things in her head and too many images of a certain young woman. 'Hot isn't it...right, better get that van unloaded...'

CHAPTER SEVENTEEN

D ay Twenty three

'G ot another one, Tommy,' Karl says, showing a
woman into Tommy's section of the big tent.

'Alright love,' Tommy says, smiling like a hungry wolf with sweat pouring down his face from the incredible heat. 'What you after then?'

She looks drained and fit to drop with deep lines on her forehead and bags under her eyes. 'Just something for the kids,' she says quietly.

'Choccy bars? Nice bit of sugar never hurt kids eh? Bit melted from the heat but they're alright...what you got for them?'

'Someone said you can pay with ciggies,' she says, opening a small rucksack. 'Pack of fags for four Mars okay? They're Marlboro...top brand. Tenner each these are.'

'Ah you see,' he says with a pained expression. 'Choccy

bars are value items now ain't they. I can do you four Mars for two packs of Marlboro.'

'You taking the piss? That's twenty quid of ciggies for four quid of chocolate.'

'Don't blame me,' Tommy says. 'If I was in charge I'd make sure everyone had exactly what they needed...none of this crap going on now. Letting the muzzies have everything for themselves. Not on my watch. I wouldn't stand for that...'

He makes the trade and shows her out, stepping into the sunshine with the delusions of his mind telling him that everyone here can be manipulated.

'Are you Tommy?'

He turns on hearing his name. A woman standing nearby. Her arms folded across her body. A dark hooded top with the hood pulled up. Her face pale and waxen.

'What's up with you,' he asks.

She shrugs, her lips cracked and dry. 'They said you're trading.'

'Might be,' he says with a wink before tutting at his humour falling on deaf ears. 'Fuck me, only trying to make a joke. Come in...what you after then? What's your name?'

'Helen. I need something to drink,' she says, her voice low and harsh. She used to be an executive until her addiction to alcohol took over. An educated woman in her thirties that has spent the last three weeks moving from house to house as she headed south. Drinking whatever she could find. Now she trembles from head to toe. Dry as a bone and desperate.

She came in yesterday with a small bottle of Tequila hidden in her clothes and found a spot under a low shelter to drink herself into a stupor. Now she's awake and clucking. Her whole body trembling. Pain everywhere. Her head pounding and so dehydrated she can't even piss, but none of that matters. Only that she needs a drink and she steps into Tommy's little room and watches as he pulls a sheet back from a pile of crap on the floor and fixes her eyes on the half-litre bottle of vodka.

Tommy can see she must have once been beautiful. She still could be if she scrubbed up a bit. 'What you got to trade?' he asks, not seeing any jewellery.

She shakes her head. Hardly able to talk. The shakes getting worse by the minute. The absolute desperation within her so very strong. 'Vodka,' she rasps.

He looks at the bottle then at her. 'Ain't for free is it...'

She finally looks at him, seeing the look in his eyes that drop down over her body. His fat, swollen gut. The tattoos and days of dark growth flecked so heavy with grey on his jaw. Hatred inside. Hatred at him, at herself, at the end of the world and everything. A surge of utter disgust. A reminder that she was once a decent, hard-working person.

Tommy sees the contempt and stiffens his frame. His own face hardening with a sneer. 'Best fuck off then...' he says angrily.

She shakes her head quickly as though snapping back to the now and her hands tremble as she unfolds her arms and grabs at the zip on her thin cotton top, trembling too much to pull it down. She doesn't care now. She needs that vodka and she grows almost desperate in her effort to unzip her top until it finally comes down and falls open to show her naked breasts. Her ribs showing from lack of food. Her stomach curved inwards with spare wrinkles of skin showing rapid weight-loss. Sickly pale too with blue veins seen under the thin flesh but he fixes on her breasts and moves forward, grabbing one to knead hard. His heart thundering at the turn of events. Lust in his face and he moves in to kiss her, scowling at the last second when she turns away.

A few seconds later she kneels on all fours. Her jogging bottoms tugged down around one ankle as Tommy paws and pokes at her from behind while stroking himself. His face flushed a deep red. The sweat pouring down as he tugs and pulls at his cock, trying to get hard. He gets it halfway up and tries to force it in, grunting and sweating while she reaches out to grab the bottle of vodka. Tears spilling over her cheeks. Sobbing silently at his rough hands grabbing too hard and the pain from forcing himself inside her. She grunts and winces but grabs the bottle, unscrews the cap with her teeth, spits it aside and drinks deep while he tugs at himself with a growing anger at his own inability to get an erection.

The smell starts to hit him. The stench of unwashed bodies. The ripeness of it. The way she drinks the vodka without care to his plight. This should be erotic and horny but it's filthy and sordid. He can't stop sweating too. So much of it dripping on her arse and back. His fat belly wobbling. His dick now completely soft. He tries again, almost hurting himself in his efforts to fuck her but it's no good.

'Fuck it,' he snaps, pushing her away. She topples to the side, crying out at spilling the booze and drinking deep once more for fear of him taking the bottle away. Lying naked on her side, tears on her face, her pale body looking so pathetic and wretched. 'Scrawny fucking bitch,' he sneers, getting to his feet and tugging his shorts up. 'Go on, piss off out of here...fucking whore...'

She scrabbles to her feet, pulling her trousers up while too frightened to put the bottle down. Doing the zip up is impossible so she just pulls her top closed and rushes out.

'You owe me,' he calls after her. 'That one doesn't count...'

She doesn't reply but runs out and into the sun and across the way back to her shelter to crawl in out of sight to drink herself into another stupor while the pressure from the sky bears down.

There's a storm coming. That much is obvious, and so the new canteen building has to be constructed fast. People hammering and sawing. Sweating and bleeding. It's a big building too and at times both John and Pardip question if they have bitten off more than they can deal with.

Pressure everywhere. Damsa feels it too, staring across to Maleek and Ameer working hard while Bashir and Tajj sweat on the beach and she bites her bottom lip, worrying and fretting at the hostile faces staring over at her. There are too many people up here not doing anything while too few are run ragged trying to do everything. They must show they have worth to be here. They must earn their place then maybe people won't hate them.

'Come on,' she says, turning to face her family. All women in black robes. 'We're not staying here...ready?'

She leaves the perceived safety of their section and leads them through tent-town. A thing to see for sure. Seven women in black robes seemingly gliding across the ground. Backs straight. Heads held high but fear in their faces. The older women holding the younger ones close as Damsa leads them to the office, to the chaos outside and the ground stacked with new tents and new sleeping bags, with people talking loudly, with piles of bedding being brought in from the gate, stacks of food and people moving in every direction that all seem to fall silent as Damsa and her group come to a stop.

'What wrong?' Lenski asks, looking at Damsa.

'We can work,' Damsa says. 'You are busy...we can work,' she nods at her group then looks to Lenski. A second's worth of silence and the world moves on as the chaos continues.

'Is good. Go to gate. Is many things to bring in yes? Bring here...'

Inside his big circus tent, Tommy curses as he opens a can of beer and glugs the hot fizzy contents down. His face dark with rage.

'Fucking bitch,' he mutters. The way she judged him too. That look of contempt. Who does she think she is? She's the one giving fucks away for free. Worse than a crack whore. No wonder he couldn't get it up. Nobody would be able to get hard with a skank like that in this heat.

On the bay they work hard too with every spare pair of hands focussing on building the wall, and with each new container slammed into place, so it grows by another twelve metres.

'It's like Lego,' Kyle shouts amidst the noise and heat.

'It is,' Norman shouts back, his face covered in grime.

Container after container. Trucks driving in with more runs done to the docks by some of Peter's men. The crane working non-stop. Diggers working the land ahead to make it flat.

Lilly stays in the middle of it all with Norman and Kyle. Seeing tweaks to make it faster. Making sure the direction is right. Working out how to make the wall curve and what to use to plug the gaps. Throats hurting from shouting so much and breathing in the hot fumes. Faces coated in sweat with every pore clogged. Clothes sodden. Feet burning.

On the beach, Mary leads a new group across the sand, going past Bashir and Tajj sweating and working to sort, stack and load wood into waiting boats.

'This is Sandy,' Mary says, helping the family into the boat. A mum, dad and two young children. 'She'll take you over to the fort...you'll be okay you will...'

'All in?' Sandy asks, powering the boat across the water. She reaches the fort shore, slowing the boat to gently hit the beach and looking ahead to the women in black robes sorting and lifting goods to be taken inside and rolls her eyes at Donald snoozing in a chair in the shade. 'Donald,' she calls out with a groan. 'Where's Pam?'

'Eh, you what?' Donald asks, sitting up and pretending he wasn't asleep.

'Where's Pam? I've got new people here...'

'Er...' Donald says, not quite knowing anything from having such a nice snooze. 'Dunno...'

'Well go and get one of them,' Sandy calls.

'I'm a guard. I can't leave my post...'

'Yeah bloody great guard,' Sandy mutters. 'I've got to get back...they need wood bringing over...'

'Excuse me, sorry. Are you looking for Lenski?' Damsa asks, moving away from the other women. 'She is inside, they are very busy I think.'

'You speak English? Brilliant!' Sandy says. 'Right, out you get,' she says to the family. 'Can you take these in to see Lenski...or Pamela...either will do...they're new arrivals.'

'Me?' Damsa asks.

'I'm meant to be on wood supply,' Sandy says as though that explains everything. The new family clamber out to stand on the beach and turn from the boat driving away to the woman in the black robes staring at them.

'Um,' the mother says, looking frightened with wide eyes. They all do. Damsa can see the fear in them.

'Hello, sorry,' Damsa says, finally smiling, her face open and friendly. 'I am sorry. It is very busy here...yes of course, I will take you to Lenski. Do you need help with your bags? Come, let me take that. It looks heavy. Are these your children? They are very beautiful.'

'Thank you, wow...this is...it's too much,' the man says, shouldering a rucksack as he glances back over the water to the bay.

'Is it okay here?' the woman asks. 'I mean is it safe?'

'I think it is, yes,' Damsa says, leading them through the gates. 'There is much work to do though. Everyone is very busy here...'

'Aren't you hot?' a young girl asks, eleven years old and ready to question the world as she takes in Damsa's robes.

'Crystal, shush, that's rude,' the mother whispers urgently. 'So sorry...'

'It is not rude,' Damsa says. 'If you don't know something you should ask. Our clothes are very light, and they stop the sun...plus we are from a hot place.'

'Are you a Muslim?' Crystal asks.

'Crystal,' her mother whisper snaps again.

'It is fine. Yes, I am, Crystal. My name is Damsa. It is nice to meet you...' she pauses as they falter to take in the fort from the inside. At the work underway and the people moving about.

'It's big,' the mother says.

'Yes. Indeed it is,' Damsa says, smiling at the children. 'We just have to go a short distance...' she leads them on, feeling their fear at coming into a strange new place, seeing the worry on their faces. 'They have an evening meal,' Damsa explains. 'The children can eat first then they call for adults...and there are showers around the walls to wash... I believe there is a place to get hot tea from too...and I think they give you some space, maybe a shelter for now and a tent when they have some...Lenski? These are new people. Do I bring them to you?'

'Yes. Is new people. Is many new people,' Lenski says under the crushing heat, cursing under her breath at Pamela disappearing again but she notices the new people and the way they look in fear at the fort and everything going on, but not in fear at Damsa. But then the Muslim woman has a friendly smile that reaches her eyes and a soft, polite tone of voice. 'Wait please,' she darts inside, grabbing a clipboard and re-appears swiftly. 'I show you how we do this yes? Can you write English?'

'I can,' Damsa says, taking the clipboard with a confused look. 'I'm sorry. You will show me how to do what exactly?'

'Greet new people. Is fine. You will be good at this...'

L illy bends forward as she pours water over her head to rid the sweat from her eyes before turning to look at the long line of containers and already a staggering achievement in just how many they have laid.

Another container goes down bringing them another twelve metres closer to the finish line and they rush on for the next. Preparing the ground and making sure the container angle is good for the curve and checking the contents. Arguing over whether three hundred boxes of fashion shoes need to be taken out before the container is put in place.

'Shoes are shoes,' Kyle yells. '

'They're high heels and sandals,' Norman shouts back at him.

'Get 'em out,' Kyle yells, waving his arms at the crane driver.

'Just slot the fucking container in place,' Norman yells after him.

The crane driver dithers and tries to do both then snaps and yanks a lever to bring one end up, letting three hundred boxes of fashion shoes spill over the ground. 'HAPPY NOW?' he yells.

'FINE,' Kyle shouts back.

'GOOD,' Norman bellows and on they go, working to get the container in place and twelve metres closer to the sea, to the finish line. They go deep into the old estate. A bad place to be, blackened and covered in lumps of twisted metal that scream out when the diggers and machines drag them free. Piles of slag and bricks. It stinks too. Chemicals and ash made up of people and objects. The arse end of the line but every container down is twelve metres closer.

'THE CURVE IS TOO MUCH,' Lilly shouts, indicating with her hands that the container has gone in at a bad angle. 'GET IT BACK UP...'

'IT LOOKS FINE,' Norman yells.

'IT'S NOT FINE. GET IT BACK UP AND DO IT AGAIN...' she waves in the air, motioning the crane driver to take it back up and bring it back down.

'BETTER,' Lilly shouts, giving a thumbs up.

'It was bloody fine where it was,' Norman says, marching on.

'It bloody wasn't,' she snaps, striding after him as they

join Kyle opening the next container up, slamming the big metal doors open. Boxes inside. Chinese markings on the sides that none of them can understand. All three go inside and at the same time they pluck knives from belts to slash the boxes open, tearing at packaging to see what's inside. Their blood up. Eyes set and hard.

'What the feck,' Kyle says, pulling a long curved rubber thing out with another smaller knobbly bit poking out the bottom. Lurid green in colour and he spots a twisty thing on the base, frowning as he turns it that makes the vibrator hum and jack rabbit up and down while the knobbly bit at the base spins.

'What the hell is that?' Norman asks, pulling a box out to look at the picture on the side. Something pink and kind of looking like a body part, but inflatable and weird. 'Is that a vagina?' he asks, showing it to the others. 'That's a vagina...'

'I think it is,' Kyle says, holding his jack rabbiting, spinning, thrusting bright green dildo as Lilly stares at a box in one hand containing an assortment of cock rings and a butt plug in the other, her head moving from side to side as she looks at them in turn.

'That's a butt plug,' Norman says, nodding at the butt plug. 'Apparently,' he adds quickly. 'That's not a gay thing... straight people use them too,' he tells Kyle and Lilly. 'And er...right...interesting...'

'Blow up dolls,' Kyle calls, opening another box.

'Whips anyone?' Lilly asks, pulling one out from a box. Long and black with a thick handle. She widens her eyes, flicking it back and forth a few times before turning to wave her arm harder. 'How do they work?'

'Flick it harder,' Kyle says, watching as she does it again. 'No, harder...really hard...like straighten your arm and...'

'I think it's in the wrist,' Norman says. 'Try it from the wrist...'

'Definitely the arm,' Kyle says, leaning past her to pull another whip out as he lets it unfold and starts trying to make it crack. 'Not enough room in here, try it outside...'

'Wrist. I'm telling you,' Norman says, taking a whip and following them out. 'Like this...' he flicks his hand out, frowning when the whip just flops about as the men nearby stop to look over with shrugs and confused glances to each other.

'I'm getting it,' Lilly says, flinging her arm about harder.

'Aye, that's better,' Kyle says, trying with his.

'Ha!' Norman says when his whip goes straighter than before. 'Definitely in the wrist...'

'What's the hold up?' Peter asks, stopping at the open doors then darting back as Lilly cracks a whip at him.

'I did it!' she says. 'Did you see that?'

'Do it again,' Kyle says, the two men watching her do it again. Flinging her arm up then down and out while moving her wrist. 'Got it...yes!' he shouts when his whip cracks.

'I gotta try this now,' Peter says, dodging the cracking whips to grab one from the box

'Mine's not doing it,' Norman says, flinging his arm up and down. 'Is it broken?'

'Harder,' Kyle tells him. 'Go on! Harder now. Crack that fecking whip...'

'I'm trying...'

Mary reaches the estate, marvelling at the length of the wall and the colours of the containers. Reds, blues, yellows and greens. A noise ahead. Harsh cracks. A container on the ground. The doors open. She rounds the end and comes to a dead stop at the view of sweaty men cracking whips as Kyle holds a whirring jack-rabbiting bright green dildo with a knobbly base. Norman next to him waving his inflatable vagina as he frowns at his whip not cracking. Then she spots Lilly in the middle, her face glistening as she smiles while holding a butt plug in one hand and cracking a whip in the other. 'Oh hell. Now that's not helping at all...' she mutters, turning swiftly about to head back to the beach while blasting air from her cheeks. 'Not good, Mary. Don't even think it...'

A few minutes later and the sex-toy container lifts into the air and pauses while one end is hoisted up for the boxes to slide out, dumping the contents on the ground before being slotted into place and the wall extends by another twelve metres as the afternoon rolls on.

CHAPTER EIGHTEEN

D ay Twenty Three

T ime becomes paradoxical. A thing of uncertainty. A measurement of the passage of existence that can no longer be relied upon to be accurate because on the one hand, it's trundling on so painfully slowly, where everything takes more effort and requires more focus and the later the day gets, the worse it seems to become.

However, time also speeds up with one hour seemingly dragging for five then suddenly it's done and gone and those people scurrying about the bay and in the fort like feverish ants all feel a sense of panic that they are not working fast enough and that somehow, they will run out of time.

There is a storm coming you see, and that approaching eventuality becomes the marker to aim for. The wall must be done before the storm. The canteen must be built before the storm. The new tents must be pitched before the storm. The shelters must be taken down before the storm.

And then, like clockwork and like every other day that has gone before, and yet coming with a sense of surprise, they start to run out of light as the afternoon wanes and evening takes its place, heralding the approaching night, and that alone prompts a fresh burst of energy.

'COME ON,' John shouts, his voice deep and booming. Clapping his hands to gee his team on.

'Come on guys,' Colin calls, his voice lighter and maybe not so deep and booming and his hand clap doesn't quite generate the same thunderous noise, but the intent is there and he spurs his team on to strip out the old tents and get the new ones up while re-organising the way they are pitched, the lines and rows, making it better, tweaking and altering.

'COME ON,' Mary shouts on the beach, clapping her hands as she works with Bashir, Tajj and the boat drivers to get more supplies over to the fort. A glance up to the sky just hinting at fading light.

'Come on,' Ann urges inside the marquee tent, gripping Simon's arm as he squirms and writhes in agony. A dislocation that needs popping back in. Anika holds him down, grim faced and nodding at the doctor who wrenches with an explosion of force and a crunch of bone. Simon screams out once then gasps as he sinks back.

'COME ON,' Lilly claps her hands hard, buoying them up. Another container down. Another twelve metres of security. She runs for the next. A mass of men trudging behind her on legs that have never felt so tired and heavy.

'Come on,' Tommy snaps at Pamela in his little room, grabbing at her clothes to tug them down so he can remove the stolen goods. His breath stinking of beer. A few empty cans already littering the floor. Karl, Matty and a couple of others in there with them, watching Tommy pull Pamela's breasts from her bra. Beer cans in their hands, a small bottle of whiskey being passed around. 'Good girl,' Tommy says, his voice too harsh, his eyes too glaring. He pats her arse too hard and pushes her too roughly out of his section. 'Go on, get some more...'

'Come on through,' Damsa says on the shore outside the main gates of the fort. The last boat full of people all clambering out. She goes forward to help, her sisters with her, helping lift children and giving steady arms for people to hold. 'My name is Damsa...I'll take you inside...'

'Thanks,' one of the men says, tall and bearded, pale and drawn from three weeks of hell. 'Is it safe here? We heard it's safe...'

'It is safe, we have food and medicine and guards,' Damsa says, smiling at them in turn. Soft and gentle, her whole manner so full of understanding and empathy for the fear and worry they are feeling. 'Are you hungry? We can get you some food. Let me take your baby while you get out,' she says to a nursing mother.

'Thank you, she's so heavy...' the mother says, looking ready to drop.

'I can carry her, it is fine...are you ready to come through? Please, don't worry. Everything will be okay...'

'Shit,' John spits the word out, exhausted, filthy, drained even. He looks up, seeing the light is fading fast, seeing his workers have nothing left to give.

'That's enough,' Pardip says to him, his head hanging low.

John nods. They've done what they can.

'Bugger,' Colin says, looking up at the darkening sky, his workers all dragging their feet and looking so very worn out. 'Okay guys, we've done what we can...let's call it a day...'

'You know what?' Mary says on the beach, shaking her head slowly as Bashir and everyone else look at her. 'That's enough it is. Enough. No more...Ann? We're done out here...'

Ann steps out, nodding over. 'Same, we'll start packing up...'

'Why pack?' Mary asks her. 'You've a wall keeping it safe now...'

'That's a very good point,' Ann says, looking at the wall.

'COME ON,' Lilly shouts, running alongside her new wall. Still as energised as before. Driven and relentless. She'll work all night if she has to. She won't stop. She'll never stop.

'Lilly,' Norman says.

'SO CLOSE,' she shouts out, clapping her hands. A few more containers and the first level of the wall will be done.

'Lilly,' Norman says again, his tone making her blink at the sorry sight of his face coated in grime and muck, at his sodden clothes. At Kyle leaning against the container wall with his hands on his knees. At the other men around them. Some sitting. Some lying down. Others almost swaying on their feet. The digger drivers hunched over their steering wheels. The crane driver yawning. Peter, Willie and Elvis still with their heads up but only through sheer will power. 'That's enough, Lilly,' Norman says. 'Enough for today...'

Frustration inside. A surge of irritation that the world isn't doing what she wants. That she cannot finish what she started right now. A flash of immaturity perhaps. A flash of something for sure.

'Not bad though,' Peter calls out, nodding at the last container laid and he turns as he looks back down at the wall stretching behind them. Nearly a kilometre of containers in a long curve.

'Aye,' Kyle says. 'Not bad at all...' he looks at Lilly with a message sent from his eyes to hers. Telling her not to be a tyrant. Telling her not to drive men to the point they break.

She draws air and nods, forcing the irritation away. 'It's very good,' she calls. 'We'll call it a day and pick it up tomorrow. Thank you...I mean that too...it's an astonishing achievement.'

Pamela walks back through tent-town, scowling at the way it all looks so different already. New tents are up. Some of the shelters have been taken down. She hurries on past the empty Muslim family patch, figuring they've all been given a swanky new super enormous tent, or maybe even the best rooms in the walls. Then she spots two of them walking past with armfuls of gear. Then another one behind them calling out as she rushes to join the first two.

Pamela frowns and moves on towards the gate, having heard a new family was coming over. The light now going from the sky. The night coming. That's good. She can go back to Tommy's tent and get drunk with them all. She's hungry too and her belly feels weird from eating too much stolen snack food.

She reaches the office, seeing Lenski outside with Sam, Pea and Joan. Stuff on the ground. Bags and boxes of new things being stacked and sorted.

'Hiya,' she calls out, waving a hand. A glance from Pea who goes straight back to work. Sam doesn't even look. Joan glares for a second, tuts and turns away.

'Where you go?' Lenski asks her, spotting what looks like chocolate smeared up her wrist.

'Eh? I was...I had to...I was working and...' Pamela stutters the words, caught out at the harsh voice.

'Is busy. I not find you...you hide in Tommy's tent all day, leave everyone else to work. Is lazy...I call you on radio all day...'

'I was fucked...I mean I was...the boys and...' she trails off at seeing Damsa and another couple of the Muslim women walking towards them with a new family. The women carrying babies, children and bags. Damsa talking as she leads them in. A clipboard under her arm. A bag on her shoulder and cradling an infant child.

'...and there are shower cubicles all around the walls. The water is cold, but you can wash. We have toilets in the middle and you can see where the food is cooking...' Damsa says, pointing over to Agatha and Sunnie working hard to get the evening meal ready. 'And in a minute I will show you to Colin's noticeboard, it has a map so you can find everywhere....and this is the main office. May I introduce you to Lenski, Sam, Pea and Joan...'

Pamela glares. Unblinking. Unflinching. Lost for words and thoughts at the sight of a Muslim in a black robe talking English and holding a baby. How dare she. How dare they. That was her job. The poor new people. They must be terrified being greeted by Muslims. She glares at them, expecting to see fear and worry, and she does see that, except the fear and worry isn't aimed at the women but at the fact that everyone they ever knew is probably dead and they are now refugees in a strange place. Then Pamela blinks with another thought. A realisation even. Sudden and profound.

'Can I go then?' she asks. Nobody listens or responds or even looks at her and she eases away, back-stepping before turning and heading off with a grin. This is great. She doesn't have to meet new people anymore. She can hang out with Tommy in his tent and eat choccy bars and drink beer and maybe he'll finger her or something. It's about time the muzzies started work anyway. Loafing about doing nothing all this time.

'What?!' Tommy snaps in his room a few minutes later. 'Are you being fucking serious?'

Pamela nods, wobbling her chins. 'Lenski was totally like *fuck you fatty, go fuck off and eat mud while my new bezzer friends take over* and I was like, *but me and Lilly got fucked and raped* and she was like *fuck off fat cunt,* and that Muslim woman that speaks English, she was like sticking her finger up at me and mouthing *fuck off fatty...*'

Karl and Matty share looks and shrugs, neither thinking that sounds quite true but who cares? They drink beer and watch as Tommy goes even redder in the face.

'But it's cool though,' Pamela says, grinning at Tommy. 'I can hang out now...fuck 'em yeah? Let the muzzies do the work...'

'You stupid fucking bitch,' Tommy says slowly, shaking his head at her. 'Who's gonna get the stuff now?'

'Eh?'

'The stuff. From the store rooms? Who's gonna get it? Are you that fucking stupid? Jesus Christ...fucking fat bitch...and that scrawny fucking crack whore too.'

'Oh but...' she pauses, frowning at what he just said. 'What crack whore? Can I have a beer now?'

Tommy grabs another can, opening it as she steps in with a smile, thinking it's for her but he moves away, tutting and muttering before drinking deep. She shrugs, grabs a can and flops down near Karl and Matty. 'Fucking muzzies,' Tommy mutters. 'This is them taking over...I'm telling you...'

'I'm telling you,' Norman says as they walk back through the camp towards the beach. 'That's nearly a kilometre of containers put down. That's a staggering thing to do. Even if the whole end of the world thing hadn't happened it would have been hard...'

'Night then, see you tomorrow!'

'Night, Willie,' Norman calls back as the lads from the camp drift off.

'Goodnight,' Lilly says, turning to wave at them before looking at Norman and Kyle.

'We'll get the bottom layer finished in the morning then start another on the next row,' Norman continues.

'You're right,' Lilly says, exhaling deeply. 'I was just frustrated.'

'I'm not criticising you,' Norman says quickly. 'We need that drive...'

'Yes we do,' Kyle says emphatically.

'That energy you have,' Norman says. 'Honestly, it's essential...I mean that. I doubt we'd have got half of this done today...'

'And don't forget you got new tents too,' Kyle says.

'What we're trying to say,' Norman continues. 'Respectfully of course, is not to be too hard on yourself.'

'Understood,' Lilly says.

'And that's not patronising you either,' Norman says. 'It did sound a bit patronising...but my god it's so hot.'

'I shall forgive the patronising on the basis of the heat then,' she says, offering a smile that he takes in good humour.

'Will ye hurry up now,' Mary calls from ahead, holding the boat ready.

'Coming coming,' Norman shouts back as they rush over the sand and climb in to sit on the low planks, groaning with tired legs as they all talk and greet each other after a very long day.

'Bloody hell,' Ann says, glancing back at the bay, as they can all turn and gawp at the sight of the wall. A solid multi-coloured line snaking across the land and disappearing from view behind the camp then reappearing on the far side, edging towards the sea.

'You think that's impressive?' Norman asks. 'Wait till you hear about the butt plugs...'

The chat comes back as the boat powers on, reaching the shore so they can spill out and trudge in through the gates.

'Welcome to the fort,' Lenski says, waiting for them with mock politeness. 'I show you tour yes? Come please...' she steps over to the side, through a recessed doorway and into a set of rooms. 'They are all clean now yes? We have many beds in here. More rooms back there with bedding too. Place to store clothes and things. We have light too. Jaspal, he put solar panels on the walls and feed wires into here. The light is not strong but is enough. I get furniture soon...'

'It's incredible,' Lilly says. 'Who is it for?'

'Single men,' Lenski says. 'Norman, Kyle, Alf, John, men who work who give hard effort, they have beds in rooms now. They share space...plus we keep them near the gates so they can fight the zombies if they come through. Yes?' she adds with a grin.

'Hey now, she's got some smarts,' Mary laughs as Norman and Kyle take it in. The pitted concrete floor. The rough walls. The bedding all mix and match. A low table to one side scratched and dented with bottles of water on it.

Norman compares it to what he had and thinks about Robert and his home. The pain is still there, so raw and terrible but maybe not so bad as it was. He's too exhausted to think about it much and this room now looks very inviting. Comforting and homely even.

'It's perfect,' he says earnestly. 'Thank you, Lenski...'

'Is no bother. Come, we go on...' she bustles out as the lights within the fort start to flicker on with the shadows growing deeper and darker. 'Damsa, she help with meeting new people. She very friendly. Pamela, I think we no use her now. We have problems there, but I explain that later, she is not nice person. I show you the canteen now. Come...'

They head across the fort, passing people flaked out by the food tables drinking tea or simply too exhausted to move. Children running about. People talking. A hubbub of noise. Lilly takes it in, seeing the change from just one more day out of the fort. The way people are getting to know each other. The way they greet each other from a day spent working in different areas. The bay workers talking to John's and Colin's teams. She spots Sam, Pea and Joan ahead with John and Pardip and blinks at the skeletal frame standing large in the middle.

'That's enormous,' Ann remarks, making them all turn to see Lilly's group heading over.

'Lilly!' Billy shouts out from nearby, rushing over to be hoisted up for a hug. The other kids running in as Lilly spots Ameer wedged between his dad and Simar, still translating.

'What do you think like?' Pardip asks them.

'Did you make it?' Anika asks. 'I wouldn't go in if they made it,' she tells Lilly, adding a wink.

'This is solid this is,' Simar calls over.

'Course it is,' Anika says, offering a thumbs up. 'But er...

I'm not a builder or anything but doesn't it need sides? And a roof? And a floor...and like windows and a door...joke!' she squeals out as Pardip lunges at her. 'It's great. Honestly... drafty mind but...'

'The frame is pretty much done,' John says. 'We'll get the sides and top on tomorrow...if the weather holds,' he adds with a glance up at the sky. 'But having Maleek has saved a day's worth of work...'

'More than that,' Simar says.

'Maleek is a carpenter?' Lilly asks, working out who Maleek is.

'Good one too,' Simar says. 'And his lad here has been translating all day...'

'It's amazing,' Lilly says. Looking at the building then past it to the new tents put up. 'Very good. Makes a huge difference...'

'Come,' Lenski says, taking her arm. 'I show you offices and rooms...want me to take Billy? You look hot.'

'I'm fine. How's it been?' Lilly asks, trying to hug her squirming brother. 'What's wrong?' she asks him.

'Want to get down,' he says, far more interested in what Rajesh, Milly and Amna are doing.

'I've just got back in,' she says. 'Not even a kiss?'

Billy kisses his sister then squirms to be released to run free and wild, to shout out and race into the offices to get chairs, the four kids laughing hard.

The adults follow them in, dumping bags and groaning with relief. Damsa inside holding sheets of paper and waiting patiently. Her eyes flicking nervously to Lilly and Mary. Remembering their faces on the beach and how close to death they all were. Remembering the fierceness of these two women. But that was then, and this is now, and time rolls ever forward, changing the world and the people in it as it goes by.

'Hello,' Lilly says to her. Not surly, not grumpy but then not overly friendly either. Distant and aloof. 'Lenski said you are helping now.'

'We wanted to work,' Damsa says politely.

'Thank you, that helps a lot,' Lilly says simply.

'Hey now, remember me? Sorry for pointing guns at you before,' Mary says, sticking her hand out to Damsa. 'What's your name again? Damsa? That's a gorgeous name that is. Is it hot in them robes? They look light though and I bet they keep the sun off...'

'Thank you, you are very kind,' Damsa says, her nerves easing somewhat as she spots the light fading outside. 'Would you excuse me...'

'Ah sure,' Mary says. 'Do you all pray when it gets dark?'

'Yes, yes we do...is that okay?' Damsa asks, her eyes once more flicking to Lilly standing nearby talking to Lenski.

'Fine with me,' Lilly says.

'Is good. Yes. Pray. Is fine,' Lenski says. 'I see you at food yes?'

'Thank you,' Damsa says, walking out.

'Are they still under a shelter?' Lilly asks Lenski quietly.

'No, I put in tent. Big tent. Has rooms inside. They have good space now, but they are big family...'

Damsa walks on towards the back with a calling inside that now is the time to offer prayer to Allah. Today has been a better day. Nervous yes, and Fearful too, but good and it feels nice to smile at people and put them at ease. Damsa was so very scared when she came here and so she knows just how hard it must be for the new people.

She heads first towards the space her shelter was in, frowning at seeing it empty then remembering with a smile that they now have a tent and she changes course, veering to go left.

'There she is,' Tommy calls out, standing with a cigarette in one hand and a can of beer in the other. Pamela next to him doing the same. Others around them. 'Time for prayers is it love?' Tommy calls.

Damsa smiles politely and walks on. Dipping her head as though to avoid confrontation.

'That the one that stole your job is it, Pammie?' Tommy asks. 'Oops, better not say anything against the fucking muzzies. They'll have that Polish bitch over here shooting everyone eh? Lining up outside like a fucking Nazi. Muzzies and Nazi's...same fucking thing really. Nah, I'm not being racist. I'm not. Honest I ain't...Pamela's British born and bred and lost her job to an emicunt. It's fine....'

A barrage of words spewing from his mouth. Humour inflected within his voice that earns a few half drunken laughs from men and women lounging about. Sucking on cigarettes. Glugging from cans of beer.

'Bet her husband can get it up in this heat...' Tommy adds with an edge to his voice.

'Why do you keep saying that?' Karl asks.

'Fucking hell, Karl. I'm only joking. Jesus mate. Can't even say nothing round here...I'm just saying is all...I'm just saying she looks fit...like her bloke can probably get it up... they're used to the heat and they breed like rats anyway... nah, you go on love. Go and pray to Allah that we all get infected so you can take over...'

Damsa rushes on, shaken as she reaches her tent to see Ameer going in ahead of her then running back out to look for her.

'Mum!' he runs over, flinging his arms about her body.

'Me and dad were building all day and he was working with Simar and he's so funny! He makes these faces and was spraying me with water and his brothers are so nice and John was there and they said that they couldn't make that building without dad and...'

She smiles at him, listening to the words rushing out as she goes inside the big tent. A communal area in the middle with smaller bubbles leading off. Basic, but enough.

'You've had a good day then?' she says, seeing her husband exuberant manner as he talks to his brothers. Everyone chatting about what they did, what they saw, what they heard.

'You have a job?' Maleek asks her as they start laying the prayer mats on the ground.

'It is not a job, I am just helping,' she replies. 'It is okay though?'

'Yes!' he says, grinning at her. 'Of course. We should work...can I show you the building later? It's so big now...I told Simar how to make a joint differently...I will show you. You will be very impressed.'

'Maleek,' Tajj says, a rebuke to his tone. 'It is already late...'

'Of course, of course,' Maleek says as they take to their mats, supplicating and getting ready for evening prayer.

'Wankers,' Tommy says, opening another can. 'Bet they're inside pointing their arses at Allah eh?' he walks out and drops to his knees, pushing his backside up and wailing in a stupid voice making the others laugh, his rasping voice going up and down as he purposefully bangs his forehead into the ground. The sight is funny and he gets good laughs, but he remembers the woman from earlier on her knees in front of him. Laughing at him not being able to get hard. That look of contempt on her face. The disgust she had for him. It festers inside. Mutating and becoming something other than what it was and he pushes up to his feet, glaring balefully at the tent the Muslim family now have. 'Fuckers...got a new tent. We don't have a new tent...and the ragheads are sleeping in the rooms now. Fucking Pammie got fired for nothing...telling you...I'm fucking telling you...if we don't do something, they'll take over and slit our throats...'

CHAPTER NINETEEN

'FOOD! EVERYONE TOGETHER TONIGHT,' Agatha shouts from the big tables, banging a ladle against a metal pot.

'I forget,' Lenksi says in the office. 'Aggie and Sunnie say to try this tonight. They say too many families want to eat together...'

'That's fine,' Lilly says, dragging a hair brush through her brother's hair. Once again red-faced and flushed but this time from getting four young children into a shower. It was meant to be one at a time until all four decided they would shower together. Lilly and Pea did try and explain about boys and girls having different bits, but it got very complicated very quickly with all four wanting to know what bits they had, and where they were, and why and why and why.

In the end it was a mammoth team effort as bit as difficult as building a wall to get them washed, scrubbed, dried and changed with one brief interlude when all four kids burst free from the cubicle to run nudey across the fort, and it wasn't until Lilly used *that voice* that they all stopped and came back.

'You four are becoming feral,' she says, pulling Billy's t-shirt straight as Pea sorts Rajesh while Sam brushes Milly's hair while Mary and Amna shrug and pull faces at each other.

'What's feral?' Milly asks.

'Wild,' Lilly replies. 'Like wild animals...just very cute ones. Come on. Food. I'm hungry...'

They go out into the fort proper, heading to join the throngs going for food. Norman and Kyle heading over. John's voice heard as he greets Pardip, Simar and Jaspal.

'There he is,' Simar calls out, spotting Maleek with his family gathered about him. 'Maleek! Alright mate. You should get double portions for what you done today.'

'More than you should get,' Anika calls from further ahead, laughing with Ann.

'Eh, we're the hard-working team we are,' Simar calls back. 'Not like you lot over there swimming about and lying on the sand...' he trails off with a laugh at the huge groan coming back and the voices all joining in. 'Yeah yeah, whatever,' he says, waving a hand at the jokey protests.

'Have you seen our wall?' someone shouts.

'Five containers makes a wall does it?' Simar asks, setting them off again. 'I'm joking!'

'Fucking listen to 'em,' Tommy sneers quietly, further back in the queue. His gait becoming a bit unsteady from the booze. 'You hearing that? They get double portions now...eh? That's where our food has gone...listen to 'em all shouting at each other in wugga wugga language...wankers... I'm telling you, they're taking over.'

'Lilly love!' Agatha says, spotting her in the queue. 'What you queuing up for? You want food you just say so. Blimey. I've heard what you did all day. They said over a mile of wall has gone up today.'

'Not quite that much,' Lilly says.

'But still. Fancy that. A new wall eh? And it looks so good too.'

'Looks amazing,' Sunnie says, bustling behind Agatha. 'Keeping us all safe...'

'She is,' Agatha says. 'Keeping us all safe...eh. And Norman's over there with Kyle sweating away and Mary getting the things we need. Pea and Sam and Joan, all working so hard they are.'

'Working so hard,' Sunnie says, bustling back the other way.

Plates loaded, cutlery grabbed and they head out to sit on the grass and eat with Lilly heading over to the side, lowering down as the others gather about her in a big circle. John and Pardip side by side next to Simar sitting near Maleek and his family. Jaspal near Lenski. Alf nearby. Mary plonks down beside Lilly, sharing a smile as she gets comfy to eat. Ann and Anika joining them. More people nearby.

'Will you look at that, Blondie,' Mary says quietly, looking around. 'You've got an Irish gypsy sharing a meal with Sikhs, Muslims, a Catholic priest and a Polish woman...end of the world is it? Doesn't bloody look like it...'

'I don't think Kyle is a priest,' Lilly replies.

'Really?' Mary asks, giving her a look. 'From everything I just said you pick out the priest bit?'

'You know what I mean,' Lilly replies with a smile.

'And our rooms are cracking aren't they? Lenski, I said our rooms the rooms are grand now.'

'Good. I hope they okay.'

'More than okay,' Norman says from across the circle.

'Am I down with you guys?' John asks.

'Yes,' Lenski replies. 'Single men down there so you can

fart and scratch your...' she pauses, casting a quick look at the children. 'Your bums, yes?'

'Nicely recovered,' Kyle chuckles.

'Need this weather to break,' Norman says.

'Not too soon,' John says.

'We need the sides and roof on yet,' Pardip adds.

'How long will that take?' Ann asks as everyone looks to Simar and Maleek.

'The lady wants to know how long it will take for your building to be finished,' Ameer translates.

'The lady is a doctor, Ameer,' Damsa says.

'I think by tomorrow evening,' Maleek says.

'My father thinks by tomorrow evening,' Ameer says to Simar.

'That's too long,' Lilly says, bringing every head over to her.

'Too harsh, Blondie,' Mary whispers.

'I mean, of course yes,' Lilly says quickly at everyone looking at her.

'They're working like demons,' Mary whispers again.

'You're all working so hard and I really appreciate that,' Lilly adds. 'I'm just concerned the weather will break...' she smiles at the faces nodding in agreement, their reactions softening from her blunt tone. 'Do you need more people working?'

Pardip shakes his head, swallowing his food before answering. 'We've got enough people...it's just the processes...it all takes time, and we've only got a few power tools.'

'It's looking grand though,' Mary says.

'Much bigger than I thought it would be,' Pea says.

'I was thinking that,' Sam says.

'Needs to be big,' Simar says. 'Lots of people to feed...'

'How's the wall?' John asks.

'Fridges,' Norman and Kyle reply together, both laughing. 'And shoes,' Norman adds.

'You and those bloody shoes,' Kyle laughs.

'And the whips mind,' Mary calls out.

'The whips!' Norman laughs. 'I brought mine over to keep practising...'

'I'm telling you,' Mary says, pointing at them all with her fork. 'You've not seen nothing till you've seen this lot cracking whips and what was that other thing you were holding, Father?'

'I've no idea,' Kyle laughs. 'Something green.'

'Something green,' Norman laughs, shaking his head as he eats but the smile becomes frozen and slowly fades as he glances up to see Tommy staring at him. Patricia and Keith with him. Karl and Matty. Gwen and more that Norman recognises from that area. All of them sullen and hard-faced. A few dozen at least. Tommy says something, sneering as he nods towards Lilly's group. A few laughs but not nice ones. Sniggering and nasty.

'...and Norman's saying *I think mine is broken, I really do...*' Kyle says, imitating a posh English voice as Norman shifts his focus from the dark to the light, smiling at the joke and pushing Tommy and his group to the back of his mind. Who cares what they do. There will always be people like that.

'Crack it,' Norman says, mimicking a strong Irish accent. 'Crack that whip...'

'Ach, I don't sound like that,' Kyle laughs.

'You do,' Sam calls out, pointing her fork at him as the laughs roll round.

'That was brilliant, Norman,' Pea says, chuckling away. 'Do it again.'

'Ach to be sure,' Norman says. 'Aye, crack that whip!'

Tommy festers with an anger growing inside at Norman making jokes and laughing. Looking tanned and relaxed and popular. 'Queer cunt,' he mutters. 'And what they laughing at?' he asks, seeing the Muslims smiling as they eat. 'They can't even speak fucking English...'

'Tommy,' Karl says, nudging his side.

'Eh?' Tommy asks, turning to see Sunnie waiting to serve him. He glares at her, tutting and shaking his head before grabbing his plate and taking a step on to purposefully grin at the white woman next to her. 'Alright love! What you got?' he asks brightly.

'Er, you missed Sunnie,' the woman says.

'Alright alright, no need to string me up. Only asking for some food.'

'Just load his plate up and get rid of him,' Sunnie says.

'You'd bloody love that wouldn't you,' Tommy says, looking at Sunnie.

'Pamela?' Sunnie asks, holding a ladle full of stew out as Pamela shuffles in front of her.

'Sorry, what?' Pamela says.

'Not again,' Sunnie snaps. 'You've been doing this all day.'

'I just can't understand her,' Pamela says, looking at the others. 'Honestly, her accent...'

'I don't have an accent!' Sunnie says, an edge growing in her voice.

'Yeah I don't understand her either,' Tommy says. 'Still, best not say anything, get shot for racism in here...or they starve you and make you work to death...'

'I give up,' Sunnie says, slamming the ladle down before striding off.

'What's all this about?' Agatha asks, not hearing the

conversation but seeing Sunnie walk off. She grabs the ladle, scooping a portion on Pamela's plate. 'Go on, keep moving. We've a lot of mouths to feed we have...'

'Where we eating then?' Karl asks, staring around at the groups spread over the eating area.

'Not fucking down here, that's for sure. This lot think they can laugh? We'll fucking show 'em...' he struts off, chest puffed up and his plate loaded with food, striding past the building site. 'And that's built all wrong too,' he says, pointing at it as they go by. 'First bit of wind and that's coming down, you mark my words.'

The sight of it offends him. The solid looking joists on the floor. The struts poking up and the roof rafters so thick and plentiful. The speed it's gone up frightens him too, not that he would ever admit it. He heard people say Lilly has laid a kilometre of containers down as a wall and that all the structures in the bay are now pulled down, and that also offends and frightens him. All of it does. That's it all moving so fast and he's not a part of it.

It wasn't meant to be like this. He's English and white and this is the new world, yet everything is already changing around him like it was in the old world. The shelters are being pulled down. They were only up for a day or so. New tents and better order. The rooms being cleared out and the people working hard being moved into them. He wants to pick fault with it all and tell everyone they're doing everything wrong.

Too many feelings inside that he can't process. A sense of panic and worry. Shame too, and insecurity from the realisation of his utter insignificance. The lack of respect that comes from not working and not giving back.

All of those things make him louder and angrier, and if that wasn't enough, his pride has taken a hit too from the scrawny crack whore who didn't care two shits when he couldn't get hard. Fuck her. Fuck them. Fuck everyone and he plonks down on the ground outside his tent and starts shovelling the food in. Chewing fast and angry as the others drift over.

'I'm fucking telling you,' he tells them. 'This is out of control. Literally out of control. Them muzzies started this...they killed everyone by spreading a jihadi fucking disease so they can take over. That's why they wear them robes. Eh? Never figured that one out did they. What they hiding? Weapons. That's what. Bottles of nerve agent and more of that...that...that fucking infection. Yeah, that's what they got. More infection. They'll kill us all they will. You saw 'em. Working in all the rooms now. Cooking our food. Carrying our bedding. Greeting new people to infect...we're fucked. We're so fucked. If we don't do something we'll all be dead...you think your kids are safe? They ain't fucking safe. That Lilly, she's made a deal with them. That's fact that is. That soldier told me. He said this is what they do...'

A drip-feed of poison. A steady flow of angered words that prey on the fears everyone already has and Tommy chunters on, the vicious righteous humiliated anger bubbling away inside.

O n the other side of the building site, everyone else lies or sits on the ground, sweating in the super-charged hot air. Bellies filled and nearly all of them feeling the buzz that only comes after a day of sheer hard work. The younger children play. Older children sit quietly, some snuggle into the sides of parents or the people who have given them care. Subi lies on her back, her head on Pea's lap while Pea plays with her hair. A deep bond growing between them. Two gentle souls that don't need to make noise like others.

'And so we left Afghanistan,' Damsa explains to a few people sitting nearby. 'It was so violent and dangerous. My father worked for the American army too which made us targets for others...' she pauses, sadness in her features. 'But here we are. Everyone has suffered and lost...'

'Ameer got into a good school did he?' Sam asks.

'He did yes,' Damsa replies, smiling at her son. 'Very prestigious in fact. I know every mother will boast of their children, but yes, he is gifted.'

'What in?' Ann asks. 'I'm guessing maths?' she ventures.

'Music,' Damsa says.

'Seriously?' Sam asks. 'What sort of music? I keep forgetting he speaks English,' she says with a tut at herself. 'Ameer, what music are you into?'

'The violin,' he says shyly, dropping his head from the gazes of so many. 'I am still learning though.'

'The Royal College of Music arranged our visas,' Damsa explains. 'Ameer has to study in a state school but at weekends he was given extra tuition in London...or at least he was,' she adds.

'You play the violin?' Mary calls over. 'I love the sound of that. Have you got it here? You should give us a blast...'

'Oh no, I couldn't,' Ameer says quickly, blushing deeply.

'Ah why not? We'd love to hear it,' Mary says. 'Unless it's awful mind, nothing worse than a screeching fiddle...ah, maybe I shouldn't have said anything now....is he any good?' she asks, looking at Damsa.

'He is very good,' Damsa says as the others laugh at the

way Mary speaks. 'Ameer, maybe you could play a little?' she switches to her language, speaking softly.

'They want to hear him play?' Maleek asks.

'Oh no, I cant,' Ameer says.

'You should,' Maleek urges. 'A few minutes and you haven't practised for weeks now...I will get it. Stay here...'

'Father, no...'

'Ameer, it's fine. Be brave...' Maleek says, pushing up to his feet and heading off through the crowds of people relaxing after the meal. He smiles at the building site, his eyes automatically going to the rafters that need doing next. Noise from the big tent where the angry people live. Lots of them all sitting outside talking loudly, drinking from cans and he spots big bottles being passed about. He sticks to the shadows and slips into his tent to find Ameer's instrument then heads back out, glancing over with a worried expression at an explosion of laughter. Tommy on his knees mimicking prayer again. Others doing it with him. The big woman that was greeting new people. A few others too. Banging their heads and waggling their backsides while wailing noisily.

He hurries back to the others and his son protesting quietly. 'There's so many people,' Ameer says.

'Ameer, there are people here that hate us,' Maleek says, opening the case on the floor. 'And your music gives pleasure...' he looks at his son, seeing the worry in his eyes. 'It will be okay, try and play, just a little...'

Ameer nods, taking the violin and stick in hands that tremble as he brings the chin rest to nestle under his jaw, his heart beating too hard now. Too many people watching him. It's too hot. He's too scared. He glances at his mother who smiles and nods him on, showing she has faith in him.

He brings the stick up, testing the strings, a scratching

noise, unpleasant, harsh and brought on by nerves and a quietness spreads out as the people all turn to stare. Another test, another scratch.

'Stay calm, close your eyes and breathe,' his mother says gently.

Ameer closes his eyes, inhales slowly and brings the bow into place while his fingertips find the strings. Another beat of his heart. Another surge of panic and Mary winces, wishing she hadn't egged the boy on and thinking they'll have to listen to an awful rendition of something terrible and then smile politely after. An awkward glance shared with Sam with a preparatory cringe factor already being projected.

Ameer starts. Still too nervous. It's been three weeks since he played, and, in that time, he has seen too much death and destruction. Corpses in the streets and screams in the air at night. He draws the bow over the strings, cursing the awful noise. It's too slow, he speeds up, but it comes too fast. His centre of mass is off. His being isn't relaxed. He plays on, trying to find his way in, trying to seek that which takes him from this world, but it doesn't come. Instead, his mind fills with the images of the horrifying things he has seen. Over and over. More and more. He tries ridding them, trying to focus, trying to blot them out and play music so people do not hate his family. But still it won't come. Still the feel evades him. He goes too fast and slows down. Then it's too slow so he goes faster. He stretches the notes out, long and wailing like the screams of the dying he heard outside while they stayed hidden and silent.

No. This isn't right. He must try harder. His father is relying on him. He cannot bring shame to his family. He must play properly. He must give pleasure and not this awful, screeching noise bringing the entire area to silence.

Everyone turns to watch. Everyone grows still. Watching a boy in turmoil playing music that floats out. Discordant for sure, but yet beautiful at the same time, and heart-achingly sad too. He goes faster then slower, seemingly trying to find a groove but what he produces holds them all rapt and entranced.

Those closest watch his face. Seeing the utter anguish in his features. Pure sadness. Terror, horror. Fear too. Tears prick his eyes, spilling over his cheeks and his bow moves faster, pushing harder, producing deeper sounds that roll out. Emotive and raw, yet so powerful too.

He plays on. Delving into the lower notes, making it dark, strong and turbulent. Hearts beat harder. The music striking all of them. Every man and woman thinking of what they have lost, of what they had, of what they saw that has hurt them so and still Ameer plays on, his body starting to move, starting to sway, his face still morphing through stages of pain and heartache.

Darker, faster, deeper. Harsher. There is only pain in this world. Only heartache. Only suffering. They're all going to die. They can all feel it. Ameer tells them this is so. Everything they do is in folly, in vain. To live is to suffer. To exist is to hurt. There is only darkness now. Only suffering. His face starts flushes with anger, his lips curling up, his brow dropping. Anger inside. Unfairness and loss that bring forth a rage.

It becomes too much. Too dark. People close their eyes, feeling themselves falling, feeling the hope dwindling, there is no hope and no reason to keep going.

Darker still. Rasping and harsh. Faster Ameer. Play faster. He feels the pain in his heart that pours into his arms, into his hands, into his fingers. Faster still. Jerking the bow back and forth. Violent, confused and angry. Consumed with Turmoil. With anguish. Adrenalin starts pumping. On and on but so something else stirs within him. A sense of resisting. Pushing back. Of knowing when to be like a willow tree and take the strong wind and when to start to rise and hold the ground.

The notes start to lift, light within the dark but so very fast, so very strong. They suffered so much. All of them. They saw so many bad things, but they are trying. By the will of Allah, by the will of God, by the will of the spark inside that drives them to live and survive and rise each day and despite the losses they are trying. To fight back. To say no. To push and resist. Not to be cowed. Not to be beaten down.

Hearts start stirring. Blood starts pumping. Everyone listens. Everyone reacts. Seeing Ameer's face and the glimpses of hope and courage seen within the pain, seeing the inner strength coming out. The inner strength they all have. They lift chins, eyes growing wet with moisture. Jaws clenching. Blood thundering as Ameer plays and plays. The music lifting them. Bringing courage and hope, each note fighting the darkness away. Saying no. Saying they will not be beaten. They can survive. Not just survive. They can live. They can rebuild and make it better. They can do this. There is hope. Not just death, and from the destruction so something new will emerge and those notes go higher and come faster. Damsa weeping openly. Pea's arms wrapped about Subi, both of them crying. So many are unable to stop the tears for the hope it gives, that a young boy from a country brought down by war can do this now in a place so very strange to him.

Sam thinks of her family. Norman thinks of Robert and the pain is so very bad. So very awful, but bittersweet too. Don't take just the bad. Remember the good. Remember the warmth and laughter and the love, and in that darkness, hidden by the shadows, Lilly feels a hand brush against hers while her heart thunders in her chest. She feels the warmth of it. The surety of it. The hardness of the knuckles against hers. She doesn't look at Mary, and Mary does not look at her, but both watch and listen to Ameer while chests heave all about them.

This is the new world. This is the world for the living. The rules of old do not apply here. The oppressive fears forced on them by whatever causes are no longer valid. Those that held power before and became corrupt and tainted from it now do not have a voice. This is cleaner than it was. Not shaped by greed or desire but by the primal instinct of a young girl that once learnt about the order of needs. Air, water, food, shelter and security. It's that simple and Lilly drives them on. Lilly makes them work till they pass out, but she does it too, from the front, and she does it *for* them, for her brother, taking only what everyone else takes. Eating only what they eat. Sleeping after them. Rising before them.

Thoughts and dreams race and surge as Ameer takes it higher still, bringing hope with every pull of his bow. His face lifting. Subi cannot take her eyes from him. She's never seen someone look so beautiful as now. So consumed with what's inside and Ameer's brow starts to rise, a smile touching his lips and the notes change, sharper, highs and lows together. Mysterious, intriguing, becoming playful and joyous. Smiles start showing. Fingers wiping tears from cheeks. People laughing at the sight of each other. Men whacking other men on the back and arms. Women grinning sheepishly and Ameer starts to smile, to play, to drift into the music. Up and down, high and low, sharp and fast.

Mary laughs, dropping onto her side to reach over

Lilly's lap, plucking the radio from her belt with a wink. 'Be five minutes...' she darts off to a few confused looks that quickly go back to watching Ameer.

The lad plays on too. Opening his eyes now and then to see people smiling and moving a little. He keeps going, happy to be giving pleasure, hoping this is what his father wants, and the people will accept them.

He tries to make it lighter still, feeling his way organically, knowing the violin can make fast, happy sounds but this is not what he trained to do. He pokes his tongue out, ad-libbing as he goes, making it up. Spotting Subi watching him and blushing deeply, feeling suddenly self-conscious and wanting to look good. He tries appearing serious and reflective, deep and mysterious and peeks again to see if she's still watching and misses a chord at seeing her staring past him. Then he spots everyone else looking past him too and pauses mid-play to turn and startles at seeing a group of people walking over from the gate. Two men in the lead. Old as time, grizzled and grey, teeth missing, faces worn, weathered and lined. Solid shoulders but their backs are starting to stoop. Knees not as strong as they once were and each holding a violin in their hands.

Eggy coughs into the silence, bringing his violin up. Uncle Jack spits to the side and counts to three as they both start playing to a ripple of noise spreading out.

Ameer grins, his eyes wide with delight at the music coming from them. Fast and lilting. The thing Ameer wanted to play but he didn't know how. Folk music but fast and strong. They come closer. Two old men leading more with Mary grinning from ear to ear. Peter, Willie, Elvis. Men and women from the camp who heard when Mary used the radio to call for her Uncle Pete to come over with Eggy and Uncle Jack.

'Come on lad,' Eggy says, dipping his upper body towards Ameer. 'Play boy...'

Ameer hesitates. It's too fast for him. The way they move isn't how he was taught, and he watches as Eggy and Jack come to either side of him, leaning forward to stare at each other. A nod between them and they slow their play, easing the speed down.

'Play lad,' Eggy urges.

'Go on, Ameer!' Kyle shouts.

'Try it,' someone else calls.

'Have a go!' another voice adds to more calling out as Ameer looks this way and that, finally spotting Subi staring at him and that's all the lad needs.

He brings his violin up, holding his bow ready as the two men slow down even more to give easy strokes, letting him join in. Simple and sweet. Long notes. A little speed. A little more. Ameer keeps up, tying to watch them both. A bit more speed. The old men start tapping their feet. Drumming a beat. Faster now. The notes not hard, just different and Ameer plays on, his mother laughing with delight at seeing her son tapping his foot as he plays.

'Faster boy,' Eggy says, speeding up, taking it up through more levels. Ameer loses it now and then, earning laughs from the two men who tell him to jump back in. On they go, louder, higher, faster. 'Ready lad?' Eggy calls, grinning with delightful mischief and the burst of energy comes without warning as the two men go faster still with little Ameer between them, doing his best to play and move and tap his feet.

Kyle rises to his feet, grinning as he rolls his sleeves up and waves his hands and starts tapping his right foot, clapping in time, the foot stamping a little harder. A jig danced, his feet moving. People laughing at the sight of the gun-toting Father dancing to the music. A whoop and Mary swishes in, dancing to Kyle, looping her arm in his, spinning round and round, both of them grinning. They break and turn, coming back to do it again.

'FASTER LADS,' Mary shouts and the music speeds up. Sam can't hold back and jumps up to run in, looping her arm with Mary then Kyle and more rise, laughing and silly. People banging on the ground. Clapping hands. A woman who took part in an annual samba band parade grabs a bucket and adds to the beat.

It's too hot for this. They've all worked too hard. They're exhausted and should be beaten and cowed. Sam grabs at John's and Pardip's hands, pulling them up. Lenski on her feet with Simar and Jaspal, looping with one then the other then off to do the same again with Ann and Anika then over to Damsa and Maleek. The other women up and clapping. Bashir laughing. Tajj sour faced, his manner stricter, his mind less open. Older than the others and not happy to be so gleeful, but everyone else is, because the old ways are gone. The old rules are not here. This is the new world and Mary dances over to Lilly looking plainly terrified at the prospect of dancing and drags her in, looping arms to turn then break and do it with someone else. Stupid. Silly. Infantile even, but bloody glorious all the same.

'FUCK 'EM,' Tommy yells, on his feet holding court at the back of the fort. Swaying from the booze. A bottle of vodka in his hands. More bottles of spirits taken from his stash of goods being passed around. 'We can sing too...RUUUUULE   BRITANNIA...BRITANNIA

RULE THE WAVES...COS WE'LL NEVER NEVER NEVER BE SLAVES...'

'He's got the words wrong,' Karl says, frowning drunkenly before shrugging and joining in with the voices singing deep and loud.

At the front they dance and jig. Arm in arm, round and round. So many have died. So many have fallen and they have so much to do, but here, tonight, they can have this time. This is earnt and paid for with sweat and blood and pain.

It's still hot though. Crushingly hot and it's mere minutes before the sweat pours down and they gasp for air, flapping hands in front of faces. Clothing once more becoming sodden. Ameer sweats too. Grinning at Eggy. Grinning at Uncle Jack. His violin now a fiddle. His aptitude and skill shining bright.

'No more,' Lenski gasps, wafting air over her face as she breaks from dancing with Jaspal, enjoying his muscular arms looping in hers. 'I hot...I too hot...'

Jaspal grins in the dark at her. White teeth showing through his dark beard. His features handsome and chiselled. She grins back, frowning at the feeling inside. Unsure of what to make of it but thinking it's nice. Maddox not in her mind at all.

'You're sweating,' Mary says, laughing at Lilly.

'It's too hot,' Lilly says as Billy and Amna dance in circles nearby.

'Ah you know what we need,' Mary says. 'SWIM! WHO'S UP FOR A SWIM?'

'RUUUULE   BRITANNIA...BRITANNIA RULE THE WAVES...something something mumble mumble NEVER EVER WILL BE SLAVES...' they sing at the back of the fort, drunk and loud, sweaty and hot, swaying and bouncing off each other. Men with tops off. Chests puffed up. Arms out wide.

Pamela blows air from her cheeks. So hot she could puke, or that could be the snacks she hasn't stopped eating or the strong cider she hasn't stopped drinking, and maybe the vodka, or the brandy. She doesn't know. She just feels hot and sick. 'I need to cool down,' she tells Tommy.

'Eh?' he yells at her while everyone sings the same line over and over.

'I'm hot,' she shouts.

'Go for a swim then,' he shouts, getting the idea at the same second he says it. 'SWIM! FUCK THIS...'

They pour through the front gate and into the sea. Gasping and crying out at the cooling waters. Lilly goes to the side, to the darker shadows where they can stack their rifles and gun belts and strip down to underwear. The shadows deep enough to not worry about being seen partially naked. In they go, splashing and cooling off. Joan paddling with her trouser legs rolled up, watching the little ones in the shallows and keeping an eye on the weapons. Norman and Kyle staying inside to listen to the music with Simar and others. Jaspal running into the sea with Lenski, then cursing and running back out to remove his turban, showing a top knot of silky black hair and not caring one bit if he's in public or private because this is the new world and these are new rules. His stomach defined with muscle that makes Lenski pull a face at Mary as he dives past them.

'I think Lenski's got the hots going on,' she says when Lilly surfaces next to her. 'This heat, it does things to the mind I reckon...' she smiles at Lilly, winking as she splashes water at her.

Kids in the shallows, splashing about, making noise. None of them caring that only a dozen or so metres away and down on the seabed lie the bodies of the fallen. Their flesh slowly rotting and floating up to be eaten by fish that in turn will be caught and consumed. The virus within the bodies now dead. The flesh cleansed.

***

At the back they do the same, but because of the alcohol they go mostly naked. Well, the men do, splashing in with big guts and heavy limbs then calling out for the women to strip down.

'Go on, get 'em off,' Tommy yells, eyeing Gwen trying to drunkenly remove her jean shorts.

Pamela wants to go in, but she hates the water, but then she also wants to be naked but then doesn't want to be naked. But then she wants everyone to look at her boobs but not her fat bits. She belches a bit too forcefully and throws her upper body over to vomit so hard she farts and shits herself.

'Dirty fucking bitch,' Tommy sneers, splashing away from her on the shore.

'I GOT FINGERED,' Pamela wails with vomit and

saliva hanging from her mouth and shit dribbling down her legs.

'Come on, time to go in,' Lilly wading from the sea, the water cascading down her body. Mary ahead of her already on the shore trying not to look while Lilly also tries not to look, while Lenski makes no attempt whatsoever to stop looking at Jaspal as he walks out.

'*His stomach,*' she mouths to Mary, pointing at her own belly then at Jaspal in front of her.

Clothes tugged on. Weapons collected, and kids gathered as they head back in to the music ending to a long applause. Ameer grinning widely while stealing glances at Subi, men and women patting his back.

'We'll play again lad,' Eggy says, winking at Ameer. 'Speed you up a bit, come over one night eh? Ask your ma though...get Mary to bring you. Night all.'

'Night, Eggy...night, Uncle Jack,' Mary says, hugging both as the party slowly breaks up.

Giggles at the back of the fort. Mirth and merriment with steam rising from the jets of piss spraying out. 'Get the sides,' Tommy urges, leaning back to aim his dick higher. Men on either side in a big circle. Women too, some of them joining in to squat and piddle, chuckling and laughing at each other. Bottles still being passed. Someone pukes, heaving up to spew but that just makes everyone else laugh even more.

They finish up and head off, swaying and singing *Rule Britannia* still loud and slurred. Into Tommy's tent. Back to his stash and more booze for the party to keep going.

'We've got to make a stand,' Tommy tells them, handing another bottle of vodka out. 'Seriously...no, no...no listen to me...we need 'em out. We need an election in here with them bitches voted out and us voted in. The common man yeah? We'll stop them coming in. The muzzies. The darkies. Muzzies out yeah?' he slurs and nods, urging them on. 'Muzzies out...muzzies out...muzzies out,' he chants softly, giggling as though trying to keep them all quiet as his words are taken up. 'Muzzies out,' they join in, laughing in delight as people move past their tent heading back from the other side.

'I t was too much,' Tajj berates as they walk back. 'Ameer should practise yes, but this culture is not ours. Singing and dancing? Our women showing their faces? What next? Drugs? Alcohol?'

'Brother, enough,' Maleek says, groaning into his hand as he rubs his beard. 'We have to fit in.'

'We must be accepted, yes,' Tajj says. 'But we are not to become them. We are not them.'

Maleek rolls his eyes at his son and daughter, making them smile. Damsa choosing to stay quiet and not aggravate the older Tajj.

'Still, it was a good night,' Maleek says brightly, making his wife and a few others chuckle while Tajj starts berating them again.

'What's that smell?' Bashir asks, stopping outside their tent. 'Has it rained? The tent is wet.'

'Wet?' Maleek asks, staring at the stains on the sides and the liquid dripping down. The smell hits him. The stench of piss as he spots the urine marks on all sides and a smear of wet vomit dripping down the main door.

'This is acceptance?' Tajj asks.

'Muzzies out...muzzies out...muzzies out...' the soft chanting coming from within the big tent across the way. Damsa and Ameer alone understanding the words.

'What are they singing?' Maleek asks.

'A drunken pop song,' Damsa replies quickly. 'I'll get some water to wash the sides...children, go inside, to bed now. Go on. Everyone inside,' she says firmly as the people in the big tent all spill out, laughing loudly. Lighting cigarettes and moaning it's too hot to stay inside with fat Pam stinking of shit and puke.

'Whoa,' Tommy calls, spotting Damsa looking over. 'Everyone hide, the muzzies are back...had a nice night?' he calls with a big grin, giving a thumbs up. 'Infected anymore countries for your Jihad have you yeah?'

Sick laughs and cheers and Damsa rushes inside, hearing them chanting and shouting. The pressure suddenly back and bearing down.

———

'We needed that,' John says, heading into the rooms at the far end by the main gates. A low bulb burning softly as the men head to bed rolls. Kyle choosing the one closest to the door. Lowering down while grinning and humming. Norman on the other side. John further down. Alf already asleep and more out the back. 'I'm beat,' John says, stripping down to shorts to flop on his bedding. 'Night lads...'

'You are such a poser,' Simar laughs, heading in with Jaspal. 'I knew you'd do that...*hey ladies, look at me, I'm a Sikh with a six-pack...*'

'Idiot,' Jaspal replies, shaking his head at his brother as they walk down to the end of the room. 'Night, gents...' he adds, waving a hand.

'Night,' Kyle says.

'Night,' Norman says, down to his shorts on his bedding. The air still so hot. 'We did need that,' he says quietly.

'Aye,' Kyle whispers, gun belt off and to his side, his clothes ready to be pulled on quickly. The end of the twenty third day and he wonders where Henry and the team are. Are they alive? Did they make it through the first few days? If they are alive then they will eventually head here. They'll hear what's happening. They'll find out and come. Then what? Is that good or bad? Kyle doesn't know. He doesn't know where Howie is either. He doesn't really know anything, only that this new found sense of hope is very, very fragile. But still, he grins in the dark, chuckling at the evening they just had. What a night. Lilly should be proud of what she has achieved.

'Seriously, Blondie. You should be proud,' Mary whispers as they strip off ready for bed. The kids already fast asleep. Exhausted from the day and night. Sam, Pea and Joan sparked out further down the room. Lilly closest to the door. 'What a night eh?' Mary adds.

'Aye,' Lilly says, not even realising she's using that word now.

'I never see stomach like this,' Lenski whispers from the other side, making them both smile in the dark. 'I go sleep now. Is good day. Is good night. We do again tomorrow...is hot. Is too hot. I no sleep is so hot...' she lies down, huffs at the heat, rolls over and falls asleep within seconds.

'It is hot,' Mary says, down to her bra and knickers as she lies back on her bedding.

'It is,' Lilly says, dressed the same. Weapons in reach, clothes ready to be pulled on quickly. The door with a string attached to the top so the kids can't sneak out. The lighting near on pitch dark.

Mary rolls on her side, edging closer to Lilly, 'can I ask you a question?' she whispers.

'Ssshhh,' Joan whispers from further down the room.

'Sorry, Joanie,' Mary whispers, smiling again as she goes closer. Their bodies touching. That energy between them still flowing. She lowers down over Lilly, bringing her mouth close to her ear. 'Do you think she can hear me now?' she asks, testing to see if Joan will reply while Lilly feels the rush of warm air blasting over her ear, making her skin prickle with a shiver running down her spine.

'You're so hot,' Lilly says, resting a hand on Mary's side.

'Is it too much? Want me to move back?'

Lilly shakes her head.

'Was that a nod or a shake?'

'It was a nod,' she chuckles. 'It's fine. What was your question?'

'Should go to sleep really.'

'I'm not tired, are you?'

'Not really. Too much going on. Do you know what I mean?'

'I do. Was that your question?'

'No,' Mary whispers down. 'Promise you won't be offended first.'

'I don't know what it is yet.'

'Ach, I'm not asking till you promise.'

'Fine. I promise to try and not be offended.'

'That'll do. Er, so...are you autistic or anything? Not like...like loads, but it's a spectrum isn't it and you could have a wee Blondie toe in that world.'

'A Blondie toe?'

'Aye, a Blondie toe. I mean, you're smart and funny and you function brilliantly, but I noticed that sometimes you don't empathise with others so good. You know what I mean? Do you mind me asking you all this?'

'It's fine,' Lilly says. 'I like talking to you.'

'Dunno why. I can't stand you personally. No, but they said what you did. You know, with the grenades and that.'

'And?'

'And it doesn't seem to bother you. Or like, you don't show it does...does that make sense? I'm not making sense. Like we had that fight with the infected things at the docks right, and we can all see they're infected and so we can make it okay in our heads to kill them.'

'It's the same,' Lilly says. 'In my head I mean.'

Mary pauses, exhaling slowly while feeling Lilly finger-tips start to move a little on her side. It's nice. It feels nice. 'Were you like this before?' Mary asks.

'I hadn't killed anyone if that's what you mean. I don't know,' she pauses, thinking while running her fingers over Mary's skin, feeling the softness. 'I don't know. I just did what had to be done. It's like that now. I can see what should be done, and I get frustrated that others don't do what I want and at the speed I want...so maybe I am. I guess it's possible. I got angry on the bay earlier and

Norman had to tell me to stop otherwise I'd have worked everyone too hard, then tonight, I couldn't understand why it would take so long to put the sides and roof on the new canteen but I didn't hear my own voice and how hard it sounds, then you said I was being harsh. Am I too much?'

'No,' Mary says quickly, smiling down at her. 'I was just wondering. You're lovely, Blondie. Don't worry...'

Lilly chuckles, digging her fingers into Mary's side to tickle for a second and making the woman drop to laugh quietly. That energy flowing faster. The spark there. The warmth of them both. Heads closer now. Lilly's hand moving up and down Mary's side, stroking further across her back. Mary almost resting her chin on Lilly's shoulder while remembering what Pea, Sam and Lenski said the first night she stayed in the fort. That it was Nick that found Lilly and eventually saved her brother. 'Do you think about him much? Nick I mean,' she asks.

Lilly shrugs, following the same train of thought and in truth she's hardly thought of Nick. 'No,' she says honestly as another door in her mind opens. One she knew was there but had been ignoring until now. She shifts a little, air blasting from her nose as Mary frowns in the darkness.

'What?' Mary asks, detecting something in the air.

'Nothing.'

'Go on, say it...'

'They left,' Lilly says quickly, giving voice to the thing that has been bugging her for days. 'Howie left. Right when it was at the very worst they packed up and went...they could have left one. Any one of them would have stopped it from happening, but they didn't, and it went wrong and I had to kill children to do that...and now I don't know which is worst. That I did that and I'm fine with it, or that they left in the first place...it's like...I don't know...' she trails off, sighing again, shuffling as though to get closer to Mary without realising she is doing it while Mary listens, trying to detect the nuances but finding Lilly near on impossible to read sometimes. Like she is closed down and projects that cold exterior while the turmoil stays hidden deep within.

'You asked me if I feel bad about killing them? No. And I'd do it again. I would have killed Damsa and her entire family to protect my brother...but not just Billy. Milly too, Raj and Amna, all of them...people who can't defend themselves. Does that make sense? They can't do it but I can and so I will. Whatever it takes. Whatever the cost. It's either right, or it's wrong...' that door opens a bit more as Lilly's hand tightens on Mary's side. 'Nick saved my brother and I will always, always be thankful for that, but he did what I would do now,' she tenses, blasting air in frustration. 'I'm not explaining it very well...'

'It's okay,' Mary says softly.

'I didn't have ability before. I didn't know how to fire a gun or...or...fight back. Now I do, so what Nick did was incredible, what they all do is incredible. Nick told me what they face every single day. Thousands of infected coming at them all the time, and they're off now keeping them away from us, trying to fix it. And that's important and it's right people here should respect them. I respect them. But...' she stops again, holding back.

'But what?' Mary asks gently.

'But they left. They fucking left,' Lilly says, the words spilling out at the same millisecond she thinks of them. The realisation of her emotional reaction dawning as she speaks. 'They left. Howie left. My dad was weak and he failed and he died because of it...'

'Blondie...'

'No. It's the truth. I loved him. I do love him, but he was weak, and he didn't protect us. I took this fort back and I fixed it and I was so worried what Howie and Paula would think when they got back. I was in knots. I could hardly go out and meet them, and Nick was there and I had this rush of emotion for him and you know what happened? Nick fucked me and they went again...'

'Hey now, I'm sure that he...'

'Where is he then? Is he here? I opened my legs and he went. He took what he wanted and went but dressed it up in honour and sacrifice and doing the right thing. That's fine. I get it. We have to do the right thing and what they are doing is vital but that doesn't mean I'm the little girl waiting for him ready to rush back into his arms and open my legs again. Nick wasn't there at the docks and he wasn't there when that van came down the road full of infected and he didn't have to scream at Damsa and Ameer...' she stems the flow of words, her hand gripping Mary's side tight now, the energy spiking harder. That door open and the raw ugliness of true emotion laid bare. She loves them all. She supports what they do and respects what they are, but she hates them for leaving. For abandoning this place. For abandoning her, but it's made her hard inside, and this world needs that now. This new world. This brave new world where the rules of old no longer hold true and it doesn't matter what was, only what is and so she frowns, breathing hard. 'I don't want to talk about Nick...'

'That's fine,' Mary whispers, sensing a finality and she drops down to kiss Lilly's shoulder, seeking to give comfort with a natural act and as her lips brush Lilly's skin so that energy changes direction again with both suddenly becoming very aware of how close they are.

'I er,' Mary swallows, pulling her head back as Lilly

turns but a fraction with her lips millimetres from Mary's cheek. She starts gliding her hand up and over Mary's ribs to the material of her bra and over the swell of her breast and up across Mary's neck, so gently, so very gently. Bringing her hand to the side of Mary's face who turns her head into Lilly without any resistance given at all, and that young woman of a singular minded determination moves in to kiss Mary. Their lips meeting. Their breath held. Fleeting. Barely touching but they hold for eternity with neither moving. The heat bearing down. Hearts whumping hard. They blast air from noses and move to kiss harder, pushing into each other and as their mouths open so Mary pulls back and away. Breaking the contact.

'I need a drink,' she says, breathing hard. 'It's hot and... you'd better get some sleep, Blondie...I'll get some water...' she pushes up and goes out, unhooking the string from the door as Lilly watches her go. Her own breath coming in gasps. Still feeling the contact of the kiss.

She rolls onto her back, blinking and wiping the back of her hand across the sweat on her forehead.

She waits a minute. Biting her lip and finally sits up before going out into the dark passage. Cool concrete floor underfoot. She heads out into the main office, looking out through the open door into the fort. A noise from nearby. The glug of water in a bottle coming from the room they use to change and wash in. She moves to the door, easing it open to see Mary inside drinking water.

'Alright,' Mary whispers in greeting, offering a tight smile. 'Needed water...' Lilly holds still, staring in at Mary's hair spilling down her shoulders and back. At the beads of sweat glistening on her body. Mary blinks at her, trying not to do the same. 'I'm not gay, Blondie. I like boys...men...I like men...'

Lilly waits. Not saying a word.

'I'm not a bloody lesbian. And you're sixteen. I'm twenty one. That's wrong that is...' she drinks again, swallowing the water and lowering the bottle. 'We're just pals. Right? Mates. Like soul mates...girls get crushes. This is a crush. I fancy you. You fancy me but like a crush, right? The weather, it's hot as anything. We're all out of sorts... Fuck off, Lilly,' she says when Lilly moves in a step. Her blue eyes fixed and staring. Her blond hair pulled back. 'Jesus. I said I'm not gay...I'm going back to bed...' she finishes the water and nods as she walks past Lilly, pausing at her side, thinking to say something, wanting to say something, and in the end she says nothing at all and walks on.

Lilly stays still, waiting for seconds, for minutes, confused, rejected, unsure of what to say or do. That awful heat pushing down so very hard and still feeling the kiss on her lips.

———

They sit together in the middle section of their big tent. Confused, scared and unsure of what to do. The women grouped together holding the children close. Maleek clutches a length of wood in his hands snatched from the building site. Bashir and Tajj the same. Arming themselves as they tremble and sit in silence, once more listening to the noises outside. The drunken yells and shouts. The chanting too. *Muzzies out. Muzzies out. Muzzies out.*

'You lot pack it in,' someone else calls from within tent-town.

'FUCK OFF!'

"GET FUCKED.'

'SHUT UP CUNT...'

Angry slurred voices yelling back. Laughter harsh and brutal. An impact on the side of the tent making them all flinch. Another empty beer can thrown. Laughter again. Footsteps coming closer.

'Muzzies out, muzzies out....' the chanting coming softly as they listen to giggles and drunk men shushing each other. Then they hear the patters of liquid as the jets of piss come again, spraying on the outside of the tent. The stench of it now so strong and the heat bears down, crushing and hot as the pressure grows.

CHAPTER TWENTY

D ay Twenty Four

'J esus,' Sam says, walking from their room into the main office. Her hair poking up, sleep lines on her face. Her clothes clinging wet to her body. 'This heat...' she stops at the table, grabbing a bottle of water to drink deep in the super-charged air. If yesterday was bad, today is off the chart. 'My head is killing me,' she says.

'It's the heat,' Ann says from the table where even the children sit quietly, rendered silent by the awful pressure. 'Painkillers over here.'

'Ta,' Sam says, walking over to mouth two white pills. 'You okay?' she asks, looking at Lilly.

'Fine,' Lilly says.

'You're up early again,' Sam remarks, watching Lilly tie her boot laces. 'Do you even sleep?'

Lilly offers a smile as she strands straight to pull her hair back. Clean trousers, a clean black vest top. Her pistol already holstered. Her grenades already pocketed. Her rifle nearby.

'Morning,' Mary says, walking in from the back. Dressed and ready. Boots on. Her face lacking the usual spark of humour and fun. 'Ready?'

'I am,' Lilly says.

'Ready for what?' Sam asks.

'Docks,' Lilly replies. 'We're doing an early run for more containers...we shouldn't be long.'

'Oh okay, cool,' Sam says. 'Are we doing the meeting when you get back?'

'Don't worry about the meeting today,' Lilly says. 'Unless Lenski wants to hold one. The canteen is the priority before this weather breaks.'

'Sure,' Sam says, looking from Lilly to Mary trying to avoid each other's eye contact. 'You both okay?'

'Aye,' Mary says. 'Just hot.'

'Very hot,' Lilly says, picking her rifle up before kissing Billy and working round the table to the other children. 'You all be good, okay? Everyone will be tetchy today because of the weather...'

'What's tetchy?' Milly asks.

'Grumpy,' Mary says, earning a quick look from Lilly. 'Laters,' she adds, smiling at Ann and Sam.

'Stay safe,' Ann calls.

'What's up with them?' Sam asks once they've gone.

'This heat,' Ann says. 'Does things to people.'

'Hang on a second,' Lilly says as they near the gate. She moves to the recessed door, leaning in to hear the rustle of people starting to wake. 'Kyle?'

'Aye?' he asks, his voice gruff and low from sleep.

'We're doing the run for the docks.'

'Are you going now? Want me to come?'

'It's fine. We'll be back soon.'

'Okay, stay safe...'

She heads out to see Mary opening the outer gate and follows her to the beach and the sea they swam in last night. Into a boat and Mary starts the engine, the chugging noise seeming so loud in the near silent world about them. The water an inky dead calm with no motion. The sky above them coming to light. The air so thick you could eat it and just moving is hard work.

'You okay, Blondie?' Mary asks.

'Fine. You?'

'Aye. Fine. You didn't sleep did you. I heard you tossing and turning.'

'No, you?'

'Same. Bloody heat. Listen, about last night...'

'It's fine,' Lilly says, cutting her off. 'My apologies.'

'Ach, don't be all posh and polite now and make it worse.'

'I said it's fine. I just got confused...'

'Confused about what?'

'Mary, it's early and I'm really hot...'

'Fine.'

'Fine.'

They hit the shore, killing the engine and heading over the sand to the road to Peter waiting with vans and men smoking as they sweat and check weapons.

'Been waiting for ages,' Elvis snaps.

'Piss off,' Mary snaps back, giving him the finger.

'Just load up,' Peter calls gruffly. Everyone tetchy. Everyone snappy. 'Your van is at the back and stay in formation this time, Mary.'

'Whatever,' she calls back, heading down the line to the

waiting van and the day starts. The twenty fourth day since the world ended.

───────────

'My head,' Pea says, walking into the main office.

'On the table,' Sam says.

'What is?' Pea asks.

'Painkillers.'

'Right. You could have just said that.'

'I did,' Sam fires back.

'Ladies,' Ann calls softly.

'Have they gone already?' Joan asks curtly, bustling in. 'They were up all night yacking on and running in and out. I'll be asking for a room on my own if that carries on...'

'On the table,' Sam says.

'What is?' Joan snaps.

'You're doing it again, Sam,' Pea says. 'Joan doesn't know what's on the table.'

'The bloody headache pills are on the bloody table,' Sam says.

'Urgh. Is hot. I have headache,' Lenski says.

'Don't say it,' Pea snaps.

'On the table,' Sam says.

'Just say there are pills here if you want them,' Pea says.

'Ladies,' Ann calls softly.

'Are they tetchy?' Milly asks.

'I think they are sweetie,' Ann replies.

'Morning morning,' Kyle says, walking in. Ruffling Billy and Rajesh's hair before spotting the packet of headache pills in Lenski's hands.

'You want?' she asks.

'Aye, right thumping brain this morning.'

'That's because you snore,' Norman says, walking in behind him.

'And you don't?' Kyle asks, giving him a look.

'Gentlemen,' Ann calls softly.

'You both do,' John says, pushing through them to aim for the drinks table at the back. 'Might go back to sleeping in a tent...anyone got any headache pills?'

'Here,' Kyle says, throwing the packet over.

'Alright,' Simar says, yawning as he walks to the table to find a seat.

'Hey,' Jaspal says, gruff and low, lifting a hand as he walks in.

'Eh up, the six pack Sikh is here,' Simar calls.

'Wasn't funny yesterday and it isn't now...' Jaspal snaps. 'And who was snoring last night?'

'Kyle,' Norman says.

'Norman,' Kyle says.

'All of you were,' John calls from the back.

'And you weren't?' Jaspal says.

'Gentlemen,' Ann calls.

'Tetchy,' Milly says, nodding at Simar.

'You're right, babs, we're all very tetchy,' Simar replies. 'Where's the boss lady then?'

'Which one?' Ann asks. 'Lilly has gone for the docks and Lenski is over there. Lenski? Lilly said you can have a meeting if you want or everyone can just get on with it.'

Lenski nods, sipping water. Her own head thudding with pain. 'I think no meeting. We just work yes? Everyone knows what to do...'

'Sides and roof,' John says. 'Soon as we can...this weather'll break any minute now...Sim, you go and get Maleek up. We can get a few bits done before breakfast while it's a bit cooler...'

'Cooler, are you taking the...'

'Language,' a few people call out as Simar cuts off, blasting air and pulling a funny face at Milly.

'Fine. I guess I'm going to get Maleek then...someone make us a brew though? Tea please...Not Jas though. He makes awful tea...it's all those sit ups he does...'

'Sim, too early,' Jaspal snaps as Simar heads out, wincing at the pain in his shoulders from lifting and carrying so many lengths of wood and doing so much work overhead yesterday. He rolls his shoulders as he walks. Stretching his arms and grimacing at the sky. Another day. Another super-hot, super-busy day.

He passes the site, checking the rafters and seeing where they need to do next as his foot scuffs an empty beer can, kicking it along the ground. He looks down, frowning at the sight of it. He spots another one nearby and walks on, seeing a few more dotted about as his head lifts to see the utter mayhem spread out as the noise reaches him.

People gathered outside the big circus tent. Men with tops off. Women stripped down to bras and shorts. Tattoos and bellies on show. Beer cans everywhere. Plastic bottles of cider and empty bottles of spirits. Snack food wrappers littering the ground. Cigarette butts everywhere. A foul stench in the air. Booze, tobacco, sweat and vomit. He slows as he walks, spotting torn off chunks of cardboard with words scrawled on them stuck to the side of the big tent.

THE FORT #2.
THE OTHER FORT.
THE ~~ENGLISH~~ BRITISH FORT.
MUZZIES OUT.
PAMMIE SHIT HERSELF

There's a lot of people too. Must be close to forty. More that joined in during the night, lured in for the booze and having heard what Doctor Lisa said about death camps and starvation and how the Muslims started it all. Scared people. Stupid people. People who just wanted to get drunk and feel safer in a mass of others. Now they're all drunk and milling about like the outside of a pub after a football match. Like a festival turned ugly.

'*Muzzies out...muzzies out...muzzies out...*' that soft chanting coming from a few here and there as Simar takes it all in. Seeing tents and shelters have been pulled down and the poles taken from them and dug into the ground in a circle. Forming a weird barrier. Like a crappy fence line.

He spots Maleek's tent and his stomach lurches at the sight. Puke and piss stains all over it. The ground at the sides littered with cans, debris and crap. Shoes and rubbish thrown over. Lit cigarettes that have singed holes in the sides. The smell of piss everywhere. A darker, uglier, nasty wet brown smear down the opening flap from someone taking a shit on it. Another side of cardboard wedged outside. The words scrawled in thick black letters.

PAKI LAND.

'Did you do this?' he calls out, anger rushing inside. 'OI...DID YOU DO THIS?' he shouts louder, his fists clenching at his sides as he walks towards the big tent. Making those closest turn and laugh at him.

'DID YOU DO THAT?' he asks again, pointing at Maleek's tent.

'Fuck off,' someone calls.

'Watch out, the muzzies are about,' Tommy shouts. 'What's up with you? Go on...fuck off...'

'YOU RACIST WANKERS...' Simar yells, striding in towards them.

'OR WHAT?' Tommy bellows, switching instantly to rage as he walks out with men puffing up to go after him. Men with sticks and hammers and pipes taken from the building site. They run at Simar who goes at them. Too incensed and too angry to think clearly. His fists bunched and swinging but against so many he stands no chance and the blows come in from all sides. Punches to his head and body. Sticks hitting his back. People kicking his legs.

'HEY...HELP!' someone in another tent screams out in panic.

'SHUT YOUR FUCKING MOUTH,' Tommy screams at them. 'Go on, that's enough...go on...back now...' he pushes his group away from Simar, chuckling at seeing his turban yanked off and he grabs the material before Simar can, laughing as he throws it into his group.

'You fucking...' Simar gets to his feet, his face cut and bleeding as another roar comes up from the crowd. Angrier and louder from seeing Maleek rushing from his tent with his brothers. All three of them armed with sticks as they rush to grab Simar, pulling him back.

'MUZZIES OUT...MUZZIES OUT...MUZZIES OUT...' the chanting starts again as more empty cans are launched at the retreating men.

That noise drifts down through the fort to the open door of the office but becomes lost to the chat inside, the scraping of chairs and drinks being made.

'What's that noise?' John asks, peering at the door as a young woman pops into view.

'Is the gate open yet?' she asks quickly, her husband close behind with their son in his arms.

'Do what, love?' John asks.

'Is the gate open? We want to go...'

'Go?' John asks, walking towards her as he clocks the way she looks frantically up towards the back of the fort.

'We're not staying,' she says, her voice shrill and panicked. 'Been fights all night, people throwing up, pissing everywhere...some guy's getting beaten up now and...'

'Whoa whoa,' John says, holding a hand out. 'What? Where?'

'We're leaving,' another woman snaps, striding down with her kids gathered about her. 'That's disgusting...you said it was safe...when we came in, they said it was safe... that isn't safe!'

'What isn't?' John asks. 'Len, come here a minute...'

'What happen?' Lenski asks.

'You don't even know?' another asks, striding past her. 'I'm going outside...I'll wait for the boats thank you...'

'I go see,' Lenski says, heading out.

'What's going on?' Sam asks as those in the office turn to focus on the happenings in the doorway.

'Something at the back,' John says. 'Fights or some-thing...said someone is getting beaten up...' he rushes off after Lenski as the office spills out, all of them seeing people walking quickly away from the back, holding children and whatever they can carry in their arms. Frightened faces. Children crying. The heat so very awful and crushing down.

Lenski goes first, walking fast towards the building site and with every step closer so the noise comes clearer.

'MUZZIES   OUT...MUZZIES   OUT...MUZZIES OUT...'

Loud chanting and it takes a few seconds for her to realise what is being said. She spots the first beer cans as John strides behind her and the others rushing to catch up. More litter on the ground. More debris. The smell reaching them as they go past the building site towards tent town, seeing forty or so people drinking outside Tommy's tent. Men with sticks and hammers and weapons. Knives and pipes. Men with tops off holding beer cans and bottles over their heads. Women too.

'MUZZIES   OUT...MUZZIES   OUT...MUZZIES OUT...'

Tommy spots Lenski coming into view. A rush inside. A smirk on his face that he is making this happen. That he is going to wipe the grin off the smug Polish girl's face and he leans back to sing loudly.

'RUUUUULE   BRITANNIA...BRITANNIA RULE THE WAVES...COS WE'LL NEVER NEVER NEVER BE SLAVES...'

'What the hell is this?' Lenksi asks, shouting to be heard as she spots Simar outside Damsa's tent. His face cut and bleeding. His turban gone, and his black hair pulled from the knot. Maleek, Bashir and Tajj clutching sticks. Damsa inside holding her children. The other woman looking as terrified as she.

'Fuck me,' John says, reaching Lenski as the others catch up, all of them staring at the mess, at the piss and puke and shit. At the massed chanting coming from the huge drunk group.

'What's going on?' Pardip yells, running towards them, eliciting more yells from the crowd. 'Sim? What happened?'

'Them racist wankers,' Simar spits the words out, blood on his mouth, split lips and his clothing torn.

Sam and Pea come to a stop. Joan with them. Norman balking at the sight of it all.

'LENSKI!' Sunnie shouts, rushing over with Agatha. Both of them looking shaken to the core. 'They've emptied the back rooms...it's all gone. All the alcohol, the cigarettes... snacks, chocolate...'

'They've been in my rooms too,' Colin yells, rushing over, his face etched in fear and worry. 'Stuff thrown everywhere...'

Lenski reels on the spot. Her head thumping. The heat rising with every minute. The air so thick. Everything so charged. Lilly isn't here either. This is down to her now.

'Did they do that to you?' Jaspal asks, finally seeing his brother cut and bleeding. 'DID THEY DO THAT?'

He turns off, pumped and ready to fight, marching towards the mass of people who break out with loud deep yells, brandishing weapons and throwing cans out.

'Jas, get back you bloody idiot,' Pardip says, dragging his younger brother back.

'I'm not having this,' Jaspal shouts. 'You've got guns... stop them...give me a gun and I'll fucking stop them...'

'Jaspal!' Sunnie snaps. 'Calm down...'

'Look what they did,' Simar shouts, pointing at Maleek's tent. 'They've shit on it...bloody animals...'

'You can't shoot them,' Norman says. 'They're not armed...'

'I bloody can,' Jaspal says.

'Okay. We think,' Lenski says, grabbing Jaspal to turn him hard. 'We think. Yes? Simar. Is not time to fight now. No...everyone listen...Simar!'

'I'm listening!' he says, wiping the blood from his mouth.

'Ameer,' Lenski calls. 'Is this happen all night?'

'All night,' Damsa calls, edging out from the tent with an instant roar from the crowd at the sight of her.

'MUZZIES OUT...MUZZIES OUT...'

'Just bloody shoot them...' Jaspal says again. 'Like shoot in the air and make them all be quiet...'

'It won't work,' Kyle says. 'They're too pumped and drunk...'

'I ask them. I say be quiet. I try this,' Lenski says.

'Don't!' Norman says quickly, pulling her back. 'They won't listen...'

'I try. I do this. Wait...' she pulls away, walking towards the big crowd. 'WE SPEAK... TOMMY...WE SPEAK...'

'Alright alright,' Tommy shouts, laughing as he tries to wave his cohorts down. 'What do you want?'

'Some English cock...' someone shouts, making them all burst into laughter with more jeers.

'THIS WRONG. YOU STOP THIS,' Lenski shouts. 'YOU SCARE PEOPLE. BREAK THINGS...'

'PISS OFF!' Tommy shouts. 'This here,' he says, pointing at the crappy fence line. 'This is our bit now...our land...no fucking muzzies or queers or fucking ragheads...'

'YOU RACIST PRICK,' Jaspal shouts, moving out with Simar as the crowd gees up, the tension ramping.

'Or what?' Tommy laughs at them, gleeful and drunk. 'This is England mate...fuck off...'

'No,' Lenski calls. 'This end now. Is trouble already... you stop before this gets worse...'

'WHAT YOU GONNA DO? Shoot people for having a drink? Protecting the fucking muzzies more like. Yeah?

Keeping it all for yourselves? Yeah? They're infected. I heard it. Soldier told me. Said they started it. This is a jihadi thing...fucking...fucking wipe out the white man...revenge for nine eleven and...and...fuck 'em! Get 'em out...all of your foreigners and queer cunts...FACK OFF BACK TO YOUR OWN COUNTRIES...'

'The world is over,' Lenski says, shaking her head. 'Is gone...why do this?'

'OUR FORT MUZZIES OUT...OUR FORT MUZZIES OUT...OUR FORT MUZZIES OUT...'

She tries shouting again but the chants get louder and she jumps back as a beer can bounces off her leg. The anger escalating quickly.

'Len, come back,' Sam says, pulling her away.

Tommy stops chanting. Standing in the middle surrounded by sweaty half naked men. A grin on his face. A nasty smirk. His drunk mind mutating the lies into truth. Convincing himself the Muslims really did start this. Convincing himself he is standing up for his rights. Thinking of the woman who didn't show care when his dick wouldn't get hard. Thinking of how everyone was working and he was being left behind. Just like before the world changed. Anger inside. Wrath and a need to lash out and hurt. A vicious, bitter middle-aged man unable to cope with his emotions who will destroy the world and claim it was everyone else's fault.

Norman watches it all, seeing the ugliness of it. The dangerous mob mentality that has brought down whole countries erupting right here, and the fort is too small and too fragile to withstand it.

'What are we doing?' Sam asks.

'Get some bloody weapons and get into them,' Simar

says. 'Round some lads up and we go in...will Peter send some guys over?'

'They're not there,' Sam replies. 'They're all on a run to the docks with Lilly...'

'There's too many of them,' Norman says. 'And they've still got alcohol too. You can see the boxes behind them. I used to prosecute and defend people in court from riots and from my experience, this could go one of three ways. They'll either blow themselves out and slowly drift off or they'll start trashing everything, or worse they'll try and break into the armoury...it's how riots start. Mass civil uprising...'

'So what do we do?' Pea asks, everyone looking at the lawyer shaking his head.

'I don't know. The police would get them into one area and drag them out one by one and cart them off...we can't do that. We don't have water cannons or horses...we don't have shields and we certainly can't fight them head on. People will get killed and if we lose they'll tear the fort apart...'

'You said three options,' Joan says.

'I did,' Norman replies. 'The third option is they'll form a lynch mob and go for anyone they think is a Muslim...'

'Rotten sods,' Colin says, shaking his head. 'Absolute rotten sods...'

'Of all the rotten, dirty, filthy bloody things to do,' Mary shouts, turning a circle in the truck car park at the Southampton docks. 'Can you believe it?'

'Aye,' Peter says darkly. The men all out of their vans

staring to where the container trucks were. The trucks that are now gone.

'Stealing our bloody containers,' Mary says.

'Someone's building a wall I guess,' Willie says.

'Do you think you thick ginger prick?'

'Mary!' Peter snaps.

'Aye, shut your mouth, Mary.'

'Willie! The pair of you just shut up,' Peter says. 'Lilly, what do you want to do? We've plenty of empty trucks here...'

'We'll load what we can and get back,' she says with skywards glance. 'It'll just take a bit longer...'

'We have to protect the armoury,' Kyle says. 'If they go for that we have no choice...'

'Agreed,' Joan says.

'Why wait for that?' Jaspal asks again. 'We have guns. We can stop them...'

'Stop saying that ye daft twat,' Kyle snaps. 'If I give you a gun what then? You think you can shoot unarmed people? You think you can point a gun and shoot people dead...do you"

Jaspal stiffens, scowling and angry.

'It's not that easy,' Kyle says. 'I've seen this before and it is damn hard to kill an army charging at you, let alone when they are unarmed and standing there. Yes, they're drunk and racists and dirty filthy shits, but I won't kill them, and I've killed more people than all of you put together...we've got to think now. Be smart and stop sounding off with your fecking pride...' he draws air, swallowing with another dark look at the chanting crowd. 'We guard what is essential...the armoury and the people. We protect them...'

'And the food,' Lenski says.

'Food can be replaced,' Kyle says.

'From where?' Sam asks.

'It's taken days to get the stores filled,' Agatha says. 'Them bastards...all of 'em...they wants stringing up they do...'

'Honestly. I'd bloody string them up,' Mary shouts. 'Robbing our containers...'

Heat and noise again. Pressure growing. Pressure unrelenting. Keys found. Trucks found. The crane made to run and the painfully slow process of plucking containers from the thousands of stacks and plonking them down on the backs of the lorries begins. Fastening chains. Unfastening chains.

'Is your head hurting?' Mary asks Lilly as they wave the next truck towards the crane.

'No,' Lilly shouts.

'Is that the infection doing that? Does it stop you having headaches? Right. Next zombie we meet is getting snogged...I'll be having some of that I will...'

A look from Lilly, an eyebrow arched. Mary tuts, pulling a face. 'Very bloody funny, Blondie. You know what I mean...shit!' she ducks from the gunshot sounding out. The sharp crack of an assault rifle firing into the air as everyone turns to see a man striding from a big white van spilling more men out. All of them armed with rifles.

'LEAVE MY FUCKING CONTAINERS ALONE,' he yells out.

'THEY'RE NOT YOUR BLOODY CONTAINERS,' Mary yells back, striding towards him. 'DID YOU STEAL THE OTHER ONES?'

'DID YOU TAKE THE FIRST LOT?' the guy shouts as Peter's men rush from trucks. 'WE'RE HAVING THEM...' he adds, pointing beyond Mary and Lilly.

'YOU BLOODY WAIT,' Mary shouts, slinging her rifle and bunching her fists.

'YOU WAIT,' the man shouts, slinging his rifle and bunching his fists.

'Wankers,' Mary shouts, charging in.

'Wankers,' the other man shouts, charging in.

'OUR FORT MUZZIES OUT...OUR FORT MUZZIES OUT...'

The chanting goes on, getting louder, angrier, deeper. Missiles sailing through the air. The crowd itching to rampage. Emboldened by the rules of society that armed authorities cannot, and will not, shoot unarmed protesters.

Lenski bites her bottom lip. Feeling helpless and stupid. She has a gun. She can shoot them, but she can't. She knows she can't. She remembers Maddox dragging a child out to shoot him dead in the compound and shudders at the memory, but then there is just no possible way of reasoning with so many drunk angry people. They've become like a single massed entity.

She tries again and again, waving her arms and shout for them to listen, trying to reason with them, but they just chant louder. Whipping themselves up into a frenzy as more missiles are launched out, making her retreat quickly for fear of being injured and even that just makes them worse. Like they are gaining a victory by her running back. The aggression rising with every minute and that awful, dreadful heat bearing down magnifying the ugly mood.

There's no choice now. She knows that. 'We have to get them out,' she shouts at the others, running towards Damsa's piss, puke and shit covered tent. 'Damsa, we go now. Come quickly...'

'No,' Damsa holds still, clutching her children as the women cluster together. 'They get worse when they see us...'

Kyle comes forward. 'I'm sorry, Damsa. I am, but we've got to get you out now...there's too many if they start charging...we'll go quickly, okay? Straight down to the gate and we'll get you over to the bay...'

'The bay isn't safe,' Norman says. 'The wall isn't finished, and Peter's taken all of his guys...'

'Kyle,' Joan says, pushing into the middle. 'We need to guard the armoury and the food and the people...there's not enough of us to do all of that...I suggest we corral everyone into the food rooms and leave two guarding the armoury.'

'The stores are too full,' Agatha cuts in.

'You won't get them in,' Sunnie adds.

'WATCH OUT...' a shout from Simar watching the crowd who spots the flaming missile sent flying high into the air. A full toilet roll of soft paper set alight that arcs high and starts to drop, plummeting with a trail of sparks and landing next to Damsa's tent.

'Shit!' John shouts out, running in to stamp the flames out with his feet.

'MORE,' Simar yells, seeing more flaming toilet rolls soaring up with a huge laugh coming from the crowd.

'GET THEM OUT,' Kyle shouts, drawing his pistols and he moves to stand between the crowd and the tent, showing them he is armed. Joan at his side holding her rifle, both of them hoping the sight will stop them, but it does nothing.

'Out, come on!' Lenski snaps, pulling Damsa and her family out of the tent and the sight makes the crowd scream louder as they spot Muslim women in black robes. Infected. Dangerous. They started this. They caused this infection. Everything is their fault.

'It's on fire,' Pardip yells, running to the back of the tent now aflame from toilet roll. Kicking and stamping the structure down. Everything in the fort is so dry. Like a tinderbox that only needs a spark. Simar, Jaspal and Maleek run to help as Sam, Pea, Lenski, Colin, Agatha and Sunnie all cluster about Damsa and her family, ushering them down and away.

'FUCKING CUNTS...' a man runs out from the crowd, faceless, angry, part of the entity of the mass. A full beer can in his hands. Heavy and solid and he launches it out, sending it hard into the group, hitting Norman on the back.

Tommy jumps up and down, screaming so hard the veins in his neck push out. Matty next to him. Karl and Gwen doing the same. Patricia and Keith, suburbanites used to fine living now drunk on vodka, yelling and feeling that thirst for blood. Feeling that rush that comes from being part of a big crowd all acting as one. The anonymity of it. The release of fear fuelled anger made so much worse by the alcohol. Ordinary, scared people that cannot stop that flow of energy as they hold lighters to toilet rolls taken from Colin's room and send them flying out. It's fine to do this. It's allowed. They're not individuals now, but part of the mob, of the whole. It's not them doing it. And anyway, the muzzies started it. Everyone said they did.

Two sides charging in the docks, and the strangest thing of all is that in the heat of the truck car park and under the pressure of that awful heat, not one of them even thinks to shoot or use a gun. Instead, and as though an unspoken rule spreads out with near instantaneous understanding, they all sling their weapons.

What both sides see, is that the other people are the same as them. Relatively clean looking survivors with guns who are clearly just trying to get containers.

Then one side see the other is made up of what mostly looks like very tough looking gypsy men, weathered and tanned with thick limbs and fading tattoos. With solid looking jaws and noses that speak of many fights and knuckles so hard they could punch through wood.

'STOP,' the lead guy shouts, holding his hands up as the two sides come together with everyone but Mary abiding his words and she slams her fist into his face, sending him staggering back. 'Ow! What the fuck...'

'Mary!' Peter yells. 'The man said stop...'

'He said stop, Mary,' Willie shouts.

'Mary, what the hell you hit him for?' Elvis shouts.

'There was no need for that,' someone on the other side shouts, helping the punched guy.

'We were going to bloody fight,' Mary shouts. 'I didn't hear him!'

'You alright there, fella?' Peter asks. 'Is he alright?' he asks the men helping the punched guy. 'Ach, Mary. You've no need to hit the man...'

'I said I didn't bloody hear him.'

'Is it broken?' the man asks, trying to stem the blood while fingering the bridge of his nose. 'It feels broken...is it broken?'

'Aye, looking that way,' Peter says. Tutting at Mary.

'I didn't bloody hear him,' Mary says again.

'I heard him and I'm half deaf...'

'Piss off, Eggy. You weren't deaf last night with your bloody fiddle were you? Ah, you'll be fine there, just a wee punch it was...'

'It doesn't feel very bloody fine.'

'Stop your whining. You shouldn't have shot your gun off now,' Mary chides him, ruffled at everyone tutting and shaking their heads at her. 'It'll add character anyway... broken noses always do...'

'I'm sorry to interrupt,' Lilly says, drawing everyone's attention to her. 'Are you here for containers?'

'Yeah,' the punched man says, somewhat huffily and somewhat nasally. 'We're building a wall as it happens...'

'We are too,' Lilly says. 'Where are you from?'

'That way,' he says, thumbing west. 'You?'

'That way,' Lilly says, pointing east. 'The rest of the keys are in that building...get your trucks and we'll get that other crane working and do both at the same time. Agreed?'

The man looks at her, holding his head back as blood drips from his nose. 'You in charge or something?'

'I am suggesting a simple cooperative process to aid us both. I am hot, grumpy and in a rush, so I suggest you either get working or get out of my way...'

'**G**ET THEM AWAY,' Kyle shouts, keeping pace behind the cluster of people ushering Damsa and her family away from their tent. Missiles coming in. Coins, stones, shoes and cans.

'The armoury,' Joan calls out, worried that they'll all go to the front of the fort and leave the armoury undefended.

'This is getting worse!' Colin shouts, seeing the crowd move out from Tommy's tent to lob more flaming toilets rolls to Damsa's vacated tent and more towards the fleeing people.

'THE CANTEEN!' Simar shouts, running to stamp on a rolling ball of fire going too close to the wooden frame of the new structure. Another roar at the sight of him.

'Ere,' Tommy yells in the midst of his group. 'Watch this...' he pours brandy over Simar's turban and scrunches it up before setting it on fire. Laughing when it goes to flame, scorching his hands as he juggles it for a couple of seconds before throwing it out. 'THAT'S FOR ALLAH... MUSLIM CUNTS...MUSLIM CUNTS...COME ON... MUSLIM CUNTS...'

Tent poles lobbed like spears and it's all the small group can do to keep moving, taking cover behind a stack of plyboard, ducking down while Joan and Kyle keep the armoury door in the back wall in view, hoping to hell none of the drunken idiots get the idea to go for weapons.

The situation escalates by the second. Lenski grabs Damsa, pulling her round to face her. 'We go now...we run for the front. Sunnie, your family too...they're not safe here...we go...ready?'

They duck from more missiles bouncing off the plyboards that sail overhead, the noise so bad, the heat so awful.

'We've got to go,' Sunnie yells out. 'Sim, Jas...'

'I'm not bloody leaving,' Simar yells.

'You have to go,' Lenski says.

'I built that bloody canteen and there's no way they're tearing it down or setting it on fire...'

'I'll stay,' John shouts. 'Go!...I'll protect it.'

'No!' Simar shouts. 'No way...'

'I'm staying with Sim,' Jaspal says.

'What's happening?' Maleek asks.

'Simar won't leave,' Damsa explains quickly. 'He and Jaspal are refusing...they said they'll burn the canteen down...'

'We are leaving right now,' Tajj says.

'Go!' Lenski urges them, angered at their delays, fearful of the situation getting worse, and it does too with Damsa's tent engulfing in fire with flames licking the sky.

'Get out you fools,' Kyle roars, wrenching people up to their feet, pushing them on. 'GO!'

'Maleek,' Damsa yells, seeing her husband falter.

'No,' Maleek says, shaking his head, glancing at Simar and Jaspal and John. 'No...I built that too...'

'You have children!' Damsa says, grabbing at her husband's arm as people push and shout for them to run now. Everything a blur. Everything happening so fast.

'Dad, please...' Ameer says, pulling at his father's wrist.

'No. I will stay. I have to stay. I built that...we must defend it...go with your mother. All of you go...'

'NOW,' Kyle snaps, grabbing at them to push on. Colin, Agatha, Sunnie and more all pulling Damsa and the women. Tajj going with them. Shouting back. Bashir with Tajj, running away then stopping, shaking his head and going back to Maleek.

'BASHIR!' Tajj bellows. Ordering him to go.

'BASH!' Simar shouts in warning, pulling him back from a glass bottle flying towards his head. More flaming toilet rolls. Clothes rolled up, set on fire and thrown too. Small pockets of flame. Smoke wafting across the fort. Adding heat hazes and hurting eyes as Kyle and Joan watch the armoury door while the men left, those that bled and sweated to build the canteen run about trying to stamp the fires out while dodging the missiles coming in and all the time that heat comes down and that pressure grows.

Truck after truck. Containers slammed on. Some not quite landing snug within the cradle, but it will do, and the loaded trucks pull forward, so the empty ones can take their turn.

Heat and noise. Diesel fumes. Everyone shouting. Everyone red faced and feeling wretched. Mouths open. Gasping for air.

'It's taking too long,' Lilly shouts, looking up. Clouds in the distance. The sky now grey. The storm is coming. She can feel it. They all can.

'Just a bit longer,' Mary shouts. 'We'll get a couple more then go...'

People at the front of the fort. Families gathering. Children being held and grouped together. Everyone crowding between the inner and outer gate as Lenski rushes over with Damsa and the others. All of them shouting to Lenski, asking what's happening, demanding to know.

'Are the Muslims attacking us?' a woman asks.

'No!' Ann says. 'Just drunken idiots...everyone stay calm. We're going to be fine. It's just a few people who got drunk...'

'Looks more like an uprising to me,' Lisa says, pushing through the crowd to Lenski and Ann. 'This is what happens when you work people too hard...'

'Not now, Lisa,' Ann warns.

'Why isn't the little tyrant here sorting her mess out? She caused this...'

'They said it's drunks,' someone says.

'And Muslims,' someone else shouts.

'Got what you wanted have you?' Lisa asks, smiling grimly at Lenski. 'How are you going to fix it? Come on... you wanted to be a leader? Where's your sixteen year old schoolgirl now?'

'NOT NOW, LISA!' Ann shouts.

Lenski thinks fast. The beach isn't safe yet. The wall isn't finished, and Peter's men aren't there. She can't take these people over to the bay, but then leaving Damsa and the children in the fort like this isn't safe either.

'Hello?' Lisa snaps, clicking her fingers at Lenski. 'I said what are you going to do now?'

'Sandy!' Lenski spots her in the crowd, calling her over. 'Get boats ready...if gets worse or if I say then get them over. Yes? Damsa and Sunnie family first. They are targets...'

'Where's Pardip?' Sunnie calls out, seeing he's not with them.

'He's back with his brothers,' Ann says.

'Stay here,' Lenski says. 'You wait...I go back...'

'I'll come with you,' Norman says.

'No, you stay. They shout at gay men too...they see you like they see Muslims,' Lenski says, nodding at him to stay before setting off. Norman hesitates for a second then goes after her. Running towards the noise and smoke and a scene looking worse by the second.

Tents and shelters on fire. The ground littered with debris and the big crowd spilling out past their boundary. Groups of them tearing tents down and kicking shelters over to get at the poles and belongings inside. Opening bags, scattering the prized possessions taken by families fleeing their homes. Smashing picture frames. Tearing photographs of lost relatives up. Kicking bags around. Throwing them into the fires. Smoke billowing up. The noise getting worse.

Tommy focusses on the canteen building, staying close to the front line of the most hardcore angry people. 'IT'S A FUCKING MOSQUE...LOOK AT IT...THEY'RE BUILDING A MOSQUE...'

Pardip stamps on another fire while John covers him with a bin lid, holding it like a shield that becomes a target for things to be thrown at. Both of them holding sticks as weapons, readying to defend themselves. Simar, Jaspal, Maleek and Bashir running everywhere to stop the building setting alight. Taking whacks from cans, faces cut from bottles and poles launched at them.

Kyle, Joan, Sam and Pea the only thing keeping the mob at bay. Still unable to fire at them, still unable to shoot unarmed drunks because the rules of society dictate you cannot shoot unarmed protesters.

'WE'RE TAKING IT BACK,' Tommy yells, strutting like a general behind his troops. Bare chested. A heavy stick in his hands. 'OUR FORT NOW...ENGLISH FORT... BRITISH...NO FUCKING QUEERS AND MUZZIES...THEY SHOULD BE KILLED SO THE

OTHERS DON'T COME HERE...WE'LL HANG 'EM FROM THE WALLS...'

'**B**londie, we need to cut and run,' Mary shouts. A glance up. Only grey above them. Only pressure bearing down. Threatening to unleash at any second.

Lilly nods, lifting her radio to her mouth. '*Peter...we need to go...*'

'We're getting out,' the guy Mary punched shouts as he rushes over. 'This weather's going to break any second...'

'Same,' Lilly says as the men left in the empty trucks drop out to clamber into the loaded ones. 'I'm Lilly by the way...'

'Gordon,' he replies, shaking her hand. 'We're at Winterbourne barracks in Dorset near the border with Devon.'

'Fort Spitbank up the coast,' she replies.

'I know it...got many there?'

'Few hundred. You?'

'Same...nice meeting you.'

'You too,' Lilly shouts.

'Sorry about your nose,' Mary says.

'It really hurts,' Gordon tells her.

'I said sorry!'

'Whatever...' he waves a hand and runs off, heading down the line of trucks on his side to the front.

'We'll take our van back,' Mary says, running down the line of trucks with Lilly as they both look to the sky and the low grey clouds coming in fast.

‘BURN THE MOSQUE...’ Tommy yells out, screaming so hard his voice rasps and breaks.

'Wanker,' Sam shouts, lifting her rifle, the most hot-headed of them all, the most fiery and she sights on Tommy who spots her aiming and laughs with delight, over-playing his reaction as he points at her and sways side to side. Wobbling his belly.

‘COME ON...’ he yells, urging her to do I while knowing she won't, and he bursts out laughing when she lowers the gun, and that inaction spurs them on even more.

'BURN THAT FUCKING MOSQUE DOWN...'

It's Keith that does it first. An educated man who worked as a financier in the City of London and who commuted daily from his leafy street in Surrey. Keith that liked to play squash and golf and always had the latest BMW. Keith that takes an empty beer bottle, pours some brandy in it, adds a strip of cloth, sets it alight and proudly shows his new mates who erupt in cheers and tell him to throw it. *Like seriously. Throw it now before it goes bang you bleedin' idiot.* Keith throws it and even takes a run up with a solid overhand motion, lobbing it high so it sails long and smashes against a side strut of the canteen frame, showering the ground in glass as the brandy spills and ignites the wood. Another cheer. Another escalation as Simar and Maleek rush to the strut, beating it with their bare hands, ripping their tops off to beat the flames out, coughing from the smoke as the wind starts to blow.

'It's coming in,' Mary says, driving the van behind the fleet of trucks laden with containers. Leaning forward to see the tree tops starting to sway. The sky streaked with grey and dark smudges of greens and blues. An intent above them. A thing coming. Foreboding and dark. The pressure now worse than ever. The air so thick they stretch their mouths, trying to pop their ears. The hairs on their arms prickling with static.

'It's going to be big,' Lilly says, her voice seemingly flat and void of depth. The resonance sucked away. 'We need to get back.'

'What do you think we're bloody doing?' Mary asks.

'No. I mean now...the water. The sea...'

'The what?'

'The sea. If the storm hits we won't get over in the boats...'

'Ah gotcha. It'll be fine. A few hours away won't hurt...'

'No. Go round...go! Put your foot down...' she urges, pulling her radio close to her mouth. *'Peter, we're going on... I'm worried about the sea getting too rough.'*

'...hear...what...' crackle and static coming back, the odd word blaring out.

'Cheap shit,' Mary says, looking at the radio. 'It's the weather, try again...'

'Peter, we're going back fast. The sea. I'm worried about the sea,' she calls slow and clear as Mary accelerates to pull out behind the last truck and powers on down the line.

'...going back...' Peter says through the radio, the transmission breaking again.

'Hang on,' Mary says, speeding up to pull close alongside the lead truck as Lilly leans out, staring up at Peter leaning down.

'THE WEATHER,' he shouts, showing her his radio. 'I COULDN'T HEAR YOU...'

'THE SEA. I'M GOING TO RUSH BACK TO GET OVER...'

'THE SEA? AYE. OKAY. GO...GO!' he shouts, motioning her on.

'Okay go,' Lilly says, giving a thumbs up to Peter as the first strong gust hits the side of the van.

———————

L enski feels the gust blowing over her face. The wind rising, but that pressure. It becomes something else. She shakes her head, feeling heartbroken inside at what's happening. She should have stopped it. She should have realised the rot from Tommy would spread out. Letting Pamela show new people about was a mistake. Taking them to the infirmary to be poisoned even more by Doctor Lisa was a mistake. A catalogue of errors all leading to this point now, and the one thing they have that can end it is the one thing they will not do. They will not shoot them.

She can't do it. None of them can. They're drunk. Stupid. They're reckless and dangerous. They're setting fires and destroying things, but the risk to life isn't immediate and so all they can do is wait for the pressure to rise and get worse.

The crowd get closer too, and as the distance lessens, so their aim gets better. Bashir goes down from a thrown pole whacking into his head. Norman rushing to his aid as Tommy mimics a rutting, fucking motion. Laughing as he does it.

'YOU GONNA BUM HIM? BUMMING A MUZZIE?'

The wind comes, catching the fire from Damsa's tent, sending it to the next as more families spill out and start heading away. Shouted at. Jeered at.

'GO ON...BURN THAT MOSQUE...' Tommy roars the words out. He's a warrior now. This is a battlefield, and these are his troops fighting for truth and justice. Fighting like the British lions they are. Like his ancestors did in the big wars.

This isn't what Tommy planned. Not at all. He was going to whip everyone up, make them react and then come in all suave and smooth to save the day and be a hero, except he wasn't intelligent enough to plan for that, so instead he does this, what he is good at. Exploiting fears and urging people on to overthrow their oppressors, and in his mind, right then, while the smoke wafts over and the wind starts to blow, while that crushing pressure comes down and the sweat rolls over his swollen gut, he feels like a king-in-waiting.

He will tear this fort down and be crowned the glorious leader. Then he can get Viagra and fuck who he wants. Power surges inside of him. Desire and greed. Lust and vengeance. 'BURN THAT FUCKING MOSQUE...' he pauses, drawing air, his face bathed in sweat. 'AND KILL THE FUCKING MUZZIES...'

CHAPTER TWENTY-ONE

'I t'll be okay,' Mary says as they feel the van buffet from the wind howling in. That awful sky coming in from the south. A wall of darkness as wide as the horizon.

'We left it too long,' Lilly says. Cursing herself. Clenching her jaw as Mary reaches over, squeezing her arm.

'We'll be fine. We're like a few minutes now...and even if we don't get back over it'll be okay...Blondie, look at me, it's fine...'

'Okay,' Lilly says, nodding at her, offering a tight smile. A feeling inside. A sense of dread. An awful feeling growing, but then she thinks about last night with Mary and about Nick and Howie and the confusion mingles in. The rejection last night. She tried to kiss Mary. No, she did kiss Mary. Mary kissed her back too. A girl. She kissed a girl. She thinks of Mary saying she isn't gay. Lilly never thought of herself as being gay. She's had girl crushes before but that's normal for both men and women.

'Jesus,' Mary says, grabbing the wheel harder as the van slides across the road. 'That bloody wind...ah look, we're okay, there's the road to the shore now. See, we're not far...'

'L ENSKI!' Sandy shouts, waving her arms while not wanting to go closer to the utter carnage across the way.

'What?' she asks, turning to see Sandy waving at her and she runs over, knowing it won't be good news.

'The sea...the wind...' Sandy shouts. 'It's not safe to take them away...the wind is too strong...'

'Okay. Take them now. Go now.'

'It's too late!' Sandy shouts.

'KILL 'EM...KILL THE MUZZIES...KILL THE MUZZIES...'

'Shit,' Sandy says, hearing the chant, seeing the flaming missiles coming in, the tents on fire at the back. Pardip and the men rushing to put fires out on the new structure 'We can't get them over...'

'Show me,' Lenksi runs with her, sprinting across the fort as the wind comes in, howling and strong. They reach the people gathered at the gates. Scared people. Terrified and confused.

'I need to get through please!' Sandy shouts, panic in her voice as she pushes out onto the beach with Lenski. The wind suddenly so much harder from the lack of shelter from the walls. The sea churning with waves growing. 'It's too strong,' Sandy shouts over the wind. 'The waves are coming from the side and they'll tip the boats over...we can't aim for the shore...I'm sorry. They'll drown if we try...'

Lenski stares out to the bay, nodding slowly before turning to go back in, crossing into the middle section.

'I want everyone in here now...come through...all come through...' she calls out, pushing through to Ann and Sunnie and the others trying their best to keep people calm. 'Is no way out now. Get people in here and chain the inner gate from this side. Lock yourselves in here...'

'Len,' Ann says in shock.

'Are you bloody stupid?' Lisa asks.

'Do this,' Lenski snaps, harsh and clipped. 'No open gate. No come through. Donald, you keep them here and wait...' she draws her pistol, hating the feel of it. Checking the magazine as tears prick her eyes. Knowing it will come to this. Hating that it will come to this. Another nod and she goes back into the fort. The pistol in her hand as those behind share looks, silent and worried.

***

L illy grits her teeth, silent and brooding as she watches the sea and the waves growing higher. The wind slamming through as they speed along the shore road.

They turn the bend, seeing the container wall ahead as Mary drives on. Both of them taking glances to the waves crashing on the beach. The wind hitting the van. Through the gap and into the bay proper. A lessening of the gusts from the containers and Lilly frowns, thinking nothing has changed here.

They go down the road, nearing the beach and the marquee tent flapping in the wind. Cars and vans parked up. A few of Peter's men left behind as guards. Old men, grey and stooped, but still it all looks the same as yesterday.

She jumps out as the van stops, rushing along while

shielding her face from the sand whipping across. 'What's going on?' she shouts at Uncle Jack. 'Did they all go back?'

'Who? Ain't nobody been here. Got new people turned up you have. None of them came over from your fort though...'

'What about Norman and Kyle?' Lilly asks. 'Ann?'

'I said nobody,' Jack snaps. 'Nothing. Figured you're all waiting for Peter to get back...'

Lilly steps away, bringing her radio up. *'Lilly to the fort...LILLY   TO   THE   FORT...CAN   ANYONE HEAR ME?'*

Nothing. No response.

'You came out garbled from here,' Mary says, holding her uncle Jack's radio.

'Something's not right,' Lilly says. 'They would have come over...' she starts across the sand, heading to the sea and the few boats bobbing in the waves.

'Blondie? Don't even think about it...'

'I have to get back,' Lilly says, wading into the crashing waves, fighting to reach the closest boat, throwing her rifle in before she clambers over the side.

'DON'T BE A DICK,' Mary shouts. 'IT'S WAY TOO BAD NOW...'

'I'M GOING,' Lilly says, heaving the anchor up and moving to the back to start the engine.

'LILLY...IT'S TOO DANGEROUS...'

'I'LL SEE YOU LATER,' Lilly shouts, twisting the grip and turning to get the boat aimed out, fighting to keep her balance as it rocks and sways on the waves.

'YE A BLOODY IDIOT,' Mary shouts, wading out to clamber in. 'SERIOUSLY...'

'STAY HERE THEN.'

'I WILL NOT.'

'FINE.'
'FINE.'

'KILL THE MUZZIES...BURN THE MOSQUE...' The chant comes solid and unbroken. Roaring out from men and women now consumed with a primeval urge to cause destruction. Drunk on booze and violence.

'KILL THE MUZZIES...BURN THE MOSQUE...'

They'll charge at any minute. Kyle can feel it. Reading the mood, seeing that build-up of raw, ugly emotion that will detonate and get so much worse. 'SAM!' he shouts the warning, barging her aside as the spinning bottle comes in hard, whacking into his side.

'GO ON!' Tommy yells. 'DRIVE 'EM BACK...THEY AIN'T GONNA SHOOT...WE'RE UNARMED...'

A shift in focus and the four take the brunt. Pea and Sam. Kyle and Joan. Missiles coming in that drive them back towards the canteen to take cover behind the ply board. Snatching views now and then to keep the armoury door in view, and still it's not bad enough to shoot them. Still they can't do it. Voices inside their heads saying no. Saying you cannot kill people for this.

Another Molotov cocktail comes in, thrown again by Keith and it smashes into the side struts of the frame. More brandy inside this one. More flames that spill out and start eating into the structure.

'PUT IT OUT,' Simar shouts, beating at the flames with his hands wrapped in clothing, his face burning from the heat. Norman at his side ripping his own top off to fight the fire. To protect the canteen. Maleek behind them, stamping on other flaming missiles coming in. John, Pardip and Bashir doing the same.

'GET OUT OF HERE,' Kyle roars at them. 'GO!'

'NO!' Simar screams out, shouting as the clothing wrapped about his hands sets alights. He tears them off, his face a mask as he fights to protect the thing he built.

'PARDIP...GET THEM AWAY,' Sam shouts, the crowd coming closer, the anger building. The tipping point is coming. The point where they will charge. What then? Do they shoot? Do they run?

Pardip can't get them away. He knows his brothers and they won't back down. Nor will he either. This is about taking a stand. This is about defending that which you hold dear.

'KILL 'EM!' Tommy roars, urging them on, egging them closer, feeling the time to charge is coming fast.

***

'Drive into the waves,' Mary shouts, holding on at the back of the small open-topped boat tossing and rolling, watching the waves get bigger, seething with mass and shape. High peaks and deep troughs. 'Aim into the wave then go along before the next one...'

Lilly tries that, turning the tiller to angle the boat at the wave, feeling the prow lift and the boat rise then crash back down before they turn and try to whip along, but the boat sides are too shallow, and the engine isn't powerful enough. She tries again, feeling it lift then crash with water smashing over the front, drenching them again. She tries to turn but the boat is too sluggish and slow.

The motion brings Mary's gorge up and she turns away, puking over the side as the boat lifts and falls like a toy in a bathtub. Wind whipping past them. Waves crashing into them. The engine screaming out. Mary grabs hold of Lilly, trying to hold them both steady as the waves and tide and power of the sea all grow worse.

They become an object to be toyed with because the storm is coming, and the sea wants to dance and sing and get bigger.

Another wave comes. Bigger and stronger, smashing into the boat to make it seesaw too far over, the edge dipping beneath the surface as water pours in, weighing it down, pulling it further in.

'BLONDIE!' Mary screams as the boat tips, sending them down into the depths, ripped from each other's embrace as they tumble and spin. Their mouths filling with salt water, making them gag and retch as they break the surface.

'MARY!' Lilly shouts, puking sea water as she spins to see Mary coming towards her. She brings a foot up, tugging at the laces, wrenching the sides apart. Desperate to get the heavy, water-logged boots off. She kicks one free and sinks down as another wave hits them. Changing the world about her to bubbles and roars and motion from within. She feels the power of the sea churning and ragging her on and feels that pressure growing as she goes deeper while working at the laces on her other boot. Pressure on her chest. A need to breathe in. A need to expel the water in her lungs. She kicks the boot free, unclips her gun belt to let it sink away and kicks hard. Legs above her. She aims for them, breaching the surface and sucking air in as Mary reaches out, terrified and panicking.

'BOOTS,' Lilly shouts. 'GET THEM OFF...' she can

see Mary isn't listening. Panic in her face. She goes closer, sucks a deep breath and drops to feel her way down Mary's body. Unclipping the pistol belt then going down her legs to her boots, yanking the laces free, tugging them down.

'BLONDIE...' Mary panics again, thinking Lilly is drowning, reaching down to pull her up while feeling her boots coming loose. She kicks them off, frantic and hard, water going in her mouth, retching and puking. A sudden release of weight as her feet become unburdened and Lilly pops up, gasping and sucking air again.

'We have to swim,' Lilly says, her voice near on lost. 'Mary...we have to swim...'

'Which way?' Mary asks, too low down to see land now.

'Hold on,' Lilly grabs her as they lift on the next wave, both craning up to see the bay and the fort as the waves crash, making them tumble down through the water.

***

Smoke and wind and noise. The last bit of time before the storm hits proper, the last bit of time before the riot detonates and the pressure gets worse. The fear of it. The sheer awfulness of it.

Karl and Matty at the front with Gwen, Keith and Patricia just beside them. Tommy behind them, urging them on, whipping them into a frenzy.

'KILL THEM FUCKING MUZZIES...THEY STARTED THIS...THIS IS A JIHADI...WE HAVE TO KILL THEM BEFORE THEY KILL US...'

'I can't see the doors,' Joan snaps. Trying to see through the press of people and smoke to the armoury doors at the back.

'Joanie,' Kyle shouts as she runs off, realising what she is doing. He tries to see the doors himself and curses. 'Stay here,' he shouts and runs off.

Sam winces, seeing Joan and Kyle rushing up the side of the fort towards the back, leaving just her and Pea here against dozens of angry drunk people getting worse by the second.

'HANG 'EM FROM THE WALLS...' Tommy roars on, urging his troops to get them ready to charge. Motion from the other side. Joan running out. Kyle running after her. Why are they splitting up? Tommy frowns, seeing only Sam and Pea left between him and the people he wants to kill and the building he wants to see burn.

They won't shoot. Everyone can feel it. The end is already decided. Tommy will win. He glances again at Joan and Kyle snaking up the side and turns, trying to see what they're aiming for. The food stores? The other rooms?

'WE SHOULD GET SOME GUNS,' Keith gets to his side, shouting over the chanting.

Guns. The armoury. Tommy's head snaps over, seeing the doors at the back. He didn't think of it. Why didn't he think of it? A room full of guns. He has to act now. He has to make them charge now.

'WE'RE GONNA KILL 'EM...' he roars out, surging forward. 'KILL...KILL...KILL...KILL...'

A new chant. A new intent and the missiles stop coming as the crowd gathers together, edgy and dark, violence rippling through them. Faces twisted and ready. There are no limits now. There are no barriers. The Muslims have to die.

'THEY KILLED EVERYONE,' Tommy bellows. 'THEY STARTED THIS...'

Simar grabs a stick, holding it ready. This is it. This is when it happens. Jaspal does the same, moving to stand beside his brother. Norman swallows, his heart thundering, his guts twisting. He spots a length of wood and bends to pick it up. His fingers wrapping about the end. Maleek next to him. Both staring at each other. Both so very, very scared but this has to be done. It must be done and so they grip their weapons and step into the line. Ready to fight. Ready to protect the canteen that has suddenly come to mean so much more than a simple building. Pardip moves to his brothers, standing tall. John with him. Both of them big men. Both armed. They'll go down. They know they will. You can't fight forty angry drunk people, but by fuck they'll take a few with them.

Bashir blinks, staring at the small line then over to the huge crowd. Just Pea and Sam between them. Both of them shaking from head to toe. He can see the tremble from here. 'Soul ja,' he says, rushing to the two women. 'SOUL JA...' he shouts, yelling at them but neither Sam nor Pea hear him but only see the crowd seething as they ready to charge. Feeling it's going to go.

Lenski feels it too. Walking from the front with dread in every step. This is her fault. She caused this. She has to stop it and she grips the pistol in her hand, held at her side as the tears stream over her cheeks.

They kick and swim. Arm over arm. Crying out and gasping. If they make progress they know not. If they are even aiming towards the fort now they know not either. Only that they rise and fall and sink beneath the surface into darkness where they kick with everything to breach the surface.

This was folly. Lilly knows that now. It was stupid to do

this, but still, that voice inside says it had to be done. She must reach the fort.

Their energy starts to wane. To wilt. They need air, to breathe, to recover, but the sea has become an animal now, throwing them about, pushing them under, taunting them. A lull. A quiet second. They swim hard. Kicking to make progress. Grunting from the effort but the lull is a foul trick played as the next big wave comes in and their world fills with the vision of white as the wave breaks and they go down, sinking deep, tumbling and spinning, crashing into each other. Images of their lives coursing through their minds. Children playing. School. Mary's dad died in prison. He was only there for a minor offence, but he was stabbed. She barely remembers him. She thinks of her mother who died a few years later. Run over as she crossed the road. She thinks of being raised by Uncle Pete and everyone else. She thinks of her life and now and Lilly and last night. She thinks of many things all in the blink of an eye, the beat of a heart.

Lilly doesn't really think of anything, only that she doesn't know which way is up or down. She doesn't know which way to swim, and that means she will die here. Her lungs are demanding air. She will soon pass out, and in so doing, she will breathe in and drown. She grows still in the turmoil. Feeling Mary beside her. Pulling her in. Both with eyes open. Both with hair splaying out. Both suddenly so very calm. Reaching out to touch each other's faces. Breaths held. Suspended in a second of calm, not seeing the bubbles starting to rise up around them. Chests urging them to breathe in. Minds preparing to die. The energy between them flowing from one to the other.

Motion beneath them. Something dark rising up that brushes past them. Bodies. Corpses. The dead from the battles before now disturbed from the seabed that still contain bubbles of air that seek to the find the surface and so some of them rise up, giving direction. Showing the way. Giving them something to push against. The frame of a big man. A snatch of dark hair glimpsed. The features now rotten and grotesque but with enough form of substance left for them to get their feet on it and they push hard. Up. Up. Kick. Go up. Hold on. Do not breathe. Not yet. Hold on. Just hold on.

T hat small line waits for the charge. Those few good people stand ready to oppose the will of a mob that wants to kill them.

A distance behind them the inner gate stands open. A strange quiet within the middle ground as the people stare out across the fort to Lenski walking on. A solitary figure with a gun held at her side. Her chest rising and falling. Her heart thundering. She has to kill. She has to end this.

Joan switches the safety off on her rifle. She will have to kill. It's going to happen. She can see Tommy shouting and pointing at the armoury doors. She can see a small group forming and organising to go for it.

Kyle thumbs the safeties on his pistols. Ready to do what must be done. Praying to God that this is righteous and proper.

'SOUL JA,' Bashir screams the word.

'Sam!' Pea shouts, switching the safety off on her rifle. 'I don't want to do this...'

'I know,' Sam shouts back.

'Get in and get them fucking guns out,' Tommy shouts at Keith, pointing towards the armoury. 'I'll get this lot going…ready?' he turns away, striding towards the front line. 'WE'RE GONNA KILL 'EM…WE GOTTA CHARGE 'EM…THEY WON'T SHOOT. WE"RE NOT ARMED…READY?'

'SOUL JA,' Bashir screams.

'What the fuck is your problem?' Sam snaps at Bashir banging his hand into his chest.

Lenski thumbs the safety off and snatches a breath. An awful sickness inside. A terrible feeling of dread and worry. Lilly isn't here to fix this. Howie isn't here. None of them are and Lisa was right. Lenski wanted to be a leader and this is what it takes. She starts lifting the gun. Readying to take life while the rules of society that say you cannot shoot unarmed protesters scream in her head.

O n and on. Air. Breathe. Water. Do not breathe. In and out. Heads breaching the surface then sinking back down. A refusal to die. A refusal to give in. The waves sending corpses slamming into them and they kick on, feeling bones and rotting flesh.

In the fort, Tommy screams out, 'ARE YOU READY?' A roar comes back. Thunderous and deep. They have good on their side. They believe the people with dark skin caused this. Alcohol. Heat. Anger. Fear. A deadly mix all fuelled on by Tommy.

'SOUL JA!' Bashir shouts over and over, frantic and loud, banging his hand on his chest. Close to Pea and Sam who stare wide eyed as the line readies to charge. Men and women gripping weapons. Screaming into the air.

Lilly feels something underfoot. Mary beside her. Both crying out as they gain the seabed, digging their bare feet into the sand as the waves still throw them about. Closer now. Greater traction gained. Veins pushing out. Teeth bared. Lilly reaches out, grabbing Mary's arm, the two clinging on to pull and fight through the waves smashing about them.

Lenski walks on. Every step taking minutes to complete. Every heartbeat taking eons to come and go.

Kyle at the back of the fort, running with Joan through the smoke. Keith going for the doors at the back. Sam and Pea moving backwards to join the line with Pardip and John. Bashir still screaming the same sounds out. Why won't they listen to him? Why won't they understand?

Lilly and Mary hit the shore within the burst of another wave slamming them down. Mouths spewing seawater. Lungs retching and burning. Eyes stinging. Everything hurting but they're on land. They can feel it. Mary sags, ready to drop.

'No,' Lilly staggers to her feet, pulling Mary up, fearful of another wave. They need shelter. They need to be inside. She pulls Mary on, both of them lurching across the shore. Bodies exhausted and spent. 'Get in,' Lilly whispers, pulling at Mary, dragging her to the gate. She bangs against it, thinking it to be locked. She bangs again and it gives, spilling them both inside.

They sprawl out. The world suddenly so much quieter from the walls blotting the wind about their ears. Gasping and crying. The two of them pawing at each other, grabbing and pulling as though still trying to swim as everyone turns from staring into the fort to look down at the two soaking wet women. 'It's not just a crush...' Lilly gasps. 'That kiss...it was...'

Mary turns her head to look at her, both staring, both gasping for air.

'Lilly!' a voice snaps as the two women bring their heads up to a sea of faces staring at them. Everyone from the fort in the middle section. Billy rushing towards her. Throwing his arms about his sister's soaking wet body.

'What...' Lilly sucks air, trying to make her mind work. 'What's happened?' she looks round seeing scared faces. Damsa and Ameer with the women but not Maleek or Bashir. Sunnie and Anika but not Pardip, Jaspal or Simar. Ann but not Norman. No Lenski. No Kyle. No Joan. No Sam or Pea. 'What's happening?' she says again, pushing to her feet.

'It's gone bad,' Ann says. 'Lenski said to stay here...'

'They got drunk,' Agatha says. 'That Tommy...racists and...'

'They're tearing it apart,' Sunnie cuts in. 'Par and the lads are trying to stop them but there's too many...'

'All drunk,' Ann says. 'They've lost it...'

Lilly staggers to the inner gate, Ann helping her. 'You need to rest,' Ann says. 'Both of you...'

'How's your empire now, Little Tyrant?' Lisa says, snapping Lilly's head over.

'What the hell?' Mary says, shaking her head as she staggers after Lilly, joining her at the gate to look through. 'Holy shit...is that fire? Is the fort on fire?'

Lilly steps through, taking it all in with one sweep of her eyes. The fires at the back. The flames from missiles thrown near the canteen. The huge crowd edging closer to a thin line. She sees Sam and Pea holding rifles. She sees Maleek and the others clutching sticks with their backs to the new building and she sees Lenski, walking alone towards them with the pistol lifting in her hand.

'SOUL JA,' Bashir screams.

'I don't know what that means,' Sam shouts back at him. Everything a blur now. Everything a mess.

'KILL 'EM...' Tommy roars out. 'NOW...KILL 'EM ALL...'

A roar and the crowd moves. The mass of them knowing they will not be fired upon. Sam and Pea freeze. Not believing this is happening. Kyle with Joan, running for the back as Keith leads his group towards the doors as the detonation of violence finally comes. The deep roar of it. The crowd now sick with bloodlust. Ready to tear that small line apart and they won't stop there. They'll burn that building down. They'll destroy and rampage. They'll kill and rape. They are the mob. Ordinary people now monsters to the last.

'SOUL JA...' Bashir yells again, turning his head from the coming crowd to Sam. 'SOUL JA...' he beats his chest, desperation in his voice.

'Stop screaming fucking sold ja at me...' Sam yells, snatching a look at Bashir.

'SOLDIER!' Pea exclaims with sudden realisation. 'He's saying soldier...'

'Soldier?' Sam gasps, looking at Bashir.

'Soul ja,' Bashir says, nodding fast. Pointing at himself.

'Give him your gun,' Pea urges.

'I am!' Sam yelps, pulling her rifle overhead to pass to Bashir who takes the weapon and sweeps an arm out, forcing them behind him as he lifts to aim and make ready.

'Here we go...' John shouts, going low while gripping the metal pipe in his hands. 'Ready lads... READY?'

Lenski aims as the crowd starts moving. Seeing the charge. Seeing the end game is right here and she will have to shoot them. She has to end it, but still she hesitates. Still she sees unarmed drunk people and her finger holds the trigger. Willing herself to do it before it's too late. She has to. She must.

Movement on her right side. Lilly stepping in with Donald's rifle in her hands. Movement on her left side. Mary stepping with her chest heaving. Both of them drenched to the bone. Both of them breathing hard and Lenski turns to look back at Lilly. At the cold blue eyes glaring from someone who doesn't give a shit what the rules of society were.

'No,' Lilly whispers. A feeling inside. A surge within. A seething, growing knot of rage building up. A rage unlike any other Lilly has ever felt. Soaking wet. Bare footed. It's been hot as hell. She's worked everyone to the point of nearly breaking them to flatten the bay, to get materials to build a canteen, to build a wall. Days of blistering heat. Days of sheer gruelling hard graft and seeing broken people pick themselves up and move on again. Working in that staggering heat to build and make something decent and now this.

'No,' she says again. Her voice stronger. Harder. The girl who took back the fort. The girl that rolled the grenade into the room full of children and right there, Lenski knows Tommy has made a very, very terrible mistake.

Without a shred of hesitation Lilly pulls the trigger and sends the first round spinning across the fort that takes a man through his chest because to Lilly there are no rules and there is nothing she will not do to protect the fort.

The second round slams into a woman who drops screaming out from her thigh bone shattering. The old world is over. This is the new world. It doesn't matter what was. It only matters what is now. What they are now.

'SEE ME...' she roars out, firing the third round that takes a man through the side, making him spin away and drop. Lilly doesn't see unarmed protesters. What she sees are the enemy who must be stopped. Those are the rules of the new world. This is the way now.

'SEE ME…' she fires again, sending a bullet through a shoulder that comes out the other side with shards of bone lacerating the faces of raging drunks behind. She shoots as the drunk, roaring crowd charge across the fort towards that thin line of terrified people who only did good.

Everything a blur. Everything happening so quickly. Bashir hears the shots but keeps his focus on the crowd coming at him. Two years in the Afghan army. Taught by British and American instructors. He sights his weapons, selects single shot and fires into a big man charging at him. The bullets slam home. The man falters with a look of confusion on his face. This isn't right. He's not armed. They can't shoot him. He spots another muzzle flash and feels the impact of more rounds hitting him, shunting his body as he sobers in a heartbeat, looking about at the fires and carnage and he drops to die, bleeding out as Tommy roars behind him.

'GO ON! KILL THE FUCKING MUZZIES…INTO THEM…KILL KILL KILL…' Tommy hears the gunfire, figuring them to be warning shots but not caring if they're not. It's too late. He'll tear this fort apart and be the king. Fuck them. Fuck the muzzies. Something whizzes past his head with a noise like a wasp. Someone drops near him, screaming out as he clutches his stomach. 'KILL 'EM… KILL THE FUCKING MUZZIES…' another wasp going by. Someone else screaming in pain.

Lilly fires single shots. Striking bodies and legs. Dropping them as they charge. Gunfire. Smoke. Chaos and noise. The pressure of the storm bearing down. Everything a blur. Everything happening so fast.

'I'm not having this,' Agatha says, muttering the words that grow louder. 'I'm not. I'm not having this...not in my bloody fort...'

Lilly fires. Bashir fires. Smoke and fire. Noise and chaos. Hearts hammering. Bashir adjusts his aim, firing again. Lilly striding in. Sending bullets into the crowd.

'No,' Agatha says, shaking her head. 'NO...' she steps out through the gate with a ripple spreading through the others. 'This is our fort...' she speeds up, rushing on towards Lenski with Sunnie at her side. Colin and Joanne share a look and go after them as the bay workers nod at each other. The boat drivers. The people who have worked and felt the change. They go through the gate. Striding after Agatha and Sunnie.

Lilly fires. Bashir fires. The crowd charge.

A roar from behind. Lilly spins to see people spilling from the gates with Agatha and Sunnie running as fast as they can. All of them grabbing heavy things to hit with. Ordinary men and women prepared to fight for what they hold dear. Dozens and dozens of them. A new mob. A bigger, louder one.

A surge inside Lilly who passes the rifle to Lenski and runs out to scoop a length of wood up, holding it aloft. Holding it high. 'INTO THEM,' she screams her battle cry. 'COME ON...INTO THEM...' She starts the counter charge. Running hard. Mary behind her. Lenski running.

Simar snaps his head over. Seeing Lilly charging. Her face a mask of pure aggression. Running ahead of everyone else. A sight to see. Fearless. Relentless.

'COME ON,' he shouts out, holding his weapon aloft, holding it high and he breaks out to run as Lilly steams by. Norman crying out, holding his stick ready. Pardip and

John roaring. Maleek screaming. That thin line going fast into the screaming crowd.

A second of silence before they hit. A second of pure energy as every man and woman in that drunken mob see Lilly coming at them. The wildness in her face. The blaze in her eyes. The sky behind her streaked with colour. The clouds rolling. A flash of lightning in the distance.

Lilly hits the line first. Going deep with a roar and striking her stick into a kneecap, smashing it to bits. Mary behind her, swinging out with huge punches. Smashing into jaws. Into noses. Into eyes and skulls.

The second line hit. Simar, Jaspal, Pardip, Maleek, Bashir and Norman. Men who would have been killed for being dark, for being gay. Now armed and fighting. Striking out wild and untrained but driven by pure aggression. Teeth bared. Eyes wide.

The third line hits. Agatha and Sunnie slamming in to lash out. Colin and Joanne. Brian Collins limping on his injured ankle using his crutch as a weapon. Martin Jones swinging a club with one arm still in a sling. Jane Parker snarling as she takes a drunk woman off her feet with Emily the librarian. The two kicking and dropping to punch and batter. Lenski steaming in behind Lilly and Mary, using the butt of the rifle to hit out, whacking left and right, screaming wildly.

Lilly takes another one down, smashing the stick into a mouth so hard the teeth fly out. She batters the man away, blood spraying over her face. In deep. In amongst them. Fighting close and hard. Mary at her back. Punching and punching the way she was taught by her Uncle Peter. Breaking bones with her hard knuckles. Her red hair flying as she twists and pivots.

John rams his stick into a man. The weapon breaks,

snapping in two. He ditches it to use his fists, fighting dirty, brawling hard. Pardip at his side, his weapon already lost. A hit across his back. He roars out and spins to see Karl lashing out with a heavy pipe. Pardip shouts out and goes in, slamming his forehead into the big man's nose, dropping him instantly.

Norman on the floor, rolling over and over with a drunk tattooed man, blood flying out. Grunts and shouts. The guy gets the better of him, experienced in street brawls and he gets Norman onto his back and starts slamming punches down as Maleek dives in from the side. Norman surges up, going after them. Diving in to punch and hit.

Kyle and Joan stopped running the second they heard the gunfire. Both of them hunkering down to see where it was coming from, but the smoke hampered their view. Wafting across, making them cough with eyes stinging. Motion everywhere. The crowd roaring as they charge. Noise and chaos. Gunfire and smoke. Everything a blur. Everything happening so fast.

'THERE!' Joan shouts, seeing figures running for the armoury door. A solid little crowd of men led by Keith. Things in their hands. Weapons and tools. They run fast. Going through the smoke and heat. Men at the door. Tools being used. Wood splintering. A jemmy cracking the lock.

'GET OUT,' Kyle shouts, aiming his pistols. 'GET OUT OF THERE...'

The men turn, seeing him coming. A burst of motion, faster and harder as the doors are wrenched open with men running in. Kyle goes faster, sprinting to get there. Firing once into the belly of a man still outside. He reaches the door, seeing men inside grabbing at weapons but he cannot shoot his pistols into a room full of ammunition and grenades. Everything a blur. Everything happening so fast. 'GET OUT,' he goes in fast, holstering his guns.

'FUCK OFF,' a man screams out, grabbing a rifle to use as a club, swinging it at Kyle's head but the old man blocks the swing and goes in low before rising up to slam the flat of his hand into the man's chin, snapping his head back. Kyle turns his foe with the force gained, slamming him down into a pile of boxes while bringing his knee up into the elbow joint. A crunch of bone. A scream of agony and Kyle steps back, pulling his knife from the sheath on his belt, ducking another punch to stab into a thigh before bringing the blade up into the stomach, stabbing hard and deep, twisting the handle, pulling it out and slicing the blade across the throat. Gunfire behind him. Joan firing her rifle into the head of another man running towards the open doors as someone else looms at Kyle, swinging fists. Kyle dances back, swaying side to side before going in to grip and roll the man over his hip, driving the blade into his throat as he drops.

'STAND DOWN...' Joan shouts, striding in, aiming her rifle at the others.

'OKAY OKAY,' Keith yells, a pistol in one hand, a magazine in the other. He was almost there. Almost armed. A flicker of rage on his face but he drops them both to fling his hands up.

'Bastards,' Kyle shouts, fuming as he stands up. 'Ye bastards...'

'We're unarmed...' Keith says, keeping his hands up.

'Ye fucking tried though didn't ye,' Kyle shouts, lashing out, punching Keith in the face with a hard hit. 'YE FUCKING TRIED THOUGH...'

Outside the armoury it feels like the battle goes on for hours. 'KILL 'EM...' Tommy roars out. He can win. He can do this. He can take the fort and be the king. 'STRING

'EM UP...' people fighting all about him. A battle waging. His troops will win with ease. He's got this.

Delusion in his mind. This isn't a battle. It's a brawl and over within minutes with the mob turning from one solid mass back to the component parts of drunks and idiots within an instant.

'COME ON,' Tommy roars, turning this way and that. A big metal pipe in his hands. His chest puffed up. His arms out wide. His belly wobbling as he struts. Sweat dripping down his red face. 'KILL 'EM...' his voice seems louder now. Penetrating further. Or maybe it's the lack of the roar from this mob now decimated. Solid hits now heard. The grunts of individual fights. Not a battle. Just a brawl. Sordid and filthy. People crying in pain. Drunk and confused. Begging for help. 'COME ON,' Tommy shouts again, spinning on the spot. His face a mask of aggression. Smoke wafting about him. His feet shunting empty beer cans and bottles. His crappy fence a few yards behind him. 'NO,' he shouts angrily. 'NO...' he roars. Seeing Karl down with Pardip straddling over him, smashing fists into his head. Emily and Jane ripping Gwen off her feet, punching and beating her as the woman screams in panic, trying to crawl away. Matty dead on the ground.

Sticks being used as clubs to beat the drunks. Breaking bones. Giving back what was threatened against them. Taking revenge. Not a battle but a brawl. Bodies everywhere. The cries and whimpers sounding through the shouts.

'FUCK,' Tommy screams. 'GET UP...GET UP...'

A whump of an impact from Lilly smashing her stick into a man, driving him to the ground.

Mary staggering back. Her fists dripping with blood. Her lips snarling as she runs the back of one hand across her forehead, smearing a wake of blood. Seeing the beatings being given. Hearing the bones breaking. 'THAT'S ENOUGH NOW,' she cries out, her voice cracking. 'ENOUGH...IT'S DONE...' she lurches to Emily and Jane kicking at Gwen, pushing them back. 'ENOUGH...it's enough...stop...STOP!' she staggers to Lenski, taking the pistol to aim over the wall out to sea and she pulls the trigger. Making everyone flinch and turn. Making them look. 'Enough...it's over...ye can't beat them when they're down...'

'OUT,' a voice at the back. Joan ordering the remaining men from the armoury at gunpoint. Kyle coming out last. Heaving for air. His knife dripping in his hand.

'Sim, get back mate,' Jaspal says, pulling his brother back from slamming punches into someone on the ground. A man whimpering. His face pulped and covered in blood. Norman and Maleek get to their feet. The man they were fighting sobbing for mercy.

Only a few of the drunks remain on their feet but they wilt back quickly. Lifting hands in surrender. Dropping to the floor to cry. Staggering and overplaying confusion.

'What's going on?' one of them asks. 'It just went nuts...'

'You fucking racist,' Simar rushes at him, seeing the guy that threw the can at Norman. Seeing one of the men that beat him down with a stick that laughed at him and called him a Muslim cunt.

'Mate,' the guy says, holding his hands up. 'I don't know what's going on...'

A punch. Solid and hard. The guy drops, gurgling and spitting teeth. Simar standing over him.

'You wanted to kill me...try it now...TRY IT NOW...'

Lilly turns a slow circle, viewing the fight, viewing the battlefield. Seeing it as the brawl it is. Her face alive. Her chest heaving. The girl who took the fort back. Blood on her face. Blood spattered over her skin. 'Who started this?' her voice calls out. Hard and ruthless. Making every man and woman turn to look at her. 'Who started this?' she asks again, her head lowered, her eyes looking up, taking in the way everyone looks to a meaty tattooed guy in the middle dropping a metal pipe as he backs up with a hunted look on his face. Feral and wild. Cunning eyes seeking a way out. Licking his lips as he thinks and looks at the faces of the men he was abusing just a few minutes ago. Norman and Maleek. Pardip and Jaspal.

'Fuck me,' Tommy says. 'What happened? Eh? Just had a few beers and it went off...this heat...'

'He steal,' Lenski says, striding to a beer can. 'See?' she picks it up, pointing at the black cross. 'Yesterday. I mark them. All of these. In the food stores...I put this mark on all...'

Cans on the ground with small black crosses inked on them. Packets of cigarettes. Snack bar wrappers. Bottles of booze. 'I mark all of them...all stolen...'

'Not by me,' Tommy says. 'That fat bitch... Pammie, she kept bringing it all over saying it was hers...honest. This just got out of hand. I had some drinks. I'll admit that. A few jokes and then they all went nuts. I was calling 'em back. I was trying to let it just blow out...these things happen don't they...'

'You're a racist, homophobic, lying, thieving fucking prick,' Simar shouts. 'Kill muzzies...that's what you said. Burn the mosque...it's not a mosque! It's a bloody canteen so you can eat.'

'It was a joke,' Tommy says.

'You said kill the muzzies...you said kill the queer cunt!'

'Me and Norm go back. It was a laugh. Norman knows me. We came in together...bit of bants innit. Fucking snowflakes, can't say anything now. Everyone going on. The bloody PC brigade censoring what you say...it's how we speak where I'm from. I don't know the terms for foreigners...just having a drink. Banter innit. Joking. Fuck me... you've killed loads of people. Shooting them for getting drunk...'

'THEY TRIED TO KILL US,' Simar roars out. 'YOU SHIT ON MALEEK'S TENT...YOU SET IT ON FIRE... you said you wanted to hang my family from the walls...you stole our food and trashed the tents people risked their lives for...YOU DID THAT...'

'Come on, look, this just got silly. I saw my wife die... right in front me...I went out and had a go to get her back. I tried...but they had her. I hid in the garage...days without food or water...then I gets here and everyone's telling me the muzzies...you know...the followers of your Islam, they did it...'

'I'm not a Muslim. We're Sikhs... WE'RE FUCKING SIKHS...'

'I dunno what you're all called. Jesus mate. I'm a Christian...I'm on meds for my slipped discs. Ask that doc. Lisa. She gave me a note...' he pauses as Lilly starts walking towards him. 'I didn't steal. I didn't! That fat bitch said we could have it. I thought it was okay and that Colin was yelling at us to work and we said we're sick and that Polish bitch...that Lenski, she said we can't eat and we got scared and...' he pauses again as Lilly stops next to Mary, reaching to take the pistol from her hand, checking the magazine and sliding the top back. Loaded, made ready. 'What you doing that for?' Tommy snaps. 'Fuck me...few beers and you kill everyone. THAT WHAT YOU DO IS IT? KILL PEOPLE?'

'Yes,' Lilly says with brutal honesty.

Tommy backs up, his wild eyes darting left and right. Everyone watching him. Faces hard. 'WE DIDN'T DO NUFFIN...I saw my wife die...' he nods fast as Lilly stalks at him. 'RIGHT IN FRONT OF ME...I tried to save her. Nightmares. Given me nightmares...I can't sleep...come on. It was just a laugh...just got out of hand...' he backs up, the fear growing in his gut at the sight of Lilly. 'I SAW YOU...I SAW YOU GIVE THAT WOMAN A KICKING... double portions...creaming it off... sleeping in beds and fuck me, just having a drink. Shooting innocent people. Fat Pam did it...fuck off...I mean it...FUCK OFF...' he rages and flushes red as Lilly walks on unfaltering in her step. The utter intent entirely clear. 'They started it...soldier told me. He said it was a jihadi...I thought I was helping...I'M SICK...GOT SLIPPED DISCS...SAW MY WIFE DIE... ASK THAT DOC...they started it...the queers, the muzzies, come on. Fucking come on...please...put that down...stop it...FUCKING STOP IT YOU CUNT...'

He trips on a beer can sliding underfoot, dropping to a knee as Lilly walks at him, lifting the pistol. Thumbing the safety off.

'No!' he scrabbles backwards, sweat pouring down his face. Tears spilling over his cheeks. 'Pack it in...FUCK OFF YOU STUPID BITCH. I've got mental health...they started it...them! I'm not armed...I'm sick. I'M SICK...' a wet patch grows on his groin with piss pouring over his bare legs from his shorts. 'Please,' he begs, whimpering and sobbing as Lilly comes to a stop, the pistol aimed an inch from his forehead. 'No...please...I didn't mean no harm...I've got learning issues...'

'He made me fuck him for a drink,' a voice calls out. Rough and harsh. Helen swaying on her feet. Her body shaking from head to toe. She hid all night under a torn down shelter and now stands with the empty vodka bottle in her hand. A small black cross inked on the corner. 'He made me fuck him for this...' she says, trying to hold it up but the shakes are too much. She coughs, harsh and bitter. 'He couldn't get it up...shoved his fingers in and called me a crack whore...'

'FUCKING LYING CUNT...' Tommy screams. 'FUCKING DIRTY SLAG...FUCKING MUZZIES DID IT...QUEER FUCKING...'

A second in time. The clouds race overhead, and the wind blows her hair across her face, but all of that becomes background noise. Tommy screaming. People calling out. All of it fades out as Lilly stands in the middle, feeling like she is the only stationary object in the universe. Her mind filling with thoughts. To see the way forward at the very worst of times. That is her skill. To think clearly when the rage is screaming inside. To know when to fight, and when to think. To take all matters into consideration and know the best course of action to take. When to kill. When to take arms against a sea of troubles, and by opposing end them. When not to kill. When to use temperance and patience. Mary said she struggles with empathy. Norman said she is too harsh. Reginald said *she is a most incredible young woman. Ruthless, capable and highly intelligent. You'd do well not to under-estimate her.*

Lilly is intelligent. She is very intelligent, but more than anything, she knows when the rot and darkness needs to be removed and so she shoots him dead. Pulling the trigger to ignite the primer that explodes the propellant which sends the bullet from the barrel into Tommy's forehead, cauterizing the wound before removing the back of his skull.

A second for his body to relax and he slumps to the side.

A second for that gunshot to roll out and bring every head over.

A second for the fort to fall silent save for the wind blowing over the tops of the walls and the flap of material on the tents and shelters.

'Too harsh?' she asks quietly, staring down at the body.

'No,' Mary says.

'No,' Norman says at the same time.

Another second for Lilly to lower the gun and turn to look about at the carnage and destruction. 'If anyone ever threatens the safety of this fort I will kill them...you need to know that. I need you to understand that...'

'Don't kill me...' a woman nearby cries out, lying on her back cradling a broken arm. Her eyes bloodshot from drinking all night, her words slurred. 'I didn't do anything! They said...they said the muzzies started it...they said they're gonna kill us all...'

'Who say this?' Lenski asks.

'That Pam did! When I came in...she said the muzzies started it and they're all infected...she said you're protecting them...'

'And the doctor,' someone else shouts. 'In the hospital... she said you'll kill us if we don't work. Said it's like North Korea...'

'She said it's a death camp...' the injured woman says, looking from Lenski to Lilly with desperation. 'Said we have to give our food over so Lilly's brother can eat the best stuff...'

Voices calling out. The wild mob now gone and back to individuals seeking a way to lessen their part and blame others.

'They're telling the truth,' Helen calls out. The woman

shaking so hard she can barely stand. Her arms wrapped about her body as though she's freezing. A sight of abject misery but the way she speaks and the manner in which she says it holds weight. A flash of the person before alcohol ruined her life. Her spirit shining, her head lifting to speak out. 'Pamela said that to me when I came in. She took us into the hospital and the doctor told us to fuck off...she said we'll be told to work or we'll get killed as Billy needs to eat... I don't know who Billy is...' she trails off, trying to lick her cracked lips. 'Tommy told everyone their belongings will be taken away...he told them the leaders are taking the best for themselves...'

'SEE!' the injured woman says, nodding quickly, seeing a way out of it. 'See...that's what they said...'

'They're still animals,' Helen says, her top lip curling up with distaste as she speaks. 'That poor family at the end... the Muslims...they were going at them all night...*kill the muzzies, burn the muzzies*...they kept saying it over and over...they stood and pissed on their tent while chanting it...'

'I didn't do any of that,' the injured woman shouts.

'I saw you,' Helen says. 'All of you...'

Lilly turns and starts walking with such a look upon her face it is clear to all what she will do, and none show the least bit of surprise when she aims for the infirmary on the other side of the fort.

Lisa has this coming. She's been baiting Lilly for days now. Undermining every decision she makes. Insulting and trying to humiliate her. Now this. Calling the fort a death camp. Telling new people they will be worked to death. Scaring and whipping them up into a frenzy. Giving sicknotes to people like Tommy. Adding fuel to a pressure cooker environment. Lisa has this coming.

Mary sets off after her. Ready to stand by her side no

matter what. Ready to do what has to be done. An awful silence spreads. An awful, terrible silence as the fort becomes what it was before. A place of misery and suffering. A place where people come to die.

A death camp for the *Little Tyrant* to stalk across with a pistol in her hand, ready to do the right thing. Ready to kill everyone to protect her brother. Defender of the weak. Defender of them all. The *Little Tyrant* with her cold blue eyes and golden hair pulled back. The *Little Tyrant* that can fix every issue with a gun. It's easy. Just point and shoot and the problem goes away.

She fixes her cold blue eyes ahead. Unblinking. Her step unfaltering. This must be done. This has to be done. Something in her view looming large. Something new. The skeletal frame of the new canteen standing high. Almost lost to fire and riots.

Her foot scuffs a can and she flicks her gaze down to see the black inked cross in the corner that Lenski put on to trap the person stealing. An effort made to prevent loss and to bring order without violence, and aren't they the signs of a society?

She looks again to the canteen with a surge of frustration that it isn't finished yet. That they had dared to gain a shred of positivity only for the rot and corruption of the old world to come and take it away. Except it hasn't been lost. It's still there. The fire never took hold because good people stopped it. Good people held the line and stood up. Bashir took a rifle and shot people to defend it. Joan and Kyle took life to defend it. Everyone else poured in and fought back to defend it too. Aren't they signs of a functioning society too? One that has values and decency?

Confusion inside and she comes to a stop within five

strides of moving off and that silence rolls on, save for the wind flapping the tents and shelters.

She goes to holster the pistol then remembers her holster is lost to the sea. Then she spots her bare feet and wonders if her socks came off with her boots, or after when she was somewhere between swimming and drowning. She doesn't know. She turns and looks back to Mary, seeing she has only one bare foot while the other is clad in a bright purple sock with pink spots. It looks weird. Almost funny. She saw those socks in the outdoor place they raided. That was a good day. The last few days have all been good days. They flattened the bay and built a wall. They emptied all the contents and got material over here so that canteen could be built. And it's big too. Bigger than she thought it would be. Higher, wider, longer. She looks to it now. Seeing the struts and joists. Seeing the thick sheets of marine ply ready to be nailed in place to make it a building, but it's more than just a building.

Understanding dawns in her mind as another thought enters. She read that firefighters in the Second World War risked everything to protect St Paul's Cathedral, and even Winston Churchill said it had to remain because of what it stood for. Not because it's place of worship, it's more than that. It's the point of unity. The rallying point. That's the line they chose to form up on. John, Pardip and the others. Even Maleek and Bashir. Nobody told them to do that.

She looks again towards the infirmary and finds the essence of her rage has shifted inside. It's still there, but it's different now, quieter. Another voice is shouting to be heard. Another ideology. She can kill Lisa with ease. Lilly has that ability. Be that right or wrong, but right now, in her mind, there are two paths stretching ahead of her. One leads to Lisa. The other to the building site. One leads to death. One leads to hope. Lilly knows such thoughts are cliched, trite even. But that doesn't make them untrue, and nor does it reduce the significance of their meaning.

She turns to look back, seeing everyone where they were. People on the ground. People standing. The sky above them filled with rolling clouds. Two paths behind her. Two ways forward from here, except to Lilly, there are always more options. She is, after all, ruthless, capable and highly intelligent, and right then, she remembers the conversation with Kyle, '*do you know what Henry did when someone wouldn't do what he wanted? Nothing at all! But then he'd call me and Frank and make them do what he wanted...*'

'Will you do something for me please,' she asks Mary, her words clear and distinct.

'Sure,' Mary says, staring into those blue eyes.

'Will you advise Doctor Franklin not to tell new arrivals that this is a death camp, and we do not work people to death, nor do we steal their possessions...'

A glint in Mary's eyes as her head lifts an inch. 'Will do,' she says. 'Anything else?'

'Yeah. Tell her to stop being a cunt,' Sam calls out. 'What?' she asks when a few people look at her. 'She bloody is...'

'Aye. Will do,' Mary says. 'Anything else?' she asks, looking at Lilly.

'Please advise her that although she is a doctor and therefore highly valued, she is not beyond being removed from this fort and exiled...'

'Exiled. Got it.'

'Thank you.'

'Anytime, Blondie.'

Lilly nods, setting off. Mary nods, setting off. Both

pausing as they pass by with shoulders brushing.

'And tell her if she ever mentions my brother again I'll slit her throat while she sleeps...'

'Aye. I figured that...'

'Were we meant to hear that bit?' Colin asks.

'I think so,' Pea says.

'Muslims did not start this,' Lilly calls out, walking back to the others. 'We have no idea where it started from and we do not work people until they are dead. We don't take food either. We ask for it, so we have enough to feed everyone. If you object to something then speak out, we have a meeting nearly every morning where we raise concerns and discuss what we are doing. This is all new...all of this is...and we're learning as we go, but don't let this stop what we are doing. This is the new world...what these people did is from the old world and there is no place for it here,' another pause to look about, to draw air. 'We have work to do...we'll always have work to do. Len, where can we put all the people involved in this?'

Lenski swallows, widening her eyes, her brain struggling to process it all and keep up. She shrugs, shaking her head. 'I er...I not know...oh yes, I do know...old armoury. Yes. Put them in there. It has lock on the door to stop children going in...they will need medical aid yes? We get this...' her legs shake as she speaks with a sick feeling in her gut from what just happened, but she fakes the energy. Forcing herself to call out. 'Some will be exiled I think. I think this must happen. They cannot stay here, but we do this later. Now we have much to do. Yes? All of us. Is our fort. We make rules. Norman, you are lawyer. Write rules and put them on Colin's notice board. If people break the rules, then they go. Exile. We make clear...'

Norman nods, his mind too shocked to think clearly.

Everyone the same.

'We must work now,' Lenski continues. 'We still need to eat today...we need that canteen finished. The rain isn't here yet...' she glances up at the sky, prompting many others to do the same, shifting their gazes from the crap about them to the world above.

John feels the same as her. Feeling like he just wants to find somewhere dark to cry and shake and a single glance round makes him realise he's not the only one feeling like that, but he clears his throat. 'Sim, let's get the roof on...and er,' he pauses, rubbing his face. 'Aggie, could do with a cuppa, love...'

Agatha looks over at the big builder and his trembling hands with an urge inside to rush over and hug him. To hold all of them. 'We'll see to it,' she says quietly instead. 'Eh, Sunnie. Let's get 'em a brew on...'

'My team,' Colin calls out looking pale and drawn. 'We er...um...right...gosh, I have no idea what I was about to say.'

'We'll get this mess cleared up,' Joanne says, looking from Lilly to Lenski.

'Good. Yes. We do this...' Lenski says, summoning calmness where none should be found. 'Where is Pamela? I not see her...'

Pamela hears her name drifting on the wind and steps further back into the gloom of a dark room littered with old debris at the side of the fort.

She stands in her underwear with dried vomit on her boobs and belly, and dried shit stuck to the cheeks of her backside. Her hair in disarray and the air fills with the soft munch of her jaws as she eats the melted chocolate bar, staring out at them all.

She slipped away when Tommy got them throwing flaming toilet rolls with an instinct inside that said it was time to go and hide once more in the old rooms and dark places. She saw the big fight though. And she saw Lilly shoot Tommy too. It made her feel funny inside. A bit sick, but a bit excited too.

Now she scratches her belly, plucking the dried chunks of vomit off. A heavy sigh and she retreats under some old material to lie low in the rat shit with spiders and bugs all about her. Pamela doesn't mind them. She has cigarettes and snack food in here, and she can go out at night when it's all dark.

A few days of hiding and she'll pop up and say they all made her do it. Another sigh and she shuffles back while staring out through a crack to Lilly.

Pretty Lilly.

Beautiful Lilly.

CHAPTER TWENTY-TWO

Day Twenty Four

A back room within the infirmary. A few boxes spilled across the floor. Coffee dripping down a wall with the smashed mug lying in bits at the base. Andrew and Heathcliff stand side by side listening to Mary speaking earnestly.

'And I bloody said I did, I said you can't get across that sea in this weather, and you know what Lilly did? She hopped straight into a boat and said *Mary, I'm going over I am*. And I said, *Lilly, don't be such a bloody idiot*, but then I got in too. Which does make me an idiot also maybe. Anyway, and then what happened? Shall I tell you? The boat only tipped over didn't it. There we were, being thrown all over the place by the waves. I thought we were a goner. I really did, but Lilly was calm as you like. She took her boots off then got mine off and away we went, swimming about...are you still listening?'

'Yes!' Lisa grunts.

'Good. Then we get to the beach and we're wet through and staggering about and falling through the gates and everyone is like *the fort's being taken over by drunks,* and Lilly is up, quick as a flash. *Donald,* she says, *give me your rifle there old fella,* and then she ran in...running mind. And right after that big swim we had too. My legs were like jelly they were...is there a medical term for that? Ach, it doesn't matter. So, then Lilly is shooting them, which she had to do mind seeing as they were all going to kill the guys with darker skin having been told that the Muslims started it all. And of course, everyone is whipped up and scared thinking they're in a death camp...and that we take food and possessions away. None of which is true mind...and we don't work people to death either. Why would we do that? There's too much work to do to go about killing everyone...don't you think?'

'Of course,' Doctor Andrew Stone says quickly, glancing at Heathcliff.

'Aye, and before that, Lisa here was going to the morning meetings being all difficult and shouty. Calling Lilly a little tyrant and this and that. I said to Lilly, I said *you need to tell her to stop.* You know what Lilly said? She said, *Mary, I can't go ordering Lisa to shut up and thereby prove I'm the tyrant she says I am now can I?* Which does make sense when you say it like that, but then I said, *Blondie, stuff like that would never be tolerated in the camp. You've got to deal with it head on.* But we didn't get to finish that conversation seeing as we got busy flattening all them houses and bringing everything over into the fort, then building that new canteen, and that bloody big wall too. Have you seen it? It's very big. And of course we had a scrap with the infected getting the containers and this and that. Lots going on...and that all leads us to now. What do you say about that?'

'Er,' Andrew says.

'Well,' Heathcliff says deeply, nodding while looking down at Lisa Franklin on her knees wedged between Mary's legs with her left arm held up against Mary's leg while Mary grips and turns her wrist the wrong way. 'Yes. Very busy all over I'd say...'

'Everyone has been busy,' Andrew says.

'Aye, they have,' Mary says earnestly. 'And it doesn't help none when you've a screaming banshee twat undermining every decision you make and telling lies. What do you think?' she asks, looking down while adding a bit more pressure.

Lisa doesn't reply but only gasps. The pain radiating down her arm through her elbow joint and into her shoulder.

'Ach, but anyway, we'll let bygones be bygones. Seeing as you're a doctor and people need help. But do it again mind and you'll be out. Is that fair would you say?' she asks, looking up to Andrew and Heathcliff.

'Very,' Andrew says.

'Yes,' Heathcliff adds.

'And I know I'm just a thick gypsy girl, but I do know what being complicit is ...do you get my meaning, Doctors?'

They both nod.

'Good. That's grand that is. Anytime you're free, pop out onto the beach or go up onto that wall and look across to the big camp. Because it won't be me coming to see you next time. It'll be my Uncle Pete and Willie and Elvis and Tyson and Patrick, and Eggy and my Uncle Jack...and if those boys come pay a visit then you are royally fecked...fair warning now? Oh, one last thing...' a sharp crack. A grunt of pain and Lisa flushes deep red from Mary breaking her little finger before releasing the doctor to slump on the floor. 'Right, I think that covers it...I'd get some ice on that now. Bring the swelling out...'

She smiles at the other two looking wild and somewhat crazy. Still wet from the sea. Still with one bare foot and the other clad in the purple sock with pink spots and a slightly manic look adorns her face as she nods, gives a thumbs up and heads down to walk back through the infirmary.

She pauses at the exit door, holding still in the darkness. Drawing air and blowing it out through her cheeks. She almost died a few moments ago. They were drowning. She's never been so terrified and even now she feels sick to her gut from panic, from adrenalin, from fighting and running. Lilly is so calm though. Like it's all just part of her normal day.

Out the door into the fort. The wind still blowing. Howling over the tops of the walls and she makes her way towards the new canteen and the many people now trying to get back to work. The hot drinks table dragged closer to it. People milling and getting mugs of hot sweet tea and coffee. Mary remembers that sweet things aren't good for you when you've been in shock, but right now a hot sweet tea is exactly what she wants.

A glance up towards the back and she spots Bashir standing guard at the broken armoury door then over to Joan and Kyle ordering the last of the drunks into another room. Ann and Anika moving here and there tending the hurt.

'Tea?' a voice brings her back to the now, back to the reality of the world about her. Norman at her side holding a mug out.

'Aye,' she says, taking it with a grateful nod and they stand together, sipping the hot drinks while looking about at shaken people trying to act normally. Everyone talking too loudly and over each other. Everyone helping a bit too much. Another glance to the back and they spot Alf pushing his wheelbarrow into the middle of where the big fight took place. Rolls of material and coils of rope in his barrow.

'How was Lisa?' Norman asks.

'Alright,' Mary replies.

'Agreeable?'

'Aye. We made a pinkie promise...' she says, sipping her tea while watching John and Pardip lift a heavy sheet of marine ply from the stack to carry over to more men and women waiting to heave and push it up to Simar and Maleek on the roof.

A minute later and they take more sheets in to fit across the floor joists and there it is, the skeletal frame making a gradual shift to a building proper.

'Nice tea,' Mary says.

'It is,' Norman replies.

The wind stops with a sudden cessation of noise, bringing forth a bizarre stillness.

'Was that it?' Agatha asks, turning from the drinks table to look up with everyone else. A moment in time of near perfect silence. Simar and Maleek both on top of the building looking up. John and Pardip standing on the first section of the new floor. Everyone poised. Everyone still.

And like a switch is flicked the rain comes. From nothing to a torrential downpour in an instant. Water falling from the sky straight down bringing an orchestra of noise. Soaking, drenching, warm and cleansing.

Norman and Mary lift their hands to cover their mugs of tea while staring up with eyes closed. Letting the clean water run over them. Listening to sounds of water striking hundreds of surfaces. Feeling the heat of the last few days ease away. Everyone does the same. Holding still. Taking but a few seconds.

'No, that wasn't it,' John calls out, answering Agatha and earning a few chuckles. 'Come on! Back to it...Aggie, give us two minutes and start bringing the food tables over...'

Noise and motion again. People working. Colin and his few at the back pulling the ruined tents and shelters down. Picking the cans, bottles and rubbish up.

'Put the bodies in there,' Alf says, pointing at Tommy's big tent. 'I'll get 'em wrapped and ready...'

'Did you get many containers?' Norman asks Mary.

'A few, saw some other people there. From another place I mean, survivors, like us.'

'Really? That's actually nice to know...'

'Aye, I thought that. After punching the fella in charge...' she looks at Norman and shrugs. 'I'll explain it later.'

'Sure,' he says, sipping his tea. 'We should jump in and help I guess...'

'Aye, can I ask you a question?'

'Of course.'

'When did you know you were gay?'

'Pardon?'

'When did you know? Did you like just wake up one day and think *I'm gay*, or was it like a gradual thing?'

'Right,' he says. Sipping his tea while glancing about at the chaos unfolding again with people hammering and others sawing. 'I think I just always knew,' he replies.

'Gotcha. Always knew. Understood...'

'Great. Er...was that it?'

'So, I have a friend right...'

'A friend.'

'Aye, a friend. A woman. She likes boys. I mean men, you know what I mean, she fancies men. She's even had sex with one of them, not a lot mind cos of her strict upbringing in a close-knit travelling community and the fact her Uncle Pete would rip the lad's dinkle off and shove it up his arse, but she's had a few fumbles, a few kisses...it's not me by the way.'

'Right. Sure,' Norman says.

'And now she fancies a girl. My friend does. She likes a woman. But she doesn't think she's gay. Is she gay? I mean, does that make her gay? I asked her, my friend that is, I said, *are you sure it's not just a crush now*. She said, *Mary, I don't think it's just a crush...*'

'Okay,' Norman says.

'What do you think about that?' Mary asks.

'Sorry, about what?'

'About my friend. Is she gay?'

'Maybe your friend is. Maybe she's just curious...lots of people are.'

'Ah, right. Yes. I never thought of that. Like bi-sexual is it?'

'Could be, yes, if you er, if you really want to put a label on it...or, more importantly you can just reflect on how you...I mean your friend, feels about the other person. Regardless of what gender they are.'

'Gotcha,' Mary says. 'So?'

Norman looks at her. She looks back at him.

'Is she gay then?' Mary asks. 'Like maybe a little bit? Can you be a little bit gay?'

Norman takes in her green eyes and red hair and thinks of how she's stood at Lilly's back through thick and thin the last few days. 'Maybe just a bit,' he replies.

'Ah right,' Mary says, nodding at him with a relieved smile. 'I thought that. I thought maybe she's just a bit gay.'

'But it's fine,' Norman adds. 'This is the new world...'

'Yep. New world. Sure...except my friend is from that close-knit community and really doesn't want her brother and cousins and uncles knowing she might be a little bit gay...'

'Of course,' Norman says. 'Best keep that quiet then. Your friend being a little bit gay that is.'

'You know what, Norman? You're a top fella. Really you are. Right, shall we go and help out or what?'

CHAPTER TWENTY-THREE

D ay Twenty Five

A new day. A new dawn and the boats set off across the water. The perfectly flat, mirror-like surface now replaced with waves and motion, and the colour has changed too. The deep blue now greener and greyer from the sediment churned up by the storm that passed through yesterday.

'Another one,' Lilly says, pointing off to the starboard side.

'Aye,' Kyle says, tutting sadly at the remains of the corpse bobbing a few metres away. 'And they all came up while you were swimming over?'

She nods, pulling a face to show how grim it was.

'Hopefully the tide would have pulled most away.'

'Hopefully. We're eating the fish from this sea...'

'Ach, I wouldn't worry. It's a big sea and the chances the

fish are eating the bodies are pretty slim,' he says as they pass a severed leg floating on the water. 'Or not,' he adds.

Neither mention the fact they are about to add more than a dozen fresh corpses, but at least these are all wrapped in sheets, bound with rope and weighed down with rocks. Which means it will just take a bit longer for the material to rot so the fish can eat the corpses.

Of the forty two that rioted. Fifteen were killed outright. Three by Kyle. One by Joan. Three at the end during the huge brawl. The rest were shot down by Lilly and Bashir.

Many more were hurt. With gunshots, with broken limbs, fractured skulls, busted jaws and noses. Concussions, contusions and lacerations.

They go further out than before. Out to sea. Out away from the fort and the bay and Lilly stares across to her wall and the trucks lined up ready for the work to carry on. The marquee tent on the beach has gone. Blown away by the storm, but that's not so bad.

'This far enough?' she asks.

'Aye,' Kyle says. She doesn't cut the engine this time but lets it idle so they can keep positioning into the waves between heaving bodies over the side. Other boats behind them manned by men and women from the fort gripping corpses that splash down into the waves.

A light drizzle comes on. A gentle wind too. The sky overhead low and grey but that heat is gone. That awful, crushing heat.

'Into thy hands dear lord. We commend the soul of thy servant departed, now called unto eternal rest and we commit this body to the deep...'

Kyle calls the prayer out. Lilly stares across the sea, not

bowing her head, not closing her eyes. Watching. Always watching.

The engines rise again as the boats head back. The breeze in their faces. Salt in the air. A cleaner scent too. Like the air is fresh and renewed. 'We'll need to have that conversation soon,' Kyle says, looking at Lilly.

She nods and stays quiet for a few seconds. 'Now?' she finally asks.

Kyle stares across to the bay thinking today is the twenty-fifth day since it started. If Henry and the old group survived then they would have gone to ground somewhere to stay low for the first month. That would be the normal protocol for an end-of-world event like this. A month gives everyone else enough time to charge about and go mad at each other, for the initial absolute chaos to unfold and vent. A month should also see the first hints of structure within communities that have survived. Those behind big walls. Those that got food, water and security. Places like the fort and Lilly said they met another group from a place down in Dorset.

Aye. And that month is nearly over so now is the time for them to set out. Henry, George, Carmen, Frank and Howard. Kyle has no idea if they all made it, or where they are. If Henry knew something big was coming he would have taken steps to find somewhere suitable to hide out, and Kyle is sure that if Henry knew it was imminent then he would have found Kyle to warn him. Dave was still working in the Tesco store by all accounts too. And Kyle heard Howie went looking for his mum and dad. All of those things make Kyle think this event was not foreseen. That it took them by surprise.

Now, if the old team are alive, staying low in an isolated property somewhere, they will soon emerge, and once they emerge they will commence intel gathering and hear about the fort, and Mr Howie. Then they will come here.

'Hard to say,' Kyle replies at length. 'Maybe a few more days...'

'In that case,' she says. 'Tell me in a few more days.'

He smiles at the reply, his craggy face lighting up, his deep blue eyes beneath his hair streaked with grey now blowing in the wind. There's something so wholly unique about how Lilly's mind words. That she looks forward with everything she has and will only consider the past if it is absolutely essential. He rubs his jaw, nodding as he looks at the young woman this new world so desperately needs. If Henry ever does come here, he will adore her. Of that there is no doubt.

'Would you look at that now,' Mary says as they head back into the fort, all of them staring across to the big canteen standing large in the middle section. 'She's looking good or what?'

The building does look good. Dominant and imposing, but it suits the fort. The wooden boards and apex roof blend so well.

They walk towards it, seeing people up and about, all of them gathering about that one place, just like they did yesterday once it was built.

'Morning,' Brian Collins says, leaning against the side of the canteen. A cigarette in one hand. A mug of coffee in the other. Other bay workers gathered about him. Martin Jones. Emily and Jane. Jillian with her hand still bandaged. 'We going over this morning?'

'Aye,' Kyle says. 'We'll have the meeting and be on it...'

They walk in to see the food tables at the back with Agatha and Sunnie bustling about behind them. Smells wafting out. Steam rising from pots. The water heater going non-stop. Generators chugging away. The clatter of crockery and cutlery. Running water from a hose pulled over and fitted to a tap inside. A hole cut into the floor that feeds to the old visitor centre kitchen drainage outlet. Thought taken in the construction.

They grab coffee and bowls of food before walking over to the main office and a hubbub of noise and once more they take seats at the big table with Lilly at the head staring out to the faces of the fort leaders. Simar still without a turban. Jaspal and Pardip. Lenski next to Lilly. Kyle, Joan, Sam and Pea. Colin and Joanne. Norman. Ann. Anika.

'I think we should start with the hardest thing first,' Lilly says as the room falls quiet. 'The people that took part in the riot…'

'Get rid of 'em,' John says quickly.

'I agree with John,' Sam says.

'Exile, yes. We should do this,' Lenski says.

'All of them?' Lilly asks.

'Bloody right,' Simar says. 'Every last one…no excuses for what they did.'

'Some are too hurt to be moved,' Ann says.

'How many?' John asks.

'Five can't go anywhere,' Anika says, checking a list in front of her. 'Two of them aren't expected to survive either…'

'There is twenty two in old armoury,' Lenski says. 'We should make good decision, yes? Smart decision. We are like a town now…'

'A society,' Lilly says.

'Yes. This. We make decision like the society now… Norman, you are lawyer. What you think?'

'Well. I guess I am,' Norman says thoughtfully. 'If I may break this down…on the one hand you have scared refugees brought into a pressure cooker environment and immediately told by the person that greets them that the Muslims started it and they are infected and so on, then they are shown to the infirmary where more fear is given and then on to Tommy where yet again more pressure is applied. All of those things, combined with the hot weather and Pamela stealing alcohol from the stores eventually led to the incident yesterday. That does give some mitigation. There are reasons why they did what they did. However,' he says, lifting a hand as Sam and a few others start speaking out. 'Plenty of people did not take part who were also subject to the same thing, and those people are now moving about freely, working and joining in...so one must really examine the values and motivations of...'

'Norman,' Mary whispers across. 'You're smart as anything and I could listen to you all day, but they want to know if the bad people should be kicked out...'

'Right,' Norman says as a few people nod. 'Understood. Yes they should. The fort isn't big enough to allow them to remain and fester with grudges, and as much as I hate to say it, it will also send a very strong message, not only that we will exile people, but also that we do things fairly. We're not executing them, we are simply saying...'

'Got it,' Mary says brightly, giving him a huge grin. 'Norman says get rid of them.'

'Yes,' Norman says, rolling his eyes. 'I said that.'

'Hands up who thinks they should be kicked out,' Mary says as everyone in the room lifts their hands. 'Ach, seems to answer that one then.'

'That was easier than I thought,' Lilly says. 'We'll do that first...other than that. The new canteen is fantastic...'

'Brilliant,' Pea says.

'Amazing,' Ann says.

'Leaks like a bloody sieve it does,' Kyle says.

'Well we kinda built it quickly,' Simar says.

'Right. With lots of holes too.'

'It was raining,' Simar replies.

'Aye, inside and out...' Kyle quips and the meeting goes on. A new day. A new dawn. A new feeling in the air.

———

An hour later and the old armoury floods with light as the twenty-two people inside shield their eyes and wake with sore heads and bruised bodies to stare up at Lilly walking in with Lenski. The two fort leaders side by side.

'You are being exiled,' Lilly says bluntly, directly. Without preamble. A few gasps. A few mutterings that grow louder. 'You need to leave...if you don't move you will be moved...'

They file out into the drizzle to see Joan standing with a rifle. To see Kyle with his hands resting on the butts of his pistols. To see Bashir now with a pistol on his side and an assault rifle strapped across his chest, a soldier once again standing ready and watchful. Sam and Pea. Mary nearby. All of them armed. All of them grim-faced. A sea of faces beyond them as everyone else stares over. Men, women and children, and Keith looks to the back of the fort, seeing Tommy's tent is still standing and he frowns, thinking they would have torn it down by now. Everywhere else looks clean and orderly. The burnt shelters gone. The ruined tents too. Order has returned. Tents in neat lines. The debris and crap cleared away.

'Move,' Lilly orders, making them shuffle and stumble towards the front, passing the new canteen, all of them gawping at the size of it with the sides and roof now on. People standing outside drinking from mugs, bowls of food in their hands. The smells of cooking in the air and on they walk in silent shame.

'Please...' the woman with the broken arm calls out, the panic building inside. 'PLEASE! You can't kick us out...WE'LL DIE...'

'I hope you do,' a voice calls in reply, lost within the crowd.

Keith walks with them. Staying silent. Staying watchful. Patricia is dead. Shot by Bashir. Matty is dead. Gwen is in the infirmary with broken bones. Tommy was executed by Lilly, but then Tommy was a fool that didn't know what he was doing. Keith doesn't cry or weep at their losses but walks on with his face impassive. His eyes taking it all in. They go through the gates to the boats and in to cross the sea.

Each vessel with an armed person at the back and Keith stares ahead to the armed men waiting on the beach, then he lifts his gaze to take in the wall made from containers. The size of it. The placement of it. He spots the trucks waiting and figures they will make it higher too.

Onto the shore and Peter's men waiting silent and brooding. Rough voices telling them to move. Hands shoving them to walk. Pushing them into vans. Telling them to sit down and shut up. Keith does as he is told. Silent and watchful.

The vans move, going along the shore road. The people inside of them crying and weeping. Regretting what they did. Trying to tell anyone that will listen and each other that they didn't do anything. They just got drunk. It was everyone else.

The vans stop. The doors open.

'OUT,' Peter orders. They spill out to see they are outside of the wall and that sends fear through them. This is real. This is happening. They are outside of the protection now.

Keith remains quiet. Standing in the middle and staring at the wall, at the gap in the middle then over to where the wall goes into the sea. He spots Bashir with a rifle. Mary, Kyle, Joan. He saw yesterday that Lenski, Sam and Pea all hesitated to shoot. Bashir did not. Nor did Lilly.

He'll remember that.

He looks down to three rucksacks being dumped on the ground.

'Food and water, enough for a couple of days,' Lilly says, viewing them all. 'Some medications too...'

'Please,' the injured woman begs, falling to her knees. 'Please don't...'

'If any of you are seen in this area you will be killed,' Lilly says. 'You have five minutes to be out of sight...'

'DON'T!' the woman screams out, on her feet, running back to the gap in the container wall. A hand in her hair and she's yanked back and pushed into her group by Mary.

Keith studies them all one last time. Each face in turn. Then he stoops to pick a rucksack up, shoulders it and pauses to look at his old neighbour Norman. Eye contact held. Emotionless and cold. Then he nods once, turns and walks away, unblinking, unflinching, unafraid.

The rest follow after him. Grabbing the bags and rushing on while casting looks to the sides as though the infected will attack them right now.

'I feel bloody horrible doing that,' Pea says into the silence.

'After what they did?' Sam asks her.

'I know but...' Pea trails off. Shrugging.

'Aye, it's not nice,' Kyle says heavily. 'But necessary... come on, we going back in?'

They file back through with Peter nodding to his men to drive the truck across the entrance, sealing the bay and the new world rolls on.

'Did you see the fella that picked the bag up?' Mary asks as they walk back down the shore road.

'Keith,' Norman says. 'Used to be my neighbour in Surrey.'

'You know him? He looked like a right weird fella. Did you see his eyes?'

'Shock I should imagine,' Norman says. 'His wife was killed last night...he's soft as anything.'

'Aye, so were you a few days ago,' Kyle says, placing a hand on Norman's shoulder. 'Look at you now eh? Building walls and fighting like a trooper...and snoring too mind. You snore something rotten...'

CHAPTER TWENTY-FOUR

D ay Twenty Five

T his was a mistake. Norman knows that now.

'What have we got so far?' Sam asks.

'No aggression,' Pea says.

'No aggression,' Sam repeats, holding a finger up.

'No abuse,' Pea adds.

'When you say no abuse,' Simar asks. 'Do you mean like no abuse at all, like zero abuse, or like can I still call Jas the six-pack Sikh...'

'Bloody idiot,' Jaspal groans as everyone else laughs.

'Friendly abuse is okay I think,' Pea says.

'Yeah, like banter,' Sam says. 'Add that one down, Norm. No abuse, but banter is okay...'

'We are not using the word banter,' Joan says.

'Ach, it's fine,' Mary calls out. 'Norman'll put it into some legal wording, like *abuse in a negative way is not allowed but friendly japery is...*'

'I don't like japery either,' Joan says. 'Don't write japery, Norman.'

Norman nods. This was definitely a mistake. He was going to write the rules up in the peace and quiet of the office, but then he figured he could sit in the canteen with everyone else. So he strolled over with his notepad and pen, sat down at a table and asked, casually, as you do, if anyone had any suggestions for the new fort rules that were going to be pinned on the notice board.

Now, over an hour later and he sips hot tea having not written a word while listening to a mass discussion going on.

He looks about the inside of the canteen. Seeing they've lined the interior walls with ply, and he saw they added insulation between the layers. They've weatherproofed the outside, fixed the leaks and sorted through the piles of furniture taken from the houses on the bay to bring over chairs and tables. Pictures too. Paintings and wall art. Even a few drawings made by the kids who couldn't play out in the rain today. It's nice. He turns in his chair, smiling at the sheets of paper pinned to the walls. Each covered in bright drawings. Stick figures and big yellow suns. Some are a bit dark and black, showing where children have used art to express inner turmoil. He spots the good one and studies it closer, marvelling at the depth and scale given. A man, a woman and a young boy. All hand in hand. The detail is really rather good. Milly did it apparently. Something about a man called Gregory and his wife Cassie and their son. Milly wouldn't say who they were. Everyone guesses it must be her family. It's the figures in the background that really make it striking. Indistinct people but all of them are clearly infected. Red eyes glowing and they all look sad with down-turned smiles.

But still. What a difference after just another day.

There's even a door at the end of the canteen now. It doesn't quite fit properly mind, but then Simar and Maleek said that's down to warping, or bad wood, or rotten wood, or many other things and nothing to do with them.

The food tables at the back. Generators chugging away. They've enough fuel for years. Fuel does go off but that's a worry for another time.

'Okay okay,' Sam says, holding her hands out to bring the hubbub down. 'No aggression, that's obvious. I think no abuse is obvious too…I mean, if you need to explain it to someone then they're a twat anyway…er, oh and no racial abuse, no homophobia…none of those things…'

'Do we need to specify all of that?' Pea asks. 'No abuse means no abuse doesn't it?'

'People should work,' Lenski says.

'We're still on the abuse thing,' Sam says.

'I just say. People should work…not make work but, Norman, you make it sound good yes. Not made to work but they should work…and no litter. I see litter everywhere in fort…'

'We need some bins,' Pardip says as Sunnie walks up behind him, resting her hands on his shoulders.

'Then you need people to empty the bins,' Sunnie says.

'Colin!' A few people call out at the same time.

'My team can do that,' he says gladly.

'Stop taking more work on,' Joanne chides him.

'Are you a section head, Colin?' Sam asks.

'I am, yes!'

'Pea was wondering…' she adds.

'Twat,' Pea mutters.

'Right stop,' Mary says. 'We're getting way off track here. Norman needs his rules…'

'I think we should ban the word banter,' Joan says.

'And stop people eating with their mouths open,' Pea says.

'Farting indoors, that should be banned,' Sam says.

'Aye, nothing worse than dirty man smells,' Mary says.

'Nothing worse than nagging women,' John mutters to a detonation of well-humoured replies.

Lilly listens on, smiling at the jokes while behind those blue eyes her mind thinks to Howie coming back. It'll be either tonight or tomorrow. The old woman said tomorrow. The old woman Lilly spoke to on the shore road just as the day was drawing to a close.

***

'Will you look at that,' Mary says, staring up at the sixteen feet high solid wall of shipping containers. Two layers now added running from the sea and stretching off across the bay. 'Are you pleased, Blondie?'

'Very,' Lilly says. The end of another busy day and the day is drawing to a close. The big engines on the cranes, trucks and plant machinery still going but everyone can see the light is fading, and so the vibe shifts too with everyone looking forward to stopping work.

'Feels different today,' Mary says, 'you know what I mean?'

'I think so. Less frantic.'

'Aye. Not so hot either...like everyone knows what they're doing now.'

'Aye,' Lilly says, not even realising she says it now. 'It does feel better.'

'And that,' Mary adds, pointing at the wall. 'Is bloody grand...'

A couple more trips to the container yard by Peter's men and the wall carried on being constructed. The first level finished and the second layer well underway.

'Mary!' someone shouts, making them turn to see one of the guards at the gap in the wall waving at them.

'What's up, Callum?' Mary shouts.

'Lady down the road,' Callum calls, thumbing back over his shoulder.

'A what now?' Mary shouts.

'An old lady down the road...will you come over, so I don't have to shout.'

'We'll come over, so you don't have to shout,' Mary says, heading over with Lilly.

'Look,' Callum says, leading them through the gap to point down the shore road. 'Just stood there she is...'

'Aye, she is,' Mary says. 'Looks old too.'

'I just said that,' Callum says.

'I know you just said that, I'm saying it too,' Mary replies.

'What do you think she wants?' Callum asks.

'How the feck do we know that?' Mary asks him.

He shrugs. A rifle in his hands. Spots on his face. 'Do you want me to go and ask her?'

'We'll go,' Lilly says.

'Are ye sure now?' Callum asks. 'Do you want a man with you?'

'I don't know. Do you want a punch in the face?'

'Ach, Mary.'

'Ach your own arse, Callum.'

'Just keep an eye,' Lilly says, nodding at Callum as she walks out with Mary. 'There's no one else about,' she adds, viewing from the sea across the road to the cleared land on the other side and beyond the old woman.

'She wearing a nightie?' Mary asks.

'Looks like it,' Lilly says, staring at the old woman standing entirely still in the middle of the road. A once white night gown reaching her ankles. Her arms at her sides. Her head up and white hair hanging down, giving her a dignified, almost regal appearance.

'She's moving,' Mary says quietly when the old woman starts walking towards without hint of old joints, bad hips or sore knees, as though age hasn't touched her, and it's that very thing that makes Lilly reach back to pull her rifle forward.

'She's infected,' she says quickly.

'How can you tell?' Mary asks, pulling her rifle forward to make ready.

'The way she's moving,' Lilly says, coming to a stop. The container wall cutting the noise from the bay. Near silence and with a light drizzle falling and the light fading quickly it imbues a nearly ethereal atmosphere.

The old woman stops. Lilly and Mary stop. Both of them aiming. Both of them now seeing the red infected eyes, but the old woman stands without show of malice or raging hunger and her hands do not claw, nor does she show her teeth.

'Are we shooting it?' Mary asks.

'We need to speak to Lilly.'

'Holy shit it spoke,' Mary says. 'Did you hear that? The bloody thing spoke...'

'Don't say we need to speak to Lilly. That sounds weird, just say I need to speak to Lilly...' the old woman says.

'What the feck is she on about?' Mary asks.

'Lilly is here,' the old woman says, the boy says in the kitchen of the bumfuck nowhere house 300 miles away in the north of the country. Cassie nods, holding him tight. 'Is she alone?'

'No,' the old woman says, the boy says, the infection says as Mary and Lilly share a confused look. 'She has another woman with her.'

'Who the hell is she talking to?' Mary asks. 'Who the hell are you talking to?' she calls out.

'Can anyone else hear us?' Cassie asks.

'Can anyone else hear us?' the infection asks, the old woman asks.

'Jesus, okay, not creepy at all,' Mary says. 'Can I just shoot it now?'

'What are they doing?' Cassie asks.

'They are standing side by side. Lilly is on the left. The other woman is on the right. They are aiming guns...' the old woman says.

'Right,' Mary says. 'Blondie, can I ask, is this a normal zombie interaction we're having right now?'

'I don't think it is,' Lilly replies. 'Who are you talking to?' she calls out, not seeing anyone else in sight.

'Okay. Same as before,' Cassie says in the kitchen of the little cottage while listening to Gregori in the shower upstairs. 'Repeat what I say...'

'This is going to be a very weird conversation,' Cassie says, the boy says, the woman says on the shore road outside the container wall. 'Lilly. My name is Cassie. We need to talk...'

'Talk then,' Lilly says. She frowns gently, thinking she has heard the name Cassie somewhere recently, but she can't recall where from.

'Oh hang on, just to avoid any confusion, the woman you're talking to isn't called Cassie. I'm called Cassie. I've no idea who you are talking to...' the old woman says.

'She is called Deborah,' the old woman then says, clearly having a conversation with herself while projecting the manner of conversing with other people that cannot be seen.

'The woman is called Deborah apparently,' the old woman continues. 'Anyway, the point is I'm about three hundred miles away in a cottage talking to you through a little boy. Which I know sounds crazy but there you go...are they still there?'

'Yes,' old woman says, replying to her own question.

'What the fuck...' Mary mumbles.

'I can't see you, I can't hear you either, which is annoying and something I hope is fixed very soon as it would make things so much easier if I could have access like the boy does,' the old woman says with a clipped, distinctly unhappy tone. 'But anyway, that's a conversation for later...' Cassie says, pausing when the shower cuts off upstairs in the little cottage. Oh, did you know Blinky is dead?'

Lilly doesn't reply.

'We didn't kill her. I don't know who did. The others are alive though. Howie and his merry bunch. They've got some new people with them since they left your fort. Danny and Natasha, and a new guy just joined them too, but I think they know him already. I also know you are called Lilly and your brother is Billy. I know you run the fort and I know you've had lots of troubles there. I also know a lot of the people you have inside. Sam and Paula, I think she's called Pea. Lenski of course. Joan...'

Lilly tenses, her eyes hardening.

'I also know Howie left you. I'm sure, that like every other sycophantic idiot you think the sun shines out of his arse, but he did leave you...didn't he...' Cassie pauses, trying to picture the young woman standing outside a big wall made of shipping containers. 'But it sounds like you have coped rather well. Tell me, what do you think of the new world, Lilly? The air is clearer isn't it? No cars, no aircraft, no noise and no traffic. I was terrified when I realised what had happened...now though? Now I'm not. Now I'm glad. This is better than what it was...' Lilly watches the old woman speaking, seeing something not quite human in her eyes. Something wild and feral, something cunning and learning.

She knows Marcy was infected and kept her own mind too. What she doesn't know is why this old woman is here now, but she remembers what Reginald said. That the infection is evolving.

'What do you want?' Lilly asks.

Cassie thinks fast while Gregori moves about upstairs. He'll be down in a minute for dinner. She has to hurry.

'It's never going to go back to what it was,' the old woman says on the shore road. 'It can't, and nor should it. I spoke with that awful little twat Reginald too and said our country was the sixth biggest economy in the world, yet we had homeless and poverty. He said I was trite. Mind you, I had just thrown people they knew at them, which was a bit dark, but I wanted their attention. But then something tells me I don't need cheap tricks to get your attention. Do I have your attention, Lilly?'

'You have about ten seconds before I shoot you,' Lilly says.

'I've offered Howie a deal,' Cassie says, the old woman says. 'I've told him if he stays inside the fort I will let you all live. I won't touch this area. You can grow crops and do what you want. Howie should be with you either tonight, or tomorrow. Probably tomorrow because I chased them all into a big room full of cocaine so they're a bit wiped out.

The point is...no I'm just going to make dinner now. Give me five minutes...sorry, there's someone else here. Are you still there, Lilly? I can't see you...'

Lilly blinks, trying to make sense of it. 'I'm still here...'

'Howie won't take the deal. He's got that self-righteous stick up his arse. He'll come back to the fort and then come straight back out to fight...but he can't win. Not against this. It's too big. Lilly, listen to me, you haven't come against me. You're defending your own and I respect that. I want you to live in freedom. I don't want to hurt you. You can stay behind your wall and we'll co-exist without ever impacting on each other...'

'If you think I will kill Howie...'

'I can do that without you. What I want is for you to tell him to stop. Withdraw your support. Make him see reason. The world is better now. This thing isn't evil, Lilly. I can feel it. I just know it's not. It seems that way because of how it acts, but it's young and learning...it has to take more hosts, but they don't feel pain and they don't hurt each other. It cures every disease and illness they have. They don't need to eat or drink as much...shit, I wish we had more time to talk but I'm playing catch-up a bit here. This isn't the devil, Lilly. This is the future...tell Howie to stop and keep me informed of his plans and in return, I will give you this whole area. Let your brother grow old...'

Lilly listens, still silent, still watchful.

'I'm coming,' Cassie says, smiling at Gregori mooching through the kitchen cupboards.

'Where is mushky peas?

'We're not having mushy peas again,' Cassie says, the old woman says as Cassie leans in closer to whisper into the boy's ear. 'Howie left you. They all left you. You went through hell in that place, and now you are thriving. Don't waste that? This is a new world, Lilly. The old rules are gone, and we've got something good going. It's so fresh. So new. I love it! And I am never going to let Howie take that from me. I'll send every host I have against him and then I'll come for you. I don't want that...'

'I hungry now.'

'Yes! Gregory, I know...'

'Is Gregori. Not Gregory...'

'Jesus, right listen, I have to go. Lilly, all I want is to know what Howie is planning. That's it. Then you can all live in your fort...blimey, she doesn't say much does she. Is she still there?'

'I heard you,' Lilly says.

'I'll be in touch,' Cassie says, the old woman says and drops dead, her heart stopped by the infection. Both Lilly and Mary staring down at the corpse in the road.

'So, let me see if I'm getting this right,' Mary says, needing to break the silence. 'Did the zombies just try and make an alliance with us?'

'I think they did,' Lilly says.

'Right. Gotcha. And there's me worrying about being a little bit gay...'

'A little bit gay?' Lilly asks, looking up into her green eyes.

Mary shrugs. 'Either that or it's just a crush.'

'Oh,' Lilly says. 'Yes, I guess that makes sense.'

———

L aughter brings her back to the now. To the canteen packed with people. Damsa and some of her family now inside. Not Tajj though. He's not interacting with people so much.

'And I'm like, *Blondie, there's no bloody way we're getting in a boat over that sea now,* and she said, *Mary, we're going over to the fort we are,* and off she runs, into the big waves and that little boat throwing us about. And I'm puking up, but Blondie is still driving it on...*it's only a wee storm* she says. I said, *Lilly, this isn't a wee storm now...*'

Laughter rolling through from Mary's story that gets a bit wilder with each re-telling. The air warm. The smells of food and coffee hanging in the big room.

'...and we get into the middle bit of the gates there and we've no idea where we are, then she jumps up *Donald, give me your gun now. I've a fort to save I have!*'

'I didn't say it like that,' Lilly says, rolling her eyes.

'Then we run in and Lenski's right there...*Lilly!* she says, *they're littering in my fort...littering I tell you!*'

'I no say this,' Lenski laughs.

'Whatever,' Mary says, not going into the rest of the story and choosing to leave it on a light note. She looks to Lilly. Green eyes meeting blue. Smiles shared. Secrets shared too.

Lilly looks to Kyle, sensing the time for a conversation is rapidly approaching. But not right now. Howie will get back tomorrow, and that gives her tonight to think.

Lilly is a most incredible young woman. She is ruthless, capable and highly intelligent. You'd do well not to underestimate her.

She may also be, as it turns out, a little bit gay. Or it could just be a crush. Either way is fine though. Norman said so.

'You okay, Lilly?' Norman asks her quietly.

'Fine,' she replies. 'But we'll need to talk later. I think I need your advice on something.'

'Sure. Anytime. I'm right here whenever you need me...'

EXTRACTED SERIES
EXTRACTED
EXECUTED
EXTINCT

International best-selling time-travel

#1 Amazon US

#1 Amazon UK

#1 Audible US & UK

Top 3 Amazon Australia

Washington Post Best-seller

In 2061, a young scientist invents a time machine to fix a tragedy in his past. But his good intentions turn catastrophic when an early test reveals something unexpected: the end of the world.

A desperate plan is formed. Recruit three heroes, ordinary humans capable of extraordinary things, and change the future.

Safa Patel is an elite police officer, on duty when Downing Street comes under terrorist attack. As armed men storm through the breach, she dispatches them all.

'Mad' Harry Madden is a legend of the Second

World War. Not only did he complete an impossible mission—to plant charges on a heavily defended submarine base—but he also escaped with his life.

Ben Ryder is just an insurance investigator. But as a young man he witnessed a gang assaulting a woman and her child. He went to their rescue, and killed all five.

Can these three heroes, extracted from their timelines at the point of death, save the world?

Printed in Great Britain
by Amazon